Escaping the Darkness

Adam Inkwell

Bubs & Gato

Paperback ISBN: 979-8274609388

Hardcover ISBN: 979-8274698986

From the author:

A good book should make you laugh, it should make you cry and it should make you think. A great book should do it in that order.

I am not a professional writer. This book was written in my spare time as an anniversary gift to my dear wife. I have no idea how I'm going to top this next year.

Dedication:

For Bubs, and Gato. And to the teenage me who never stopped dreaming up worlds.

Wilderness of the North
Great Sea
Husnah
Mandel
Norton
Yalif
Zoar
(The Flying City)
Walmond
Najrah Desert
Hafahl
Avalar
Valmere
Cavandel
Salem
Petuel
Ural
Tower Isles
CONTINENT OF
FERALON

Contents

1

Echoes in the Dark

Location: Cavandel, The Mines

"That son of a cave rat!" Aria spat, her voice echoing off the narrow walls of the mine. "He stole my bloody loot," she muttered, disbelief roughening her tone.

She lifted her torch high, then turned the dial at its base. The semi-rusted metal had a satisfying heft to it; however, unlike traditional torches, it ended not in a flame but in a dome-shaped glass enclosure, smooth and warm to the touch. As she turned the dial, the light brightened, spilling into the shadows and revealing more of her surroundings.

The cave's air felt dense, carrying the metallic taste of crystal dust and iron. Aria's hands curled into fists as she paced through the warm glow of the torchlight. Her eyes darted around the space, searching, hoping she'd missed something.

It's all gone, she finally realized, the dread sinking deep. *A whole day's work, gone, just like that.*

He must have followed me here.

She shifted her gaze to the dark, narrow tunnels ahead, searching for signs of movement.

The mine was a winding labyrinth, its walls rough-hewn and ancient.

Jagged rocks jutted out, casting shadows that danced in the torch's warm glow.

Dust motes drifted lazily through the air, shifting only when she moved; their patterns briefly illuminated before fading back into stillness.

Rusted metal supports held up broad spans of ceiling, pockmarked with countless holes that stood as silent witnesses to generations of miners before her. Water trickled through the cracks in uneven rhythms, gathering in shallow pools that caught and reflected the light.

"Just wait till I get my hands on him," Aria growled, "I'm going to—" She cut herself off mid-rant.

Drawing in a steady breath, she muttered, "No, Aria... as Gran would say, 'Think nice thoughts, dear. Think nice thoughts.'"

It didn't work.

"Nope! I'll break every last bone in his body," she snapped.

"Hogan!" Aria screamed. The name tore through the open caverns, its echo swelling into a deafening roar. "You filthy rat!"

And then, amid the silence that followed, she heard it, a faint, mocking laugh from the direction of the cave's entrance.

Hogan.

She wouldn't let him get away with this, not now, not when she was so close. She had spent the entire day digging out those crystals until her hands went numb. Nearly two pounds of them, and for what? Nothing?

Aria's rage simmered at the loss, cooling into a dull ache that pressed against her chest. She sank slowly against the rough cavern wall, her eyes stinging with unshed tears. "You've got to be kidding me," she whispered, the words scarcely more than a breath.

She closed her eyes, releasing a hollow sigh as despair crept in. Her grandmother's face surfaced in her mind, worn and lined, yet still smiling through the pain that gripped her frail body.

She pictured her by the hearth, humming their favorite melody, a gentle tune that always filled their small home with warmth. The place was little more than a hollowed-out alcove, barely enough for two, yet her grandmother made it feel like a home from the Stratum.

Aria's fingertips traced the rough wall behind her, absorbing every bump, every crevice. She drew her hand back, her gaze lifting as a hint of movement swept the edge of her vision. A cluster of Lightmoths hovered near the ceiling, their wings pulsing with faint amber light.

What would Gran do?

She could almost hear her voice: *"Quit moping about, child, and do something."* And she would be right.

This was no time for self-pity.

She'd seen Hogan loitering near the mines earlier and had known he was scheming, but she hadn't imagined he'd stoop so low as to steal someone else's work while they were on the privy.

She rose and steadied herself, determination hardening her features. *Enough.*

She turned and surged toward the laughter, her boots striking the uneven stone in a hurried rhythm. The torch lurched in her grasp, casting fractured shadows that rippled across the jagged walls.

She rounded a sharp bend just in time to catch Hogan's paunchy silhouette squeezing through a narrow crevice.

"Stop, you thief!" she shouted, her voice raw with the strain of pursuit.

Hogan's laughter rang out, mocking and cruel. The sound cut deeper than it should have, stirring something sharp within her. She gritted her teeth and pushed on toward the opening.

She didn't slow. She thrust herself into the crevice, the rough stone biting into her shoulders as she forced her way through.

She stumbled forward, bursting free of the narrow gap, breath catching as her boots struck open ground.

The tunnel opened into a vast cavern, its ceiling swallowed by darkness. Ethereal purple light pulsed from crystalline veins in the walls, their glow casting otherworldly shadows that twisted and shifted like living things.

Aria spotted Hogan again, barreling toward a rickety bridge that spanned precariously across a gaping chasm. The boards groaned and shifted beneath his weight as he lumbered across, ropes creaking and swaying with each step.

By the time she reached the edge, the bridge had begun to quake, its wooden planks clattering against one another. Aria froze, heart pounding, her mind warring between caution and determination. One wrong move and she'd follow him straight into the abyss.

She gritted her teeth, then surged forward, pulse hammering in her ears. Her boots struck the weathered planks hard, each step sending tremors through the ancient bridge. The chasm yawned beneath her—a void so deep it seemed to swallow the light.

A sudden, bone-chilling screech erupted from below. Aria stopped mid-stride, her blood turning to ice.

Screechers?

In the mines? Impossible!

They hadn't been seen this high up in over twenty years.

The screech came again—closer this time. A chorus of chittering and clicking rising from the darkness.

Aria's breath caught in her throat.

She dared not move.

Her pulse thundered in her ears, every heartbeat reverberating through the open cavern—too quick, too loud. Her gaze swept the shadows, searching for the slightest flicker of motion in the depths below, while her mind fought to keep from conjuring their forms.

Rocknids.

The creatures were nightmares given form—massive, spined, reptilian beasts with gnarled fangs, human-like arms, and the sinuous bodies of serpents; relentless hunters with jagged claws, venomous bites, and eyes that glowed with spectral purple light. The miners called them *Screechers*—a name earned from the piercing wail that echoed through the tunnels whenever they hunted.

Though she'd never seen one herself, everyone in Cavandel knew the tales. And now, one of them—or perhaps two—lurked somewhere right below her. If she made it out alive, she'd have to report it.

Seconds stretched into eternity. Then, at last, the sounds faded, retreating into the void. The silence that followed was deafening. Aria exhaled slowly, her heart still racing from the encounter.

She forced herself to move, taking a tentative step forward. The bridge groaned but held. She swallowed hard and peered ahead, but Hogan was already gone.

Cursing under her breath, Aria moved carefully across the rest of the bridge. When she finally stumbled onto the other side, her legs trembled with exhaustion and fear.

The cavern's exit opened into a sprawling network of tunnels, each indistinguishable from the next. Aria paused, straining her ears for any sign of Hogan's retreating footsteps.

Nothing.

She steadied herself, letting instinct guide her toward the path that led back to the Mining Camp. The walk would be at least fifteen minutes—fifteen long minutes alone with her thoughts and the lingering echo of what she'd heard in the dark.

Her shoulders slumped as the adrenaline drained from her body. Hogan was long gone, along with her entire day's work.

Lost forever.

The cavern's eerie beauty mocked her failure. Each step felt heavier than the last, every echo a reminder of what she'd lost. Droplets of water fell from the ceiling along the dank path, their steady rhythm a melancholy metronome marking her slow trek forward.

As Aria made her way back, her mind refused to settle. The echoes from the abyss still clung to her, faint and hollow, as if the tunnels themselves whispered reminders of what lay below.

Everyone said the Rocknids had retreated into the Abyss, so far below the mines they were no longer a concern. But what if they were wrong? The thought shadowed her through the dark tunnels until the air began to shift, carrying the acrid scent of oil, sweat, and iron—the unmistakable sign of the Mining Camp ahead.

***

Aria emerged into the massive cavern of the Mining Camp, which served as the central hub of the Mines. Here the pulse of the underground city carried the weary rhythm of those who labored beneath its weight.

Jagged rock loomed overhead, swallowed by darkness and broken only by the faint gleam of lanterns strung across the camp. They offered little more than a trembling haze, enough to see by, but never enough to banish the dark. Down here, the light barely lived. Even the artificial glow of the District above failed to reach this depth.

The camp sprawled beneath the vaulted ceiling, a haphazard collection of stone and clay structures surrounded by scattered tents. What had begun as a humble gathering of hopefuls had, over the years, grown into a labyrinthine settlement, each shack and tarpaulin shelter whispering stories of endurance and struggle.

The buildings leaned against each other like old friends, their exteriors patched and weathered, adorned with relics of past labor. Rusted tools hung from their walls, while faded posters offered fleeting glimpses of what time had worn away.

The heart of the camp was marked by the Lift, a gargantuan iron structure of rattling gears and chains that vanished into shadow. It carried dozens of miners up toward the District, or farther down, into the Abyss, where the light died and the unknown took shape.

Coal dust clung to every breath, mingling with the quiet ache of exhaustion and despair. Miners shuffled past, their faces smeared with grime and etched with exhaustion. Aria scanned the crowd, frustration simmering in her chest as she searched for Hogan's hulking form, but he was nowhere to be found.

She gasped and whirled as a hand gripped her shoulder, her fists instinctively rising in defense.

"Whoa there, firecracker," came a familiar voice.

Aria froze, recognition flooding through her. It was Jace, one of the older miners, his weathered face creased with concern. "What's got you so riled up?"

Aria's clipped words tumbled out in a rush. "Hogan. He stole my haul. Almost two whole pounds, Jace! Gone!"

Jace raised an eyebrow. "What? That's more than a day's work. At least—"

"I know," she cut in, her voice low.

Jace rubbed the back of his neck, a weary grimace tightening his jaw. "He's probably halfway to the Treasury by now. The Lift's already gone and with the recent slowdowns, it'll be at least an hour before it's back."

Aria exhaled, her shoulders easing downward. "That's not the worst of it," she muttered.

"Did you bump your head, lass?" he asked, his tone rough with concern. "What's worse than losing more than a full day's haul in one go?"

She let out a low, humorless laugh. "You won't believe me."

Jace crossed his arms. "Try me," he said, his tone carrying more concern than challenge.

She hesitated, then blurted, "Screechers." She grimaced as the word left her, bracing herself for his reaction.

Jace snorted. "So you *did* bump your head."

"I'm serious, Jace," she insisted, her voice firm. "They were right there—right under me."

Jace's smirk faded. "Look, I hear you... but Screechers? This far up?"

Something in his expression tightened, then he forced the thought aside.

"Haven't seen one of those in years. Not since the Big Collapse."

He paused, jaw locking. "Took ten men to bring it down."

"I know," she said quietly. "And to be fair, I didn't really see them, but I did hear them." She glanced away, embarrassed by her own uncertainty.

Jace's expression settled, the unease buried beneath a practiced calm. "Alright. Leave it with me. I'll make sure word gets out. If what you heard out there really were Screechers—"

He paused, concern flickering across his face. "Get some rest, Aria. You're stuck down here for a while. Clean up, get something to eat. We'll talk later."

Feeling defeated, Aria nodded and turned to leave.

"And Aria," Jace called after her, his tone more serious now. "Please don't go back in there alone."

She lifted a hand in quiet acknowledgment.

"Not until we sort this out," he added, his voice trailing after her.

Aria made her way toward the inn, grateful for the few coins still tucked away in her pocket. Her shoulder throbbed with every step, yet all she could think about was the promise of warm water and a hot meal.

The path to the inn wound through narrow lanes of packed dirt and scattered debris. Lanterns flickered in the gloom, tracing veins of light through the camp. Their glow bled across puddles of black water, reflecting the silhouettes of miners moving like shadows through the haze. Shanties leaned into one another, their roofs patched with scrap metal and tar. Two miners trudged past, dragging an ore cart along the muddy path, the wheels sinking into the earth with slow, laboring effort.

The inn stood near the heart of the encampment, its faded sign creaking in the stale air. The paint—once a tired shade of blue—had long since chipped and peeled away, like the hopes and dreams of the miners who passed beneath it.

The walls bore the marks of age and hard use, patched together with whatever the innkeeper could find. Scrap metal overlapped splintered boards and clay bricks, the seams packed tight to keep out the drafts. Each section looked added out of necessity rather than design, a structure held together by the same stubborn will that kept the camp alive.

Small flickering lanterns hung from rickety beams, their warm glow struggling against the oppressive shadows, offering meager comfort to the weary souls seeking refuge within.

As Aria drew closer, she noticed the uneven stones forming the threshold, their surfaces worn smooth by countless feet treading the same path. She pushed the heavy wooden door open, releasing the mingled scents of fried roots, roasted meat, and damp earth.

Inside, patrons lounged on mismatched chairs and benches, swapping stories of their toil as bursts of laughter punctuated the low murmur of conversation.

Behind the bar stood Marielle, a burly woman with her hair drawn into a tight braid that swung like a pendulum when she poured ale.

Aria stepped forward, her stomach growling in anticipation. Marielle glanced up, sharp eyes sweeping over Aria's weary form with a mix of recognition and concern.

"You look like you've wrestled a Boulder Bug," Marielle said, setting two frothy mugs on the counter.

"Just a long day," Aria replied, forcing a smile that barely masked her fatigue.

"What'll it be?"

"Something hot, if you have it," Aria said. "And a bath, please."

Marielle wiped her palms against her apron, her calloused fingers a testament to years of serving miners. "Aye, I can do that. The stew's bubbling in the back—hearty and filling. And I can get you some hot water for the bath." She paused, studying Aria closely before adding, "That'll be four Grottos altogether."

Aria's heart sank as she fished through her pockets, fingertips brushing the worn fabric until they found the coins. Their weight offered a small measure of comfort amid the turmoil of the day.

Marielle took the coins and dropped them into a small wooden box behind the bar, her hand lingering for a heartbeat as if drawing strength from its contents.

Aria nodded her thanks, then slipped away from the bar, her mind swirling with thoughts of the day's dangers and betrayals. The warmth of the inn wrapped around her like a comforting blanket, the low hum of conversation and the soft lanternlight a gentle balm against the chaos outside.

She made her way to one of the back rooms—a small sanctuary where she could escape the noise of the main area. The hallway was dim, shadows pooling in the corners like secrets waiting to be uncovered. At the end stood a narrow door of solid, worn wood, its surface reinforced with iron bands. She stepped inside and turned the lock behind her.

A single lantern hung from the low ceiling, its weak flame casting restless shadows across the cramped space. Boxes were stacked high along one wall, filled with remnants of old mining equipment, while an aging wooden table occupied the center. Spread across its surface lay maps of Cavandel's tangled tunnels and old mining charts—trophies from miners who, long ago, had faced their fears and survived.

Aria drew a slow breath, letting the exhaustion settle over her like a heavy cloak. Then, almost absently, she began to rummage through the clutter, through the remnants of discarded lives.

As she rifled through the papers, thoughts of Hogan swirled in her mind—a mixture of anger and determination igniting within her.

Who did he think he was? How dare he take what wasn't his?

A sudden knock at the door jolted her from her reverie. She straightened, pulse quickening and called out, "Who is it?"

"It's Marielle," came the familiar voice, warm and reassuring. "I've brought your bath, love."

Relief flooded Aria as she unlatched the door, swinging it open to reveal Marielle standing there, her broad shoulders framed by the low light. At her feet sat a dented metal bucket filled with steaming water. Aria's tension eased at the sight of her, a quiet warmth stirring in her chest as Marielle smiled.

"Thanks, Marielle." Her voice softened, the weight in it easing just a fraction. "You always know what I need," she added, stepping aside to let the woman in. The room instantly felt warmer, the rich scent of herbs cutting through the ever-present tang of coal dust and damp earth.

Marielle set the bucket down carefully, then rummaged through a worn leather bag slung over her shoulder.

"You need time for yourself, child," Marielle said as she pulled a small pouch of fragrant herbs from her bag and sprinkled them into the bucket of warm water. "You can't carry Cavandel on your shoulders alone."

Aria watched as the herbs drifted across the surface, releasing oils that shimmered in slow, colorful swirls.

"It feels impossible sometimes," she admitted, pulling her dark hair over one shoulder. "With everything happening..."

"Your grandmother is a strong woman, Aria," Marielle interjected.

The reminder stung, yet it steadied her. She had to stay focused—for her grandmother and for herself.

Sensing the shift in mood, Marielle finished preparing the bath and stepped back with a satisfied nod. "It's ready when you are," she said, her voice softening before she moved toward the door. "Just lock up behind me, will you?"

The gentle click of the closing door felt like permission to exhale. Alone now, Aria released a long breath and turned toward the bucket. Even this—a bucket of warm water and a handful of herbs—felt like luxury.

She dipped her fingers in. The heat clung to her skin, seeping into the raw scrapes along her knuckles. Marielle's special blend floated on the surface, releasing a faint, earthy scent that dulled the ever-present grit of mining life.

Aria leaned forward, gathering her long dark hair over the bucket. Carefully, she dipped the ends into the warm water, then cupped handfuls to wet the rest without soaking her clothes. The water trickled over her scalp in rivulets, carrying away days of dust and grime. Beside the bucket sat a small glass vial—one Marielle had left, filled with fragrant oils. Aria worked a few drops between her palms and massaged them into her scalp.

Her fingers moved in practiced circles, working the oils through to the ends of her hair. The familiar motion loosened something inside her—not just the tangles and dirt but the weight of the day itself. She rinsed as best she could, wringing the excess water back into the bucket. The damp strands clung to her cheeks as she tied them back with a leather cord, droplets tracing cool paths down her neck.

She removed her boots and socks, loosened her collar and rolled up her sleeves. As she moved, her fingers brushed the fresh bruise blooming across her shoulder—a reminder of the chase through the tunnels earlier. She barely registered the pain.

She wrung out the coarse cloth Marielle had left and started with her face, wiping away the day's grime. The tingling oils soaked into her skin, easing the tightness in her muscles. Methodically, she cleaned her neck and arms, then reached beneath her shirt to wipe her torso, dipping the rag back into the increasingly murky water.

For a moment, she just sat there, the quiet pressing in. The lantern flickered softly, casting uneven light across the cramped room—the bucket, the cot, the faint shimmer of steam rising through the chill. That's when she noticed the mirror.

The old, tarnished glass leaned against the wall at an odd angle, its warped surface bending the light. And in that distortion, her reflection stared back at her—both familiar and foreign. The lanternlight carved hollows beneath her cheekbones and deepened the shadows around her eyes. There was something sharper there now, something unyielding.

Aria studied herself for a moment longer, wondering when she'd started to look like this—tired, older, someone she barely recognized. Then she sighed and let the thought drift away.

She reached for the rough-woven towel hanging from a rusted hook, its fibers softened by years of washings and dried herself off. Damp skin met coarse fabric as she adjusted her sleeves and pulled on thick woolen socks, patched in places. Her boots waited nearby—sturdy leather that had seen more miles than most would believe.

Finally, she ran her fingers through the tangles of her damp hair, working out the knots with practiced efficiency.

The room smelled faintly of herbs, softening the ever-present trace of coal dust. It wouldn't last, but for this brief moment she allowed herself to breathe.

Sounds from the inn filtered through the wooden door—the low rumble of conversation, the clank of mugs, the occasional burst of laughter. The lantern flickered, casting long shadows across the walls as Aria tried to collect her scattered thoughts—Hogan, the stolen crystals, the phantom sounds of Screechers still echoing in her mind.

Her stomach grumbled, drawing her back to the present. *Yep,* she thought. *Time to eat.*

She fastened her rope, torch and pick-hammer to her belt and stepped out.

The familiar murmur of voices greeted her as she sank onto a wooden bench, its boards creaking beneath her. Before her sat a steaming bowl of Marielle's famous stew—a hearty concoction that was more rumor than recipe.

Dark chunks of root vegetables floated alongside thick cuts of salted meat, suspended in a broth so rich it gleamed with an oily sheen. Tiny flecks of green herbs danced on the surface, their fragrance cutting through the heavy mineral smell that clung to everything underground. A thick slice of dark bread—dense and nearly black—rested beside the bowl, its cracked crust giving off a faint warmth.

Aria dug in, her spoon breaking the surface with a soft splash. The first bite—a complex flavor of salt, earth, and something almost sweet—spread warmth from her chest to her fingertips. Steam rose in delicate tendrils, blurring the edges of her vision. She closed her eyes, savoring the taste.

Around her, the inn's ambient noise—murmured voices, the scrape of utensils, the occasional burst of laughter—folded around her like a lullaby.

She was midway through her second bite when Jace's familiar shadow fell across the table.

"Mind if I join you?" he asked, his gruff voice breaking the spell. Without waiting for an answer, he slid onto the bench across from her.

Aria didn't look up, the stew demanding her full attention. The day had been relentless and this fleeting moment of sustenance felt sacred.

He watched her eat, arms folded, his silver-streaked hair catching the warm amber glow of the lanterns. "I spoke to a few people," he began, his voice low and measured. "About those Screechers you mentioned."

Aria's spoon paused—the briefest hesitation—then continued its journey. She chewed and swallowed but said nothing.

"If what you heard was real," he continued, "it changes everything."

"Just another day in Cavandel," she muttered, her tone laced with weariness. "What else can go wrong?"

Jace leaned forward, his weathered hands clasped on the table, eyes studying Aria's face with a mixture of concern and curiosity. The lantern's flicker cast his features in a warm glow, softening the lines that years in the mines had etched into his skin.

"Aria," he said gently, his voice barely audible above the din. "I've known you since you were knee-high to a Rockbeetle. I can tell when something's eating at you." He paused, his gaze unwavering. "What's really going on?"

Aria set her spoon down, the clatter against the bowl unnaturally loud in the stillness that followed. She drew a slow breath, her shoulders sagging as if "It's Gran," she whispered. "She's getting worse," her voice catching on the words, "and I don't know how much longer she has." The thought of her grandmother—once so vibrant, now fading under the cruel grip of Shatterblight—sat in her chest like a stone.

Jace nodded slowly, understanding her unspoken fears. He reached across the table, his hand rough from years in the mines but his touch gentle. "I'll come visit her soon," he promised, his words a quiet oath amid the tavern's noise. "It's been too long."

The promise hung between them, a small light in the encroaching darkness of their lives. Aria felt a flicker of hope—or perhaps it was only the warmth of the tavern—but she managed a faint smile. "She'd like that," she said softly. "She's always talking about the 'good old days.'"

Jace chuckled. "Aye, and I've got a few tales she hasn't heard yet. Might lift her spirits, eh?"

Aria nodded, her mind already picturing her grandmother's face lighting up at the sight of an old friend. In this moment, amidst the noise and the grime of Cavandel, there was a brief respite, a reminder that even in the darkest tunnels, there are points of light.

Jace's expression softened. "And listen to me," he said earnestly. "Don't forget to take care of yourself too, okay?"

Aria looked away for a moment, her gaze drifting over the humming tavern. She knew he was right. The relentless work in the mines, the worry for her grandmother's health—it was all consuming her bit by bit. Yet acknowledging it felt like a betrayal to her own strength.

"I know, Jace. I will," she muttered, her voice a mixture of defiance and exhaustion. Jace watched her for a moment longer before speaking up again.

"Word's spreading," he said. "And the guards have been notified." Aria nodded, but her mind was already elsewhere.

"You'd better hurry, though," he added. "The Lift's here."

Aria's head snapped up. The Lift—Cavandel's massive iron contraption that served as the city's main vertical transport, linking its sprawling levels like arteries through stone. Her heartbeat quickened. Missing it would mean another hour or more of waiting—hours her grandmother would spend worrying.

"How long?" she asked, already pushing her nearly empty bowl aside. Jace's weathered fingers drummed an urgent rhythm against the table.

"Twenty minutes, maybe less."

Aria shot to her feet. Her chair scraped against the floor, drawing curious glances from nearby patrons.

"I owe you one!" she called over her shoulder as she dashed for the door.

***

The Lift station was a chaotic blur of motion and noise. Dozens of exhausted miners crowded the platform, their faces streaked with dirt and fatigue.

Aria pushed through the press of bodies, the swarm closing in around her. She reached into her pocket and brushed her fingers over her last few coins—just enough for the ride home.

After handing them to the attendant, she slipped toward the back of the Lift, weaving between clusters of weary workers until she found a narrow space by the wall. Pressing herself into the corner, she felt the chill of the metal seep through her clothes.

A horn blared, followed by the groan and rattle of chains as the Lift began its ascent, the massive iron cage creaking beneath the weight of passengers and loaded crates.

Voices rose and fell around her—a dispute over Crythium quotas, rumors of Rocknids creeping into higher levels, someone laughing bitterly about a broken pick-hammer. All noise.

None of it really mattered.

Her thoughts were fixed on one thing only—her grandmother's face, pale and drawn, the once-strong features now frail under the strain of illness.

I'm coming, Gran, she thought, gripping the wall as the Lift shuddered upward.

I'll be home soon.

2

A Flicker of Hope

Location: Cavandel, The Outer District

Aria's eyelids fluttered open, a groggy haze clouding her vision. Shadows clung to the corners of her dimly lit room, reminders of the restless night that had tangled her thoughts.

The unforgiving stone of Cavandel offered no comfort; its chill seeped into her bones. She lay still for a moment, willing her body to shake off the weight of sleeplessness.

She had stumbled home late, her grandmother already fast asleep. Aria had slipped into bed without a word, unwilling to disturb the fragile peace that sleep granted the old woman.

Now, as she pushed herself upright with a low groan, her muscles ached in protest—a silent testament to the labor that waited for her in the mines below. A wave of frustration swelled within her chest, threatening to spill over. She stretched until her joints popped, then drew a deep breath, forcing strength back into her limbs.

The artificial dawn spilled through the window, cast by the great glow-lamps high above the caverns of the District. Aria fought against the weight of exhaustion, her mind racing as the events of yesterday replayed in fragments—the theft, the Rocknids, and the gnawing sense that something larger was stirring in the depths of Cavandel.

"Today," she muttered under her breath, determination flaring as she swung her legs over the edge of the bed. She padded across the room, the soles of her feet barely making a sound on the cool stone.

Today needed purpose, action, even if her body screamed for reprieve.

The smell of cooking drifted past her door—her grandmother was already up. Aria steadied herself, forcing a smile she didn't quite feel. There was no need to burden the old woman with her worries.

In the kitchen, the aroma of seared roots and boiled meats cut through the ever-present scent of iron dust. Her grandmother stood at the stove, back turned, humming an old lullaby. The sound tugged at Aria's heart as the gentle melody drifted through the cramped space.

"Morning, Gran," Aria said, her voice steadier now, betraying none of the weariness that gnawed at her.

"Ah, there's my girl." Her grandmother turned, a warm smile creasing her weathered face. "Sleep well?"

"Like a baby," Aria lied, leaning against the doorway. Her gaze lingered on the bubbling pot, her stomach betraying her hunger with a quiet rumble.

"How about you, Gran? How's the leg today?"

A flicker of pain crossed the old woman's face, then vanished. "Oh, same as always, dear. Nothing to fuss over."

Aria's chest tightened. *Shatterblight.* A merciless illness born from overexposure to Crythium. It infected the system and crept through the body like a curse. The disease advanced relentlessly, claiming one limb after another, leaving its victims trapped in their own failing bodies.

The word alone sent a shiver down Aria's spine. It was the miners' shadow, lurking in every jagged shard they unearthed—a slow crystallization of flesh and bone until the body became a fragile monument to its victim's suffering. Some had tried amputation to halt its spread, but the disease always returned—more aggressive, more unrelenting than before.

Her grandmother had fallen ill months ago. The first signs were subtle—a persistent ache in her left leg and a faint purple shimmer beneath the skin. Now, with her mobility reduced to a painful hobble, she could no longer work the mines alongside Aria.

Aria swallowed hard against the lump in her throat. In Cavandel, there was no place for the weak—if you couldn't mine, you didn't matter.

"Smells good," Aria said as her grandmother set a bowl in front of her.

"Good. Eat up—you need your strength," the old woman said, easing herself slowly into her chair. "And besides, you know how much I love cooking for my favorite granddaughter."

"I'm your only granddaughter," Aria said with a smirk.

"All the more reason, then," her grandmother chuckled.

They ate in companionable silence for a few moments. Aria could feel her grandmother's steady gaze on her, searching. She kept her focus on her bowl, willing her face to remain neutral.

"You're awfully quiet this morning," her grandmother said at last. "Something on your mind?"

Aria looked up, forcing a smile. "Just thinking about work. You know how it is."

Her grandmother's brow furrowed. "Aria," she said softly—her tone gentle but probing.

"It's nothing, really," Aria cut in, the words spilling out faster than she intended. "Just the usual. Long hours, tough quotas—nothing I can't handle."

Her grandmother's eyes narrowed slightly, concern and helplessness mingling in their depths. Aria's heart ached. This was why she couldn't tell her the truth. The old woman had enough to worry about without Aria adding her own troubles to the mix.

"You work too hard," her grandmother said softly, her voice edged with regret. "I wish—"

"I know, Gran." Aria reached across the worn table, taking her grandmother's frail hand in hers and giving it a reassuring squeeze. "But we're okay,

I promise. Now—tell me about your plans for today. Any exciting knitting projects on the horizon?"

Her grandmother pursed her lips, a knowing glint in her eye. "Don't think I don't know what you're up to, child." She paused for effect, then gave a playful wag of her finger. "But since you asked..."

A smile tugged at Aria's lips as her grandmother launched into an animated description of her latest creation—a blanket with a swirling pattern inspired by her favorite story, *The Tale of the Starchild*. Her face lit with excitement and for a moment, the heavy shadows of their lives seemed to fade. The crisis was averted—for now.

When they had finished, Aria stood and began clearing the table. "All right, Gran," she announced, her tone deliberately cheerful. "Time for your medicine."

Her grandmother grimaced but gave a small nod of resignation.

"You're too good to me, you know," she muttered as Aria fetched a small vial from the nearby shelf.

"Someone's got to keep you in line," Aria teased gently as she guided her to the rocking chair.

Carefully, she measured out the dose, her hands steady despite the worry gnawing at her. Her grandmother accepted the vial without protest, sipping it with a faint wince before handing it back.

Within minutes, the older woman had drifted into sleep, her breathing soft and steady, the lines of pain on her face easing into tranquility.

Aria watched her for a long moment, the faint rise and fall of her chest pulling at something deep within her. The weight in her own heart shifted—just enough to let her breathe again.

"Sleep well, Gran," she whispered, brushing a strand of hair from her forehead before tucking the worn quilt closer around her still form.

She lingered, listening to the gentle creak of the chair before moving to the far corner of their cramped living space. With practiced ease, she slid aside a loose stone in the wall, revealing a narrow alcove. Her pulse quickened as her fingers brushed the cool edges within, closing around the worn leather cover of the book hidden there. She drew it out carefully, pressing it to her chest as though her heartbeat might stir the voices of those who had once guarded it.

Her grandmother had always insisted the book be kept secret—*their* secret. It had passed through their family like a quiet inheritance, whispered about in candlelight, shared only among those who could be trusted to protect it. Now, with her mother and father gone, swallowed by the mines, the secret belonged to just the two of them. The thought made her chest ache.

Aria traced her fingers over the faded golden lettering etched on the cover, the texture worn smooth by time and secrets. A thrill of excitement and fear rippled through her as she whispered its name—*Above and Below.*

This book was her lifeline, a bridge between two worlds—the one she knew and the one she dreamed of. Its pages were a tapestry of mystery, some familiar, some cryptic. It spoke of the labyrinthine depths below, the harsh world she navigated daily, but more importantly, it whispered of the skies, the rivers and the boundless freedom of the world above—the world she longed for.

Aria opened the book and pored over the words, her lips moving soundlessly. Each page was a silent promise, a testament to the lengths to which one would go to protect knowledge—or hide it.

Some of it she understood; some of it she didn't. Charts, diagrams, and maps filled its pages, each marked with careful, deliberate detail.

The book was both beacon and burden, its pages whispering long-held secrets as she turned them. It spoke of a world beyond their reach—one Aria yearned for with every fiber of her being. Yet here she was, tethered to the depths of Cavandel. Her eyes drank in the vivid scenes and intricate sketches of a realm so unlike her own.

Tales of what was called *The Sun*, a large lantern floating freely in the sky, bringing heat, light, and darkness as it pleased. Fanciful creatures of varying shapes and sizes, and strange drawings of eerie looking things called *Trees*.

Her fingers traced an image of a vast blue expanse. "The ocean," Aria whispered, trying to imagine so much water gathered in one place. A lump rose in her throat as she turned the page to a night sky scattered with countless stars. How many times had she dreamed of seeing such a sight? The delicate lights seemed to pull her in, mocking the dull, artificial glow of Crythium that filled her underground world.

"One day," she muttered in a silent promise, closing the book with a soft thud. "One day, I'll see it all."

Aria returned the book to its hiding place, her movements quick but careful. As she replaced the stone, her jaw clenched with renewed determination. "First things first," she muttered, straightening up.

She glanced at her grandmother's sleeping form, hesitating for just a moment before grabbing her worn jacket.

"I'll be back soon," Aria whispered, more to herself than to the sleeping woman. "Time to make things right."

***

Aria paused at the end of the lane and glanced back at their home—a small hovel pressed into the rock, its crooked chimney trailing a thin thread of smoke toward the cavern's ceiling. It wasn't much, just enough space for two, yet it had endured, as they had, through every hardship Cavandel had thrown their way.

The narrow door, patched from weathered wood and scraps of metal, sat within a wall of uneven stones—some broad and flat, others jagged and small—all darkened by years of smoke and damp. Beside it, a small window of warped glass—salvaged long ago from the Stratum above—caught the light within, its surface clouded and uneven but glowing faintly all the same. That soft glow was enough—a quiet promise that her grandmother was safe for now.

Turning away, Aria's boots rang softly against the stone as she started toward the Treasury in the Inner District. The path wound through the Outer District's maze of leaning walls and narrow walkways, their railings slick with soot and condensation. Overhead, a web of bridges crisscrossed the gloom, trembling beneath unseen footsteps and casting shifting shadows that wove across the stone.

Far above, the artificial glow from the cavern's lights poured down in a steady, amber heat, washing the lane in its false daylight. Beneath that harsh brightness, the air carried the mingled scents of metal, smoke, and damp stone—the perfume of labor that marked life in the District.

The homes she passed were much like her own—humble shelters pressed shoulder to shoulder against the rock. Outside their doors, lanterns guttered low in their iron brackets, left burning from the night before, casting thin ribbons of gold that vanished into the brightening haze above.

Around her, the city stirred to its restless rhythm—traders calling from shadowed alcoves, miners exchanging rations and gossip, the distant hum of rail lines echoing through the stone. The familiar weight of frustration settled in her chest, but a flicker of hope remained. The thought of her grandmother's illness pressed heavy in her stomach, yet determination sharpened her every step. The rocky path to justice lay ahead and she would not falter.

She rounded a corner and almost collided with two familiar figures. Her childhood friends, Sylas and his older sister Heidi.

"Whoa there, Aria!" Sylas stepped back, arms flung out theatrically. "You almost took out Cavandel's greatest hero."

Heidi rolled her eyes with exaggerated patience. "Ignore him. He's been unbearable all morning."

"If by unbearable you mean *awesome*," Sylas said, throwing his arms out wide as if greeting an audience, "then guilty as charged."

He winked, and Aria laughed before she could stop herself, surprised by how good it felt to sound like the world wasn't falling apart.

"Where are you off to in such a rush?" Heidi queried, her eyes narrowing with concern.

"Treasury. Got a bone to pick about yesterday," Aria said, her voice clipped.

"What kinda bone?" Sylas asked.

"I'm off to reclaim my dignity—or what's left of it," she replied, her breath catching slightly as she prepared to spill the details. "Hogan stole my haul and I need to report it."

"What?" Heidi blinked, her tone sharp with disbelief. "How?"

Before Aria could form an answer, Sylas cut in, his brows furrowing. "That's low—even for Hogan."

Aria exhaled slowly, forcing calm into her voice. "Doesn't matter how—what matters is getting it back. I'll file a report, make them take it seriously."

Heidi's expression softened. She reached out and touched Aria's arm. "It'll be okay," she said quietly.

The three stood in the narrow street as the chatter of distant voices ebbed and flowed. For a moment, no one spoke. Sylas glanced from one to the other, the tension clear in their faces. Then, with a faint grin and a shift in his tone, he tried to break the gloom the only way he knew how.

"Well, fear not, fair maiden," he said, bowing low and exaggerated, "for Sylas is here to—"

"Save it, Sylas," Heidi interrupted, though her tone carried more weariness than bite. "So, what's the plan?"

"Get some answers. Make 'em listen," Aria replied, her fists clenched. "Dunno. Whatever it takes."

"We're coming with you," Heidi announced, "but I doubt they'll listen."

Together, they strode toward the Treasury as Aria filled them in on the events of the previous day. The rhythmic sound of their footsteps became a drumbeat to the cadence of their shared purpose.

They followed one of the main lanes until the houses began to thin, their clustered walls giving way to broader passages carved smooth into the stone.

The air grew warmer as they drew closer to Inner District, where the high ceiling lights burned stronger, flooding the lanes in a steady amber glare.

The crooked bridges and makeshift walkways of the Outer gave way to wide iron spans and reinforced beams—bridges built to last, humming faintly with the energy that coursed through the city's veins. The stone façades here were even, cleaner, their edges sharp against the dim haze. At each doorway, Crythium-powered glow-lamps burned with quiet precision, their pale brilliance casting smooth pools of light across the street—so different from the soot-stained lanterns and torches of the Outer District.

Aria lifted her gaze toward the towering shape that loomed in the distance—the Lift. Its massive frame stretched from the cavern floor to the ceiling far above, a vertical artery of steel and power connecting the many layers of the underground city.

As they neared the Treasury, Aria's resolve hardened. Whatever happened, she knew she could count on her friends. In the oppressive dark of Cavandel, their bond was a light she clung to fiercely.

The Treasury, one of four in the Inner District, loomed ahead—its stone facade cold and unwelcoming. A fortress within a city of shadows, its heavy iron doors bore the marks of time and authority. Intricate reliefs depicted miners at work, glorifying the labor that fed Cavandel's heartbeat while omitting the suffering that came with it.

When Aria pushed through the massive doors, a wave of sound greeted her—dozens of uneasy voices blending into a low, restless hum. Her heart quickened, nerves coiling tight in her stomach. She scanned the hall, eyes sweeping over the line of miners shuffling forward, each clutching their precious sacks of crystals.

Several city guards stood sentinel near the entrance, their imposing figures casting long shadows across the polished stone floor. Each carried a spear-like weapon tipped with a faintly glowing metal blade. Its purple hue pulsed in a slow, steady rhythm, washing their leather armor in a strange, living light. Brown capes hung from their shoulders, swaying with each subtle shift, while the sharp click of their boots echoed through the hall.

Their presence was a living emblem of authority—a constant reminder of the divisions that ruled Cavandel.

Aria's heartbeat quickened at the sight of the guards, her palms growing clammy against the worn fabric of her jacket. She came here every week to exchange crystals for coins, yet the unease never faded.

From the front of the line came a commotion. "These are worth way more than you're offering!" a man shouted, his voice hoarse and raw. Dirt streaked his cheeks, veins bulging at his neck as he leaned over the counter, jabbing a finger toward the clerk's indifferent face.

"That's enough," the clerk said flatly, barely glancing up from his papers. His tone made it clear the discussion was over. "Get him out of here," he added, nodding toward the guards.

Two guards stepped forward, their faces blank, devoid of compassion. They seized the man by the arms, their grip like iron shackles. His protests echoed through the hall—frantic, desperate—filling the air with the sound of wild indignation.

"Let go of me!" he shouted, his voice cracking with fury. "I'm telling you—those crystals are worth more than you think! This is robbery!" He thrashed against their grip, boots scraping across the floor. As the guards dragged him toward the heavy metal doors, his voice rose to a desperate, almost primal wail. "You're all just pawns in this twisted game!" he cried. "They don't care about us!"

Aria's heart pounded as the scene unfolded before her eyes. She felt a sharp pang of sympathy for the man—her own frustrations simmering just beneath the surface. She had seen too many like him silenced by violence or fear.

By the time her turn came, her nerves were raw, her pulse thudding in her ears. As she stepped forward with Sylas and Heidi, the clerk looked up—a thin man with beady eyes that seemed to look through her rather than at her.

"How much?" he asked out of habit, his tone lifeless as his gaze searched for the sack of Crythium Aria wasn't carrying.

"I'm here to report a theft," she said, steadying her voice.

The clerk sighed, his expression barely changing. "What kind of theft?"

"My haul—" She hesitated, then corrected herself. "I mean, my Crythium, sir. A whole day's worth of it. Stolen in the mines."

The clerk remained unmoved. "And?" he said flatly.

"I know who did it!" Aria blurted. "Hogan. Did someone named Hogan cash out a bag of crystals yesterday?"

"Young lady," the clerk intoned, glancing up from his papers. "Look around you. Do you see all these people waiting?" He paused, as if expecting an answer that never came. "We don't have time to chase after every piece of Crythium that goes missing."

"Wait—" Aria protested. "This is important—"

"Next!" the clerk barked, the word slicing through her plea.

Aria's jaw tightened, anger simmering just below the surface. "If you'll just let me explain—"

"Next!" the man repeated, already turning to the miner behind her.

Sylas stepped forward, indignation flashing in his eyes. "Hey, you can't treat us like—"

The clerk's gaze slid toward the guards. They didn't move, but their attention locked on him, fingers curling tighter around their weapons. Sylas's tone faltered, the edge draining away as if he'd suddenly remembered where he was. "—like that," he finished, quieter now, the fight gone from his voice.

"Fine," Aria snapped, frustration tightening like a knot in her chest. She caught his arm before he could recover the moment. "Don't," she murmured, low but steady. Heidi slipped to his other side, her voice soft yet urgent. "Let's just go."

Together they ushered him out, their movements quick and deliberate. The heavy doors of the Treasury slammed shut behind them, the metallic echo chasing them into the street. Anger and humiliation rolled off the three of them in uneven waves. Aria's fists clenched at her sides, her nails biting into her palms as the artificial heat of Cavandel's day pressed down—thick, oppressive and unrelenting.

Without a word, they made their way toward a nearby outcropping of rock, their boots scuffing against the uneven stone.

"Well," Sylas grumbled, kicking at a loose pebble, "that was about as useful as a Screecher in a mineshaft." The pebble skittered away, disappearing into a narrow crevice.

The rock formations surrounding the Treasury entrance loomed above them, twisted spires of stone that seemed to mock their defeat. Aria slumped onto a jagged boulder, its surface cool against her palms. Sylas paced back and forth, his movements jerky and agitated, while Heidi leaned against a pillar, arms crossed tightly over her chest.

"Can you believe that guy?" Sylas exploded, gesticulating wildly. "It's like we don't even exist to them!"

"I can't believe they just dismissed us like that," Heidi added, her voice barely above a whisper.

"Well, that's life in the District," Aria sighed. Her gaze swept over the bustling street before them. Miners trudged by, shoulders hunched under the weight of their loads, faces streaked with dirt and exhaustion. The constant hum of machinery filled the air around them.

"What we need is a plan." Heidi said, trying to ease the tension.

"I know," Sylas declared, "let's get a drink. It'll help us think."

"It's barely midday, Sylas," Heidi replied, feigning outrage with theatrical precision.

Aria nodded, her muscles tight with frustration. "I'm sorry, you two," she said quietly. "You could've been in the mines by now—and here I am, wasting your time."

Sylas waved his hand dismissively, a mischievous glint in his eye. "Oh please, Aria. Time wasted with friends is hardly time wasted at all." He paused for dramatic effect, then added with a wink, "Though I do charge by the hour, you know. My rates are quite reasonable—only ten Grottos per hour of dashing heroics and witty banter."

Heidi snorted, elbowing her brother in the ribs. "As if anyone would pay for your 'half-witted banter.'"

"You wound me, dear sister of mine," Sylas clutched his chest in mock agony. "I'll have you know my wit is highly sought after in many circles."

"The circle of village idiots, maybe," Heidi teased, her grin giving her away.

Aria couldn't help but smile at their familiar bickering. It was a welcome distraction from the weight of her troubles.

They headed down the crowded street toward one of Cavandel's many taverns. As they made their way through the winding avenues, the great guard towers of the District loomed above them—a constant reminder of the divide between those who ruled and those who served.

"Ever wonder what it's like in there?" Sylas mused, gesturing to the tall building. "Bet their floors don't shake when the mines rumble."

"Just keep moving," Aria hissed, feeling the weight of watchful eyes upon them. "They don't like us being this close. It's not a place for people like us."

"Maybe," Sylas whispered back, a smirk playing on his lips. "But one day—who knows?"

Heidi rolled her eyes but said nothing.

The trio rounded a corner and suddenly the narrow street opened up into a sprawling marketplace. Aria's senses were immediately overwhelmed by the vibrant tapestry of life. Glow-lamps cast a soft, ethereal light over the scene, their gray hue lending an otherworldly quality to the bustling crowd.

Makeshift stalls lined the market's walls, their colorful awnings a patchwork of faded fabrics. Vendors' cries echoed through the crowd, each attempting to outdo the other in volume and enthusiasm. "Fresh mushrooms! Get your fresh mushrooms!" one shouted. "New shipment of lumber! Directly from the Stratum!" bellowed another. "Look your best at the festival! Fitted corsets at only half price!" an older woman called out.

The very air seemed infused with the mingled aromas of sizzling meats, pungent herbs and the ever-present metallic scent of iron.

As they made their way down the crowded street, the air shimmered under Cavandel's false daylight, the heat spilling from stone and metal walls into the crush of bodies around them.

Suddenly, a small figure darted out from an alleyway, nearly colliding with Aria. She stumbled back, startled, as two children—a boy and a girl, no older than six or seven—skidded to a stop in front of them.

"Whoa, there!" Sylas exclaimed. "Careful where you run now."

The boy's eyes widened as he took in the trio. His clothes were patched and worn, but his face was alight with curiosity. The girl beside him clutched a battered doll to her chest, her tangled hair framing a face smudged with dirt.

"We're not supposed to talk to strangers," the young boy informed the group.

Aria exchanged a glance with Sylas and Heidi. "That's good," she whispered, crouching down to the child's level. "But what are you two doing out here all alone?"

The girl shuffled closer to her companion, eyes darting nervously. The boy puffed out his chest. "We're not alone. We're on a mission!"

"A mission, eh?" Sylas grinned, playing along. "Sounds important."

"It is," the boy nodded vigorously. "We're gonna be heroes, just like the Dwellers."

Aria's breath caught. She felt Heidi stiffen beside her as well.

"The Dwellers?" Heidi asked, her voice carefully neutral. "Where'd you hear about them?"

The girl tugged on the boy's sleeve, shaking her head frantically. He ignored her. "The Dwellers are going to save us. Papa's fighting the bad guys, to make things fair."

Aria's mind raced. The Dwellers. The resistance.

"Can you tell me—"

Then the world exploded in a deafening boom.

The ground lurched beneath their feet, sending shockwaves through the stone. Aria stumbled, catching herself against the wall. Dust billowed from the direction of the guard tower, choking the air with a sudden, terrifying darkness.

"Explosion," Heidi coughed out, "from the guard tower," her voice barely audible over the ringing in Aria's ears.

"Run!" Aria yelled, grabbing the children by the arms and hauling them along to safety.

They sprinted, dodging falling debris and the panicked surge of bodies. Aria's lungs burned with the effort, her mind reeling from the chaos. Her heart pounded.

What was happening?

Aria pulled the children close, shielding them with her body as they raced through the panicked crowd. Debris rained down around them, forcing them to weave and duck to avoid the falling wreckage. Sylas and Heidi flanked them, Sylas' usual bravado replaced by genuine alarm as his eyes darted, searching for a safe path.

Finally, they reached the relative safety of a narrow alleyway, the crush of the crowd thinning. Aria ushered the children into a sheltered alcove, her hands trembling slightly as she checked them for injuries.

"Are you both alright?" she asked, concern threading through her voice. The girl clutched her doll tightly, her eyes wide with fear, while the boy stood protectively in front of her, his chin jutting out defiantly.

"We're okay," the boy replied, his voice laced with a bravado that belied the tremor in his hands. "We have to find papa. He'll know what to do."

Aria's heart raced as she processed the boy's words. The Dwellers—the resistance group that they've been hearing so much about lately.

Could it be true? Were these children somehow connected to them?

Before Aria could question the boy further, a woman's frantic voice echoed down the alley.

"Jem! Lyla! Where are you?" The children's heads snapped up, their faces lighting with recognition.

"Mama!" the girl cried, darting out of the alcove. The boy followed close behind, calling out, "We're here, Mama!"

Another bomb blast rocked the District.

"Run!" Sylas shouted, grabbing Aria's arm and pulling her into motion. She looked around, but the children were long gone. *At least they were safe now.*

"Alleyway!" Heidi shouted, pointing to a narrow opening between two buildings, her eyes wide with fear.

They veered left, the alley's shadows swallowing them whole. Aria's pulse hammered in her temples; every breath a battle.

"Stay close!" she called out, gripping Heidi's hand.

"Of course!" Sylas gasped, barely audible over the noise. He ducked beside them as debris clattered in the street behind, the echo of the blast still rolling through the District.

They pressed deeper into the alley, huddling together with their backs to the cold stone, waiting for the world to stop shaking. Eventually, silence fell over them like a curtain—heavy and suffocating.

"Everyone okay?" Aria's voice was a whisper, her throat raw with dust.

"I think so," Heidi said, a small victory in her tone.

"Still kicking," Sylas managed, though his usual humor was gone, replaced by something else.

"Let's try to keep it that way," Aria said, her resolve hardening once more. Together, they would face whatever came next.

***

Grit and sweat mingled on Aria's skin as they staggered into the dimly lit tavern, its usual raucous atmosphere subdued to a low murmur. She scanned the room, noting the tense postures and furrowed brows that mirrored their own. Sylas leaned against a rough wooden column, his breaths short and clipped, while Heidi slumped onto a bench, her hands trembling.

"Did anyone see them?" Aria whispered, her voice steady despite the adrenaline still coursing through her veins.

Sylas shook his head, glancing around with narrowed eyes. "No. I don't think so."

"What in the depths is going on?" Heidi murmured, wiping a smear of dust from her cheek. "We could've been—"

"Think it was them? The Dwellers?" Aria cut in, her thoughts racing.

"Aren't they supposed to be the good guys?" Sylas said, meeting her gaze. "Either way, the Warden won't be happy. Not after this."

Their conversation hung in the air, laced with the possibility of change—of upheaval. And danger. Aria could taste it, metallic and sharp on her tongue. Her thoughts drifted to her grandmother, asleep in her rocking chair, then to the tremors that had threatened to shake their world apart.

"Hey," Heidi's voice cut through the noise, her hand reaching across the table to touch Aria's arm. "You're still with us, right?"

"Of course." The words came automatically, though she wasn't sure she believed them. It all felt like too much—the injustice, the exhaustion, her grandmother's failing strength and now the chaos outside. Doubt gnawed at her like a half-remembered dream. The world seemed to be closing in and Aria could only wonder how much more she could bear.

"Good," Sylas said, a half-smile flickering across his face. "Because we stick together. No matter what."

Aria nodded, summoning a smile that felt brittle.

Together, yes, she thought, *but how long before it all slipped away?*

Her heart wrestled with the question, even as she pushed it aside.

"Let's lay low for now," she said quietly, her eyes scanning the room once more. Every face seemed a blend of fear and resolve—a mirror of her own conflicted soul.

"Agreed," Heidi sighed, and for a moment none of them spoke—the weight of the day settling heavy on their shoulders.

As the tavern's low hum continued around them, Aria's thoughts drifted upward, to the sky she'd never seen, to the chains she yearned to break. *One day*, she promised herself. *But not today.*

Today, she had a grandmother to protect and a mystery to unravel. The surface would have to wait.

***

The man waited silently in the cramped alcove, tension coiling along his spine. From the corridor beyond came muffled echoes—distant shouts, urgent footsteps, the faint groan of shifting stone and timber. The glow-lamp sputtered against the rough walls, casting restless shadows across his face as he listened, waiting.

At last, hurried footsteps approached. The door eased open and two figures entered quickly, supporting a third between them. The woman stumbled, her hand finding the wall for support. Her eyes were wide, unfocused, her face streaked with soot and ash.

"Anna," the man breathed quietly, stepping forward. "You're safe."

She lifted her gaze sharply, blinking as recognition flickered through the haze. "Pike?" Her voice was hoarse, threaded with disbelief. "Did Sebastian send you?"

Pike hesitated only briefly, his expression carefully neutral. "He's too cautious. There was no other way."

"No other—" Anna shook her head slowly, her gaze drifting toward the corridor. "You didn't need to go this far, Pike. Was this for me, or *her*?"

For a moment, Pike said nothing. He held her gaze steady. When he spoke, his voice was calm, measured. "It's done. And we have work to do."

She studied him, searching for something in his face. Between them hung a weighted silence, punctuated only by the distant echoes from the passage outside.

One of Pike's men cleared his throat gently. "We need to move. Guards will sweep this section soon."

Pike nodded sharply. "Take her through the secondary route. Quickly."

They moved without hesitation, guiding Anna gently toward the exit. At the threshold, she paused, glancing back to meet Pike's gaze. Her words fell quietly but with unmistakable clarity.

"Sebastian won't forgive this."

Pike's gaze softened slightly, resigned. "I know..."

She lingered only a heartbeat longer before vanishing into the shadows. Pike stood quietly for a moment after they'd gone, breathing slowly as the distant murmurs faded into silence. Yet as he turned away, a faint scent of smoke seemed to follow him—imagined, perhaps, but enough to tighten something in his chest. Finally, he slipped out after them, disappearing swiftly into the darkness.

3

Shadows of Rebellion

Location: Cavandel, The Stratum

Cavandel was a cage of stone and iron—one that its people were born and buried beneath. Only dignitaries from the surface were ever granted passage downward—envoys, merchants bearing fine goods, and haulers sent to collect the latest shipments of Crythium. For everyone else, the city's boundaries were absolute.

The pride of Cavandel was its uppermost level, known as the Stratum. Perched just beneath the surface of the Emerald Mountains, it served as the subterranean city's gateway to the world above—a world that no one from Cavandel ever saw.

The walls of the Stratum stood like sentinels, heavily guarded and unyielding, forming an impenetrable barrier between the ruling elite and the chaos that festered in the District below. Every inch of it gleamed with mechanical precision—a monument to order and control. Rows of glow-lamps cast a muted golden haze across the streets as passersby moved quickly beneath them, their faces half-lit, half-lost in shadow. Light caught on glass, stone, and the polished curves of rail lines, bridging the silent avenues in a seamless flow of motion and machinery, while steam drifted from air vents and grates like silent whispers, coiling lazily through the arches before dissolving into the dim expanse above.

At the heart of the Stratum stretched the market square, overshadowed by the Administrative Hall—an imposing cluster of iron and glass that loomed above the city. Their façades gleamed beneath the lamplight, ornate yet austere, each pane mirroring the ceaseless motion below. Within those walls, decrees were penned and orders sealed, shaping the fate of every soul in Cavandel—from the Warden's office at the summit to the miners laboring in the depths beneath.

It was here, in the dim confines of a richly furnished yet oppressive office, that Thaddeus Blackthorne, Warden of Cavandel, sat brooding. His gaunt figure cast skeletal shadows across the walls, illuminated by the faint glow-lamp. The rhythmic ticking of an antique clock—a relic salvaged from the surface—filled the room. Each second punctuated his dark thoughts, amplifying their weight.

The clock's golden hands ticked steadily, marking the passage of time in the city above—a place bathed in sunlight and freedom. But here, deep within the bowels of the Emerald Mountains, time had no meaning. The endless dark of the mines blurred the lines between day and night, creating a timeless void where only the rhythms of labor and rest gave structure to existence.

Thaddeus leaned forward, his bony elbows pressing into the grooved surface of a massive wooden desk. The desk itself was a relic, its rich grain a stark contrast to the dull stone walls. Its surface, scarred and stained from a lifetime of use, bore witness to countless decisions made upon it.

Sprawled across the desk lay an intricate map of Cavandel, its parchment cracked and curling with age—a patchwork of history where faded tunnels met sharp, fresh ink marking new excavations.

Scattered around it were crystal decanters, their contents glowing faintly in the low light. Each held a different shade of amber liquid—the finest spirits from the surface world. A half-empty glass rested near Thaddeus's right hand, condensation beading on its rim.

His pale eyes swept the room—a space both utilitarian and indulgent. The walls were lined with charts, production reports and schematics, each pinned with ruthless precision. Interspersed among them hung rare artifacts from the surface: a pressed flower, its fragile petals frozen in time; a faded photograph of a sun-drenched landscape; a tattered book of poetry, its spine dulled and cracked from years of use.

In one corner loomed a filing cabinet, overflowing with ledgers and records—every gram of Crythium extracted, every Grotto minted or dispensed, every infraction punished. The cabinet's surface was marred by scratches and dents, each a testament to the countless times Thaddeus had slammed it shut in frustration—or in triumph.

Across from it stood a forgotten mirror, veiled beneath a dusty drape. Thaddeus hadn't looked at his reflection in years. He didn't need to; he already knew the hollow-eyed specter that would greet him.

On the desk before him, a shard of Crythium gleamed with an otherworldly violet light. Thaddeus stared at it, his fingers drumming the desk's edge.

Bombings. Chaos. Disorder.

His jaw clenched, the muscles in his face drawn taut. He had been entrusted—no, destined—to maintain the balance, to ensure the precious Crythium kept flowing.

How did it come to this? How had these vermin—these Dustborn—managed to put a crack in his perfect system?

Thaddeus reclined in his seat, his gaze fixed on the radiant shard. Its glow danced across his features, casting shifting patterns that seemed almost to mock him. Cavandel had been perfect once—a masterpiece of order, a city balanced on precision and will. But now—

He closed his eyes, savoring the memory of a city bent to his will. The miners toiled in the depths, content in their stations. The guards patrolled with unwavering vigilance, their brutality swift and unquestioned. And he—above it all—where he rightfully belonged.

But it hadn't always been this way. Thaddeus Blackthorne had not been born into power or privilege. No, he had clawed his way here, inch by agonizing inch, through darkness and shadow.

He opened his eyes, the violet glow of the Crythium shard still flickering across his gaunt features. It sat on his desk like a piece of fate itself, its edges sharp enough to wound. In its glow, he saw the echoes of his past—the hunger, the desperation, the unrelenting will to survive.

His fingers traced the deep grooves etched into the wooden desk, feeling its scars beneath his fingertips. This desk, massive and imposing, had once belonged to men who dictated his actions. Now, it was his kingdom. Every decision, every order, now flowed through him.

But there was a time when his hands held only a pickaxe too heavy for his boyish frame.

As a child, hunger gnawed at him like a parasite, a constant ache that twisted in his belly. He had lived on the outermost fringes of Cavandel's society, where the walls of their ramshackle hovel leaned inward, weary as the people within.

The gruel in their bowls was thin, their clothes thinner. His father, a miner, came home every night with soot caked beneath his fingernails and despair clinging to his skin. No matter how many hours his father gave to the mines, poverty held them captive.

Thaddeus's gaze shifted toward the cabinet of ledgers by the wall, each drawer swollen with records of wealth now bound to his command. The irony wasn't lost on him. His father had died counting minutes until payday, while Thaddeus now controlled the pay of countless thousands. The weight of that power had once thrilled him, but tonight it pressed down on him, as heavy as the cave-ins he had barely survived.

He remembered his mother's cough—the wet, rattling sound that heralded the end. Her handkerchief had always come away spotted with blood, like a canvas splattered by a cruel artist. Shatterblight had stolen her breath when he was just ten, and with her passing, the fragile tether holding his father together had snapped.

Thaddeus leaned back in his chair, the leather groaning under the shift of his weight. His eyes glanced to the covered mirror in the corner, the place where he buried what little remained of the boy he once was.

He had entered the mines at twelve—a child forced to grow up with blistered hands and lungs full of dust. The tunnels had been cruel to him at first; every swing of the pickaxe made his shoulders scream, and every slip of his grip tore new blisters into his palms.

His first year had been a trial by fire, but failure was never an option. His body was weak, but his mind was sharp. He quickly realized that survival underground wasn't enough to escape poverty's grip. His first real chance had come when he least expected it, in the crowded, chaotic market square of the Inner District.

He still remembered the girl who had captivated him then—the scent of warm bread drifting from her mother's stall, mingling with the heavy, metallic air that always lingered in Cavandel. One moment he was helping stack crates of bread; the next, the wheel of a wealthy merchant's cart cracked, leaving the man stranded in the market's busiest lane.

Would any of it have happened if that wheel hadn't broken? If his haphazard fix hadn't held long enough to impress the merchant? If he hadn't said yes to the offer—and goodbye to that girl?

He could still see the fear and excitement in her eyes as he walked away, the weight of her hopes pressing against his back.

He had left everything behind for that chance. His father hadn't noticed his departure. The girl had understood.

The transition from laboring the mines to working for the merchant wasn't easy. The role was grueling in its own way—ledgers to balance, quotas to calculate, shipments to monitor. The merchant demanded perfection, and failure wasn't tolerated. But Thaddeus thrived under the pressure.

That had only been the beginning. Power had its own rhythm in Cavandel, and Thaddeus had seized it the way he did everything else—quietly, efficiently, and without looking back.

He wasn't the boy waiting for orders anymore. The same streets that had once echoed with his hunger now trembled beneath his calculated gaze.

He ran a hand over the map spread across his desk, tracing a path through tunnels he hadn't set foot in for years. His eyes burned as he thought of the girl, who hadn't been fortunate enough to find her way out.

She had been his first friend, the girl who sat with him when the shifts felt endless and recited simple poems her mother had taught her. "Words can take you anywhere," she'd told him once, "even if only for a moment."

Her laugh—bright and hopeful—had been a light in his otherwise dim world. But hope, like everything else in the mines, eventually crumbled under the weight of reality.

Her memory followed him, whispering through his thoughts like the faint ticking of the antique clock.

He downed the rest of the amber liquid from his glass, the burn of it fading too quickly.

His gaze returned to the Crythium shard, its glow casting jagged shadows across the map. Cavandel was his now, a city shaped by his ambition. But tonight, the weight of its flaws pressed in on him—bombings, dissenters, cracks in the system he'd built.

He set the empty glass aside and leaned forward, tracing a path across the map. His eyes burned with determination.

The boy who once dreamed of escape was gone, buried beneath the weight of decisions made in dimly lit rooms like this one. Regret, like the dust on the covered mirror, would remain undisturbed.

Because in Cavandel, survival was power—and Thaddeus Blackthorne was nothing if not a survivor.

He allowed himself a fleeting smile, thin and bitter. He could still recall the early days when he was first named Warden of the Vein. The fear in the eyes of the District's residents as he walked the streets. The averted gazes, the way they scattered like insects before him.

That was respect.

"Respect," he muttered under his breath, the word tasting like ash. The smile faded from Thaddeus' face, replaced by a glowering scowl.

His eyes snapped open, narrowing as he glared again at the Crythium shard.

The Dwellers. That's what they called themselves. Filthy rats crawling in the shadows, gnawing at the foundations of his rule. They had forgotten their place, they had forgotten the importance of balance.

Thaddeus rose abruptly, his chair scraping against the floor. He snatched the Crythium shard, its sharp edges biting into his palm. The pain grounded him, sharp and immediate, a fitting reminder of the cost of power.

If respect had to be earned again, then so be it. He would descend into the chaos below, and he would remind them who truly ruled Cavandel.

But first, he needed to find Commander Grask—and, of course, deliver a little message to the good people of Cavandel.

***

Drazic Grask sat in the dark. Just the way he liked it.

The glow-lamps embedded in the walls barely flickered, their dim light casting trembling shadows that crept and shifted like things with minds of their own. The cool, damp air clung to his skin, but he didn't mind. Not when she was with him.

Gently, he traced his calloused fingers down her full length, his touch slow and deliberate, like a man savoring a secret. She didn't pull away. She never did.

"Scarlet," he whispered, leaning back against the cold stone. Her name felt warm on his tongue, like a promise waiting to be fulfilled. "You've always understood me."

A smile flashed across his lips as he felt her familiar form beneath his fingertips. "You are the only one I can trust," he muttered, "I'll do anything for you, as long as we're together." His fingers paused, resting on a familiar ridge, a flaw that only he knew how to find. "You've shown me that pain isn't something to fear. It's the one thing that defines us all."

Her silence wasn't empty. It was patient, waiting.

Drazic exhaled slowly, letting the tension bleed out of him. "Do you think Thaddeus will be pleased?" he asked, tilting his head forward, but only he could hear her faint whisper.

He closed his eyes, the weight of the day's accomplishments pressing down on him. "That miner was lying to us," he murmured, his voice barely more than a breath. "He knew something about the bombings. Thought he could hide it from us." His grip tightened, knuckles whitening.

The glow-light flickered again, casting her magnificent form across the wall. He smiled faintly and whispered, "Are you still hungry?" The answer was already there, humming in his veins, but he liked asking her anyway.

"It's not wrong if it gets us results, is it?" he said, repeating the words under his breath. "It's not wrong if it keeps the Warden's trust."

A knock came at the door, sharp and deliberate. The Warden's voice followed, cutting through the silence. "Grask!"

Drazic's eyes snapped open, and for a moment, he stared at the door, disoriented, as if Thaddeus's interruption didn't quite belong in the world he had just shared with her.

He stood slowly, fastening her in place at his side.

The lamp flickered one last time, its glow illuminating the coiled form of Scarlet, the whip that lay snug against his hip. Her leather was dark, stained with years of secrets and confessions pulled from unwilling tongues. Drazic patted her handle, his fingers lingering for a moment.

"You're always right," he muttered to himself before pulling the door open and stepping into the corridor where the Warden waited.

***

A few minutes earlier, the Warden of Cavandel had paused before a plain gray metal door in the barracks wing of the Administrative Hall. He rapped lightly, the sound carrying down the narrow corridor. These quarters belonged to Drazic Grask—his chief officer, his enforcer.

Posted at the door was a watchman standing guard—a young man of maybe twenty-five. His eyes were sharp and unyielding, flickering briefly toward the Warden before snapping back to the corridor ahead.

His face was a mask of discipline, carved from stone, but there was a tension in his jaw, a subtle quiver that betrayed the weight of the Warden's presence. He stood frozen in place, his posture rigid, his hands clasped behind his back. A dim glow-lamp, affixed to the ceiling cast long shadows across his broad shoulders, emphasizing the polished brass of his uniform buttons.

After a few seconds, Thaddeus knocked again, but louder this time.

That lunatic, the Warden thought, *what could he be up to now?*

"Grask!" the Warden shouted, banging louder this time.

"Is he in there?" Thaddeus asked the guard.

"He is, Warden," the guard replied. His voice was clipped, almost swallowed by the oppressive silence of the corridor.

Thaddeus's pale eyes narrowed, his jaws clenching in frustration. He raised his hand to knock again, but before his knuckles met the cold metal, the door let out a low, grating creak. It swung open just enough to reveal a sliver of darkness beyond—a void that seemed to pulse faintly with an unsettling stillness.

Thaddeus hesitated, his hand hovering in mid-air. A chill prickled the back of his neck, something he hadn't felt in years. The air smelled faintly of burnt metal and something else—something acrid and sharp.

Drazic's stocky frame filled the narrow gap of the doorway, his broad shoulders blocking any view of the room behind him. The chamber was a mystery, a void of darkness.

His left cheek bore the jagged, raised scar of an old burn, the skin pulled tight in a permanent sneer that seemed to deepen as his eyes met Thaddeus's. His steel-tipped boots scraped against the stone floor as he shifted his weight, the sound sharp and grating in the silence. The whip coiled at his side swayed slightly, its leather tip brushing against his thigh like a restless serpent.

"Warden," Drazic drawled, his voice low and rough. He didn't step aside or invite Thaddeus in. His face stayed half in shadow, but his eyes caught the light—something glinting there, not fear or guilt, but a flicker of defiance, carefully masked.

"We—uh, I wasn't expecting you." His eyes darted to the guard—who somehow stood even stiffer—before returning to Thaddeus.

Thaddeus's lips formed a thin line, his gaze cutting through the dim light to fix on Drazic. "Am I interrupting something, Mr. Grask?"

For a moment, only the faint hum of distant machinery filled the air between them. Then Drazic looked down at the whip at his side—a wicked instrument named Scarlet for its crimson-stained tip.

"Scarlet and I had a prior engagement," Drazic replied, his tone unapologetic, laden with a sinister undertone. The implication was clear—something unpleasant, an interrogation perhaps, was in progress or about to commence within these confined walls.

The Warden's eyes flickered, the mere hint of a scowl crossing his pale face. "I sometimes wonder why I keep you around, Grask," he said, his voice cold and even. "Your tastes for dramatics are unseemly." His gaze fell pointedly on Scarlet, then back up to meet Drazic's unwavering stare. "It's only because you're efficient, remarkably so. But let's be clear—you're a bit too—peculiar, for my tastes."

Thaddeus took a step forward, forcing Drazic to move back, relinquishing control of the space as Thaddeus peered beyond him into the darkened room. He only saw faint outlines—strange instruments and shadows that moved too erratically to be anything benign. The air inside felt charged, heavy with something unsaid, something done.

"This engagement of yours—" he probed sharply, eyes glinting with both curiosity and disdain. "Never mind," the Warden muttered with a scowl. "Come with me."

Drazic hesitated, his gaze lingering on the shadowy depths of the room. Reluctance etched across his features as he finally closed the door with a definitive, muted clink. He turned, the narrow corridor now framing him against the backdrop of glow-lights that cast long and wavering shadows across his scarred face.

"Very well, Warden," Drazic grumbled under his breath, falling into step beside Thaddeus as they strode through the narrow corridor of the Administrative Hall.

Their footsteps echoed unevenly in the passage, a stark juxtaposition of two distinct rhythms.

In the shadowed corridor, the distinct cadence of Thaddeus Blackthorne's boots echoed with authoritative precision, each step a declaration of ownership over the space and silence around him.

His ensemble—a sleek coat of darkest leather, accented with golden buttons and a trim belt—gleamed, untouched by the underground's grit, a testament to his meticulous nature. A dark cravat peeked from under his high collar, its knot as sharp as his gaze, while his coat moved with sculpted grace, every fold a stroke of dark elegance.

Contrasting sharply, Drazic Grask's presence was marked by the heavy thud of his practical boots, their worn leather telling tales of the depths he controlled.

His robust brown coat, edged with golden epaulets and reinforced with functional buckles, bore the marks of a life amid dust and discord. It was a garment of utility, seasoned by skirmishes and by the relentless demands of overseeing the guards and maintaining order across the rugged domain.

Together, they moved through the Stratum, a study in contrasts—Thaddeus, with his regal, calculated demeanor, and Drazic, rugged and unpolished, each bearing the weight of their respective roles. Their attire not only declared their rank but also narrated their history—a warden's precision and an enforcer's resilience etched into every thread.

They stepped out of the Administrative Hall and made their way south toward the Lift, passing through the market and several guarded checkpoints. Each post was manned by imposing figures, their silent vigilance a stern reminder of order within this subterranean world. At last, they reached an overlook—a high ledge that opened onto the vast sprawl of the District below.

The caverns stretched out like the gaping maw of some giant beast, swallowed by shadows and intermittent bursts of harsh, artificial light. Below, figures moved—little more than specks from this vantage point—but each one a miner, a Dustborn, their lives hanging by a thread as fragile as the veins of Crythium they extracted.

"I've heard the rumors about the Screechers in the Mines," he said, his tone as measured as a wire pulled taut. "Miners whispering about chittering in the dark."

Drazic Grask stood beside him, arms crossed, his gaze steady on the distant glow of the District below. "I've heard the same. Enough that I sent a team to investigate."

He let the silence stretch before continuing. "They found claw marks near a collapsed tunnel. Deep ones."

For a moment, only the low hum of distant voices stirred the air between them.

"Do you think it has something to do with—"

Thaddeus exhaled slowly, his breath rising like steam into the cold. "No," he murmured, his hand closing around the iron rail in a quiet, almost imperceptible squeeze. "What we're doing is for the greater good."

He paused, then added, quieter still, "Maybe it'll work to our advantage. Let the fear spread—just enough to remind them what lies beneath. When the time comes, they'll remember who holds the line between order and chaos."

After a few moments he spoke again. "And our rat problem is getting worse," he stated flatly, his eyes scanning the city below with a predatory intensity.

"Indeed, Warden," Drazic agreed, his voice a gravelly echo to Thaddeus's frosty tone. "They're getting bolder."

Thaddeus's eyes narrowed slightly. "We need to flush them out. Cut off their escape then eradicate every last one of them."

"Agreed." Drazic's confirmation was swift, as if he relished the upcoming hunt.

"And do you know the best way to catch a rat, Mr. Grask?" Thaddeus paused, his thin lips curling into a semblance of a smirk.

Drazic's brow furrowed slightly, intrigued by the question. "Good bait?" he answered.

"Correct, Mr. Grask," Thaddeus replied, "and patience." He turned, gaze sweeping once more across the dim expanse. "Every successful hunt requires both—something most overlook." His voice dropped, low and deliberate. "It's not enough to merely set a snare. You must first observe—wait for the vermin to grow comfortable, to establish a pattern before you make your move."

Drazic grinned, the scar on his cheek pulling tight with wicked anticipation. "And, when they reveal themselves?"

"Then you strike," Thaddeus assured him, his voice as cold as the stone walls surrounding them.

"And the festival, Warden—do we cancel it?" Grask inquired.

The question lingered in the air, met by silence.

Thaddeus didn't answer immediately. His sharp features remained unreadable, but a flicker passed through his eyes—an unspoken weight pressing in. His gaze stayed fixed on the sprawling cavern below, yet his thoughts drifted elsewhere.

The question stirred something in him, something buried deep beneath the layers of command and cold efficiency.

He thought of *her*.

Gloria. The miner's daughter with quiet eyes and a smile that softened the edges of the world. He could still see her at the Founders Day Festival all those years ago, her hair catching the golden glow of the lanterns as she handed him a slice of her mother's bread. She hadn't laughed that day; only smiled—a small, fleeting thing, but it had been for him.

He had promised to return for her, back when ambition had yet to sharpen his edges. Before the merchant from the Inner District had swept him away with promises of wealth and opportunity. *Wait for me*, he had told her, *I'll come back to pull you out of this place*. And he had convinced himself there would be time to do so.

But when he finally returned, it was too late.

He stood in the doorway of her family's empty shack, the stale air thick with dust and abandonment. The neighbors barely remembered her name. Gone, they had said. Lost to the mines, like so many others.

Thaddeus inhaled slowly, exhaling through his nose. He forced the thought away, locking it behind the same door where all unnecessary sentiments were kept. Regret was a weakness. The past, a distraction. Gloria's fate had taught him a valuable lesson—balance was everything, and sacrifices were necessary.

At last, he spoke.

"Mr. Grask," he said, his tone sharp and deliberate. "Founders Day has taken place in Cavandel for over four hundred years—every year. It is more than a festival; it is the foundation of our purpose, our balance." He straightened, his voice dropping to a quiet edge. "Do you know what it would make me, if we canceled it under my watch?"

He turned his head slightly, just enough for his cold gaze to meet Drazic's, but the man remained silent.

"It would make me a failure. And tell me, Mr. Grask—am I a failure?"

Drazic stiffened, his shoulders rigid under the weight of the Warden's words. "Of course not, sir," he replied firmly.

"Good." Thaddeus exhaled slowly, smoothing out the front of his coat.

His features returned to their cold, calculated stillness. "The festival will proceed, Mr. Grask. Just as it did last year, so it will this year, and every year after that."

Drazic gave a brief nod. "Understood, Warden."

Thaddeus turned his attention back to the depths of Cavandel, to the endless movement of its citizens below. The past no longer mattered. Gloria no longer mattered. Only balance mattered—and balance would be maintained.

4

The Sanctuary

Location: Valmere

On the surface world, many miles directly above the underground city of Cavandel stood the illustrious city of Valmere. It was all marble, glass, jade, silver, and stone.

Nestled within the protective embrace of the Emerald Mountains, in the heart of the province of Avalar, the city of Valmere stood, a radiant symbol of prosperity and elegance. It rose like a jewel amidst the rugged peaks, its stately domed towers and graceful spires piercing the boundless azure sky. Sunlight bathed the city in warmth, casting a golden glow over its majestic rooftops and white stone walls.

Pristine cobblestone streets were woven like intricate threads throughout the city, their patterns forming a tapestry of meticulous planning. Lush gardens surrounded the thoroughfares, their manicured hedges and colorful flower beds arranged in perfect symmetry.

Fountains dotted these green oases, their crystalline waters dancing in the sunlight, accompanied by the melodic laughter of children at play.

Elegant townhouses and stately manors lined the broad avenues, their façades adorned with intricate carvings that told tales of the city's storied history.

Windows framed in gilded casings shimmered like jewels, catching and refracting the sunlight in dazzling displays.

Several buildings were crowned with ornate ironwork balconies, where residents would sit to enjoy the view or converse with neighbors, their voices mingling with the faint hum of activity below.

The streets themselves were a marvel of excellence, their polished surfaces free of debris. Horse-drawn carriages glided smoothly over the cobblestones, their wheels scarcely making a sound.

Ornate bridges arched over sapphire canals that crisscrossed the city like veins of light. These waterways, lined with ivy-covered stone walls, carried barges laden with goods: barrels of fine wine, crates of fragrant spices, and bolts of luxurious fabric. The canals were a lifeblood of commerce and beauty, reflecting the sunlight in shimmering patterns that danced along their surfaces.

In the marketplaces, the city's diversity was on full display. Artisans showcased their craft, from gleaming jewelry that sparkled like captured starlight to richly hued fabrics that rippled in the breeze.

Vendors in colorful stalls stood proudly beside their wares, their friendly calls adding a lively rhythm to the air. Stands overflowed with fresh fruits, their vibrant hues rivaling the flowers in the gardens, while the aroma of baked goods drew passersby like moths to a flame.

The mingling scents of exotic spices, sweet confections, and blooming flowers created an intoxicating blend that was uniquely Valmere.

Merchants hawked rare spices, intricate ceramics, and delicately embroidered tapestries.

Street performers captivated audiences with their acrobatics, music, and storytelling, their performances drawing laughter and applause from onlookers. The market square pulsed with energy, its vibrant chaos a testament to the city's thriving spirit.

High above the bustling markets, the sky teemed with life of its own. Sleek airships that glided through the sky like majestic leviathans, their polished hulls gleaming in the sunlight.

Massive envelopes, taut with gases, kept them aloft, their surfaces adorned with intricate patterns and the crests of noble houses. The largest vessels were floating palaces, their decks lined with ornate railings and glass-enclosed observation rooms. Flags snapped in the wind, vibrant splashes of color against the azure backdrop. Propellers whirred, driving the vessels forward with a steady hum that blended seamlessly with the city below.

Towering above it all, the grand Palace of Valmere crowned the city like a beacon, a symbol of the kingdom's wealth, power, and aspirations. It gleamed in the sunlight, its brilliance casting an aura that seemed to bless the city below.

And as the day waned and the sky deepened into twilight, the city's lights would flicker to life, transforming Valmere into a glittering jewel set against the dark canvas of the Emerald Mountains.

The palace itself was more than just a symbol of power; it was a testament to the kingdom's enduring legacy. Its spires pierced the heavens, their tips designed to catch the first light of dawn and the last rays of dusk.

Grand balconies overlooked the city, their railings intricately wrought with motifs of stars, vines, and celestial beasts.

The palace housed not only the royal family but also scholars, diplomats, and artists whose presence cemented Valmere's reputation as a center of intellect and culture.

Even beyond the palace's imposing presence, the city brimmed with architectural wonders. Libraries with towering stained-glass windows stood as sanctuaries of knowledge, while theaters, adorned with marble columns hosted performances that drew crowds from across the kingdom.

Temples of various faiths rose in quiet reverence, their bells chiming softly to mark the passing hours.

Every corner of Valmere spoke of prosperity and harmony, from the lavishly decorated inns that catered to wealthy merchants and travelers, to the lively taverns where friends gathered over frothing mugs of ale.

Even the smallest details—the polished lampposts that lined the streets, the mosaic-tiled plazas and the neatly trimmed trees shading the walkways—reflected the city's dedication to order and beauty.

It is said that no other city in the province of Avalar, in fact, no other on the entire continent of Feralon compared to its majesty.

Yet for all its splendor, Valmere was not a city without its faults. Beneath the shimmering facade, the whispered tales of those who toiled below could sometimes be heard.

Everything came at a cost and Valmere knew this well, for everyone traded with Valmere for its priceless Crythium.

***

Far beyond the city walls of Valmere, among the thick bramble, a figure stood hunched over. Ragged breaths tore from his lungs as he stumbled forward, one unsteady step at a time. The pristine walls of Valmere loomed in the distance, a shimmering beacon that taunted the battered traveler. Crimson-soaked rags clung to his frame. Each labored movement sent fresh waves of pain through his wounded side.

The traveler's vision swam, the gleaming towers of Valmere blurring and doubling before his eyes. He blinked hard, willing the world to steady itself and pressed on, his feet dragging through the undergrowth.

High atop the city walls, a guard shifted his weight, scanning the horizon.

Sunlight glinted off his polished white leather armor, highlighting intricately engraved golden clasps and the embossed emblem at his chest. Tapered leather tassets flowed from his waist, accentuating his authoritative bearing, shifting gracefully with each measured step along the ramparts.

His eyes, sharp beneath furrowed brows, swept methodically over the verdant fields beyond the city walls—past the orderly gardens and flourishing orchards whose bounty fed Valmere. The seasoned lines on his face deepened as he scanned the horizon, poised, vigilant and ready.

Something caught his eye—a flash of movement in the distant thicket.

He squinted, shielding his eyes from the glare. There—a figure stumbling through the undergrowth. The guard's hand instinctively moved to the hilt of his sword, the Crythium-enhanced blade at his side glowing faintly in the sunlight.

"Oi! Markus!" he called to his fellow guardsman. "Take a look over there."

Markus joined his comrade at the wall's edge, peering into the distance. The figure's ragged form stood out starkly against the pristine landscape.

"Looks like trouble," Markus muttered. He raised a spyglass to his eye. "Stars above," he whispered.

"What is it?" his comrade asked.

"He's injured. Pretty badly." Came the response.

They watched as the figure stumbled closer, weaving unsteadily through the brush, crimson-stained rags fluttering in the breeze.

"Alert the gate captain," Markus ordered. "I'll keep watch."

His partner nodded and jogged off, boots clanking on the stone ramparts.

Markus leaned forward, straining to make out more details. The figure was male, he could see now. Young, perhaps in his thirties, with dark hair matted with sweat and dirt.

Within minutes, a small contingent of guards assembled at the city gates. The captain strode forward, his white cloak billowing behind him.

"Hold your positions," he commanded. "Let's see what we're dealing with." The men stood still, cautious.

"Open the gates!" he bellowed.

The massive gates groaned open. Markus and the other guards fanned out, weapons at the ready. The injured man stumbled forward, his legs finally giving out as he collapsed just inside the threshold.

"Please," he whispered, his voice raw. "Help..."

The captain approached cautiously. "Who are you? What happened?"

The man's eyes rolled wildly, unfocused. He struggled to push himself up, arms trembling. "I'm a soldier," he rasped, "...from Salem."

"And what happened to you?" the captain questioned.

"A little over four days ago, we received word from Petuel," the soldier coughed. "They were attacked by the Nomads..."

"The Alveraki?" the captain pressed, his grip tightening on the hilt of his sword.

"Yes," the man wheezed, his voice barely audible.

Markus knelt beside him. "Easy now," he said reassuringly, "You're safe."

"No," the man whispered as his eyes fluttered shut. "You don't understand. No one's safe."

Suddenly, the soldier's eyes snapped open, wild with urgency. He clutched at Markus's arm, his grimy fingers leaving streaks on the pristine white leather.

"The airship," he gasped. "Our airship..."

The captain's brow furrowed. "Salem only has three royal airships. Why would they—"

"The King," the soldier interrupted, his voice cracking. "He insisted that we take it. The news was too urgent..."

Markus exchanged a glance with the captain. The use of a royal airship spoke volumes about the gravity of the situation.

The soldier's chest heaved as he struggled to continue. "We set out immediately. But the sky was angry."

His eyes grew distant, reliving the memory. "Captain Thorne. We advised him to go around. But our orders..."

"You flew into the storm?" the captain of the guard asked in disbelief.

The soldier nodded weakly. "Lightning—like I've never seen. It danced across the hull. And the wind," his fingers dug into Markus's arm. "We were thrown about like leaves. The envelope tore, then flames erupted from the engine room."

Tears welled in the soldier's eyes. "We fell..."

"I've heard enough," the captain said to the wounded man. Then, turning to his men, he barked, "Get him to the infirmary—now!" He gestured for the gates to be closed, then added, "We'll question him later."

Two guards came forward, lifted the man and began carrying him off. The captain's eyes narrowed as he watched the injured man being taken away. He turned to Markus, his voice low and urgent. "Double the patrols, just in case."

Markus nodded sharply. "Yes, sir."

"I'll bring word to the palace," the captain added. "We need to inform the King."

As Markus hurried off, the captain's gaze swept the horizon. The peaceful fields beyond the walls now seemed ominous, their tranquility potentially concealing untold dangers. He clenched his jaw, his mind racing through all the grim possibilities.

***

Within the opulent council chambers of the palace, King Aleric sat at the head of a massive table carved from a single slab of polished obsidian. His presence was as immovable as the throne behind him—broad-shouldered and cloaked in a robe of deep crimson, trimmed with white fur that caught the sunlight like frost.

A crown of blackened gold rested on his silver-streaked hair, the metal forged in the old style, unadorned but unmistakable in its weight. His eyes—steady and discerning—swept the chamber with a gaze honed by decades of rule.

Around him, delicate tapestries adorned the walls, depicting scenes of Valmere's storied history in vibrant threads of gold and silver. Sunlight streamed through the stained glass windows, casting kaleidoscopic patterns across the marble floor.

The air hummed with laughter and animated conversation as the king's advisers and state officials gathered for their monthly assembly. Fine wine sloshed in goblets as hands gestured in animated debate, their ruby contents glinting in the warm light of crystal chandeliers suspended from the vaulted ceiling.

"To Councilor Elias!" A portly official bellowed, raising his cup. "May your new son bring you as much joy as the last five!"

A chorus of cheers erupted around the table. Elias, a tall man with sharp features and piercing eyes, accepted the congratulations with a thin smile that didn't quite reach his eyes. "You're too kind, my lords," he said smoothly. "I daresay young Theo will be the brightest of the bunch."

King Aleric chuckled, his stern features softening for a moment. "At this rate, Elias, you'll single-handedly populate the next generation of Valmere," he jested.

The chamber erupted in laughter.

Servants glided silently between the revelers, refilling goblets and offering platters of delicacies. A string quartet played softly in the corner, their melodies weaving through the jovial conversation.

Prince Gideon leaned back in his chair, observing the scene with a critical eye. His youthful features belied a sharp intellect that assessed the room with ease. At nineteen, he carried himself with the poise of someone far beyond his years.

His dark hair, neatly styled, framed a face beginning to harden with the angles of manhood, though traces of youth remained. High cheekbones and a strong jaw hinted at the regal bearing he would grow into, while his eyes—a striking steel blue—held a depth of perception that often unnerved those who met his gaze.

His skin, unblemished and lightly tanned from hours spent in the palace gardens, contrasted with the deep burgundy of his doublet.

A faint smirk played at his lips as he watched Councilor Elias soak in the praise of their peers.

His fingers drummed absently on the armrest, scanning the faces around the table. Laughter and banter flowed freely, but beneath the veneer of joviality, he sensed undercurrents of tension.

A commotion at the chamber doors drew his attention. The captain of the guard burst in and the room went silent.

"Your Majesty," the captain said, bowing low. "Urgent news from the gates."

King Aleric's smile vanished. He raised a hand, silencing the murmurs that had broken out. "Speak."

"An injured soldier sire, from Salem. He spoke of nomads attacking Petuel."

The room erupted. Councilors leapt to their feet, shouting questions and demands. Gideon's eyes narrowed, watching his father's reaction.

"Silence!" the King commanded. The room fell quiet. He turned to the captain. "Go on."

"The man's wounds were severe, sire. He said his airship crashed in a storm just a few days ago."

Councilor Elias's lips twisted into a disdainful sneer. "Nomads? Preposterous. Petuel is a military stronghold, its walls rivaling that of our own."

His voice carried the sharp edge of condescension as he continued, "And besides, everyone knows the Alveraki don't attack established cities. The tribes are little more than wandering savages, too preoccupied with preying on each other."

Gideon leaned forward, his eyes glinting with intensity. "Perhaps, Councilor Elias, but we cannot afford to dismiss this threat so casually." His voice eased through the murmurs like a blade.

He gestured toward a window overlooking the city below, commanding the room's attention. "Consider the reports we've received over the past few months. Merchant caravans ambushed with increasing frequency. And now, a soldier from Salem, one of our staunchest allies, arrives at our gates with tales of a Nomad invasion in Petuel."

Gideon's gaze swept the chamber, meeting each council member's eyes in turn. "We sit here, surrounded by luxury, while the winds of war may be gathering strength beyond the mountains. If Petuel has fallen—"

"If, my prince," interrupted Councilor Brovish, a wizened man with graying hair. "We must not leap to conclusions based on the ravings of a single, injured soldier."

Murmurs of agreement rippled through the chamber.

King Aleric raised his hand, silencing the room once more. His weathered face was etched with concern as he considered his son's words. The chamber fell into a tense hush, all eyes fixed on the monarch.

"My son speaks wisely," the king said, his deep voice resonating through the chamber. "We cannot afford to be complacent."

He rose from his seat, his regal bearing commanding attention. The king strode to one of the grand windows, his velvet robes rustling softly with each step. He gazed out over the shimmering cityscape of Valmere, its marble spires and jade-tiled roofs gleaming in the evening sun.

King Aleric turned back to face the council, his eyes grave. "We must act, but with caution."

The chamber remained silent, tension thick in the air. The soft rustling of silk robes and the occasional clink of jewelry were the only sounds as the councilors waited for their King to continue.

Councilor Brovish cleared his throat, his face creased with thought. "Your Majesty, if I may suggest a course of action?"

The king nodded, gesturing for him to continue.

Brovish gestured skyward. "We have at our disposal the finest fleet of airships in all of Avalar. Perhaps we could put them to use in this matter."

Murmurs of interest rippled through the chamber. The councilor continued, his voice gaining strength. "I propose we send a contingent to Salem by airship. It's but two days' journey, so we could have confirmation of these reports within four days."

The chamber buzzed with whispered conversations. Gideon leaned forward, his interest piqued.

Brovish wasn't finished. "Furthermore, we could dispatch our swiftest and most agile vessel to Petuel itself. A scouting mission, if you will. The journey would take ten days each way, but within three weeks, we could have eyes on the situation."

The council erupted into animated discussion. Councilor Elias's voice rose above the din. "And risk our prized airships on a fool's errand? The very thought is—"

"Most prudent," Gideon cut in, silencing the room. "Councilor Brovish's suggestion is sound. We have the means to gather intelligence quickly and discreetly. It would be foolish not to use them."

King Aleric nodded slowly, his eyes distant as he weighed the options. The chamber held its breath, waiting for his decision.

"Very well," the king said at last. "We shall proceed with Councilor Brovish's plan." He turned to the guard still standing at attention by the door. "Make the necessary arrangements. I want our finest pilots and most experienced scouts on this mission."

The captain bowed low. "At once, Your Majesty."

As the guard hurried from the room, King Aleric addressed the council once more. "Let us prepare for all eventualities. I want reports on our grain stores, our weapons caches and the state of our defenses. If war is coming to our doorstep, Valmere must be ready."

"Father, allow me to lead the mission to Salem." Gideon's words hung in the air, charged with determination, his piercing blue eyes fixed on his father. The council chamber fell silent, the tension palpable as all eyes darted between father and son.

King Aleric's brow furrowed, his weathered face a mask of conflicting emotions. Pride warred with concern in his eyes as he regarded his heir. For a moment, Gideon saw not the stern monarch, but the father who had taught him to wield a sword, to ride a horse, to lead with compassion and strength.

"Your eagerness to serve is commendable, my son," the king said, his voice low and measured.

Gideon's jaw clenched, but he held his tongue. His mind raced, imagining the perilous journey to Salem. He saw himself at the helm of a sleek airship, cutting through storm-tossed skies, racing against time to uncover the truth. The thrill of adventure called to him, a siren song promising escape from the gilded cage of the palace.

But more than that, Gideon yearned to prove himself. To show his father, the council and all of Valmere that he was more than just a prince in waiting. He wanted to be the one to bring back vital intelligence, to play a crucial role in safeguarding the kingdom. The weight of future responsibility pressed down on him and he longed to demonstrate that he was ready to bear it.

King Aleric seemed to read the thoughts churning behind his son's eyes. He stepped closer, placing a hand on Gideon's shoulder. "I have a different task in mind for you." He looked the young man square in the eyes. "You are of age now, Gideon—the age I was when my own father began to share the deeper burdens of the crown with me."

The king's voice dropped lower, meant for Gideon's ears alone. "It's time you learned about making the truly difficult decisions. The ones that shape the fate of our people."

Gideon's curiosity sparked, momentarily overshadowing his disappointment. He searched his father's face, noting the new lines of worry etched around his eyes.

King Aleric turned to address the council, his voice ringing with authority. "My lords, I thank you for your counsel. You are dismissed. Prince Gideon and Councilor Brovish will remain."

The councilors exchanged surprised glances but rose without protest. They filed out, along with the musicians, bowing to their king and prince as they departed. As they exited the chamber, Gideon caught a significant look passing between his father and Councilor Brovish.

The old councilor's eyes gleamed with something Gideon couldn't quite name. Anticipation? Apprehension? The prince's mind whirled, trying to piece together the puzzle unfolding before him.

The heavy doors swung shut with a resonant thud, leaving only the king, Prince Gideon and Councilor Brovish in the chamber. Silence stretched between them, broken only by the soft crackle of flames in the ornate fireplace and the distant chiming of bells from the city below.

King Aleric moved to a side table laden with decanters of amber liquid. For a brief moment, the king's regal mask slipped, revealing a man weighed down by untold secrets. Crystal clinked as he poured three measures, the rich aroma filling the air. Gideon accepted his glass with a nod, noting the tremor in his father's hand—barely perceptible, but there.

"Walk with me, son," the king said, gesturing towards the balcony and the two men followed.

The view from the balcony was stunning. The sun hung low on the horizon, painting the sky in hues of gold and crimson. Below them, the city of Valmere sprawled out in all its glory.

Gideon's eyes swept over the familiar landscape, drinking in details he'd seen a thousand times before, yet now viewed with fresh intensity.

King Aleric broke the silence first. "Gideon, do you know where our Crythium comes from?"

Gideon frowned slightly, a little puzzled by the question. "From the mines, of course," he responded.

"And where are these mines located?" the king prodded further, his gaze not leaving the horizon.

"In the mountains." Gideon replied, his voice trailing off as he sensed there was more to his father's questions.

"But *where* in the mountains, Gideon?" the king pressed, turning to face his son, his eyes searching Gideon's face for signs of comprehension. The question lingered in the air.

"I don't know, father." Gideon finally admitted.

Aleric nodded slowly, his expression unreadable. "And have you ever wondered, truly wondered, who toils in these mines?" His voice was soft, yet carried a weight that pressed upon Gideon's chest.

Gideon's heart quickened as he processed his father's words. He faltered as the seeds of doubt began planting themselves deep within his mind. He had heard the whispers, the rumors of dark places deep and hidden, far beneath the earth. "Father, are you really suggesting that—"

The king interrupted. "There is much that has been kept from you Gideon, for it wasn't the kind of knowledge a child should bear."

"Surely you jest, Father?"

King Aleric turned back to the horizon, his face lit by the dying light. "No jest, Gideon. Sometimes the truth is a heavy burden, one that you must now begin to bear." Gideon was speechless, his mouth going completely dry.

"The Crythium Capsules that powers our city, that lights our homes and defends our walls—" The king paused, gazing out towards the setting sun. "Cavandel," he whispered.

Gideon felt a chill despite the warmth of the whiskey in his hand.

"The underground city?" His voice was barely above a murmur.

"Yes. Cavandel," Aleric confirmed solemnly. "The city beneath our feet, entwined with ours by fate and necessity, much as the roots of a tree sustain its branches."

"But at what cost?" Gideon asked, his brows knitting together in confusion.

The king turned to face the sprawling landscape below them once more. He gestured towards the vibrant greenery that bordered Valmere—the lush fields and dense forests that seemed to stretch endlessly.

"It's the law of nature, son. There is balance in all things—day and night, rain and sunshine, growth and decay," the king said, "Each element must exist in harmony with its counterpart. Roots do not yearn to see the sunlight," he said finally.

Slowly, Gideon raised the glass of amber liquid to his lips. He took a shaky sip while trying to regain his composure.

"Cavandel mines the Crythium and we refine it to create capsules that provide energy for everyone. Just like my father and his father before him." The king paused for a heartbeat, before continuing. "Everyone, Gideon. From Yalif all the way to Petuel, they all depend on us for power, for protection."

King Aleric's words hung in the air, heavy with implication. Gideon's mind reeled, struggling to process this revelation. He stared out at the city below, its gleaming spires and elegant boulevards suddenly taking on a sinister cast.

Gideon shook his head, disbelief etched across his features. "This is madness, father. Surely this can't be true. Cavandel is just—just an old wives' tale," he stammered.

His mind raced, recalling fragments of stories whispered by nursemaids and servants. Tales of a vast underground city, shrouded in eternal darkness and mystery. Of pale-skinned people who never saw the sun, toiling in endless mines. Of monstrous creatures that lurked in the depths, waiting to devour the weak.

But those were just stories, weren't they? Fables told to frighten children into obedience.

King Aleric's eyes softened as he watched the turmoil playing across his son's face. He placed a weathered hand on Gideon's shoulder, his touch anchoring the young prince in the midst of his thoughts.

"I understand, my son," Aleric said, his voice low and tinged with memory. "Remember, I too was once in your place." His gaze grew distant, lost in the mists of time. "But in time, Gideon, I came to accept the way things are. To embrace it, even."

Gideon's head snapped up, shock evident in his eyes. "Embrace it? Father, how can you even—" Aleric held up a hand, silencing his son. "Look at our city, boy! Really look," he commanded, gesturing to the city and beyond.

Gideon turned, his eyes sweeping over the city he'd known all his life. But now, everything seemed—different. Tainted.

The gleaming spires that had once filled him with pride now loomed like accusing fingers pointed at the sky. Their polished surfaces no longer reflected glory, but shame. Each glint of sunlight off a golden dome or jeweled window became a mocking reminder of the wealth built on hidden suffering.

He gazed at the broad avenues, lined with their stately manors and lush gardens. The carefully manicured hedges and vibrant flower beds now seemed grotesque, nourished by the sweat and blood of unseen laborers toiling in the darkness. The tinkling of ornate fountains in the squares took on a sinister quality, each droplet a tear shed by those trapped below.

His eyes darted from one familiar landmark to another, each now transformed by the revelation.

Even the palace itself, his home since birth, took on a menacing aspect. Its gleaming walls and soaring towers felt like a cage, built on the backs of those who would never see its splendor.

As twilight deepened, the city's lights began to flicker to life. Gideon watched as glow-lanterns and street lamps cast their warm glow across Valmere, transforming the city. He turned to his father, searching the older man's face. "How can we allow this, father?"

King Aleric's expression remained unreadable, though his jaw tensed, a subtle clenching that betrayed the weight of years and decisions. He exhaled deeply, the sound carrying more than air—it carried regret and something else Gideon couldn't quite identify. Resolve, perhaps.

"We do not allow it," Aleric said at last, his voice firm yet measured. "We command it—because without Cavandel, there would be no Valmere."

Gideon flinched as if struck.

"The world is not as simple as you wish it to be, Gideon," Aleric continued after a moment's pause. "Valmere thrives because of what lies beneath it. Every advancement we've made—our defenses, our prosperity, our very survival—" The king paused, studying his son's face.

Gideon's jaw tightened. He wanted to argue, to shout, but something in his father's tone gave him pause. This was not the voice of a man making excuses; it was the voice of a king bearing the weight of countless lives.

"There's still much to understand, son. In a fortnight, during the next major delivery, I'm sending you to Cavandel."

Gideon's eyes widened. "You mean—"

"Yes," the king nodded. "You will journey down to Cavandel, and you will witness the mines firsthand."

Gideon's heart raced. A thrill of anticipation mingled with dread.

Aleric's lips quirked in a humorless smile. "In the meantime, there are some things the good Councilor and I must discuss in private. Good night, son."

The king turned, his broad silhouette framed by the dying rays of sunlight. He glanced briefly at Councilor Brovish, who stood quietly a respectful distance away. With a single nod from Aleric, the elder statesman inclined his head in understanding and stepped forward. His usual measured grace, his piercing eyes betraying nothing.

"Your Majesty," Brovish said smoothly, his voice a silken thread weaving through the heavy air. "Shall we adjourn to the inner chambers, sire? The matters at hand require—delicacy."

Aleric's gaze lingered on Gideon for a moment longer. There was something unspoken in his eyes, a faint flicker that seemed to convey both sorrow and inevitability. Then, without another word, he pivoted and strode toward the double doors leading back into the palace. Bovish followed the king with measured steps.

The heavy doors closed behind them with a soft thud and for a brief moment, Gideon felt utterly alone.

The wind picked up slightly, tugging at the edges of his tunic as if urging him to move—or perhaps to stay.

His father's words replayed in his mind like a haunting melody. *We command it. Without Cavandel, there would be no Valmere.* It wasn't just the words themselves but the weight they carried—decades of decisions justified by necessity, by survival.

Gideon stood rooted to the spot. He gripped the marble railing tightly, leaning forward as he scanned the city below. The balcony suddenly felt both vast and confining. His eyes roved over Valmere, seeing it anew.

To most, this view would be a source of pride—a testament to human ingenuity and resilience. To Gideon, it felt suffocating.

5
Forging in Firelight

Location: Cavandel, The Mines

The Mines formed the heart of Cavandel's labor—a vast network of tunnels stretching beneath the District, where the city's workers spent their days chipping away at stone. Glow-lanterns and battered torches swung in tired hands, their halos shifting across the walls and leaving long stretches to the dark, while the shimmer of Crythium veins offered flickers of hope amid the grind of exhaustion.

Deeper still, beneath the Mines, waited the Abyss—a place spoken of more in whispers than in plans, where the lure of untouched Crythium drew the desperate and the daring alike. Those who descended were either chasing fortune or fleeing reason, and few ever returned to say which it was.

Within the relative safety of the Mines, high above the Abyss, Aria and her companions toiled away in a dimly lit cavern.

"It's not working!" Aria's voice rang out, filled with panic and desperation. She screamed in frustration as rocks and debris flew all around her. Her heart raced as she frantically tried to regain control of Heidi's latest invention—*The Jack-Driller*.

The contraption was as bulky as it was heavy, a patchwork of various scraps of discarded metal, fused together in a trembling mass of hoses, wires, iron, and copper. It shuddered violently in Aria's grip, threatening to tear itself apart.

Months of planning, building, and testing had led to this moment—a creation Heidi swore would be their ticket to the Inner District. Yet as it rattled and screamed, Aria couldn't shake the thought that it might instead be the end of them.

The device drew its strength from a faulty Crythium capsule—one of the rare treasures Heidi had salvaged from the mounds of refuse cast down from the Stratum. The dump site, one of four scrap heaps in the District, served as both graveyard and goldmine, where scavengers clawed through the wreckage from above in search of anything still worth saving.

"Hold it steady!" Heidi's voice cut through the roar. "Adjust the angle—like this!" She gestured through the haze of dust and steam, her words nearly swallowed by the grinding of gears.

All the while, Sylas kept his distance, shifting uneasily as his gaze darted between the chaos and the narrow exit. Aria gritted her teeth, her arms trembling as she fought to steady the machine. The tip screeched against the stone, sparks bursting outward and flooding the cavern with brief, violent light.

"I'm trying!" Aria shouted back, her voice trembling with strain. The machine lurched her forward, nearly toppling before grinding to an abrupt halt. Her stomach dropped.

"I... think it stopped working," she managed between ragged breaths.

Heidi stepped closer, pushing a strand of hair from her face, frustration edging her tone. "Yeah," she muttered dryly, "I can see that."

Silence settled over the cavern, broken only by the hiss of steam escaping the stalled machine. Heidi crouched beside it, studying the damage while Aria stood gasping, her chest rising and falling as she stared down at her former foe. Sweat traced jagged lines through the dust on her skin, leaving pale streaks across the grime.

The group remained silent, the air taut with unease.

Sylas cleared his throat, breaking the silence. "Well, that was... drilling." He winced but forged ahead. "Get it? Thrilling? Drilling?" When no one responded, he scratched the back of his neck and sighed. "Tough crowd."

Aria shot him a withering look, though a reluctant smile tugged at her lips. The cavern seemed to exhale now, the heavy tension finally easing.

Heidi rolled her eyes but allowed a faint smirk, before prying open the service panel. She studied the mess of melted connections with a sigh that carried more weariness than surprise. "Oh dear," she murmured, disappointment threading through her voice.

Both Aria and Sylas looked at her with curious glances.

"Capsule's broken," she groaned, as she extracted the small glass cylinder from the device. She traced her fingers along the cracked surface, then examined the once purple Crythium core, now blackened and covered in soot. Aria and Sylas watched as she inspected each of the cone shaped metal tips, before announcing with finality, "Yep. It's Fried."

Next time, Heidi thought, *I'll just need to find a bigger one.*

Aria's eyes widened in disbelief. "Well—can't we fix it?"

"Fix it?" Heidi replied with a low chuckle. "Looks like we're back to digging the old-fashioned way."

Location: Cavandel, The Outer District

The next day, Aria trudged along the winding paths of the Outer District. The events involving Heidi's Jack-Driller had taken its toll, and her body still ached with each step.

She had made plans to visit the market with Heidi—a necessary trip to stock up on supplies before their next descent. Cavandel's artificial lights had only just begun to brighten when she left her grandmother safely tucked away at home.

The air was damp and carried the faint aroma of earth as Aria set off, her boots thumping softly against the path. She drew her cloak tightly around her shoulders to ward off the lingering chill, her thoughts already drifting to the day ahead.

Heidi's place wasn't far—a modest structure just big enough for her and her brother Sylas—but it was their home. Aria quickened her pace, eager to get the preparations underway.

The narrow street wound its way between sagging buildings and shadowed alcoves, their crumbling façades etched with cracks and streaked with the grime of countless seasons. Faint wisps of fog clung to the uneven path, muting the sound of Aria's footsteps as she approached.

When she reached Heidi's door, her friend was already there, waiting patiently. Heidi leaned against the weathered frame, her arms crossed, her expression calm but expectant. The faint glow of a lantern hanging above the doorway cast a warm light over her features, softening the sharp edges of the surrounding decay.

Heidi was the embodiment of practicality. Her short, wavy brown hair framed a soft, round face that radiated quiet determination.

A green fitted tank top clung to her frame, partially concealed beneath a long beige duster coat brimming with pockets, each one promising utility over ornamentation.

Her brown cargo pants, functional and worn, were tucked neatly into sturdy, knee-high leather boots, scuffed from countless adventures.

Around her waist was a wide leather belt, rich with loops and compartments that hinted at her resourceful nature, and the tools of her trade.

Completing the ensemble was a medium-sized backpack, bristling with gadgets that spoke of preparation, and an ever-curious mind.

"You're late," Heidi grinned. "Again." Despite her teasing tone, her light brown eyes sparkled with warmth.

"You know how it is," Aria replied, as she pulled her friend into a tight embrace. "Gran wasn't feeling her best. I had to make sure she was settled before heading out."

Heidi pulled back, her expression softening. "How is she doing?"

Aria sighed, tucking a loose strand of hair behind her ear. "Worse, I'm afraid. She doesn't eat as much these days."

Heidi's hand was warm and gentle, as she placed it on Aria's shoulder, her fingers slightly calloused but comforting. "I'm so sorry," she said, her eyes filled with understanding and sympathy.

"Thanks," Aria nodded softly.

Her grandmother's worsening condition weighed heavily on her—a cruel reminder of the toll the mines had taken on her over the decades.

Aria attempted to cut through the tension, by forcing a smile. "So, where's that idiot brother of yours?"

Heidi's eyes brightened with amusement. "There was a drop from the Stratum, so that idiot brother of mine went scavenging at the Junkyard. He'll catch up later."

The Junkyard, was the closest scrap heap to their location. A towering, mountain of discarded machinery, old equipment and various detritus from the Stratum—all tossed unceremoniously to the District below.

To some, these dump sites were an unsightly blight, a testament to the ruling class's excess and disdain for those beneath them. But for resourceful residents of the District, the scrap heaps were a treasure trove of useful items and raw materials just waiting to be discovered. Every seven days, a fresh deluge of cast-offs would cascade from above, covering the slopes in a glistening new layer of possibilities.

"I'm hoping he'll find a larger capsule," Heidi said, thoughtful. "One strong enough to handle the Jack-Driller without—well, you saw what happened."

Aria chuckled at the memory. "Oh, I definitely saw what happened," she said, rolling her shoulders with an exaggerated wince. "I felt it too. I think it's time you find someone else to test your deathtraps."

Heidi gave her a playful swat on the arm. "Don't be so dramatic! A few bruises never hurt anyone. And be honest, without some excitement, you'd just end up complaining about that."

They laughed, and the conversation continued as they set off towards the market. Aria allowed herself to get swept up in Heidi's infectious enthusiasm, her mind already racing with possibilities.

They passed a group of haggard miners returning home from their shift, faces etched with exhaustion. They shuffled by, eyes downcast, shoulders slumped under the weight of their labour.

A child's cry echoed from a nearby alley, then was quickly silenced. Aria quickened her pace.

The air grew thick with steam as they neared one of the markets of the Outer District. Large metal pipes snaked overhead, hissing and clanking. Condensation dripped from rusted joints, forming puddles on the uneven ground. Aria sidestepped them, her worn boots offering little protection against the dampness.

Heidi adjusted the straps of her harness, tools jangling. "So have you seen that slab-toothed dirtbag Hogan lately?" She spat his name like rancid dust.

Aria shook her head grimly. "Not since he ransacked my carry-bag a few days ago." Her jaw clenched at the memory, heat rising in her chest. "He seems to be avoiding us."

"He'd better be!" Heidi spat.

"I still don't get why he would even follow me all the way in there," Aria added.

The whole idea made little sense to her. Hogan was only able to steal her day's work because of her own negligence. He couldn't have planned that. So why would he waste a whole day just shadowing her?

"You ever wonder," Heidi began, breaking into Aria's thoughts, "if maybe he's just got a crush on you?"

Aria stumbled slightly, caught off guard. "A what?" She shot her friend a sharp look, half-laughing, half incredulous.

"A crush," Heidi repeated, her grin widening. "You know, the kind where a boy acts like a complete moron because he doesn't know how else to get your attention?"

She raised an eyebrow, enjoying Aria's discomfort far too much. "Think about it—why else would he follow you into the mines like some lovesick puppy? It's not like he's smart enough to have a better plan."

Aria scoffed, though her cheeks burned faintly. "Hogan? Really? That's ridiculous. He's younger than me, for one."

"So?" Heidi grinned. "Seventeen, eighteen—what's the difference?"

"The difference is—he's just a cowardly thief. That's it."

"Uh-huh," Heidi teased, a knowing lilt in her voice. "Sure, he does. And I'm just a humble genius with no sense of adventure."

Aria rolled her eyes, but her mind wandered back to Hogan's strange, persistent behavior. Could it really be that simple? The idea was absurd—wasn't it?

They turned a corner and the market came into view, filling the air with mumbled voices and the occasional hiss of escaping steam from overhead pipes. The clang of metal and the low rumble of conversation grew louder as they approached.

"Anyway," Aria muttered, her voice low with resolve, "if I ever see him again, I'll make sure he regrets stealing from me."

"You do that," Heidi said, grinning. "Just don't hurt him too bad. You might break his poor little heart."

Aria rolled her eyes, but her cheeks burned faintly as she quickened her pace.

The market was a riot of sights and sounds—a clamour that assaulted Aria's senses. Rickety stalls overflowed with an eclectic array of wares, from rusted tools, and colourful masks for the upcoming festival, to strange contraptions of indeterminate purpose.

Shopkeepers barked their sales pitches, voices rising and falling in a heated chorus. The air buzzed with haggling, punctuated by the clink of coin and the shuffle of trade.

The scent of roasting mushrooms and simmering broth mingled with the ever-present tang of iron and damp earth.

Aria and Heidi weaved through the chaos, their boots crunching over loose pebbles and discarded scraps of metal. The market was always a mess, but today it seemed especially alive with movement and noise.

Heidi kept her eyes sharp, scanning the crowd out of habit. Aria, meanwhile, clenched her fists at her sides, still simmering from their conversation about Hogan.

Ahead, flickering light spilled from a stall adorned with an assortment of torches. Some were rudimentary—just metal shafts wrapped in oil-drenched cloth—but others gleamed with intricacy. Metal casings engraved with swirling patterns cradled glass cylinders that pulsed faintly, those were powered by Crythium Capsules.

"That's the one," Heidi said, pointing toward the stall with a glint in her eye. "Let me handle this."

Aria followed as Heidi strode up to the merchant, a squat man with grease stains on his apron and soot smudged across his face. His thick fingers tinkered with a Crythium-powered torch. "You here to buy, or gape?" he barked, without looking up.

"Depends," Heidi replied smoothly. "How much is that one?"

The merchant finally glanced up, eyes narrowing as he followed Heidi's pointing finger to the intricate Crythium torch on the stall's edge. "That one ain't cheap," he grumbled, wiping his blackened hands on his apron. "Fifty Grottos. Non-negotiable."

Heidi snorted, crossing her arms. "Fifty? That's two day's wages! For that piece of junk? You're dreaming, old man."

The merchant gave her a hard look, his expression shifting to one of annoyance. He leaned forward, the light from the torch casting odd shadows across his face. "This 'junk', happens to be top-tier craftsmanship. Hand-forged casing, reinforced filaments, and a Crythium capsule that's stable enough to last a year—maybe two. You don't know what you're looking at, girl."

Heidi smirked. "Oh, I know exactly what I'm looking at," she said calmly, "the casting is so scratched and dented, it looks like it barely survived a rockfall.

She picked up the torch, turning it over with practiced familiarity, her fingers tracing the etched patterns as though deciphering them. "And look—the filaments are uneven." Her gaze shifted to the shopkeeper, as if checking off a mental list. "Reduced brightness," she intoned, then turned to the base, unscrewing it with brisk precision. "Let's see the capsule."

The merchant's face darkened, though whether from anger or embarrassment was unclear. He snatched the torch from her with a grunt, his eyes narrowing into slits. "You've got a sharp tongue," he said, "for someone who clearly ain't got fifty Grottos to rub together."

"Sharp enough to know when someone's trying to sell me rocks for crystals," Heidi shot back.

Aria winced, her eyes darting between Heidi and the merchant. The tension between them crackled like a frayed wire.

"Alright," Heidi said, raising her voice just enough to be heard over the din of the market. "Thirty Grottos," she offered, her tone suddenly crisp and businesslike. "That's more than enough, considering the state it's in. Take it or leave it."

The merchant let out a barking laugh, leaning back against his cluttered stall as if he'd been told a joke so absurd it required him to steady himself. "Thirty? You're funny, girl. Real funny." His thick fingers drummed on the worn wooden counter, leaving faint smudges of soot behind. "Try finding something like this anywhere for less than Forty-five," he grumbled. "Won't go lower than that."

Heidi's eyes narrowed. "Forty-five?" she scoffed, throwing a hand into the air as if he'd just asked her to hand over a month's haul. "For an overworked Crythium core that's probably on its last legs? Be serious." She shot Aria an exaggerated look. "Can you believe this?" she said, incredulous. "I could slap together something much better in my spare time."

"Then maybe you should," the merchant grumbled, his grin hard and toothy. "But if you want something that won't fall apart two minutes into a tunnel crawl? Forty-five."

Aria coughed lightly.

Heidi didn't flinch. Her eyes stayed locked on the merchant, her smirk sharpening into something colder, more calculating.

"Forty," she said flatly, her tone like a hammer striking an anvil. "And that's me being generous. I might be desperate, but I ain't stupid."

The merchant's drumming fingers stilled and for a moment, the only sound was the hum of the market around them—the shouts of other vendors, the distant clatter of a mining cart trundling down the cobblestone path. He leaned forward slowly, his thick elbows resting on the counter like twin hammers. His face was unreadable now—a mask of careful consideration.

"Generous, huh? Generous would be paying full price for goods that'll save your hide down there." He jabbed a finger downward, as if the mines were just beneath his boots. "You think you're clever, but those tunnels chew up clever and spit out desperate. Forty-five is already a bargain."

"And forty is my final offer," Heidi said firmly, stepping closer to the stall so the flickering torchlight threw sharp shadows across her determined face. She pulled a handful of coins from one of her many pockets and placed them on the counter with deliberate force. The coins clinked together, their dull metallic sound swallowed by the sounds of the bustling market.

The merchant's eyes glanced to the pile of coins, then back to Heidi's unflinching gaze. For a moment, neither moved.

"You're stubborn," he muttered finally, shaking his head slowly.

"Stubborn keeps us alive," Heidi said evenly. Her voice remained steady, but Aria noticed the faintest flicker of a grin tugging at the corner of her lips.

Heidi had won.

The merchant grunted and swept the coins into his apron's pocket. He shoved the torch toward Heidi without ceremony. "Fine. Forty," he said, his voice sounding defeated, "but don't think I won't remember your face."

He wouldn't.

She had haggled with him for a lantern only two months ago and he had threatened her with those exact words.

Heidi snatched the torch from his hands and turned on her heel without another word. Aria followed, throwing an apologetic glance over her shoulder as they slipped back into the flow of the crowd.

"You're unbelievable," Aria muttered, once they were out of earshot.

"What? I got us a deal, didn't I?" Heidi said, inspecting the torch as they walked. She twisted the base with a knowing ease, checking the capsule inside. "Besides, he was trying to rip us off. This thing is barely holding together—typical market junk."

Aria shook her head, but she couldn't suppress a smile. Heidi's stubbornness could be bothersome, but it was also why Aria trusted her. She wasn't afraid to stand her ground, even when it meant pushing things to the edge. "Well, let's just hope that 'market junk' doesn't fall apart when we need it most."

The market pressed in around them as they weaved through the maze of stalls when Heidi stopped abruptly.

"What's wrong?" Aria said, as she bumped into her.

"Look. Over there." Heidi's voice dropped to a whisper and Aria followed her pointed finger through the shifting crowd. At first, it was difficult to make out what Heidi had spotted—But then, almost hidden beside a cluster of towering crates—she saw him.

Hogan.

"What do you think he's up to?" Heidi murmured, but Aria was already on the move.

Her heart raced as she pushed through the crowd, eyes locking on Hogan's bulky form. *He would not get away this time.* She darted forward, weaving between shoppers.

Just a few more steps.

Hogan turned at the very last moment, eyes widening in shock as he spotted her.

"You!" Aria snarled, as she lunged at him, her body propelled by determination and rage. The world blurred around her as she flew through the air, arms outstretched.

Her fingers grazed the rough fabric of Hogan's shirt, then clenched, gripping tightly. They crashed to the ground in a tangle of limbs, sending up a cloud of dirt and grime. The impact knocked the wind from Aria's lungs, but she held on, her fingers digging into Hogan's shoulders like talons.

They rolled across the uneven ground, knocking over a nearby crate. Its contents—a jumble of mismatched gears and springs—scattered across the path with a musical clatter. Shouts of surprise and anger rose from the crowd as people stumbled to avoid the mess.

Aria's world spun as they tumbled, her vision a blur of flickering torchlight and shadowed faces. She was dimly aware of Heidi's voice calling out, but it was drowned out by the pulse pounding in her ears.

The acrid scent of sweat and fear filled her nostrils as she grappled with Hogan, her fingers digging into the coarse fabric of his shirt.

As they rolled to a stop, Aria found herself pinning Hogan to the ground. Her hair had come loose in the scuffle, dark strands falling across her face as she glared down at her captive. Hogan thrashed beneath her.

Aria's chest heaved as she glared down at him, sweat beading on her brow, her eyes blazing with fury. The crowd around them had fallen silent, their collective breath held in anticipation of what would happen next.

"You owe me big time, you thief," Aria snarled, her voice low and dangerous. She leaned in closer, her knee digging into his side. "And you'd better start paying up."

Hogan's eyes darted wildly, searching for an escape, his face a mask of fear and desperation.

"Do you enjoy spying on girls while they're on the privy, Hogan?" Aria spat, "then stealing from them?"

"I—I don't know what you're talking about," he stammered, his voice cracking. "I didn't see anything. I promise! I just thought it'd be funny."

Aria's grip loosened slightly as she studied Hogan's face. His eyes were wide with terror, pupils dilated in the dim light. A thin sheen of sweat glistened on his forehead and his lower lip trembled. For the first time, Aria noticed the dark circles under his eyes, and the dirt on his cheeks.

"Why'd you do it, Hogan?" she demanded, her voice sharp like flint sparking against stone.

Hogan squirmed beneath her, coughing. "Why not? Everyone takes what they can down here. You're just mad because I beat you to it."

Aria's jaw tightened. "You didn't beat me at anything. You stole from me."

Hogan laughed, short and bitter. "What's the difference?" he scoffed. "Smart girl like you—you'll bounce back." His eyes shifted to the crowd gathered around them, watching.

For a moment, Aria's grip loosened, confusion clouding her gaze. "Bounce back? Look around you, Hogan. What are you talking about?"

"You wouldn't understand," he said, a hint of disgust in his tone, "what it's like to always come last. To always watch someone else win." His face tightened. "But I don't care anymore."

Aria looked down at him, then up to the crowd around them, who now shifted uncomfortably. She took a deep breath, exhaling through her nose and her fury began to waver, replaced by a twinge of unease. "You're not worth it," she seethed, releasing him completely.

As she stood, the intense silence was broken by the crackle of loudspeakers coming to life. Located high above the District was a network of devices that served as the public address system of Cavandel.

It was the Warden.

The crackle echoed through the cavernous expanse, reverberating off iron and stone. The familiar hiss of static swept through the crowd, silencing conversations mid-sentence as every gaze turned upward.

Warden Blackthorne's voice boomed through the air, each word dripping with a veneer of false warmth that did little to mask the underlying threat.

"Greetings, my dear citizens," his voice oozed, dripping like poisoned honey. "I trust you're all enjoying another productive day in our most—glorious city."

The market fell eerily silent, all eyes remained upward as if the Warden himself might materialize from the shadows above. Aria felt a chill run down her spine, her recent scuffle with Hogan suddenly trivial.

"It has come to my attention," the Warden continued, his tone shifting ever so slightly, a razor's edge of threat beneath the veneer of civility. "That some among you may have—*forgotten*—the delicate balance that keeps our society functioning."

The cavern seemed to grow colder, the air thick with tension. Aria caught Heidi's eye across the crowd, a silent exchange of worry passing between them.

The Warden's voice droned on, each word a carefully crafted barb designed to instill unease and compliance.

"Dissent, dear citizens, is an illness. A malignant growth that threatens the very existence of our great city." His tone was almost conversational, as if discussing an unpleasant but necessary truth. "And like any illness, it must be purged, for the greater good of all."

A murmur rippled through the crowd—a blend of fear and morbid anticipation. The Warden's public addresses were rare and always signaled a tightening of control, a reminder of the iron fist beneath the velvet glove.

"There are forces beyond your control threatening our great city," the Warden continued, "forces lurking in the depths, clawing their way upward. But do not mistake their hunger for hope. We will not be deceived. Order will be maintained."

Aria's heart pounded in her chest as she stared up at the speakers, her recent triumph all but forgotten. Beside her, Heidi stood rigid, her face a mask of apprehension.

"In light of recent events," Blackthorne continued, his voice taking on a sharp edge, "I have found it necessary to implement certain—" he paused for effect. "Measures, to ensure the continued safety and prosperity of our great city."

The Warden's words rang out like a death knell. The words still hung in the air, as the public address system let out an ear-splitting screech.

The sound tore through the cavern, ricocheting off stone and steel. Market-goers clapped hands over their ears, faces tightening in pain. The screech faded into a guttural crackle, like the death rattle of some monstrous beast. Static hissed through the speakers, punctuated by occasional pops, before ebbing to complete silence.

The crowd shifted, a sea of worried faces bathed in the city's glow-lights. Aria's thoughts spiraled through the possibilities, each darker than the last. What would those measures be—increased patrols, harsher quotas, random searches?

In the silence that followed, the crowd stood frozen, eyes still fixed on the speakers above. The air thrummed with tension as they waited for the pronouncement to continue, but nothing came.

Aria's heart pounded in her chest, each beat echoing in her ears. She glanced at Heidi, whose face had gone pale, her knuckles white as she gripped her newly acquired torch.

A child's whimper broke the silence, quickly hushed by a parent's desperate shushing. The sound seemed to break a spell and a wave of whispers swept through the crowd.

What did he mean by new measures?

Purged?

The words rippled outward, growing in volume and urgency. Fear and speculation mingled in the air, almost palpable, as the artificial day slowly turned into night.

6

Trial by Fire

Location: Cavandel, The Outer District

Each morning in Cavandel, the air seemed to grow denser, like simmering unrest ready to boil over.

The Warden's cryptic announcement had rippled through the streets like a silent storm, leaving whispers in its wake. The markets buzzed with half-formed rumors—of stricter work quotas, of disappearances in the night, and of punishments harsher than ever before. Miners shuffled to their shifts with lowered gazes, murmurs barely escaping their lips as if the walls themselves could listen and betray them. Fear had taken root in the cracks of the city, growing quietly but surely.

Aria awoke with the familiar soreness of overworked muscles, her thoughts already tangled in the duties of the day. She moved through the habitual rhythms of her morning, her hands nimble as they prepared the scant breakfast their dwindling coin could afford.

The mines consumed her daylight hours. She worked alongside Sylas and Heidi, their presence a small comfort in the dim, winding tunnels.

By evening, the world above the mines felt distant, as if the entire day had been swallowed by the underground. When she finally returned home, the faint ache in her arms reminded her that exhaustion was now her closest companion.

Her grandmother sat near the hearth, the pale light of a single lantern casting a warm glow over her frail body.

Aria forced a lightness into her expression, but her grandmother's keen eyes pierced through the facade. "You've got something on your mind, child," she murmured, her voice thin but underpinned with the iron of her spirit.

Before Aria could muster a reply, the silence fractured—a faint, almost imperceptible scrape of boots against rough stone reached their ears. In Cavandel, unexpected visitors often brought trouble.

In the dim alley outside, a figure loomed, its shadow stretched long and dark along the path; It was cloaked in a garment so dark it seemed to drink in the scant light. The stranger's hood concealed his features, leaving only a faceless silhouette—a specter from the miners' lore, lurking in the shadows to ensnare the unsuspecting.

Aria's heart skipped as the knock came.

She reached for the nearest object and gripped it hard. Grim possibilities flashed through her mind—Hogan seeking retribution, guards enforcing the Warden's new measures, or worse yet—

Her grandmother's voice, remarkably steady and with an air of annoyance cleaved through the tension. "Aria. Get the door."

Aria blinked, forcing herself to breathe. She stepped toward the door, fingers tightening around the handle until her knuckles whitened. The cold metal pressed into her palm, grounding her as she pulled it open.

The figure stirred at her movement and lifted his hood. Beneath the shadow was no stranger, but the familiar, weathered face of Jace. His eyes, though dulled by years underground, still held a glimmer of warmth—a trace of the grin he once wore in brighter taverns.

"Good evening, young lady," he said, his voice warm yet edged with gravity. "Just thought I'd keep my word."

He glanced at the cooking utensil in Aria's hand and laughed, a rough bark that came from somewhere deep. "If I'd known you'd greet me with a spoon, I'd have brought my pot to make it a fair fight." His grin turned sly. "Or is this just practice for the next thief foolish enough to knock?"

Relief unraveled the knot in Aria's chest, warmth rising to replace it. She lowered the ladle, the tremor in her hands fading as her lips curved into an unguarded smile. Then, without thinking, she embraced the man.

Her grandmother's eyes brightened with recognition as Aria stepped aside, letting him in.

"Jace, you old coot! It's been ages!" the old woman declared. The joy in her voice was a rare melody, lifting Aria's spirits. Yet at the back of her mind, the image of the shrouded figure lingered—a reminder that in Cavandel, even friends could become phantoms in the dark.

Once inside, Jace shrugged off his cloak and hung it on a nearby hook, revealing a sturdy frame clad in well-worn clothes. He chuckled as he set a familiar bundle on the table—a gesture that sparked immediate recognition in both women's eyes.

Aria's breath hitched as Jace unwrapped the bundle, revealing a small trove of treasures. First, fresh herbs from the Inner District—lush and fragrant, their earthy scent cutting through the stale air. Then a used power capsule, still good for a few more months. And finally, a glass vial of syrup, its rich sweetness drawn from elusive mushrooms that thrived in the depths below.

From her chair near the hearth, Aria's grandmother leaned forward slightly, her gaze lingering on the jar with something close to reverence. "Well, well," she murmured, her voice touched with amusement. "Jace brings gifts like it's Founders Day already. What's next?"

Jace huffed a quiet laugh. "Now, now, old friend," he said, his tone light but steady. "And here I was, just trying to be nice."

A smirk tugged at his lips, as he accepted a plate from Aria.

"Just in time for leftovers," she said. "Have a seat."

The worn lines of his face deepened with the gesture as he pulled up a chair. They lingered in easy conversation for a while—old stories, half-remembered names, bits of gossip that carried more comfort than meaning. It was talk meant to steady the heart, not stir it.

Then the laughter faded, and in the quiet that followed, Jace's tone softened. "How are you holding up?" he asked, his gaze steady on the old woman. His voice was gentle and tinged with the kind of concern that couldn't be hidden.

"Ah, Jace, you old softie," she replied, a flicker of her former vigor warming her tone. "I'm as well as can be expected, given the circumstances." Her hand swept vaguely across the cramped room.

Jace's eyes glanced briefly to her leg, hidden beneath a thick blanket. "And the leg?"

She sighed, the sound barely audible over the crackling fire. "I wish I had better news," she admitted, regret lacing her words. But then her voice lifted, a feigned cheerfulness softening the truth. "It is what it is. But enough about me, Jace. How are the mines these days?"

Jace didn't answer at first. His silence lingered, pressing against the walls like an unspoken confession.

"I've heard rumors," he said at last, his tone careful, as though testing the weight of each word. "That they're close to finding a cure. A real one."

Aria's ears pricked at the mention, but her grandmother only chuckled, the sound weathered but warm. "Come now, Jace, you know better than to go around spreading rumors." Her smile deepened, wry and familiar. "Some things never change, it seems."

They shared a glance, brief but meaningful—an untold story passing silently between them. Aria watched the exchange, a flicker of emotion stirring in her hazel eyes. Jace had been a fixture in their lives for as long as she could remember, a steady presence who had outlasted both her parents and many others who had come and gone.

Jace cradled his cup, eyes lowered as though the grooves in the table held the answers he couldn't find. "I was thinking about the old orders the other day," he said quietly, voice soft enough that Aria had to lean closer. The weight of something unspoken lingered in his tone.

Her grandmother tilted her head, a faint smile playing at the corner of her lips. "I'm surprised you remember them. We had to change the plan more often than not."

Jace chuckled under his breath. "It was never about the plans, was it? It was about who was leading them." His gaze lifted briefly to meet hers, a glimmer of something warm flickering behind the weariness.

The old woman hummed thoughtfully, her fingers tracing the rim of her plate. "Well, we did what we could, with what we had." She paused, eyes distant. "Though I'll admit, sometimes it felt like we were running blind."

"Blind or not, you always found a way," Jace said. "You made sure of that." His voice carried the quiet respect of someone who had trusted her through every peril and survived because of it. "Not many could've done it."

Her smile deepened, but it didn't reach her eyes. "Not many are left to say so."

They shared a quiet glance—brief but heavy with the weight of names unspoken and friends lost along the way.

Aria shifted in her chair, her gaze darting between them. "What orders?"

"Oh, nothing you'd be interested in, dear," her grandmother said smoothly, waving off the question. "Just the kind of choices that demand more than most are willing to give." She turned back to Jace. "You weren't so bad at them yourself, you know. Quick to adapt."

Jace smirked, the lines around his eyes softening. "Quick to do what was needed."

"And that," she replied, her voice low, "was exactly why we made it through."

Silence followed, but it was rich—like the aftermath of an old battlefield, marked by both victory and loss, with only the survivors left to tell the story.

Jace rose slowly, as if the act of leaving carried a burden of its own. He reached for his cloak, the worn fabric slipping through his fingers before he pulled it over his shoulders. "I should be going," he said, the words soft, as though reluctant to break the moment.

Her grandmother folded her hands in her lap, watching him with a calm understanding. "The road didn't let you rest for long, did it?" she said quietly. "But it kept you sharp."

Jace chuckled under his breath, the sound barely audible. "Sometimes sharp. Sometimes—just tired." He looked back at her, his gaze lingering a moment too long. "You've always been good at surviving, Luce, but take care anyway."

The old woman smiled faintly. "You too."

Jace turned toward Aria, his expression softening as he met her gaze. "Take care of her," he said, and though his words sounded like an order, there was something fragile beneath them—a request, almost a plea.

"I always do," Aria replied, her voice steady. Then she stood, her hands brushing the folds of her cloak. "I'll see you out."

Before following him, she glanced back at her grandmother. "I won't be long," she said softly, the promise in her tone clear.

Her grandmother nodded, a knowing look flickering in her eyes. "I'll be right here."

Satisfied, Jace nodded once, and pulled the door open.

Aria followed him out, the door clicking shut behind her. The night greeted them with its chill, carrying the scent of damp stone and earth. Lanternlight flickered weakly against the walls of nearby homes, casting shadows that stretched and shifted like they had a life of their own.

Jace moved a few steps down the path, his boots scuffing softly against the dirt. Aria lingered, the weight of the darkness pressing close. For a fleeting instant, she felt it—eyes on her, watching from somewhere unseen. She turned, scanning the alley behind her, but found only restless shadows and the low hum of the city beyond.

"Jace," Aria called, her voice gentle, like a hand on his shoulder.

He paused, turning just enough for her to see the outline of his hood in the dim lanternlight.

"About those rumors," she said softly. "I'm not asking for much—just to be pointed in the right direction.

Jace exhaled, his breath misting in the cold air. "The people behind those rumors aren't just talk, Aria. They're dangerous," he said. "They deal in favors, secrets and debts. Their help always comes at a price—sometimes more than what's bargained for."

He glanced briefly toward the shadows stretching beyond the path. "You've seen how things work down here—sometimes it's not the threat you see that gets you, but the one waiting quietly, just out of sight."

Aria absorbed his words, her gaze thoughtful. "I understand."

He studied her carefully, his brows furrowed. "They're getting desperate, Aria, especially with the recent blackouts, and the bombings—"

The bombings?

Aria's chest tightened. "Are you talking about the Dwellers?"

Jace took a deep breath, the weight of the name hanging heavy between them.

"They'll help if it benefits them, Aria, but their loyalty is as thin as a knife's edge. Don't think for a second they won't turn that edge against you."

"And you?" Aria asked softly. "Are you one of them?"

Jace's gaze fell to the ground, as though the memories were stones pressing against his shoulders. "Not for a long time," he said, "and way before they became what they are today." He straightened. "I doubt even they know what they're fighting for anymore."

And Gran? she thought.

The question probed to the surface, but she pushed it back, deciding to address it at a later time.

Aria hesitated, the chill of his words cutting deeper than the night air. "I'm not looking to get tangled in their business, Jace. I just want the truth, even if there's a slim chance of helping Gran."

Jace sighed, the sound carrying a hint of something personal, like a regret he hadn't let go of. "You're still young, Aria. Think about your future. I don't want you chasing shadows," he said quietly. "You've seen what false hope can do."

"She's all I have left, Jace," Aria admitted, her voice heavy with emotion.

Jace looked at the young woman standing before him—brave, yet naïve—and in that moment, he saw another woman, years ago.

Lucinda.

The woman he had looked up to, the one he had risked his life for and followed without question. His eyes narrowed as he studied her, and somehow, Aria felt as though her worthiness was being measured on an intangible scale.

Finally, he relented.

"I have a contact," he said flatly, lifting a hand in protest as Aria's face lit up. "But don't mistake this for hope. I'm not making any promises and I won't be able to protect you if things go wrong. I'll set up the meeting, but after that, you're on your own."

Jace sighed, then added, "Meet me at Jaco's tavern in the morning, but be early. I'll have the details you need."

"Thank you!" Aria said, wrapping her arms around the older man in a tight hug.

Jace sighed deeply and gently pried her away, but the worry in his eyes didn't ease. "Be careful," he said. "Some places are even darker than the deepest mines."

"I'll be careful," she replied softly, her words a promise.

He gave a gentle squeeze of her arm, nodded his goodbye, then turned and walked away.

As the shadows swallowed Jace, Aria stood alone under the dim glow of the lanterns, the cold night pressing against her like an invisible weight. She pulled her cloak tighter, but it wasn't the chill that made her shiver—it was the uncertainty of the path ahead. The truth she needed to chase down, no matter how dangerous.

She thought about the Dwellers—a name that had haunted the whispers of the mines since she was a child, now suddenly within reach. Dangerous. Unpredictable. But maybe—just maybe—her only chance. The thought left a bitter taste on her tongue, yet she clenched her fists, forcing herself to hold steady.

She stared down the dimly lit path Jace had taken, her heart racing not from fear, but from the flicker of hope—a hope she could no longer extinguish. If there was even a sliver of truth to the rumors, then she would try. She owed Gran that much.

But she couldn't do it alone.

Her breath trembled as it met the night air, curling into mist before fading away. Gran had always said that survival wasn't about waiting for things to change—it was about taking action, even when it terrified you.

She exhaled slowly, watching the mist of her breath disappear into the cold darkness.

She would tell Heidi and Sylas about the book.

They were the two people she could trust, even when the world seemed to crumble around them. She would have to trust them now—with the truth and with the risk that came with it.

Aria bit her lip. Deep down, she knew they would help her, but would they still trust her? Would they even understand?

With a final glance down the empty path, she turned and headed back toward the house.

The spark Jace had ignited wasn't just hope—it was determination. Whatever the Dwellers demanded, whatever secrets she had to reveal—it was time to stop waiting.

***

The next morning, Aria, Sylas, and Heidi made their way to the Junk-yard—one of the four sprawling dump sites where refuse from the Stratum rained down in endless, glittering heaps. With the Lift temporarily shut down, they'd decided to spend the day scavenging.

Their boots crunched over broken glass and loose scraps as they followed a familiar path through the chaos. They were on the hunt for salvageable parts—wooden boards, discarded pieces of wire, and sheets of metal that could be repurposed before rust and decay claimed them completely.

The steady hum of machinery filled the air as they sifted through the refuse. Overhead, the glow-lights flickered in uneven pulses, throwing restless shadows across the mounds of discarded purpose.

Sylas wiped his palms against his trousers, smearing a layer of grime rather than removing it. He tilted his head toward the Lift. "What d'you think happened?"

Heidi shrugged, tossing a bent nail into the dirt. "Who knows."

"Could've been halfway to the Mines by now," he said, casting a look at Aria, who had yet to say a word.

"Yeah," Heidi replied, her tone dry. "Must've been serious to shut it down like that."

"Probably another mess in the Abyss," Sylas muttered. "Still, I'd rather be alive with nothing to show for it, than completely dead with a haul I couldn't even carry."

Heidi gave a short laugh. "Completely dead? As opposed to?"

"Mostly dead," he said, flashing a crooked grin. "Don't overthink it."

She shook her head, smiling despite herself. "Come on. Maybe we'll actually find something useful."

Around them, twisted wires and warped circuit boards mingled with broken boards and cracked plastic crates. Fragments of glass glittered faintly beneath the glow-lights, while strips of faded fabric, damp from the morning air, clung to the wreckage like forgotten banners.

Aria lingered by a mound of corroded machinery, lost in thought. She ran her fingers along a rusted panel, flakes of grime breaking loose beneath her touch. The air was heavy with metal and mildew—thick, stale, and oppressive, seeping into her lungs and coating her tongue with the taste of rust.

"How's the search going, sis?" Sylas called from ahead as he pried open a rusted panel. A dull clatter followed, then the scrape of metal as he drew out a used capsule from the hollow inside. His grin caught the dim light as he held it up.

"A few bits," Heidi replied, brushing grime from her palms. "But nothing to brag about."

Sylas turned the capsule over in his hand, checking for cracks. It was sound. "Then pick up the pace," he said. "Or are you just here for the sightseeing?"

"Unlike you, little brother, I'm multitasking." Her tone was even, distracted but sharp. "I can find junk and ignore you at the same time."

"Ignoring me?" He pressed a hand to his chest in mock offense. "Careful sis, you might miss my next brilliant idea."

"I'll risk it," Heidi said flatly. "Your last brilliant idea got us stuck in a tunnel for over three hours."

Sylas laughed, the sound bouncing between the heaps of scrap. "I still say we would've made out it if you'd trusted my shortcut."

"Yeah, well maybe next time you can trust me when I say a tunnel's about to collapse." She kicked a rusted plate aside, the clang echoing through the Junkyard before she turned back to her search.

Aria barely heard them. Their familiar banter drifted around her like a hum she couldn't quite tune into. Her thoughts circled back to a single truth that refused to let go—Jace's words, steady and impossible, repeating in her mind.

A cure.

Aria tightened her grip on the sheet of metal until its jagged edge bit into her fingers. She'd known this moment would come—but now that it had, her heart drummed like iron striking iron.

Heidi and Sylas had always been her closest friends, but this wasn't another secret whispered in passing. Once she spoke the words aloud, there would be no taking them back.

"Aria, you alright back there?" Sylas's voice cut through her thoughts. "You've been poking that same hunk of scrap like you're trying to be its friend."

She blinked and forced a faint smile. "I'm fine."

But the effort caught in her voice, thin and uncertain.

Heidi brushed off her hands and stepped closer, concern softening her usual sharpness. "Come on, what's wrong? You've been quiet since we got here."

Aria hesitated, breath catching as she searched for the right words. "Jace came by last night."

Sylas crossed his arms, one brow lifting. "Okay... and?"

The weight of his gaze pressed against her, steady and unyielding.

"He said something," Aria finally admitted, her voice quiet but steady.

Sylas leaned back against a stack of rusted panels, a faint smirk tugging at his mouth. "Gonna keep us guessing, or are you gonna say it?"

Aria drew in a breath, the metallic taste of rust coating her tongue. "He said there's a rumor going around." Her voice steadied, even as her pulse refused to. "A cure for Shatterblight."

Silence followed—thick, suspended, as if the air itself had frozen between them.

Heidi's gaze sharpened, suspicion flickering in her eyes. "And you believe it?"

Aria met her stare. "If there's even a chance it's real, then yes."

Heidi tilted her head, doubt still clouding her expression. "And where is this cure?"

Aria hesitated, her fingers tightening around the edge of the metal sheet. "Well... that's the crazy part."

Sylas arched a brow. "What do you mean, *the crazy part*?"

She drew in a slow breath, steadying the tremor beneath her words. "You remember the explosions?"

Sylas froze. The faint trace of humor drained from his face. "The Dwellers?" he asked quietly—his voice little more than a whisper, as if speaking the name might summon them.

Heidi's eyes widened. "You're serious?"

"I am." Aria's voice wavered, but she forced it steady. "Jace set up a meeting with one of his contacts. I'm supposed to meet them tonight."

Sylas rubbed the back of his neck, releasing a sharp breath. "You're talking about the same people who've been setting off bombs, Aria. That *is* crazy."

"I know." Her hands tightened around her cloak until the fabric creased between her fingers. "But if they have what we need, I have to try."

Heidi crossed her arms, her jaw tightening. "You do realize who we're talking about, right? Last I heard, the Dwellers don't go around just handing out favors."

"They won't take more than I'm willing to give," Aria said, her voice firm.

Sylas snorted, the sound somewhere between disbelief and frustration. "Yeah? You think that's how it works? You can't just barter with them like it's some market stall."

"I know the risks," she replied, her voice catching before she forced it steady. "But I also know that doing nothing is worse." She swallowed hard, her throat tight. "I'm not asking you to come with me if you don't want to. But—" her voice softened "—I don't know if I can do it alone."

Sylas exchanged a glance with Heidi, a silent conversation passing between them. Heidi sighed, rubbing at her temples before finally nodding.

"I don't think you really know the risks," Sylas said quietly, his tone losing its edge. "But when you put it that way... what choice do we have?"

He glanced toward Heidi again, then back at Aria, a faint grin tugging at his mouth. "Guess someone's gotta make sure you don't get yourself killed."

Heidi huffed a small laugh. "You really know how to drag people into trouble, don't you?"

Aria's throat tightened, but this time it wasn't from fear. Warmth swelled in her chest. "I don't know what I'd do without you two."

The scent of rust and oil still clung to the air, but for the first time that day, she felt like she could finally breathe.

They turned toward the exit, boots crunching over scattered debris.

After a few steps, Aria slowed, glancing down at the worn leather bag slung over her shoulder. She hesitated, then drew back the flap, revealing the corner of an old, weather-stained book.

"There's something else I need to show you," she said softly, her words barely above the hum of the city.

Heidi and Sylas traded questioning glances and slowed their pace.

As Aria caught up, the acrid scent of the Junkyard faded from her senses, replaced by the weight of what she was about to reveal.

***

The meeting spot wasn't exactly what Aria had imagined—or maybe it was. A narrow alley carved between jagged walls, buried in the southernmost slums of the Outer District. The trio had never ventured this far south before. Until now, they'd never had reason to.

Cavandel's artificial daylight had begun to fade, its flickering glow receding into dimness as the city settled into night. The last of the light pooled weakly between the walls, glinting off wet stone before sinking into shadow. Rusted pipes wound along the ground, leaking ribbons of murky water into shallow puddles.

Sylas kept a hand near his satchel, his eyes scanning the shadows as if they might move on their own. Heidi stayed close, her gaze sharper than usual, darting between the far corners of the alley.

Aria's grip tightened on her bag. The book inside pressed against her—a weight she tried not to think about, but couldn't quite ignore.

They had eaten quickly at the tavern, whispering over half-finished meals as they finalized their plan. But no amount of words had quieted the knot in her stomach. Now, standing here, with the unknown waiting just beyond the dark, she felt how unprepared they truly were.

A metallic clink broke the stillness, followed by the crunch of boots on gravel. From the mouth of the alley, a figure emerged—moving with the practiced ease of someone used to not being seen. Aria's breath caught as he stepped closer.

He stopped just beyond the reach of their glow-torches. The faint light caught the edge of his silhouette, a lean frame beneath a worn jacket, a hood drawn low. When he lifted his head, the shadows parted just enough for his eyes to catch the light, dark and steady and sharp as steel.

"Punctual," the man rasped, his voice low and unhurried. "I like that." He shifted, the motion quiet and deliberate. "He said you'd be interesting. Didn't mention you'd bring backup."

Aria's breath steadied, though instinct warned her to stay cautious. "Pike?" she asked at last, the name heavy on her tongue.

His smile vanished. He stepped forward, his gaze cutting through the dim light. "I suggest you forget that name," he growled. "Real fast."

Aria's throat tightened. Her hands trembled as she lowered them to her sides. "Sorry," she whispered. "I understand."

The silence stretched between them until Pike's expression shifted again. The smile returned—thin, calculated, dangerous. He exhaled slowly, his gaze sliding toward Sylas and Heidi.

"These two supposed to protect you?" His smirk deepened. "I've seen cave rats with sharper claws."

Sylas squared his shoulders. "We can handle ourselves."

Pike chuckled, the sound low and amused, but there was steel beneath it. "We'll see." He took a measured step closer. "Let's make something clear, girl. If you're expecting a favor, you're already in over your head."

"We're not here for charity," Aria said, her voice firmer than she felt. "We just need information."

Pike studied her small frame, head tilting slightly, like a predator sizing up its prey. "Information, huh?" His gaze lowered to the bag at her side. "What kind—and how badly do you need it?"

Aria hesitated, words catching before they found breath. "We heard about the cure. The one for Shatterblight."

Pike's smile widened, his tone silken and edged with danger. "Did you now?" His voice lowered, almost gentle, though his eyes stayed cold. "Word travels fast."

Aria's breath caught. "Is it true?"

Pike tapped a finger against his chin, savoring the moment. "That's the kind of answer that costs, girl. Nothing's free—that least of all."

Aria swallowed hard and reached into her satchel, her fingers brushing the worn edge of the book before closing around a small pouch. She drew it free, the faint clink of coins breaking the hush between them.

"We'll pay for the information," she said, forcing her voice steady. "And I'll work to get whatever's needed for the cure itself."

For a heartbeat, Pike didn't move. Then a low chuckle slipped from him, soft at first, growing louder until it filled the alley. Heidi's brow furrowed, Sylas's fists tightened, but Pike only wiped a hand across his mouth, still grinning.

"A few Grottos?" he said, shaking his head. "You think that's what we're after?"

He gestured toward the walls around them as if the city itself were the punch line. "Kids," he said, his tone flat and edged with disdain. "You don't get it, do you?"

Sylas's jaw flexed. "We're not kids."

"Maybe not," Pike said dryly, "but you're still trying to play a game you don't understand." He stepped closer, his shadow stretching across the uneven ground. "Grottos can buy food or bribe a guard, but they won't buy what we're building. They don't buy power."

His gaze drifted from Sylas back to Aria, sharp and unrelenting. "Power isn't about counting coins—it's about knowing the right people, and knowing what they don't want you to know."

He sighed, brushing dust from his sleeve. "I knew this would be a waste of time," he muttered, half to himself. Turning, he started toward the alley's exit. "You've got guts, I'll give you that. But this? It's not how the real world works. Go home, children."

"No, wait," Aria said quickly, the words tumbling out before she could stop them. "What about information? Not just money—information."

Pike froze mid-step, then turned—slowly. The gleam in his eyes had shifted, sharper now, more dangerous.

"Information," he repeated, the word rolling off his tongue like a dare. "And what kind do you think would buy you a favor?"

Aria hesitated. The book pressed against her side, its edges rough beneath her palm. Her pulse thundered in her ears, steady and relentless.

This was Gran's chance—maybe her only one.

She drew a shaky breath and met his stare. Her hand trembled as she pulled the book from her satchel, the worn leather soft against her fingers. Fear coiled tight in her chest, but beneath it burned a flicker of resolve. She couldn't let it stop her—not now.

She held the book out, her heart hammering.

Pike stepped closer, his eyes narrowing as they caught the faint seal pressed into the cover. His fingers twitched at his side, but he didn't reach for it.

"Where did you get that?" His voice was quiet now, stripped of mockery.

Sylas glanced from the book to Aria, his breath shallow.

Pike's gaze didn't waver. "Something valuable enough for a favor, then," he said, the edge of a smile curving his mouth. "Well. Don't just stand there, girl. Let's take a look."

7

The Resistance Rises

Location: Cavandel, The Outer District

The alley stretched before them like a scar through the heart of the city—narrow, winding, and slick with runoff. Dim light scraped across walls of stone and crumbling brick, barely revealing their sheen. Pike moved quickly, his strides long and deliberate, as if he'd walked this path a hundred times before. The others kept close, boots splashing through shallow puddles.

Aria's breath came a little faster than she liked—not from exertion, but because her nerves refused to settle. The deeper they went, the more the city seemed to close in around them, as though they were being swallowed whole.

Behind her, Sylas muttered loud enough to break her focus. "Do you guys feel as lost as I do?"

Aria kept her eyes ahead, but Heidi wasn't as patient.

"Lost?" Heidi snorted from the rear. "I'm just waiting for the part where he sells us to smugglers."

Sylas chuckled. "Yeah. Classic ambush material." He leaned closer to Aria and whispered—just loud enough for everyone to hear—"If he tries anything, we go for the knees."

Pike sighed from up ahead without turning. "I can hear you, you know."

Heidi laughed, and Aria bit her lip to suppress a smirk, though her nerves still hummed beneath the surface. Humor was Sylas's way of handling tension, but it didn't help. Her thoughts churned with worst-case scenarios. What if this was a trap? If Pike was leading them into an ambush—or worse, straight into the hands of someone who wanted answers they didn't have? What if the book wasn't enough to make the Dwellers help them?

She clenched her fists, forcing herself to focus on the rhythm of their steps against the damp ground. The book had to be enough. *It had to be.*

The alley narrowed, forcing them to walk single file. Lost in thought, Aria didn't notice when Pike stopped abruptly at a rusted metal door set into the dead-end wall.

She bumped into him, and Sylas, close behind, bumped into her. Heidi, still laughing, was the last to crash into the pile.

Pike let out a long, exasperated sigh, turning his head slightly to glance at the mess of them behind him. "You know," he said dryly, "I don't think you're cut out for this sort of thing."

Sylas smirked, brushing off his jacket. "We're doing great," he said. "Right, Aria?"

She shot him a quick look but said nothing.

He turned back to Pike, rubbing his shoulder. "Next time, maybe call it out before slamming on the brakes."

Pike didn't respond. He just sighed again, then turned to the door and rapped twice. After a pause, he knocked once more.

The metal groaned as it cracked open, revealing a man with a thick beard and sharp, suspicious eyes. His gaze swept over the group, lingering on Aria just long enough to make her skin prickle before returning to Pike.

"You're back," the man said, his voice rough.

"Yes," Pike replied. "Let us in."

The man stepped aside and they filed in single file. The cool air inside hit Aria immediately, wrapping around her like a damp cloak. The hideout wasn't what she'd imagined. The rough stone walls were stained with moisture and patches of worn, mismatched rugs covered the cracked floor. Dim lanterns hung from iron hooks, casting flickering light that barely touched the room's corners. Wooden crates lined the walls, some marked with faded labels, others sealed shut.

"So, this is it?" Sylas sniffed and stepped over a loose board that creaked under his weight. He gave the room a slow, exaggerated scan, his brow creasing in mock disappointment. He sighed. "This is the legendary hideout of the Dwellers?"

Pike turned, his gaze hard but tinged with amusement. "Relax," he said flatly, "this is just one of many and trust me—we don't trust you enough to reveal more."

Sylas folded his arms. "Either way," he said, "it's a little lacking."

Orvin, the man standing by the door, grunted, his face contorting in offense as if Sylas had struck a nerve. He shifted his weight, the lanternlight carving deep shadows along his frame, making him seem larger than he was. Veins corded his forearms like coiled cables beneath the skin, and his scowl carried its own warning—he wasn't a man to be trifled with. Even the way he stood, feet planted wide and steady, spoke of someone used to making others regret their words.

His glare fixed on Sylas. "That scrawny one likes to run his mouth, doesn't he?"

Heidi elbowed Sylas sharply and whispered, "Why are you trying to get us killed?"

Before Sylas could answer, Aria cut in, her voice firm. "Yeah, Sylas, please be quiet."

Sylas raised his hands, his face settling into a look of meek surrender, as if apologizing for the mere offense of existing.

Orvin folded his arms, his sharp gaze never leaving Sylas. "If you don't like it, I can help you leave."

Before the tension could stretch any further, Pike sighed, the sound heavy with exasperation. "They're just kids," he said, his tone level. "Why are you letting them crawl under your skin? Don't waste your breath playing tough with them."

Orvin grunted but didn't let go of the scowl creasing his brow. His eyes narrowed on the group, lingering on Aria and Sylas. "Who are they, anyway?"

Pike's lips curved in the faintest trace of a smirk. "These little adventurers," he said, his voice dripping with sarcasm, "seem to have gotten their grubby little hands on something very precious."

Orvin's eyes narrowed as his voice dropped to a low murmur. "Why don't we just get rid of 'em and take it?"

Aria studied his face, unable to discern whether genuine threat lurked behind his words or mere theatrical posturing. His rhetoric slithered through the room—danger disguised as reason. Her stomach twisted, her fingers instinctively tightening around the spine of the book, as if it might shield her from whatever came next.

Pike's smirk lingered, unfazed. "The thought did cross my mind," he admitted, his tone deceptively casual, as though they were discussing something as routine as tunnel repairs. "But if they're holding something this valuable, imagine what else they might be useful for." He leaned slightly toward Orvin, voice lowering just enough to sharpen the edge of his reasoning. "And you don't know what else they've seen—or what they've already hidden."

Orvin didn't respond, but the shift in his stance was subtle. He wasn't fully convinced, but Pike had planted the seed.

Pike turned to Aria, his gaze steady but expectant. "The book," he said, holding out his hand.

Aria hesitated. The book felt heavier than usual—not just in weight but in the enormity of what it could mean. Her fingers tightened around the worn leather, the familiar texture grounding her as fear threaded through her thoughts. What if this wasn't enough? What if the moment Pike saw what was inside, he dismissed them altogether?

Her mind flashed through the possibilities, being abandoned here in this cold, dark place, the Dwellers turning on them in an instant. She could almost hear Sylas's voice making light of it, but that wouldn't save them if things went wrong.

The air felt heavy, clinging to her skin like damp stone.

This was why she was here, she had no choice but to trust that Pike would see value in the book. She swallowed hard, willing herself to be steady.

"Relax," Pike said evenly, his voice devoid of comfort, carrying only the weight of someone accustomed to witnessing fear.

But how could she relax? Her mind kept circling the same question. *What if this was a mistake?*

With a breath that felt entirely too loud, she held the book out to him. Her hand shook as he took it, his grip firm, steady.

Without another word, he crossed the room and sat at an old barrel that served as a table. He gestured for the others to take their places on the bench lining the wall. The wood creaked as they shifted into position, each sound punctuating the silence that followed.

"Now, I need a little quiet while I look at this," he warned.

Heidi nudged Sylas. "He's talking to you," she whispered.

Sylas didn't respond. Instead, he lifted his hand slowly, palm up, as if to ask the room what offense he'd committed this time.

Pike set the book in front of him, his fingers brushing its worn edges before tracing the seal embossed on the cover. The symbol of the early resistance was faint but unmistakable—a relic from a time before the Dwellers were the Dwellers. His eyes narrowed as he studied it, as though searching for proof of its authenticity.

His thumb drifted over the faded lettering stamped across the front: *Above and Below: The Natural and Mechanical Foundations of Cavandel and Beyond.* The title suggested a simple premise—at first. A guide to survival aboveground, and an exploration of Cavandel's inner workings below. But Pike knew better. There was nothing simple about bridging two worlds so different, yet so intricately connected.

The natural half held the expected lessons—rivers, wildlife, edible plants. But the mechanical half was where the secrets lay, buried like relics waiting to be unearthed. It wasn't just a guide to survival—it was a roadmap to power, for those who knew how to read it.

Aria's stomach twisted. The silence pressed in, heavy and suffocating. "That's just the cover," she blurted, the words slipping out before she could stop them. "You have to open it."

Pike lifted his head slightly, giving her a sharp, deliberate look. His gaze lingered for a moment, heavy with annoyance, before he turned back to the book.

Without another word, he flipped it open, the brittle crack of the pages cutting through the oppressive silence like fire.

The room felt even quieter now, as though the act of opening the book had pulled something vital from the air. The flickering lanternlight cast shadows over Pike's face, accentuating the furrow of his brow as he began to examine its contents.

He traced his fingers over the encoded symbols on one of the pages, his expression tightening in concentration. He said nothing for a long moment, and Aria could feel her heart thudding in her chest.

"I don't understand," she said quietly, glancing at the unfamiliar writing. "What's so important about that page? The rest of the book talks about useful things—plants, rivers, weather, things people need to survive up there." She leaned closer, as if proximity alone could help her decode the mystery Pike seemed so focused on.

"That's just the surface," Pike muttered, almost as an afterthought, before turning the page. His voice had lost its dismissive edge, replaced by something colder—calculating. "The surface won't save us. I'm interested in what can."

Aria blinked, stunned by the casual dismissal. "*Just* the surface?" she echoed, as though the word itself were offensive. "The surface is everything we've ever—" She stopped herself, biting down on her next words. She wasn't sure whether she was more frustrated with his indifference or shaken by how easily he'd brushed off something she had thought was so important.

Pike didn't look up or offer an explanation. His focus was already fixed on the next page.

He flipped carefully, stopping occasionally on diagrams that made Aria's head spin—detailed blueprints of structures she had barely glanced at before. Pipes overlapped in complex grids, spiraling toward something labeled *central intake,* though most of the notes had faded over time. Aria's eyes traced the intricate lines, but her mind struggled to make sense of them.

She'd skimmed over this section before, dismissing it as dry, technical descriptions of Cavandel's inner workings—useless to someone who had never planned to stay underground, whose dreams had always reached for the open sky above. But now, as Pike's fingers moved over the diagrams with purpose, she realized how wrong she might have been.

He kept flipping until he landed on a series of sketches with annotations scrawled along the margins, still legible despite the wear.

Aria squinted at the intricate lines. "What is that? More maps?"

"Schematics," Pike replied, leaning closer. His finger tapped the corner of one drawing. "That's part of the Lift system running through Cavandel. It's old, but this design hasn't changed much." He turned to the next page, which featured a sketch of cylindrical capsules lined in rows, annotated with diagrams of power lines feeding into the walls. "Capsules," he muttered.

Aria felt a jolt of unease. She had barely skimmed this part of the book.

"There's more," Pike murmured, flipping ahead until he reached another section. A diagram spread across two pages, depicting something massive and central, its lines branching out like veins. The heading was smudged, but the words Power Core remained visible in thick, blocky writing. Pike's lips thinned. "The core that powers the entire city."

Aria's fingers twitched at her sides. "Why would that be in a book about the surface?"

Pike's gaze didn't leave the page. "Because this isn't just a book about the surface." He flipped back toward the earlier sections, his movements growing more deliberate, until he reached a chapter titled *Subterranean Fauna and Threats.* His expression shifted slightly—still controlled, but sharper. He scanned a sketch of a creature with spiked limbs and a hard, segmented exoskeleton. The words *Rocknids* stood out in bold ink beneath the image.

Aria leaned forward slightly. "That's the section on Rocknids," she said, her tone casual, as if the information were no more important than the diagrams she had dismissed earlier.

"Not just information," Pike said. He ran his finger along a passage of neatly organized notes detailing the creatures' habits and growth cycles. His finger stopped on a small block of text buried in the margins—half-faded but still readable. His eyes narrowed. "This is about their venom," he muttered, almost to himself. "Its toxicity levels, extraction methods, and potential medicinal properties."

Aria frowned, the meaning just beginning to dawn on her. "Medicinal?"

Pike nodded once. "Anna will want to see this." His voice lowered as he read further, the gears turning in his mind. "This might be the clue we've been missing. If their venom or saliva interacts with Shatterblight the way this hints at, then—" He snapped the book shut, cutting off the thought.

Aria's breath hitched as the sound of the closing book seemed to echo louder than it should have. Her fingers curled against her knees, gripping them tightly as she leaned forward. "You can't take it," she blurted, her voice sharper than intended. She forced herself to breathe, but her chest tightened as panic swelled inside her. "We—we didn't come all this way to lose it."

Pike leaned back slightly, his gaze cool but unwavering. "This book is coming with me," he said, his tone steady but carrying the weight of an unspoken warning. "And if that means dragging the lot of you along, then so be it."

Before Aria could respond, Orvin stepped forward. His shadow stretched long across the room, casting jagged shapes on the walls.

"You're assuming this isn't some elaborate setup," he said, his gaze flicking from the book to Aria. "The Warden's crackdown didn't just start out of nowhere. He's been tightening the screws ever since that announcement. And you walk in here with this?" His voice lowered, the accusation barely hidden beneath it. "Awfully convenient, don't you think?"

Heidi sat up slightly, her arms crossed. "Out of nowhere?" she repeated, her tone flat and sharp. "Maybe if you didn't set off an explosion in the middle of the city, we wouldn't be dealing with this mess."

Orvin's eyes narrowed, but he didn't argue. The shift in his stance was subtle, but telling.

Sylas leaned back, drumming his fingers lazily against the bench. "What, you think we walked in here on purpose?" he laughed, "Love the hospitality, by the way."

Orvin didn't even flinch. His eyes stayed locked on Aria. "For all we know, you've led them right to us. The Warden's been tightening control because someone's feeding him information and you expect me to believe your timing is just a coincidence?"

Aria sat forward, fists clenched in her lap. "We didn't lead anyone here. No one knows where we are. We don't even know how to get back!" Her voice trembled slightly at the end, but she held Orvin's gaze, refusing to let him see how deeply his words rattled her.

Orvin tilted his head slightly, his eyes narrowing. "The Warden's reach goes deeper than you think."

The room fell into a tense silence until Heidi spoke, her voice calm but firm. "Look, you don't trust us and we don't trust you. I get it. But think about this—Aria just handed you a book with secrets that you yourself said could change everything. She's risking as much as you are. If this goes wrong, it's not just you who will pay the price. It's all of us."

Orvin opened his mouth to argue, but Aria spoke first, her voice quiet, as if admitting something she hadn't fully processed herself. "I wouldn't be here if I had any other option." Her gaze lowered briefly, her fingers brushing against the worn fabric of her sleeves. When she looked up again, her eyes held a fragile determination. "Like we said earlier, we heard that there might be a cure and it might be my grandmother's only chance—maybe the only one she'll ever get."

Pike's gaze shifted, softening ever so slightly before he spoke. "Well, the cure isn't ready yet," he said evenly, his words measured. "We're close. We've been close for a while now, but this"—he tapped the cover of the book—"might be just what we need to make it happen."

Aria's throat tightened, but she managed a small, tentative nod.

"When it's ready," Pike continued, "you'll be the first to get a sample."

Aria blinked, momentarily stunned by the certainty in his voice.

Then Pike's expression sharpened again, his eyes narrowing slightly. "Are you willing to put her life on the line for this deal?"

Aria's breath hitched, but she didn't hesitate. "Her life is already on the line," she said softly. "That's why we're here."

The weight of her words hung over the room and for a moment, even Orvin seemed to be reconsidering his position. Then Pike's expression changed—his posture relaxed and a faint, almost mischievous smile tugged at the corner of his mouth.

"Great," Pike said, his tone suddenly light, as though they'd just settled the terms of a friendly business deal. "We'll let you keep the book." He leaned in slightly, his gaze locking on Aria. "Cross us, and I'll come back for it—and anyone standing in the way."

Sylas tensed and Heidi's hand tightened on the bench, but Aria didn't flinch. She met Pike's gaze head-on, her voice steady. "Then you won't need to come back."

Pike straightened, adjusting his cuffs as if the discussion had been nothing more than a formality. "Tomorrow," he said, his voice cool and measured. "Meet us in the Mines."

"The Mines?" Heidi's voice was tight, suspicion lurking beneath her words.

Pike's smirk returned, a glint of amusement sparking in his eyes. "You're not getting cold feet, are you?"

Heidi bristled, her jaw clenching. "No," she snapped. "Of course not. I was just curious."

"Curiosity is a wonderful thing," Pike replied, his tone infuriatingly casual.

Aria's stomach churned. She had been wondering the same thing, but the weight of her question felt heavier now. She swallowed hard. "Why there?"

Pike's gaze locked on hers, calm and unwavering. "Because it's big enough to swallow the entire city and far enough from the Warden's watchful gaze. There's more hidden down there than you'd believe."

He smirked faintly but didn't elaborate. Instead, he tapped the cover of the book with two fingers. "Bring this tomorrow. Orvin will be waiting. You'll find him by the blacksmith's shop near the Lift."

He handed the book to Aria, his gaze shifting between them. "And remember"—his voice softened, though the threat lingered beneath it—"we can find you wherever you go."

Orvin, the burly man at the door stepped forward, his voice gruff. "Hey, are you sure about this?" His eyes darted to Aria and the others, distrust etched in every line of his face. "What will your brother say?"

Pike didn't look at him. "Leave that to me," he said coldly.

He paused, his eyes locking on Aria one final time, as though testing the weight of her resolve. "Orvin will take you back to the alley."

And just like that, he was gone, slipping through the doorway and vanishing into the shadows of the underground. The sound of his footsteps faded, leaving only the flicker of the lantern and the heavy silence he left behind.

***

Later that night, Aria laid in bed, the flickering lantern casting shifting shadows across the cracked ceiling. The room was cold, but it wasn't the chill that kept her awake. Heidi's words echoed in her head—*Aria is risking as much as they are*—and so did Pike's warning: *Cross us, and I'll come back for it.*

Her life is already on the line, she had said.

Aria knew time was running out. The truth of it sat in her chest like a knot she couldn't untangle, tightening with every breath. Her grandmother had developed a cough recently—persistent and sharp—and the medicine Aria scraped together to buy had done little to ease it.

Every decision she had made—bringing the book, revealing its secrets, trusting the Dwellers—had been for her grandmother. But now that they had made the deal, the enormity of that choice wrapped around her like invisible chains.

She rolled onto her side, the blanket tangling around her legs as if it, too, were conspiring to trap her. Sleep felt impossible, just beyond reach no matter how hard she tried to grasp it. Shadows flickered across the walls, their shapes twisting into familiar outlines before vanishing.

For an instant, she thought she saw her grandmother's frail form hunched over a kitchen table, coughing into a handkerchief stained crimson. Then, just as vividly, she could almost see Heidi and Sylas beside her—offering comfort, trying to hold her together. Their presence faded quickly, swallowed by Orvin's voice—cold and accusing.

For all we know, you've led them right to us.

Her fingers curled around the thin blanket as doubt crept in, coiling tighter with every question she couldn't answer. What if Orvin was right? What if someone had seen them and they'd unknowingly led the Warden's eyes straight to the Dwellers' doorstep? What if she had given him exactly what he needed to tighten his grip on the underground? She pictured guards swarming the hideout, dragging Heidi and Sylas away in chains, and it made her stomach twist painfully.

I should have done more. I should have been smarter.

Her gaze shifted toward the book lying beside her things. Its worn cover looked fragile in the dim light, but she knew better. It wasn't the book itself that mattered—it was what it represented.

Knowledge. Hope. A cure. But tonight, it felt heavier, as if its secrets were thrumming beneath the leather cover, waiting for their moment to be unleashed.

She traced the edges of its binding with her fingertips, grounding herself. Heidi and Sylas had believed in her and Pike had given her a chance.

They're depending on me, she thought, her throat tightening.

I can't let this chance slip away.

She imagined her grandmother's face again, lined with exhaustion but still managing a small smile. She had always been the steady presence in Aria's life, the one who told her stories of the surface world when they still had the luxury of imagining a better life. But now, her strength was fading and Aria didn't know how much time they had left.

We've come too far to turn back.

Her breath was slow and measured as she willed the racing thoughts to quiet. She closed her eyes, letting the hum of the underground fill her ears. It was a sound she had grown used to over the years—a low, constant murmur of pipes and distant machinery humming beneath the city like a restless giant. Tonight, though, it felt like a lullaby, calming and steady.

She let her fingers drift away from the book and pulled the blanket tighter around her shoulders. Tomorrow would bring more questions and challenges, but she would face them, one step at a time. The flickering light dimmed as her eyelids grew heavy.

In the quiet, just before sleep claimed her, Aria made a promise to herself: *I won't let them down.*

And with that, she surrendered to the darkness, her doubts unraveling into the silence of the room as the stillness of the underground finally lulled her to sleep.

8

The Undercity's Depths

Location: Cavandel, The Outer District

In the days that followed, Cavandel sank deeper into unrest. The once-steady rhythm of the mines gave way to unease, the air thick with tension so palpable Aria swore she could taste it. Guard patrols doubled throughout the District, their heavy boots echoing sharp, ominous rhythms against mud and stone.

The Warden's second announcement struck like a blow to the chest: the going rate for Crythium would be halved—at least for now. The news spread like wildfire through the city, sparking a wave of frustration and despair.

Miners gathered in grim-faced groups, their voices low but filled with anger as they imagined the extra shifts, the sleepless nights, and the mounting pressure that now lay ahead. Already struggling to make ends meet, they would have to work twice as hard just to scrape together the same meager pay.

Rumors spread as quickly as the despair they left in their wake, stoking fears of rebellion, betrayal, and desperation.

But nothing stirred the city more than the bounty notice plastered across every wall, market stall, and street corner in Cavandel: five hundred Grottos for any information leading to the capture of a Dweller, fifty thousand for

114

the capture of their leader.

The numbers were staggering. The promise of such wealth had the citizenry whispering in shadowed corners, their faces betraying a mix of fear, greed, and desperation.

As Aria moved through her neighborhood, she caught snippets of hushed conversations—neighbors speculating about who might turn on whom next, and others debating whether the Dwellers were heroes fighting for freedom or reckless rebels dragging the city toward ruin.

She passed a group of miners huddled near the entrance of a dilapidated shack, their faces half-hidden by the light. One of them whispered something and the others nodded quickly before disappearing into the shadows, their footsteps swallowed by the oppressive quiet.

Each breath told stories of the poverty that clung to the Outer District, where glow-lights flickered faintly above, casting broken halos across the damp stone. Aria drew her cloak tighter as distant echoes undulated around her like silent whispers—impossible to ignore.

***

The next morning, Aria stood by her grandmother's bed, gently tucking the worn quilt around her frail frame. The soft glow of a lantern filled the cramped room, bathing it in a hush of warmth. Her grandmother stirred, her eyes fluttering open. For a moment, Aria saw a flicker of worry within them.

She hesitated, her hand lingering on the edge of the quilt. The weight of the moment pressed down on her like a boulder. What if this was the last time she tucked her grandmother in? What if she didn't make it back in time? She tried to swallow the thought, but it lodged in her throat, thick and unforgiving.

I'm doing this for her, Aria reminded herself, gripping the quilt tighter. *I have to.*

"You're leaving again, aren't you?" her grandmother coughed softly, her voice a blend of sleep and concern. Aria hesitated, then forced a weak smile as she smoothed a stray strand of hair away from her grandmother's forehead. "Just for a little while, Gran. Jace is going to visit you every day while I'm gone. He promised."

Her grandmother's hand, delicate but steady, reached out and clasped Aria's. Her touch was warm, reassuring, despite the frailty beneath it. The gentle pressure spoke volumes—a lifetime of love, worry, and hope pressed into that single connection.

"You've been so busy, child. You don't need to keep running yourself ragged," her grandmother murmured.

"I'm not running," Aria whispered, squeezing her hand gently. "I'm just trying to do what's best for us. That's all."

Her grandmother sighed, her breath rattling softly. "Be careful," she murmured, her gaze lingering on Aria as though trying to memorize her face. "It's cruel out there."

Her eyes, usually steady, seemed dimmer now, flickering with a heaviness Aria hadn't noticed before. Then, a faint smile touched her lips—weary but sure. "Hold on to who you are, child."

Aria's throat tightened. She nodded, forcing a small smile. "I will, Gran." For a moment she lingered there, the words hanging between them, before she leaned down and kissed her grandmother's forehead. "I'll be back before you know it."

Her fingers lingered on the quilt as her heart waged war between staying and going. The warmth of her grandmother's hand felt like home, but the weight of what lay ahead pulled her toward the door. She knew she couldn't stay, not if she wanted to bring back the hope they so desperately needed.

She lingered for a moment longer, letting the soft hum of her grandmother's breathing steady her thoughts. Then, with one last glance, she slipped into the hall and eased the door closed behind her.

The front room lay hushed, faintly lit by the dying glow of the hearth.

Aria crossed to the door and took her cloak before stepping out into the chill.

Outside, Heidi and Sylas waited near the entrance, their faces shadowed by the dim glow-lights overhead. Heidi adjusted the straps on her utility belt, while Sylas leaned casually against the wall, tossing a small rock between his hands.

Aria took a deep breath, steeling herself before speaking. "Before we go any further, I just—I really need to say this." She exhaled slowly, her gaze shifting to the ground for a moment before lifting again.

"Things are getting dangerous—you've seen it yourselves." Her voice wavered, but she pushed on. "Guard patrols have doubled and the Warden's got half the city ready to sell out the Dwellers for a few coins."

She swallowed, the weight of her words sinking deep. "This isn't just another one of our adventures. If you have second thoughts..." She paused, letting the silence stretch. "Now's the time to say so."

Heidi froze mid-motion, then looked up. A breath escaped her—half disbelief, half irritation. "Are you serious? After everything we've been through, you think I'd let you meet with them alone?"

"We're a team, Aria," Sylas added, pushing off the wall and stepping closer. His grin was there, but behind it was something more sincere, more serious. "You don't get to walk into danger alone and you certainly don't get to leave us behind. We're in this together. Always."

Aria's throat tightened, emotion welling in her chest. She blinked quickly, willing herself not to tear up. "I just—I don't want to drag you into something you'll regret later. This isn't just risky. It could cost us everything."

"And that's why we need to stick together," Heidi said firmly, her gaze hardening. "We've faced dangers before but this time, we can't just hope that things will get better—we have to fight for it."

Sylas spoke up again. "We know what's at stake," he said, his voice softening. "We're not doing this just for you. We're doing it for everyone. We've lost people too and any one of us could be next. We're doing this because it matters."

Emotions surged within Aria, barely contained. She nearly broke down when Sylas added softly. "If there's even a chance that this could lead to a cure, then we're all in."

Aria exhaled shakily, a mixture of relief and gratitude flooding through her. She nodded, a small, genuine smile breaking through the tension. "Thank you. I don't know what I'd do without you two," she murmured softly.

"Probably something reckless," Heidi teased, though her tone was warm.

Sylas grinned. "Reckless and dramatic. Classic Aria."

Aria let out a quiet laugh, the sound easing the weight in her chest. "Alright, then. Let's do this. But if anyone wants to change their mind, now's the time."

Heidi tightened the straps on her belt one last time. "We're not going anywhere."

Sylas tossed the rock into the shadows, dusted off his hands and shrugged. "Lead the way, fearless leader."

Together, they set off down the winding stone passages of the Outer, the air around them thick with anticipation. The distant echoes of the city seemed to follow them, a constant reminder of the risks ahead. But as Aria glanced at her friends—Heidi's determined stride and Sylas's easy grin—she felt a renewed sense of purpose.

Whatever lay ahead in the mines below, she wouldn't be facing it alone.

But they weren't as alone as they thought. From a narrow side passage, Hogan watched, his silhouette blending seamlessly with the shadows.

The harsh illumination of Cavandel's lights brushed against the edge of his jacket, yet his face remained hidden, lurking at the edges of their awareness.

His gaze followed them, tracking each step with patient precision. The hint of a smirk played at the corner of his mouth as they disappeared down the winding path, unaware of the eyes that lingered in their wake.

Without a sound, he slipped into motion, his footsteps measured and deliberate. He kept his distance, careful not to disturb the loose gravel beneath his boots, but close enough to ensure that they could never truly escape his watchful gaze.

***

The next leg of their journey began with a railcar rattling through a dim tunnel, sparks flaring as its wheels shrieked along the metal. The air was heavy with oil and rust, every breath thick enough to taste. Shadows rippled along the walls, racing ahead toward the heart of the Inner District.

At its center loomed the Lift system, a towering monolith rising through a vast vertical shaft that stretched from the Stratum near the surface down to the lightless depths of the Abyss. It wasn't just a structure—it was Cavandel's spine, binding worlds of privilege and labor, ambition and despair.

As they neared the Lift station, the air grew colder, edged with a faint metallic bite. The structure rose before them—familiar, yet ominous—as though the very air trembled in its shadow.

It stood like a steel giant, tethered between the known and the unknown, vast enough to carry hundreds of work crews and their equipment. Iron beams crisscrossed the shaft's walls, slick with condensation and streaked with rust. Chains thick as tunnel columns coiled into the cavern's shadowed heights, groaning beneath the weight of the colossal deck and its cargo.

The rhythmic clank of gears echoed through the stone chamber, blending with the hiss of steam venting from rusted pipes embedded in the rock. Glow-lights flickered around the walls, their pulse casting shifting patterns, as if the Lift itself breathed with the heartbeat of the city.

The scent of oil, earth, and cold metal filled the air, clinging to Aria's cloak like a second skin. Her boots scuffed softly against the damp metal plating as they moved through the station. They passed a hunched figure slumped against a rusted support beam, his face buried in his hands. He didn't look up, and Aria's gaze lingered only a moment before she forced herself to move on.

She cast a quick glance at the guards stationed near the Lift's deck. They weren't searching for anyone in particular, but she knew that one wrong move—or a glimpse of the forbidden book hidden beneath her cloak—could change that in an instant.

The queue for the Lift stretched longer than usual, winding down the dim corridor like a sluggish river of grumbling miners.

"Stay calm," she whispered to herself, her fingers brushing the edges of the book.

"It's shut down again?" Heidi muttered, her gaze darting to the group of guards. "So what do we do now?"

"Only thing we can do," came a gravelly voice from behind them. "Stand here an' grow older."

Aria turned to see an older miner standing just a few steps away, his face weathered and smudged with grime. His beard was streaked with gray and looked like it hadn't been trimmed in years. He leaned on a rusted pickaxe, eyes gleaming with mischief.

"Incident down in the Abyss," he muttered. "Same story every year."

"Again?" Heidi asked, lowering her voice. "Let me guess—"

The old miner leaned in before she could finish, glancing around as he spoke. "Heard it was bad—real bad," he whispered, tapping his pickaxe against the floor. His gaze shifted toward the distant hum of machinery, "Lift's been shut down while they figure out what went wrong. Name's Guss, by the way."

He exhaled sharply, his gaze lingering on the worn metal rails leading down into darkness, as if measuring the weight of every disaster he'd seen before. "Seen my fair share of shutdowns each season—none of 'em ever good."

Aria's stomach twisted. "Was it a full team?"

The miner scratched his beard thoughtfully, as though weighing how much to say. "Aye, that's what I heard—ten of 'em went down, but only seven came back up. Poor souls. You'd think they'd know better by now."

He paused, his gaze drifting distant, as if replaying a memory too vivid to ignore. When he spoke again, his voice dropped lower. "Must've gotten greedy. Must've ventured too far."

"Especially during mating season," Heidi added.

"Aye," the old miner said with a shrug. "That's why you won't catch me down there. Ten times the loot"—he gave a short, bitter laugh—"a hundred times the danger." He leaned back against the wall, his grip tightening on his pickaxe. "Nothin' good ever comes crawlin' outta those depths."

Sylas exhaled softly. "I'm glad we never have to go down there."

"Yeah," Aria said quietly, steadying her voice against the fear creeping up her spine. "Me too."

Location: Cavandel, The Mines

After what seemed like an eternity, the Lift shuddered back to life. Aria and her companions merged into the flow of miners boarding, their footsteps lost in the steady clang of boots on metal.

No one around them betrayed a hint of suspicion. The miners' weary faces masked the tension Aria felt simmering beneath the surface. She moved carefully, every step measured to blend into the sea of exhaustion and routine.

The gate to the immense deck groaned open. After paying the fee, they shuffled in with the rest of the crowd. The grated floor and iron walls were streaked with rust and grime. Steam hissed from vents along the base, curling into the dim light. The low hum of machinery vibrated beneath their feet—a constant reminder of Cavandel's pulse.

Aria leaned against the cold iron wall, releasing a breath she hadn't realized she was holding. The compartment was as massive inside as it looked from the outside—an iron cavern alive with motion.

Crates thudded into place one after another as the loading crews worked in rhythm with the machines. Steam-powered haulers rolled across the grated floor, their wheels hissing as pistons drove heavy arms that hoisted cargo into neat, towering stacks. Overhead, cranes groaned on rusted rails, chains clattering as they swung crates into position. The air shimmered with heat and noise: gears grinding, steam venting, the low murmur of engines pulsing through the deck like a heartbeat.

Miners shuffled for space, some settling on overturned buckets, others leaning against the walls, heads bowed in fatigue. Glow-lights flickered through the haze of steam, turning the air a muted gold. Oil slicked the seams of machinery, dripping down in slow rivulets as its acrid scent hung heavy in the air.

As they waited, Aria's pulse slowed to the rhythm of the engines, though the tension never quite left her chest. Beneath the roar, the hiss, the movement, a strange awe rose quietly—an uneasy wonder at the scale of it all. Each clang and rattle of heavy chains reminded her how deep they still had to go—and how small she seemed beneath it all, how easily she could disappear in its shadow.

Sylas nudged her gently. "See? Just a bunch of tired miners heading to work. Nothing suspicious here."

Aria managed a small smile, but her fingers tightened around the edges of her cloak. Heidi adjusted her belt again, her gaze darting toward the towering gate as it began to close.

The massive iron panels ground together, metal striking metal in a deep, resonant clang that shook the walls before fading into the steady pulse of the engines.

Aria released a breath as the sound settled, sealing them in with the hum of machinery. For a moment, the air felt still—thick with heat and quiet anticipation—until the deck shuddered and jolted downward, sending a brief ripple through the floor. Aria shifted her weight, steadying herself, while Sylas grabbed the edge of a crate and Heidi planted her feet firmly, her gaze hardening with purpose.

Large chains rattled overhead as the Lift descended, each metallic clank echoing through the shaft like a distant rockfall. The steady rhythm marked time itself, counting down the moments until they reached whatever waited in the dark below.

Glow-lights outside the platform flickered faintly, casting fleeting flashes across the jagged rock walls. As they plunged deeper, the temperature fell, the cold seeping through Aria's cloak until it prickled her skin. The air grew dense with the scent of damp stone and oil—heavy, metallic, and close—like the depths themselves were conspiring to draw them in.

The light faded, swallowed by the encroaching darkness as the Lift sank deeper into the Mines. The faint clatter of tools and distant voices faded behind them, replaced by a heavy silence broken only by the hiss of steam and the slow grind of chains.

Aria's heartbeat quickened, falling in step with the rhythm of the Lift. The pounding filled her ears, a low drumbeat that echoed the danger waiting below. She drew her cloak tighter, her throat dry as she swallowed against the rising unease.

Sylas, as if sensing the shift in the air, began humming an old mining tune under his breath. The melody wavered, thin and hollow, swallowed by the iron cage that enclosed them.

Heidi stood still, her gaze distant. Though she maintained her usual composure, the subtle twitching of her fingers betrayed her.

For a moment, none of them spoke. The only sound was the low hum of the engines, steady and unyielding beneath their feet.

The Lift shuddered, a sudden jolt that turned Aria's stomach. The chains above groaned, each creak a heavy reminder of the weight they carried. She drew a steady breath, fighting back the wave of dizziness.

"Focus," Aria murmured to herself, fixing her gaze on the shifting shadows beyond the grated walls. The Mines loomed below, waiting—along with the answers they had risked everything to find.

At last, the platform slowed with a heavy groan, the chains rattling in protest as the massive gate rumbled open to the Mines. Several miners stepped off, boots striking the grated floor as they hauled crates and supplies across the decking. The air was slightly warmer here, tinged with the familiar scents of heated machinery and freshly mined ore.

Far off in the distance, Aria could see the faint silhouettes of the Mining Camp's buildings, their flickering lights standing in defiance against the cavern's suffocating darkness. Her thoughts wandered to Marielle at the inn, likely bustling about with her usual grace, tending to patrons with the same care she gave her family each day.

The imagined glow of lanternlight bathed Aria's thoughts, mingling with the distant hum of conversation and the memory of the inn's cozy bustle—a comforting vision, fleeting and fragile against the unknown waiting ahead.

As they stepped off the Lift, the cavern of the Mines enveloped them—vast and consuming. The small lanterns embedded in the walls struggled to pierce the heavy gloom, casting flickering shadows that danced like sparks off a dying forge.

Blending in with the remaining miners, Aria, Heidi, and Sylas made their way toward the blacksmith's shop, their boots scuffing softly over the gravel path. They kept their heads down, their movements casual, but the tension in Aria's chest refused to ease.

Scents wafted through the air, a tapestry of coal dust and damp stone, mingling with the metallic tang of oil. No one spared them more than a glance, but Aria couldn't help feeling like eyes were on her all the same.

Miners trudged toward small shacks and supply stations, their shoulders hunched, faces coated in grime. But it wasn't the weary miners that made Aria's pulse race—it was the city guards.

"They've increased patrols," Heidi whispered as they passed a pair standing at the corner of a supply shed. "Even down here."

Just ahead, the sound of a man protesting caught Aria's attention. She turned her head just enough to see two guards dragging him toward the

Lift, his boots scraping against the ground as he struggled. His shouts were muffled, but the panic in his voice was clear. The guards didn't slow, their grips firm as they hauled him into the shadows beyond the path.

Aria swallowed hard and kept moving, her boots crunching softly against the gravel.

Don't stop. Don't draw attention.

The path ahead was dimly lit, the lanterns spaced far apart, leaving large patches of darkness between pools of light.

A shadow flickered at the edge of her vision and she tensed, her hand instinctively brushing against the edge of her cloak. She turned her head just enough to catch a glimpse of a figure slipping between two structures, their movements quick and calculated.

As they neared the blacksmith's shop, the clang of metal striking metal filled the air, its rhythmic noise blending with the distant murmur of miners haggling over supplies.

Before they could reach the building, a hand shot out of the shadows and grabbed Aria's arm. She hissed, stumbling as she was yanked into a narrow alleyway. Heidi and Sylas followed quickly, their footsteps barely audible over the noise of the camp.

The figure released her, the glow of a nearby lantern illuminated his face—Orvin.

Aria's heart pounded in her chest, but she managed to exhale a shaky breath as recognition settled in. His broad frame, thick jacket and sharp, calculating eyes hadn't changed since their last encounter. He was as imposing as ever, but the slight nod he gave her was enough to ease the fear.

"Did you bring it?" he asked, his voice low but expectant.

Aria nodded, her hand pressing against the spot where her cloak concealed the precious volume. "We have it," she whispered.

"Stay out of the open," Orvin grumbled, his voice low but steady. "The guards are questioning people at random. If they decide to search you, it's over."

The weight of his words pressed down on Aria and for a moment, her breath caught in her throat. She glanced at Heidi, who nodded slightly, as if to say they didn't need the reminder. They knew what was at stake.

"Stay close," Orvin added, his gaze scanning the alley behind them. "And keep it down."

They moved through the shadowed alleyways in silence, Orvin's steps deliberate and quiet.

The lanternlight from the main paths barely reached them here, leaving only faint outlines of buildings and tents to guide their way. Aria's breath was shallow, each step making her more aware of the book hidden beneath her cloak.

But it wasn't her fear that kept pulling at her attention—it was Sylas's silence. She glanced back at him, her eyes meeting his, but his usual grin was nowhere to be found. His shoulders were hunched slightly and his gaze swept from shadow to shadow as if he expected something—or someone—to leap out at them. His lips, usually quick to form a joke or sarcastic remark, were pressed into a thin line.

He hadn't said a word since Orvin pulled them into the alley. Not one.

Aria felt a chill creep down her spine. In all the time she had known him, Sylas had never been truly silent. Even in the most dangerous moments, he found a way to slip in a comment, a joke—something to make them laugh, even if it was out of place. But now, his silence was louder than any quip he could have made and that terrified her.

He's scared, she realized. *Really scared.*

A part of her wanted to reach for his hand, to tell him it was going to be okay, but she couldn't bring herself to do it. The weight of the book pressed against her ribs, a reminder that they didn't have room for reassurances. They had to keep moving.

Orvin stopped abruptly at the mouth of another alley, pressing his back against the wall as he peered around the corner. Heidi and Aria mirrored him, their breaths shallow. Aria's heart thundered in her chest as she waited, her ears straining to pick up any sound beyond their own.

The faint echo of boots crunching against gravel reached her ears, but the noise faded as quickly as it had come. Orvin waited a moment longer, then motioned for them to follow.

The winding paths of the camp felt endless, the flickering lanterns doing little to light their way. Orvin doubled back twice, pausing to check behind them before moving on. Each time, they huddled in the shadows, waiting as their nerves stretched taut.

Finally, they rounded a corner and the familiar outline of Marielle's inn came into view. Its lantern-lit windows glowed warmly against the dark backdrop of the camp, the soft hum of conversation drifting through the night.

Aria exhaled, the tension in her chest loosening just slightly. "Marielle's place?"

Sylas's voice was soft when he finally spoke. "You've got to be kidding me..."

Orvin led them to the side entrance, pushing the door open and gesturing for them to enter. The warmth of the inn wrapped around them immediately, carrying the scent of roasted meat and freshly baked bread. But they didn't linger. He led them down a narrow hallway, the sound of their footsteps muffled by the smooth stone floor.

At the bar, Marielle was pouring drinks, her warm smile lighting up the room as she spoke to a group of regulars. But when her eyes met Orvin's, her expression shifted subtly. She gave him a small nod before returning to her work, her smile never faltering.

They reached the end of the hallway, where Orvin unlocked a reinforced wooden door and pushed it open. A narrow staircase descended into a low-ceilinged cellar, dimly lit by glow-lamps embedded in the walls, their warm light casting soft shadows along the steps.

"This way," Orvin grumbled, stepping aside to let them through.

As Aria descended the stairs, the cool air wrapped around her like a second cloak. Heidi and Sylas followed close behind, but Aria couldn't shake the thought that kept circling in her mind.

All this time. Marielle's inn, the place they visited every day without a second thought, had been hiding the Dwellers right under their noses. The laughter, the warmth, the smells of home—none of it had hinted at the resistance moving deep beneath the floorboards.

How had they missed it?

Her breath hitched as they reached the bottom of the stairs. The wall ahead seemed unbroken, solid stone from floor to ceiling. But as Orvin stepped forward, his fingers traced along a nearly invisible seam, finding a point only he seemed to know. With a quiet press and a subtle shift, the stone gave way, revealing a hidden passage beyond.

Orvin's words echoed faintly in her mind: *If they find what you're carrying, it's over.*

The time had arrived. There was no turning back, no second guessing. She had risked everything for this moment and now, she was standing on the threshold of the unknown. Her pulse raced, each beat a reminder of what was waiting on the other side of that door—and what failure would cost.

With her heart pounding and the weight of the book pressing against her ribs, Aria took a deep breath and stepped forward.

The door creaked shut behind them, the sound echoing like a distant warning.

9

Shadows of Doubt

Location: Cavandel, Dweller's Base

The narrow corridor stretched before them, lit by glow-lamps embedded along the ceiling. Their steady light washed over the stone walls, casting faint, wavering shadows. The air was cool and clean—a stark contrast to the metallic bite of coal dust still clinging to their clothes.

Aria glanced around as they passed a series of open doorways leading into small rooms and workspaces. One contained rows of neatly stacked crates marked with symbols she didn't recognize.

Another was filled with maps pinned to the walls, their lines tracing what looked like mine tunnels and hidden passageways beneath Cavandel. The hum of quiet conversations and the occasional metallic clink of tools echoed faintly through the hall, but nothing felt chaotic. Every movement, every task, seemed purposeful.

Several Dwellers passed them on their way to or from nearby rooms. Most spared Aria's group only a brief glance, though a few lingered, their eyes narrowing slightly before moving on.

A man carrying a bundle of supplies shifted his grip as he walked by, his posture stiff as if ready to bolt at the first sign of trouble. A woman standing near a table of medical equipment whispered something to her companion, her gaze darting briefly to Aria before she turned away.

There was tension in the air, subtle but unmistakable, like the undercurrent of a storm waiting to break. Aria didn't need anyone to tell her that they were being watched closely.

Sylas glanced around, his eyes sweeping over the walls and neatly arranged workspaces. "This place is beautiful," he said with a grin. "Think they're recruiting?"

Heidi rolled her eyes. "Please try not to embarrass us."

"I'm serious," Sylas replied, his voice light but carrying an edge of tension. "The last place felt like it was one gust of wind away from collapsing."

Aria smiled faintly, though her gaze remained fixed ahead. The steady hum of activity did little to steady her thoughts. They were deep in Dweller territory now, surrounded by people who had every reason to distrust them. If this meeting didn't go well, they wouldn't have a clean path back to the surface.

A figure stepped into view ahead, moving down the corridor with the slow, measured ease of someone who belonged everywhere. Orvin's stride hitched for the briefest instant before he forced it steady again.

"Kegan," he said with a curt nod.

Kegan didn't return it. His eyes drifted over Aria and her friends instead, the glance cool and thorough enough to make her stomach tighten.

"New faces," he murmured.

"They're here for Pike," Orvin replied quickly, already angling himself to keep the group moving.

Kegan's gaze lingered a heartbeat longer. "Interesting."

He stepped aside without another word. As they passed him, the air felt colder, as if he'd taken something with him.

Orvin stopped at another junction in the corridor and motioned for them to follow. "This way," he said over his shoulder. "They should be waiting in the lab."

***

In the lab, the warm hum of glow-lamps cast a soft golden light over Anna's table, illuminating rows of meticulously organized vials, surgical tools, and worn notebooks filled with handwritten notes. The air smelled faintly of herbs and metal, but the tranquility of the room was deceptive. Beneath the calm surface, tension coiled, ready to snap.

Anna set down a beaker with a controlled clink, her fingers curling into fists at her sides. "You always make things sound so simple, Pike."

Pike leaned lazily against the wall, arms crossed. "Things usually are."

"Not everything needs to be solved by drastic measures," she said sharply, her voice low but edged with restrained anger. "People could have been hurt—the very ones we're trying to save." She hesitated, the next words catching. "I'm grateful you got me out, but that doesn't make what you did right."

Sebastian sighed from his place near the workbench, rubbing at his temple. "We're going in circles."

Anna turned to him, frustration flickering in her eyes. "Because we're talking about another reckless choice made with little or no consideration—again."

Pike's gaze didn't waver. "We've been *carefully considering* things for years, Anna—and what has that gotten us? You captured, half a cure, and our people losing hope."

"That doesn't justify throwing caution to the wind," Anna said, her tone taut but measured. "You think making an even bigger gamble will give people hope?"

Pike shifted, a faint tension crossing his face before he smoothed it away. "What I—no, what *we've* done—is get you out of that tower and back where you belong. You might not like my methods, but you can't deny they've kept you safe—and kept us moving forward."

"That's not fair," Sebastian murmured, rubbing the bridge of his nose.

There was no anger in his voice—only exhaustion.

"Fairness doesn't interest me, brother." Pike straightened, his tone cool and even. "Survival does. And if this book holds even half the answers we need, then I'm not interested in debating who invited whom."

Anna let out a sharp breath and dragged a hand through her hair, fingers trembling before she forced them still. "And if this leads the Warden's men straight to us? What then, Pike?"

Pike gave a slow shrug, a faint smirk tugging at his mouth. "Then we adapt—like we always have. It's gotten us this far."

Anna's jaw tightened, her frustration shifting into something quieter, heavier. She turned toward Sebastian, her voice barely above a whisper. "Why do you always let him talk you into these things?"

Sebastian met her gaze steadily, the weight of his position reflected in his tone. "Because there's a balance to strike and you know that as well as I do." He exhaled softly. "We can't afford to ignore any more options right now—not with what's at stake."

Anna closed her eyes briefly, frustration ebbing into weary acceptance. She turned back toward her workbench, the soft tapping of her pen filling the ensuing silence.

Pike broke the quiet, his voice calm but unwavering. "When this is over—when we finally have a cure—you'll see I did what had to be done. And you'll thank me."

Anna's pen stilled mid-scratch. "I already did," she murmured, not looking up. "And it didn't change a thing."

"Enough!" Sebastian's voice was firm this time, cutting through the tension. His gaze moved slowly from Pike to Anna, his shoulders stiff with the weight of the decision he knew they were edging toward. "We'll keep moving forward, but we do it carefully. No risks we can't control."

Anna's fingers flexed against the workbench as she struggled to swallow her frustration. "This isn't a game," she said softly.

"No," Pike agreed, his smirk returning. "It's war. And in war, the winner isn't the one who plays fair. It's the one who does what others won't."

The quiet that followed felt heavier than the argument had. Anna lowered her head, her hair falling like a curtain as she gathered herself.

A quiet cough from the entrance interrupted them and all three turned sharply. Orvin stood just inside the doorway, looking like he'd rather be anywhere else. "They're here."

Behind him, Aria, Heidi, and Sylas stepped into the room, the tension hitting them like a wall. Orvin didn't leave immediately. He stood there for a moment, his posture steady, his gaze flicking between Anna's clenched fists, Pike's lazy posture and Sebastian's carefully guarded expression. His eyes lingered, as if silently assessing the danger simmering beneath the surface. Then, with a slight nod to himself, he stepped out and closed the door behind him.

The hum of glow-lamps and the faint scent of herbs couldn't mask the charged atmosphere. Aria's gaze darted from Anna, whose knuckles were white where she gripped the edge of the table, to Sebastian, whose shoulders seemed to bear the weight of the entire base. But it was Pike who held her attention the longest.

He leaned against the wall, one foot resting casually on its heel, his arms crossed as if the argument they'd just had barely concerned him. There was something in his posture that made Aria uneasy—not the casual confidence, but the way his gaze seemed to penetrate them, assessing.

He exhaled softly, his fingers tapping once against his arm before he shifted positions. A fleeting gesture, but one that spoke of something deeper—calculation masked beneath charm. His smirk hadn't faded and before Aria could fully process her unease, Pike's voice cut through the silence.

"Well, if it isn't our little adventurers," he drawled, his tone laced with sarcasm. His gaze swept over them, lingering briefly on Aria as though her presence amused him most. "Enjoy the grand tour of our humble home?"

Aria and Heidi stayed silent, but Sylas let out a short, nervous laugh—awkward, out of place—then quickly fell quiet.

Pike pushed off the wall and gestured lazily toward the workbench, as though inviting them into his own quarters. "Go on," he said, the mock warmth in his voice edged with bite. "Make yourselves at home. We're all friends here, after all."

He paced a few steps, stopping near Anna, who didn't bother to look up. "Now," he said, tapping his fingers lightly against the bench, "let's get down to business, shall we?" His gaze slid back to Aria. "Our little friend here"—he tilted his head toward her, that same mocking smirk in place—"is interested in our cure for Shatterblight."

Aria winced. The word struck harder than she'd expected, the weight of it digging into her chest like an old wound reopened. She tried to keep her face neutral, but Pike's smirk told her he hadn't missed her reaction.

"The cure," Anna said, her voice low and deliberate, "is far from ready."

She stepped forward, her presence as cold and clinical as the sterile walls around her. "We've tested fragments. Isolated compounds," she continued, folding her arms tightly across her chest. "Most were based on partial Crythium extractions and decay models, but we're barely holding them together."

She pressed her lips into a thin line, then turned sharply toward the table, where numerous folders were stacked neatly into a pile.

"The stabilizers fail. The bioreactive agents corrode faster than anticipated." She sighed heavily, tension radiating from her posture. "The current patients—" She paused, exhaling sharply, as if she hated what she was about to say. "The early trials slowed necrosis in some cases. But the side effects? Nerve deterioration. Vascular collapse. Or worse."

Invisible currents carried whispers of dread, pressing against Aria's chest until every breath was a struggle. Even Sylas, who never took bad news seriously, had gone silent, tapping a restless rhythm on his knee.

Anna didn't flinch. "Best case?" she murmured. "We're months from stability. Worst case?" She paused, letting the weight of it hang between them. "You'll stop the suffering—just not in the way you're hoping for."

Her words fell like stones into a deep cavern, the echoes slow to fade.

Aria's hand trembled at her side. She curled it into a fist, trying to steady herself, but her heart was already racing, betraying her calm.

"I understand," Aria whispered, but her voice wavered, each word slipping like frayed threads unraveling.

Anna's gaze softened, just enough to reveal she wasn't heartless—just realistic. "Then be sure you're ready for what you might lose," she said softly.

Silence settled like fog, heavy and suffocating. And yet, beneath the weight of it all, she held onto a fragile truth: hope wasn't about certainty. It was about risking everything when you had nothing left to lose.

"As I was saying," Pike cut in. "In exchange, she's agreed to provide us with some—valuable information." His eyes lingered on the satchel half-hidden beneath her coat, where the book rested inside.

"And of course," Pike added, his voice dripping with faux humility, "me being the helpful chap that I am, thought it prudent to oblige her."

He smiled—but it wasn't warm. It was the kind of smile that made Aria feel as though she were being sized up and sold at the same time. She sat stiffly on the edge of her seat, her fingers digging into the fabric of her cloak. The hum of glow-lamps overhead buzzed faintly, but it did little to ease the knot of tension twisting in her stomach. Across the room, Anna's sharp gaze shifted between Pike and Sebastian, her expression unreadable.

The silence in the room felt alive, heavy with things unsaid. Sylas shifted uncomfortably beside her, tapping his fingers lightly against his knee. Heidi, ever composed, leaned forward slightly, arms crossed, gaze sharp.

Aria exhaled slowly. Her heart pounded, but something deeper stirred within her—a quiet determination she hadn't realized was there.

She stood, her legs still shaky, but each step deliberate as she crossed the room, every movement a choice.

When she reached Anna's workbench, she hesitated only briefly before holding the book out to her. The worn leather cover was cool against her fingertips. Anna accepted it wordlessly, her fingers brushing over the surface as if testing its weight.

Aria exhaled again and retreated to her seat, folding her hands tightly in her lap, willing herself to stay steady.

Anna placed the book gently on the table, her fingertips tracing the faded emblem embossed on the cover—a sigil worn and weathered, its meaning long obscured by time and secrets. Her brows furrowed, the corners of her lips pressing into a thin line. Without looking up, she ran her fingers along the spine and opened it.

The room seemed to draw closer, the air tightening with anticipation. She flipped through the pages slowly at first, her eyes tracing lines of faded ink and notes in the margins. Occasionally, she muttered to herself, the words too soft for Aria to catch. Her brow furrowed deeper with each turn of the page, her fingers gliding over intricate diagrams and hurried annotations.

Pike leaned back in his chair, smirking. "I think you'll find Chapter Sixteen quite interesting," he drawled, as though offering a revelation only he fully understood. His gaze lingered on Anna, his smirk deepening as if savoring the moment he knew would come.

Anna's fingers hesitated for the briefest second, but she didn't acknowledge him. Her hand moved methodically as she flipped forward to the chapter, her movements deliberate. The faint crease between her brows deepened as she leaned in, her lips moving silently as she read. After a moment, she turned back a page and read it again, her gaze locked on the words as if decoding something fragile.

The room held its breath. The occasional rustle of paper was the only sound, broken only when Sylas shifted slightly. Even Pike, normally nonchalant, had straightened slightly in his chair. Aria didn't dare look away from Anna, her pulse racing, her thoughts a blur of hope and dread.

Then, without warning, Anna snapped the book shut. The sound was sharp and final, slicing through the room like a blade. She exhaled, her fingers still resting on the cover, as though holding something volatile.

She stared at the book for a long moment before speaking. "Where did you get this?" she whispered.

"It—it was my grandmother's," Aria said, forcing her voice to stay steady.

Sebastian walked closer, running his hand lightly over the book's worn cover. "You don't see something like this every day in Cavandel," he murmured, his gaze shifting between Aria and the book. "And where did your grandmother get it?"

The question landed harder than she expected, stirring a swirl of conflicting thoughts. For as long as she could remember, her family had been careful, secretive even. Her grandmother's warnings echoed faintly in her mind—about protecting the past. She could almost see the suspicion curling at the edges of his gaze, even if it was only her own fears projecting it.

"She didn't steal it," Aria said firmly. "It's always been in our family."

"Your family," Sebastian's gaze sharpened. "And what family is that?"

Aria's breath hitched. The answer hovered on her tongue, familiar and well-rehearsed—a false name meant to shield her family, to keep them safe.

Say it, move on, survive.

Doubt gripped her. Sebastian's eyes were sharp—too sharp—and she couldn't decide if they held curiosity or suspicion. Was he expecting deception, or hoping for something real?

Her grandmother's voice whispered: *Never give them the truth, never tell anyone our real family name. Our secret is our protection.*

Her pulse quickened.

And yet—hadn't she had enough of hiding?

What if this time, the truth wasn't a mistake but a step forward? What if it wasn't safety she needed—but trust?

"Averlock," Aria said softly. The word carried weight, but she kept her chin high. "Averlock from the Outer District."

For a moment, Sebastian looked puzzled, then asked, "As in *the* Averlocks?"

"And your grandmother," he asked coolly, "what's her given name?"

Her fingers curled inward, nails biting against her palm. This was her last chance to backtrack—to retreat into half-truths and safety. But she was done hiding.

"Lucinda," Aria said evenly. "Lucinda Averlock."

The room froze.

Then Pike laughed.

It wasn't a small chuckle—it was a full, unrestrained laugh that echoed off the stone walls. He leaned forward, wiping at the corner of his eye as if the sheer absurdity of it all had undone him. "Lucinda," he said, shaking his head. "The Silent Hawk. Of course." He exhaled, still grinning. "I should've seen that one coming."

Sylas let out a nervous laugh, then fell silent just as quickly.

Aria's breath caught, her grandmother's name hanging in the air—quiet, undeniable. She'd always known Gran had a past, but the way the Dwellers reacted—as if struck by a shockwave—made her realize how little she truly understood.

Gran had kept her secrets close, and even when Aria had tried to peek behind them, she'd always closed the door gently and said some things were better left buried.

Pike leaned back against the wall, his grin fading into something more thoughtful. "Your grandmother was a legend," he said. "The things she pulled off during the resistance—" he gave a low whistle. "I'm impressed she managed to stay hidden from the Warden this long."

Anna, still recovering from the revelation, ran her fingers over the cover of the book as if it had transformed in her hands. "Lucinda," she murmured, almost to herself. "No wonder."

Aria felt the weight of their gazes pressing down on her. She shifted slightly, her fingers curling into the fabric of her cloak. "I'm just trying to help her," she said softly.

Sebastian, who had been watching her quietly, nodded once. "Then it's a good thing you brought this to us."

The room still hummed with the weight of her words when Sebastian cleared his throat—soft, but certain. His gaze turned to Anna, who was thumbing through the pages, her eyes darting across dense notes like she was piecing together something long lost.

"What did you find?" he asked, his tone gentle but deliberate. "Anything we can use?"

Anna looked up, her fingers still resting on a passage. "Possibly more than we expected," she murmured. Her voice was calm, but there was a spark of something underneath it—hope, tempered by caution. "Early research on the Rocknids. It delves into their biology, their immune systems and how they interact with Crythium."

She traced her fingertips over a section filled with annotations. "This is where it gets interesting. We've been trying to treat Shatterblight by focusing on removing the Crythium contamination from the system. The idea has always been to extract or neutralize the crystals before they spread too far. But we've hit a wall—by the time the symptoms show, the contamination is too advanced. Once it reaches the nervous system or the bone marrow, there's no reversing it."

Sebastian's expression darkened. "Then what's different about the Screechers?"

Anna's brow furrowed as she turned the page, revealing a detailed sketch of Rocknid anatomy. Her finger tapped sharply against the margin. "That's the key. Rocknids live in Crythium-rich environments—their bodies are constantly exposed to it, but they don't suffer from crystallization like we do." She paused, tapping again, softer this time. "This explains why."

She tapped a passage circled in faded ink. "They seem to have a specific enzyme that prevents the Crythium crystals from binding to their cells. The enzyme effectively neutralizes Crythium particles before they can embed themselves in tissue. Their immune systems treat Crythium as something harmless, passing it through their bodies without damage."

Pike snorted softly and gave an exaggerated shrug. "So what you're saying is, the bugs had a stroke of good fortune. Meanwhile, we're dropping like flies. How poetic."

Anna didn't look at him, though the corner of her mouth twitched in irritation. "Exactly. And here's where it gets even more interesting. The notes suggest that this enzyme doesn't just prevent Crythium contamination—it actively stops the spread of existing crystals by breaking down the molecular structure before it can expand."

Aria's breath hitched. "So, we could use it to cure Gran?"

Anna hesitated, her eyes softening. "Not exactly." She exhaled slowly, closing the book for a moment and pressing her palms against its worn cover. "I don't think we can reverse Shatterblight, at least not with what we have. Once the crystals have invaded the major organs or the nervous system, the damage is done."

Aria's chest tightened, but she didn't interrupt.

"What we *can* do," Anna continued, "is stop the spread. If we develop a treatment using the Rocknid enzymes, we could halt the progression of the disease. That means anyone who's in the early stages—like your grandmother—could live without it getting worse."

"And for those who haven't been infected?" Heidi asked.

Anna's gaze sharpened, a flicker of excitement returning. "We could create a preventative treatment. If we can synthesize the enzyme and introduce it into their system, it could act as a barrier, preventing Crythium from taking hold in the first place."

Sebastian leaned back slightly, arms folded, his thoughtful expression shadowed by the dim light. "How close are we to making that happen?"

Anna exhaled, her fingers tapping the edge of the book. "We've already gathered small Crythium samples and studied their interaction with human cells. But until now, we didn't know what to target. This changes that. If we can isolate and replicate the Rocknid enzyme, we can begin testing it on controlled samples of contaminated tissue."

"Ah," Pike drawled, giving a short, humorless laugh as he rubbed a hand across his beard. "So all we have to do is find a Screecher that doesn't tear us apart, steal its venom, and pray we don't botch it in the lab? Perfect."

Anna shot him a look that balanced exasperation and restraint. "No," she said evenly. "That's one possibility. But according to this, the enzyme in their venom originates from something the Rocknids consume—which means we may be able to extract it directly."

Sebastian frowned, his brow creasing beneath a shock of dark hair. "And how would we even know what to look for?"

Anna turned a page in the weathered tome and nodded to herself. "The notes mention trace compounds with structures similar to those found in Glowcap mushrooms."

Sebastian blinked. "Glowcaps?" he said, voice low. "From the Abyss?"

Aria's stomach tightened at the word. The image of Guss's weary face and his grim warning flickered through her mind. She glanced toward Sylas, who met her look with a quiet, uneasy frown.

"Yes," Anna said quietly, tracing her finger along a faded illustration. "The venom's potency appears to result from a chain reaction. Smaller creatures eat the mushrooms, the Rocknids consume them, and somehow they're able to synthesize it for their benefit. We just need to replicate that process."

Sylas leaned forward slightly, wry amusement flickering in his eyes. "So all we need is a basket and to be pointed in the right direction?"

"Unfortunately, it's not that simple," Anna replied, her voice dropping slightly. She paused, fingers tightening on the book's worn leather binding. "Glowcaps are mildly toxic and they're only viable when harvested in bloom."

Pike gave a knowing smirk. "Why don't you tell him the fun part?"

Anna shot him a pointed look. "The *fun part*," she said, voice cool, "is that during mating season, the herbivores devour most of the Glowcaps down there as they're driven out from the deeper tunnels. If we want to find any still in bloom, we'll have to go deeper—into Rocknid territory."

She hesitated, fingers brushing the book's worn cover before closing it. "But the deeper we go, the less control we have over what happens."

The air seemed to weigh heavier around them, dense and unmoving, like the very walls of the underground were closing in, listening.

"But if we succeed," Anna finally said, her voice steady despite the tension, "we may be able to stop Shatterblight in its tracks."

She glanced between them, quieter now. "I can't make any promises, though. There are still a lot of unknowns."

Sebastian's gaze remained fixed on the group, his voice calm but firm. "Then we'll make sure there are no mistakes."

Aria's breath trembled as she thought of her grandmother—of the laughter they once shared, now dulled by illness. But for the first time, her thoughts didn't stop there. She thought of the faces she passed every day in Cavandel: the miners leaning on their pickaxes, coughing into their sleeves; the parents who worked through the pain just to feed their children; the hollow expressions of those who had already lost someone.

This wasn't just for Gran anymore. This was for all of them. All those who had watched Shatterblight take and take until there was nothing left.

She wouldn't let Shatterblight take anything else.

"We'll do whatever it takes," she whispered, the conviction in her voice unshakable.

The tension in the room hung like moisture in a cave, dense and suffocating. Anna exhaled sharply and closed the book with a soft thud, her fingers resting on its worn cover as though anchoring herself.

"This isn't something we can solve overnight," she said, her gaze sweeping over the group. "There's still a lot of data to sift through and the book alone won't hand us all the answers. I need time—cross-referencing what we already know with what's in here could be the difference between progress and failure."

She leaned back slightly, tapping the cover of the book. "I'll start with the enzyme pathways and the notes on their compounds, but this isn't just about following instructions. The answers will take work."

Sebastian gave a thoughtful nod, but before he could speak, Pike stepped forward, arms folded, his smirk firmly in place. "I'd say this is the part where we admit that bringing my 'little adventurers' here wasn't such a bad idea after all."

Anna's glare could have scorched him. Heidi groaned softly and Sylas stifled a laugh, but Pike wasn't done. "Go on," he added, his grin growing smug. "A simple 'thank you,' will do."

"That's enough," Sebastian said, his voice cutting through the room like the snap of a whip. He stepped forward, his calm but commanding presence leaving no room for argument. "You've made your point. But this isn't about credit or gloating—it's about what we need to do next."

Pike shrugged, as if Sebastian's words slid off him like water, but the smirk faded just slightly. The room felt quieter, more grounded, as though something unspoken had been settled.

Sebastian exhaled softly and turned back to Anna. "We'll update the team. Keep at it and let us know as soon as you have something solid."

Anna nodded, already flipping through the next set of scribbled notes. "I will."

"We need to act fast," Pike said, arms still crossed.

Sebastian's fingers drummed lightly against the table. "Timing isn't ideal."

Pike scoffed. "It never is."

Anna let out a slow breath, setting down her pen with deliberate care. "It's not mining season, Pike." Her voice was even, but the weight behind it was unmistakable. "We can't just head into the Abyss without a solid plan. We'll be torn apart."

Pike tilted his head. "Plenty of things down there can tear us apart—Cave Rats, Horned Boars. Never stopped us before."

Anna's eyes flashed. "And yet somehow, we've managed to keep our people safe." She leaned forward slightly. "It's one thing when the Rocknids are not searching for mates, when they keep to their burrows and their patterns are predictable. But now—" Her fingers tapped once against the table. "They're restless. More aggressive."

Sebastian leaned back slightly, considering her words. "That's exactly why we need to be careful."

Pike let out a quiet chuckle, the sound dry, almost amused. "Careful doesn't get us what we need, brother."

Sebastian's jaw tightened, but he didn't argue. His gaze shifted to Pike. "Fine. Have Kegan select some of our best men."

Pike's smirk was faint but sharp. "On it."

"Ahem." A pointed cough cut through the room. Heidi.

Everyone turned as she raised an eyebrow before crossing her arms. "Even if they *can* pull it off, how do you expect them to get down there? The Warden's not exactly making things easy."

Sylas let out a short laugh. "Right—sneaking down is one thing, but hauling a dead Screecher onto the Lift, past the guards, and straight through Marielle's inn? That's a whole different kind of stupid."

Pike actually looked amused. "Well, if you're volunteering—"

Sebastian cut in before the exchange could escalate. "The Lift isn't an option."

Sylas raised an eyebrow. "So, what, we just drop down through the ceiling?"

Pike gave him an unimpressed look. "Something like that."

Sebastian's gaze lingered on Pike before returning to Sylas. "We use our own routes—the ones that don't come with a welcoming party."

Then he turned to the trio. "And when you leave tonight, don't take the inn's exit. Pike will show you another way."

Suddenly, the lights overhead flickered, their glow surging briefly before dimming again. Shadows stretched and contracted across the walls as the glow-lamps sputtered, pulsing like a heartbeat out of rhythm. For a moment, the room fell into darkness, the faint hum of electricity barely audible. Then, the lights flickered back to life—weak, unsteady, casting a dim and uneven glow over the lab.

"Not again!" Anna snapped, slamming the book shut. Her voice cut through the flickering light—sharp, frustrated. "It's the generator."

Sebastian rubbed the back of his neck, exhaling slowly. "I'll check on it," he muttered.

Heidi shifted her weight, a flicker of excitement crossing her eyes as she adjusted the straps on her tool belt. Her posture straightened, fingers flexing at her side as though itching to dive into the problem.

"I could come with you," she said, her voice measured even as her body betrayed her anticipation. "Just in case."

Sebastian hesitated, studying her with a slight, almost imperceptible frown. "Maybe another time," he said quietly, as he stepped to the door.

Heidi shrugged, her hand dropping to her side. "Just trying to help."

Anna tapped the cover of the book lightly, more as a gesture of thought than urgency. "I've got work to do," she muttered, already flipping back to her notes. "A lot of it."

Pike clapped his hands once, the sound sharp and brisk. "We'll get out of your hair," he said, casting a glance at Anna before shifting his attention to Aria. "Why don't I take our little adventurers on a tour of the place?"

Aria hesitated, her eyes drifting instinctively toward the book still resting in Anna's hands. "And the book?" she asked, her voice quieter than she intended.

Anna didn't look up. "Don't worry, it's safe."

The response, simple and final, left little room for protest. Aria exhaled, the knot in her chest loosening slightly, but the hesitation lingered until Pike's voice cut through it.

"And here I thought we were becoming the best of friends," he said with a grin that was both teasing and knowing.

Sylas, who had been leaning quietly against the wall, stepped forward. "Don't worry," he said, his voice calm and steady. "We're with you."

He turned to Pike, nodding toward the corridor. "Lead the way."

Aria squared her shoulders, her breath steadying as her gaze lifted. The knot of doubt in her chest loosened just enough for something stronger to slip through—determination.

Pike caught the shift in her expression and smiled. "That's more like it."

The base stretched farther than Aria had expected, its labyrinth of tunnels and chambers weaving like veins through the underground. The dim light flickered as they moved, the uneven glow casting distorted shadows that danced along the walls.

As they followed Pike, Aria's thoughts drifted to the world above them—the Mining Camp, the dimly hovels, the soot-streaked faces of workers bent beneath the weight of quotas and fear.

They don't know what's happening down here.

Just as she hadn't.

Aria took it all in, struck by the quiet ingenuity of it—how nothing was wasted, how every cramped space served a purpose. The Dwellers' world was a hidden current beneath the surface, pressed into the rock, buzzing with intent, while the miners above carried on, unaware of what stirred beneath their feet.

They passed by the infirmary room first, where the scent of herbs and antiseptic was cut by something harsher—like burning stone.

Cots lined the walls and the flickering light reflected off the crystallized patterns of Crythium spread across the arms and torsos of patients lying motionless beneath thin blankets. A nurse knelt beside one of them, murmuring softly as she applied a damp cloth to the shimmering veins. The patient didn't stir.

Aria's breath hitched, but Pike didn't slow. They followed him past rows of storage rooms where crates of tools, rations, and weapon parts were stacked in precise columns—every detail a reminder that the Dwellers were preparing for more than survival. They were preparing for something bigger.

Pike turned down another corridor, the tunnels here carved with deliberate precision—a blend of stone and metal, wide enough for steady foot traffic yet narrow enough to feel close. With each step, the air grew warmer, carrying the faint scent of charred wood and something spiced.

A low hum of conversation reached them before they saw it.

The passage widened into an open chamber, its ceiling high enough for glow-lamps to hang freely, casting pools of warm light across the stone. Tables filled the space—some occupied by weary figures nursing drinks, others crowded with plates of steaming food. The scent of roasted meat, roots, and ale thickened the air, mingling with laughter and the occasional burst of argument.

"This," Pike said, stepping aside to let them take it in, "is the Cantina."

Aria hesitated on the threshold, taking in the unexpected warmth of the space. It *felt* different from the rest of the tunnels—alive, humming quietly with sound and movement.

A scarred wooden counter lined one wall, where a few Dwellers leaned, trading stories between sips from dented tin mugs. Toward the back, a man strummed a makeshift lute, his foot tapping softly against the stone in time with a quiet tune.

Sylas let out a low whistle. "Didn't expect a place like this down here."

Pike smirked. "What, you think we sit around sharpening knives in the dark all day? Even we need a place to eat, drink, and forget that tomorrow might kill us."

Aria's gaze swept the room, catching the flicker of curious glances aimed their way—some neutral, others openly appraising. They were still outsiders here.

Pike must have noticed, because he only shrugged. "They'll get used to you. Or they won't. Either way, this is where you'll be spending most of your time, so try not to get yourselves stabbed."

They continued their tour of the Dwellers' hideout before finally, Pike stopped in front of a heavy wooden door and pushed it open.

The training hall was smaller than Aria expected, a compact space carved into the rock, its walls lined with worn training dummies and crude weapon racks. The very air seemed infused with the scent of sweat and old leather, the glow-lamps overhead casting uneven light.

"That's Kegan," Pike murmured, nodding toward the man sparring with a few others. "Watch yourself."

Near the center of the room, Kegan dodged a staff, moving with the kind of fluidity that came from years of practice. His opponent—a stocky man with a determined stance—lunged again, but Kegan sidestepped the blow, pivoting smoothly and driving his knee into the sparring dummy beside him. The impact knocked it off balance, but Kegan didn't break rhythm. He twisted back toward his opponent, catching his wrist and disarming him with a sharp, efficient motion.

Aria's gaze stayed locked on Kegan's movements—the precision of each strike, the fluid way he anticipated every move as if he could read his opponent's mind. He wasn't just training—he was moving like someone who already knew the outcome.

As his sparring partner lunged again, Kegan met the strike head-on, blocking with ease before sweeping his opponent's legs from beneath him. The man hit the ground hard, breath leaving him in a sharp exhale, but Kegan was already moving, already positioning himself for another attack.

The answer pressed against the edges of Aria's thoughts, forming in pieces, sharp and unavoidable.

The Warden. His guards. The growing pressure pressing down on the Dwellers, constant and unrelenting.

Her gaze drifted to Pike, leaning casually against a post near the doorway, arms crossed. But his eyes betrayed something quieter, something watchful.

"How long has he been training like this?" she asked, keeping her voice steady.

Pike's eyes sharpened just enough to give her pause. "A while," he said, the answer vague but weighted. "Long enough."

Aria studied him, waiting for more, but Pike wasn't offering anything else. Instead, he straightened and gestured toward the next corridor. "Come on," he said, slipping back into his usual carefree charm. "There's plenty more to see."

They followed him out, but the rhythmic sound of Kegan's strikes echoed behind them, each thud pounding like a heartbeat syncing with Aria's thoughts.

Her gaze fell to her hands as she walked. They looked steady, but she knew better.

Could those hands really defend her?

Could they wield a weapon with the precision she just saw?

Heidi and Sylas walked alongside her in silence, taking in their surroundings, but Aria's eyes remained fixed on her palms.

Was she in over her head?

The thought twisted in her chest, heavy and suffocating.

But she didn't stop walking. Even as doubt coiled tighter inside her, she kept moving, each step forcing her forward.

And still, the Warden's presence loomed over her thoughts, settling in like a weight she couldn't shake.

Was this why they trained? Not for rebellion. Not for ambition. But for survival.

10

The Price of Duty

Location: Valmere, The Palace

High above Aria and her companions, on the surface world, in the opulent city of Valmere, Prince Gideon sat on an utterly boring chair located in an utterly boring room, surrounded by utterly boring people.

He shifted in the stiff-backed seat, fingers tracing idle rhythms along the carved wood armrest. The laughter of nobles drifted through the air, distant and hollow, as if the echoes themselves had learned to imitate joy.

Golden candelabras flickered against velvet drapes, their flames swaying gently like conspirators whispering secrets to one another. Gideon wasn't sure if it was the chair or the suffocating weight of conversation that made his back ache, but neither offered any reprieve.

He cast a glance toward the grand clock above the ballroom entrance—already an hour into the dinner party.

Too soon to excuse himself, but long enough to imagine being anywhere else.

The banquet hall shimmered under the soft glow of crystal chandeliers, casting fractured light over golden plates and polished silver goblets. It was a room built for spectacle, where even shadows seemed carefully arranged for effect. Servants moved like whispers between tables, their steps light and measured as they refilled goblets and delivered trays of delicacies that glistened beneath the candlelight.

The music, delicate and lilting, barely reached above the hum of conversation. Gideon found it difficult to discern individual words—just the ebb and flow of laughter, the rise of voices that spoke of hunting seasons, family estates, and gowns imported from distant cities. Every sound seemed to carry a weightless charm, floating like mist over still water, evaporating before it could leave an impression.

A servant approached, bowing slightly as he offered a tray of seared pheasant adorned with slivers of candied lemon. Gideon waved him off with a curt smile and a slight shake of his head, the gesture practiced, almost unconscious. His appetite lost to his churning thoughts of duty and dread.

This morning's news had confirmed what they had all feared—the airship sent by the King of Salem had not carried rumors but truth. Petuel had been attacked. The Nomads were no longer a whisper on the wind; they were a real threat. Their scouts to Petuel had not yet returned, but Gideon already knew what they would find—ruins, ashes, and the echoes of battles lost.

Yet here, within the gilded confines of the palace, the urgency seemed to dissolve like sugar in wine. The grand hall thrived with laughter, as if the world beyond Valmere's walls did not exist, as if danger could be charmed away by music and excess.

A woman across the table laughed, her jeweled fingers resting lightly against the edge of her goblet. Gideon watched her for a moment, not out of interest, but to observe the ease with which she existed in a world untouched by consequence. She spoke of fashion trends and scandal, her laughter polished as the pearls at her throat.

He turned away, his fingers tightening briefly on the armrest. Another servant passed by and Gideon caught the faintest scent of something sweet—figs, perhaps, or dates soaked in honey. His stomach churned, but not from hunger.

It was strange, he thought, how easily people could detach themselves from the weight of the world when surrounded by silk and gold.

"Gideon." His mother's voice cut through the haze—soft, but with the weight of command. He turned to find Queen Elara seated beside him, her emerald gown draped in perfect folds over the carved arm of her chair. Her smile was warm, but her eyes missed nothing as they swept the room, assessing every nuance of the gathering.

"I trust you've been paying attention," she said, tilting her head ever so slightly toward the crowd of nobles.

"As much as anyone could in a room like this," Gideon replied, his tone polite, carefully distant.

Elara sighed, setting her wine glass down with the kind of grace that came not from habit, but from intent. "You know why you're here."

"Because I had no other choice," he said evenly.

"Because you're the future king," she corrected smoothly, her gaze locking onto his. "And the kingdom expects you to choose a queen."

Gideon leaned back in his chair, the tension in his shoulders easing only slightly as he exhaled. He'd heard this speech so many times it had carved grooves into his mind.

"I know, Mother."

"Good," she said, as though the matter had been resolved. She stood with a fluidity that drew no attention, her movements practiced to perfection. Extending her hand toward him, she added, "Then you won't mind indulging me."

Gideon hesitated for the briefest moment, glancing toward his father, before rising to take her hand—the weight of expectation settling over him once more.

The nobles stirred, their silk sleeves and jeweled cuffs catching the candlelight as a ripple of curiosity swept through the room. Gideon caught it instantly, reading the moment with the precision of someone who had lived his entire life under scrutiny.

He knew exactly what his mother was doing—parading him like a prized stag before a hunting party, reminding them that the young prince was still an unclaimed prize in the marriage market. But refusing her would cause more trouble than the momentary humiliation was worth.

He stood, took her hand, and let the music draw them into the waltz. The musicians struck up a soft, lilting tune as they moved toward the center of the room. Elara's touch was light but firm, her poise unshakable as he guided her effortlessly through the steps. Even as they danced, her eyes moved across the room like a hawk circling its prey, taking in every nod, every whispered remark exchanged behind jeweled fans.

"Charlotte is watching you," she whispered, her voice smooth as silk. "She's a fine choice and she adores you."

Gideon's jaw tightened, but his reply remained measured. "Are you sure it's me she favors?"

Elara's smile didn't falter, but her eyes sharpened, catching the faint bitterness beneath his question. "Does it matter?"

"Yes," he said quietly. "To me, it does."

Elara sighed, a sound too soft for anyone but him to hear, as though she had prepared for this argument but was already tired of it. "She values what you can offer her—security, power, a future as queen. She knows her role, Gideon, and that's more valuable than you realize."

He met her gaze, unwilling to let the words go unchallenged. "You didn't marry just for an alliance."

For a heartbeat, Elara faltered, her steps slowing. The brief pause would have gone unnoticed by anyone else, but Gideon caught the flicker of something—pity, perhaps, or a memory that had long since hardened into something else.

"No," she said softly, her tone shifting. "But your father and I were the exception, Gideon, not the rule."

The words hung between them like a thread stretched to its limit, ready to snap. Gideon kept his gaze steady, though his chest tightened. "So something real can survive in a place like this."

Her smile remained, but it turned brittle, like porcelain on the verge of cracking. "It can. But not without a fight, and not without wounds."

He studied her for a long moment, the weight of her words settling over him. "Is that what it left you with, Mother? Wounds?"

Her gaze didn't waver. "It left me with a crown, and a son I raised to understand that sacrifices aren't meant to be easy."

Gideon allowed the silence to settle. She had worn her crown as both armor and burden, shielding him from the cost of her decisions for as long as she could. But tonight, she wasn't shielding him. She was passing the weight to him, piece by piece, whether he was ready or not.

The final notes of the waltz swelled and Elara released him with an easy grace, her fingers brushing his wrist as though imparting a final piece of wisdom. "It doesn't have to be love, Gideon," she murmured. "It just has to be enough."

Before he could respond, she gave him a gentle but unmistakable nudge toward the noblewomen waiting at the edge of the ballroom. Reluctantly, he approached as Charlotte stepped forward.

She stood beneath the soft glow of the chandeliers, her gown of pale gold shimmering like sunlight over water. The jewels along her neckline sparkled with every movement, but it was her carefully crafted smile that caught his attention. Radiant, flawless—perfect in every way except that it never reached her eyes.

Gideon took Charlotte's hand as the waltz began, his grip poised, his expression as smooth as the polished marble beneath their feet. He led her into the first steps with effortless control, feeling the weight of expectation settle around him like a well-worn cloak.

"You must be enjoying yourself," he said before she could speak, his tone light, inviting. "You've hardly sat down all evening."

Charlotte's lips curved into a knowing smile. "Should I take that as a compliment, Your Highness?"

He tilted his head slightly, as if considering. "It depends—do you measure success by how many dances you steal away?"

She laughed, the sound practiced but pleasant. "I'd say it's a fair indicator of one's desirability."

"Then you must be the most desired woman in the room," he said smoothly, his voice warm enough to convince, but never indulgent.

Charlotte's grip tightened almost imperceptibly. "And what of you, Your Highness? You don't seem to suffer from a lack of admirers."

"I suspect it has less to do with my charm, and more to do with my station," he said softly.

Her eyes gleamed with amusement. "You speak as if the two cannot coexist, Your Highness."

He allowed a slow, measured smile. "A flattering assumption—but dangerous all the same."

She hummed, as if enjoying this game. "And yet, you humor me."

"As any good prince would." His tone carried just a touch of irony, just enough to amuse himself, though no one beyond Charlotte would detect it.

The waltz carried them through a sweeping turn and Gideon took the moment to glance toward the crowd. His mother's gaze fixed in his direction—watchful, assessing. She was waiting to see how well he played the part.

So he did.

"Your gown," he said, returning his focus to Charlotte, "it suits you."

She beamed, her fingers grazing the silk at her waist. "I had it made in the capital—the brocade is from Estra and the embroidery was done by hand."

"A deliberate choice."

"Of course," she said, pleased that he had noticed. "One must always be intentional in their presentation."

Gideon nodded, thoughtful. "Presentation is powerful."

Charlotte leaned in slightly, as if sensing a deeper meaning beneath his words. "And yet, you don't seem particularly concerned with yours tonight."

He laughed, low and smooth, letting it slip out just naturally enough to disarm her. "On the contrary—I find it requires far more effort to appear effortless."

Her brow lifted, intrigued. "Is that what you're doing now?"

"You tell me," he said, with an ease that made it feel playful rather than calculated.

She considered him for a moment longer, then smiled. "Perhaps I'll decide by the next dance."

A clever answer. He inclined his head in acknowledgment.

The conversation shifted, drifting into the easy rhythm of courtly pleasantries. He let her speak of the banquet, the upcoming hunting season, the latest import of silk dyes from the east. He listened, offering well-placed nods and occasional remarks—just enough to keep the exchange fluid, never allowing the silence to stretch too long.

When she mentioned her necklace, adjusting it lightly so the diamonds caught the light, he made sure to acknowledge it, though not with the indulgence she might have hoped for. "Your father has good taste," he said simply.

She smiled, satisfied enough. "He says they suit me."

Gideon hummed in quiet agreement. The compliment cost him nothing and if it pleased her, all the better.

The music swelled, signaling the final steps of the waltz. As the dance concluded, he released her hand with careful grace and inclined his head. "Thank you for the dance, Lady Charlotte."

She curtsied in return, her gaze lingering. "Shall I expect another before the night's through?"

Instead of avoiding the question or giving a vague non-answer, he allowed just the right amount of diplomacy to slip through.

"If the opportunity arises, I'd be honored," he said smoothly.

It was neither commitment nor refusal and from the way her smile remained, she was content with that answer.

As he stepped away, he caught his mother watching. A slight tilt of her head, the barest flicker of something unreadable in her gaze.

Gideon didn't linger. He moved through the shifting silks and murmured pleasantries, offering nods where required, a word here, a glance there.

The steps of this dance—the one off the ballroom floor—were just as practiced, just as necessary. And yet, as the music swelled behind him and laughter rippled through the air, he was already reaching for something beyond it.

Something just out of sight.

The weight in his chest tightened, making it hard to breathe. And once again, the thought he had swallowed earlier clawed its way back to the surface:

Dreaming about being anywhere else.

As the evening wore on, his mother's gaze followed him like a shadow, watchful and unrelenting. She wasn't waiting for mere politeness or compliance—she was searching for something deeper: a spark of interest, a moment of approval, anything she could seize upon to nudge him closer to a decision. But Gideon had made his decision long ago. He wouldn't let duty dictate his heart, not in this.

He danced with a few more noblewomen, offered the necessary compliments and endured the hollow conversations as if walking through a fog. Each passing moment felt like a tether tightening around his chest, suffocating and unyielding.

But then the opportunity presented itself—a lull between dances, a shift in the crowd's focus. Gideon slipped quietly from the ballroom, weaving through the marble corridors with the ease of someone who had memorized every twist and turn.

The distant hum of music faded behind him, replaced by the soft echo of his footsteps against the marble floor. The air grew cooler as he neared the palace gardens, the heavy warmth of the banquet hall giving way to the crisp breath of night.

He pushed open the terrace doors and the night air greeted him like an old friend. It rushed over his skin, filling his lungs with something he hadn't realized he'd been missing—relief. The scent of jasmine, faint and sweet, mingled with the earthy aroma of damp soil. The stones beneath his feet were slick with dew as he walked along the winding path, past hedges trimmed to perfection and flowerbeds bursting with late blooms.

Above him, the stars shimmered, cold and distant, scattered like fragments of forgotten promises. They stretched endlessly beyond the palace walls, vast and untouchable—like the adventures he longed for.

He paused beside a marble fountain, the gentle trickle of water breaking the stillness. Reflections of the night sky rippled across its surface, stars bending and reforming with every movement. Gideon braced his hands against the edge, head bowed slightly. And for the first time all night, he allowed himself to breathe without restraint.

Out here, the weight of expectation didn't press as heavily. There were no nobles watching his every move, no conversations wrapped in layers of hidden meaning. Just the night, vast and indifferent, offering him the space to think.

He traced a finger along the edge of the marble, his gaze fixed on the sky. How many nights had he spent like this, staring upward, wondering what lay beyond the kingdom's borders? He could almost see himself there—riding across unknown lands, breathing in air untouched by courtly politics, his sword at his side and nothing but the wind and stars to guide him.

Freedom.

Adventure. Purpose beyond these walls.

But then his mother's words echoed in his mind, soft yet persistent. *It doesn't have to be love. It just has to be enough.*

He leaned forward, the weight of those words pressing against him. What if she was right? What if this life—this carefully constructed cage—was all there was? Could he carve out a version of happiness within the constraints of duty, or would it always feel like a hollow performance?

The cool night air did little to quell the ache in his chest. He closed his eyes, listening to the rustle of leaves in the breeze. Part of him wanted to disappear into the darkness, to keep walking until the palace and its obligations faded behind him. But he couldn't. Not yet.

Duty, for now, still had its chains.

He turned slowly, brushing the dew from his hands. The night had given him a brief reprieve, but dawn would come—and with it, the weight of what lay ahead. Tomorrow, he would descend into Cavandel, a place he had known only through whispered tales, now made real.

He had pictured it in fragments—dark tunnels winding endlessly beneath the earth, veins of Crythium glowing faintly like trapped lightning, miners with hollow eyes and calloused hands toiling in a world far removed from the polished marble of the palace.

What would he find there? Would he see desperation etched into the stone walls, or a glimpse of something more—something his father and the council had never spoken of but had always known? He wasn't sure which possibility unsettled him more.

The garden's tranquility couldn't quiet the thoughts circling his mind. Cavandel wasn't merely a visit—it was the heart of everything his kingdom depended on, the hidden engine that powered Valmere's splendor. For the first time, he would see what lay beneath the surface of the life he had been born into, and he couldn't help but wonder if it would change him—or worse, if it wouldn't.

He exhaled slowly, the cool night air brushing against his face. Tomorrow would be a reckoning and tonight, all he could do was try to prepare for it.

But as he turned back toward the ballroom, a quiet thought bloomed in the back of his mind—defiant, stubborn, and quietly persistent. *Not all adventures are meant to be caged. One day, I'll find mine.*

And this time, he wouldn't look back.

***

The morning light had been gray and reluctant, barely filtering through the heavy mist as Gideon's carriage set off at dawn. Now, as the wheels rumbled over the uneven path leading into the Emerald Mountains, the world felt even farther removed from the confines of the palace.

The air here had teeth—it bit at his skin, sharper with every passing mile and carried the scent of wet earth, pine, and something raw beneath it, something ancient.

He shifted in his seat, fingers trailing idly along the polished wood of the carriage's interior. His thoughts were tangled, a web of anticipation and unease. This was his first visit to Cavandel, the place he'd only ever heard spoken of in hushed voices, but now the veil was about to be stripped away, revealing the weight of what lay below.

Outside the window, the scenery shifted from the soft greens of forested hills to the jagged edges of stone cliffs. The trees thinned, their skeletal branches reaching upward like hands grasping for something they'd never catch. Mist coiled around them, clinging to the crags and ridges as though reluctant to let go. The grandeur of Valmere felt like a distant dream, its marble towers and decorated domes fading into memory.

He leaned back, exhaling through his nose. The air inside the carriage was warmer than the chill outside, but it wasn't enough to ease the cold knot in his chest. Gideon wasn't sure what he expected to feel—curiosity, perhaps, or determination. Instead, he felt suspended between two versions of himself. The prince who had been raised to inherit a kingdom and the boy who once dreamed of escape.

The carriage slowed, jolting him forward slightly. Through the fogged glass, he saw the entrance carved into the mountainside—a jagged wound in the rock, heavily guarded by soldiers in dark uniforms. Their presence was a reminder that Cavandel wasn't just a mine; it was a fortress, a secret too valuable to be left unprotected. The soldiers' hands rested on the hilts of their swords, their expressions unreadable as they scanned the area with practiced vigilance. After speaking to Gideon's men, one of the guards gave a curt nod and the gates creaked open.

Gideon felt the carriage lurch forward, its wheels groaning as they passed through the heavy iron gates. Beyond them lay a descent into shadow—a path that spiraled downward through the mountain's core. The glow-lamps lining the walls flickered faintly, their soft light barely cutting through the gloom. The scent of damp stone and metal grew stronger, filling the carriage like an unspoken warning.

As they descended deeper, carts laden with crates of refined Crythium rumbled past. This wasn't just a resource to be mined; it was the very thing that sustained his kingdom, the reason Valmere's streets were lit and its defenses were strong. But seeing it here felt different—like they had ripped something raw and living from the earth, something that wasn't theirs to take.

The carriage rolled forward, and the light of day slipped away, replaced by the dim radiance of glow-lights embedded along the tunnel walls. The artificial illumination flickered faintly, casting muted pools of light that played over the uneven stone.

They entered a small cavern where the tunnel opened into a wide chamber, its walls lined with equipment, crates, and scaffolding. The path ended abruptly and the carriage slowed to a stop beside a small platform connected to a metal hoist. Workers moved past them, their boots scuffing on the stone floor, heads bowed under the weight of crates and tools.

Gideon stepped down from the carriage, the chill biting at his skin as he adjusted the cuffs of his gloves. The hum of machinery vibrated faintly beneath his feet, like a distant heartbeat in the mountain. He exhaled, watching his breath form clouds in the cold air.

A guard in a thick coat and gloves nodded respectfully, gesturing toward the waiting platform. "Your Highness," he said quietly, his breath visible as he spoke. "We'll be taking you down to the Stratum."

Gideon stepped onto the platform, the grated floor swaying slightly beneath his boots. A guard pulled the lever and the chains groaned to life, lowering them into the mountain's depths.

The shaft walls pressed in around them, flickering with pulses of light as the Ascender rattled downward. The scent of oil mixed with the dampness of the earth thickened, growing stronger as they descended. He gripped the iron rail tightly, his mind circling around what lay ahead.

When the platform slowed and the shaft opened, the Stratum stretched before him in a wave of light and shadow. He stepped off the Ascender onto the grated metal floor, his boots clicking softly as he took in the vast expanse. The ceiling soared high above, supported by iron beams, while the faint hum of voices surrounded him like the pulse of a living thing.

Glow-lights lined the vaulted concourse, their amber light spilling across polished stone. The cavernous space stretched upward into an iron canopy, where steam drifted like breath through the rafters.

Balconies and arched walkways bridged the upper levels of buildings, each one gleaming with rows of illuminated windows that shimmered through the haze. Below, a tram rumbled along one of many tracks, the hum of its engine blending with the quiet rhythm of footsteps, tools and murmured voices.

The air carried a faint metallic warmth, alive with motion yet steeped in a strange, mechanical calm—as though the city itself were holding its breath between pulses of light.

Gideon adjusted his gloves again, exhaling slowly. The sheer scale of the place sank into him, heavier than he had imagined. His gaze swept the expanse, following the passersby who glided through their routines with quiet efficiency, their faces unreadable.

There was a hum in the air, constant and relentless, as if it too were part of the mountain's essence. For a moment, Gideon stood motionless, absorbing the magnitude of the Stratum. It wasn't a mine—it was a machine, a kingdom carved from stone and metal, built on necessity and survival.

Ensure the Crythium flows, his father's words whispered once more. He exhaled, steadying himself before taking a step forward. Beneath the hum of machinery, he could feel it—this place had its own pulse and for now, it was waiting to see if he could keep up.

There was awe here, yes, but it was tempered by something else—a discomfort that settled deep in his bones. This wasn't just a visit. This was a reckoning.

A figure approached—a man in a dark coat and eyes sharp as flint. His boots clanked against the walkway and when he stopped, he extended a hand. "Your Highness," the man drawled with a respectful nod, though his gaze remained assessing. "Welcome to Cavandel."

11

The Iron Fist Strikes

Location: Cavandel, The Stratum

Drazic Grask sat at an unremarkable desk in an unremarkable room. Across from him, one of the Dustborn of Cavandel lounged comfortably, feasting on a lavish meal that had been laid out before him.

"Would you like some more?" Drazic asked, lifting a decanter of fine ale.

"Certainly," the man replied with a greasy grin, gesturing lazily as Drazic topped up his mug. He let out a loud burp, wiping his mouth on his sleeve.

"Boy, I could get used to this," he said, grinning through a mouthful of food. Drazic resisted the urge to grimace, forcing a faint smile instead. "Oh, I bet you could," he drawled, his voice laced with dry amusement. The man was a bottom-feeder, the worst of the worst—a scavenger who'd eagerly taken up the Warden's offer of Grottos in exchange for information on the Dwellers.

Drazic couldn't help but take in the man's revolting state. Mismatched boots, scuffed and filthy, worn without socks. His pants, frayed and caked with grime, were held up by a makeshift belt of fraying rope. A shirt that might have once been gray hung loosely on his gaunt frame, while a torn jacket—clearly stolen—barely clung to his hunched shoulders.

His sunken eyes gleamed with greed beneath a mop of unkempt, greasy hair. But it was the man's beard, matted with oil and food scraps, that truly turned Drazic's stomach.

"Go on," Drazic prompted, offering a curt smile. "You were saying, about the Dwellers?"

"Oh! Yes!" the man erupted in laughter, spraying bits of food across the table. "Scum, the lot of 'em!" he spat, bits of half-chewed meat tumbling from his mouth. "Always stirring up trouble!" He swallowed noisily, pounding his chest to clear his throat. "I hope you get every last one of 'em!"

"As do I," Drazic said smoothly, leaning back in his chair.

The man jabbed a finger in the air, grinning triumphantly. "But like I was sayin' earlier, there's this fellow—down the lane, 'bout two houses down from me. He's one of 'em. No doubt about it!"

"Fantastic," Drazic said, his expression unreadable. "And is there anyone else you suspect?"

"Nah, just him. Always lurking about, that one," the man said, shoveling more food into his mouth.

"Great," Drazic said, standing slowly.

The man's eyes drifted upward, briefly following Drazic as he rose, before returning to his plate. He leaned back in his chair, chewing loudly.

"Now, about the Grottos," the man said, licking his greasy fingers. "Five hundred, right? That's what you promised."

"Yes," Drazic replied, his voice calm. "It's time for your reward. Let me get it for you."

He stepped away from the desk and crossed the room to a cabinet in the corner. Sliding open a drawer, he reached inside—not for a pouch of Grottos, but for Scarlet, his trusted whip. He let the coils slip through his fingers, the leather flexing, creaking as if awakening from slumber. She was ready. She always was.

One stroke, she whispered. *One lesson*—it would set the tone for the remainder of the day.

Drazic rolled the handle against his palm, contemplating. He exhaled, winding the leather once more around his fist. "Not now," he murmured under his breath. "The Warden doesn't like to be kept waiting. We'll have plenty of time later."

Scarlet coiled against his grip, defiant.

From across the room, the miner stirred. "What was that?"

Drazic glanced up, a subtle smirk playing at the corner of his mouth. "Oh, nothing at all," he drawled softly, his tone deceptively mild. He secured Scarlet at his hip, allowing the coils to settle against his belt with their familiar weight before moving toward the door with unhurried ease.

As he stepped into the corridor, the guards straightened at once. Drazic shot them a passing glance, then reached back and drew the door closed. It groaned in protest before the bolt slid home with a decisive scrape.

A muffled yelp echoed from inside and Drazic's smirk deepened as his boots carried him away—measured, composed, without so much as a backward glance.

Location: Cavandel, The Outer District

Aria, Jace, and the Silent Hawk sat around the small wooden table, silence stretching like shadows across the walls. The faint scent of soup lingered in the air, mingling with the rhythmic ticking of the wall clock that seemed louder than usual.

Aria, arms crossed, drummed her fingers lightly on the wood. Lucinda idly stirred her tea, the spoon clinking softly against the cup. Her gaze shifted to Jace, whose eyes traced invisible patterns on the floor as though it might hold the answers they'd all been avoiding. The silence was thick—broken only by the occasional sip of tea.

Aria cleared her throat with dramatic flair, leaning forward like a magistrate about to cross-examine. "So, which one of you is going to confess first?"

Her grandmother blinked, her expression serene but unmistakably amused. "Confess to what, dear?"

"Oh, I don't know, Gran," Aria said, her voice edged with sarcasm. "Maybe the whole *secret resistance* thing? The part where you've both been living double lives while I've been stuck chipping away at rocks."

Her grandmother sipped her tea. "Oh, don't be so dramatic."

"I'm serious," Aria insisted. "Resistance groups, forgotten legacies—what else are you hiding?"

Her grandmother took a long sip of tea and cast a playful glance toward Jace. "See? I told you she'd figure it out. You owe me five Grottos."

Jace sighed. "I don't remember agreeing to that."

"That's what you always say when you lose," her grandmother replied.

Aria's mouth fell open. "You two are unbelievable."

Jace shrugged, the corners of his mouth curling into an easy grin. "It's not like there was much else to do."

She gestured wildly between them. "Okay, but seriously. How long has this been going on? When did you two decide to play the heroes of Cavandel without telling me?"

Jace offered a humble shrug. "We weren't heroes, Aria. Just people trying to do the right thing and hoping it was enough."

The laughter in Aria's voice faded as her gaze lowered. "Why didn't you trust me with this? I thought we shared everything."

Her grandmother's face softened, her fingers drifting over the table's worn surface as if tracing old memories. "It wasn't about trust, love. It was about protection. The less you knew, the safer you were."

"Safe from what?" Aria's voice was barely above a whisper.

"From ending up like me," her grandmother said quietly. "From getting pulled into something that could take more from you than it gives."

Jace leaned forward, his voice gentle but firm. "It's not just the guards or the Warden, Aria. It's the weight of knowing things you can't unlearn. I've seen good people get crushed by it." He paused, his gaze shifting toward her grandmother. "Once you're in, you don't get to go back to being a kid. It's not fair," he said, "but it's the truth."

Aria drew a steady breath, her expression soft but resolute. "I'm starting to see that, but I'm not a kid anymore."

The weight between them began to lift when Jace cleared his throat and rubbed the back of his neck, eyes darting toward the floor. "Also," he said, "what if you turned out to be better at it than we were? My ego isn't ready for that."

Aria snorted, the sound breaking through the heaviness. "Admitting defeat already? That's fast even for you."

He leaned back, a grin tugging at his mouth. "I said *what if*. There's a big difference."

Her shoulders loosened. She laughed—a small, genuine sound—and tipped back in her chair, tapping her fingers lightly against the table. "Well, now that the cat's out of the bag, maybe you can teach me some of your skills."

"Which ones?" Jace asked, his eyes glinting. "The ones that got us into trouble, or out of it?"

"Both. Definitely both."

Her grandmother chuckled softly and set her empty cup aside. "Oh, we'll teach you, but there's one thing you'll need to learn on your own."

Aria raised an eyebrow. "What's that?"

Lucinda looked at Aria with a rare tenderness, her eyes reflecting both pride and sorrow. "You need to know when to run and when to stand your ground," she said, her voice soft but steady. "No one can teach you that. It's something you feel right here." She tapped her chest lightly, as if passing down a lesson carved into her very soul.

"And for the record," Jace added, leaning back with a smirk, "running is often underrated. "

Laughter swelled through the room, warm and unrestrained, brushing away the lingering weight of unspoken truths. They sat together, their shared laughter echoing softly off the walls, as if it, too, were part of the family.

When the moment quieted, her grandmother reached across the table and squeezed Aria's hand. "No more secrets. I promise."

Aria nodded, her smile lingering as she looked between them. For the first time in what felt like forever, she could breathe freely. Whatever trials lay ahead, she wouldn't face them alone.

The lantern flickered gently, casting their shadows against the walls as the clock ticked on. And tonight—despite her grandmother's worsening condition—the weight of the unknown felt just a little lighter.

Location: Cavandel, The Stratum

The wind whispered softly through the stone and metal walkways of the Stratum, carrying with it the faint scent of dust and iron. Prince Gideon Everhart stood at the edge of the lookout, his hands resting on the cool railing as he gazed down at the District below. Artificial daylight spilled across the maze of narrow streets, market stalls, and tightly packed homes. Far beneath him, miners drifted through the passages like scattered shadows—small, indistinct figures swallowed by the city's vastness.

Had he expected something different—something grander? The reports in Valmere had spoken of order, efficiency, and pride. Cavandel had been painted as the beating heart of Valmere's success, its people thriving beneath a shared purpose. Yet from up here, the hum of life felt muted, as though the District itself were holding its breath. The miners below didn't move like cogs in a well-oiled machine—they moved like people who had been given no other choice.

Footsteps approached from behind, their faint cadence threading through the still air. Gideon turned slightly as Warden Thaddeus Black-thorne arrived, his boots striking a measured rhythm across the stone. The man bowed his head in deference before joining him at the railing, his hands calmly folded behind his back.

"A remarkable sight, isn't it, Your Highness?" Thaddeus's voice was calm and practiced, with the smoothness of someone who'd given this speech many times before. He gestured toward the view below. "Every movement, every exchange—it all contributes to Valmere's strength."

Gideon's gaze lingered on the distant streets. "It seems efficient."

"Efficiency is survival," Thaddeus replied, his thin smile never faltering. "And Cavandel knows how to survive."

For a moment, neither man spoke. The wind brushed past them again, stirring the distant hum of activity below. Gideon pressed his lips into a thoughtful line. "The reports focus on production quotas and resource management," he said finally. "But they don't mention much about the people."

Thaddeus hesitated, just for a moment, before recovering. "Our people know their role, Your Highness. They take pride in their work, knowing it sustains the kingdom."

Gideon's gaze lingered on the streets below. "And that pride," he said quietly, "does it bring them contentment?"

The question hung in the air like a spark waiting to ignite something dangerous. Thaddeus's fingers twitched briefly behind his back before he spoke. "Contentment, Your Highness, is a complex thing to measure. But I assure you, Cavandel's people understand their purpose. And with purpose comes fulfillment."

Gideon's gaze didn't waver. "Purpose and contentment aren't the same."

The smile faded briefly from Thaddeus's face, but he quickly recovered. "No, they're not," he admitted. "But pride can carry a man through much."

Gideon pushed off the railing and turned toward him. "I'd like to see the District—up close. Speak to the people myself."

Thaddeus's shoulders tensed almost imperceptibly. "With respect, Your Highness, the District is a hard place. Not one meant for someone of royal lineage."

The Warden's gaze drifted briefly toward the massive Lift in the distance, its heavy chains visible even from this height. "It's not the work that concerns me," he said carefully. "But the environment. The noise, the crowding—it's chaotic. There's no need for you to see the District in its daily state. It wouldn't give you the understanding you seek."

Gideon studied him, the silence between them stretching just long enough for the Warden to shift slightly on his feet.

"Then when would be the right time, Warden?"

Thaddeus exhaled softly, his mind calculating. "In a few weeks, the Founders Day Festival will be held. It's a time when the District is at its best—cleaned up, decorated, and alive with celebration. You'll see our people as they truly are, without the distractions of daily toil."

Gideon didn't immediately reply. His gaze returned to the District below, his thoughts turning over the idea.

Thaddeus's shoulders eased, though his expression remained neutral. "We'll be honored to have you, Your Highness. I'll ensure everything is prepared for your visit."

"Why wait for a festival to see Cavandel?" Gideon asked as they walked. "Wouldn't seeing it now give me a clearer picture of reality?"

Thaddeus chuckled politely, though the sound didn't quite reach his eyes. "Reality, Your Highness, can be—overwhelming. The festival will show you Cavandel as it's meant to be seen. Not just its daily struggles, but its spirit."

Gideon remained silent, weighing the Warden's words. The mention of the festival lingered with him. If it offered the miners even a fleeting escape—a moment of genuine joy, a breath of relief from their burdens—it might reveal something the Warden wants to keep hidden.

After a moment, he nodded. "Very well. I'll return for the festival."

They made their way back toward the junction at an unhurried pace, their footsteps lost amid the rumble of merchant carts and the low murmur of streetgoers.

They boarded a tram that carried them north along the Central Line, the city unfolding ahead through a faint veil of mist. Light from the upper walkways wavered across the windows before giving way to the stately façades that marked the heart of the Stratum. From there, the walk to the Warden's office was quiet—not tense, but deliberate—filled with the kind of courteous remarks that kept distance intact.

At the door, Thaddeus gestured for Gideon to enter first. He inclined his head and stepped inside.

The office was dim and warm, glow-lamps casting an amber hue across polished wood. Maps of the District and production ledgers lay neatly arranged across a large oak desk. Near the edge sat a small trinket—a worn ribbon tied into a simple knot—unnoticed by Gideon but impossible for Thaddeus to ignore.

Gideon sat across from the Warden, resting his arms lightly on the chair's wooden frame. "I'll return for the festival," he repeated, his gaze steady. "I only hope there's more to witness than mere ceremony."

Thaddeus inclined his head with a measured smile. "Naturally, Your Highness. I'll ensure that your visit is... memorable."

As the conversation turned to formal matters—Crythium quotas and logistics—Thaddeus's thoughts drifted. The Founders Day Festival was more than a matter of appearances for him; it was a reminder of Gloria, of what he'd lost, and of what Cavandel had endured. The weight of her memory pressed close, but he buried it quickly, as he always did.

When the meeting concluded, Gideon rose, his expression still thoughtful. "I'll see you in a few weeks, Warden."

Thaddeus bowed low. "We'll be ready for your return, Your Highness."

The door closed behind the prince, leaving Thaddeus alone in the soft, violet glow of his office. He exhaled slowly, his fingers brushing against the worn ribbon on his desk. The prince's curiosity was dangerous—but Thaddeus had time. If he could control what Gideon saw during the festival, the balance he had maintained for so long would remain intact.

His gaze hardened and he turned toward the maps lining the walls. He had time to prepare. He just needed to make sure Gideon saw exactly what he wanted him to see—and nothing more.

Location: Cavandel, Dweller's Base

Aria hit the ground hard. The padded dirt floor did little to soften the impact, though she was grateful it existed at all; without it, her training would have left her bruised beyond repair. Every tumble landed with a dull thud, her body folding awkwardly as she fought to keep her footing. She winced, pressing her palms to the worn surface as she pushed herself upright, the sting of failure gnawing at her pride.

"Get up," Pike ordered, his voice cutting through the silence like a whip.

Her breath came in sharp bursts, sweat trailing down her brow and dripping along the curve of her neck. She pushed herself upright on trembling legs—only for Pike to send her toppling again. The frustration burned hotter than the ache in her muscles, but she bit back a groan and prepared to rise.

The walls of the training hall gleamed faintly with moisture, the air thick with the scent of metal, sweat, and worn leather. Glow-lamps wavered overhead, casting restless shadows across swaying punching bags and stacks of iron weights. Pike stood at the center, arms folded across his chest, a figure carved from stone, his gaze heavy with judgment. He had agreed—reluctantly—to train the trio, but now it was Aria who began to regret the arrangement.

Pike remained silent as Aria dragged herself back to her feet, but the hard line of his mouth said everything—failure wasn't an option and neither was quitting.

From a bench along the wall, Sylas watched with his usual half-grin, elbow resting on his knee while Heidi sat beside him, arms crossed. "You know," he said as Aria straightened, "if falling were a sport, you'd be undefeated."

Aria was in too much pain to pay him any attention.

Pike clapped his hands once, the sharp sound echoing through the damp hall. Sylas straightened instinctively, his grin fading, while Heidi's arms dropped from their fold as her gaze snapped to Pike. "Enough jokes," he said, his gaze hardening as he stepped forward. "There are basic principles you need to understand before you can defend yourself—and they have little to do with brute strength."

He began pacing slowly, his boots punctuating each word. "The first is balance. Without it, you're defeated before the fight even begins. Balance doesn't just keep you upright—it allows you to move without hesitation, to pivot when your opponent thinks they've got you cornered. Lose your balance, and you lose everything."

Pike stopped, turning to Aria. "The second is awareness. Don't just watch your opponent's hands—they'll lie to you. Watch their torso, their feet. The core is where the truth lives. If you can read their intentions, you'll be the one in control."

He resumed pacing. "Next is reaction. This isn't about thinking—it's about instinct. Muscle memory becomes your closest ally. You train your body to move before your mind catches up—and that's what keeps you alive."

His voice softened slightly, though it lost none of its authority. "Finally, endurance. It's not about ignoring pain—it's about knowing when to embrace it and when to push past it. Every fighter feels the burn, but those who prevail learn to carry it without letting it slow them down. Remember, your opponent doesn't care how exhausted you are—in fact, he's counting on it."

He stopped, letting the words settle before nodding toward Aria. "Now—show me you've been listening."

Aria swallowed hard and took her stance again, adjusting her footing as Pike had shown her. Knees bent, arms raised, weight balanced, she exhaled slowly—determined to prove him wrong.

Without warning, Pike stepped in, his foot hooking behind her ankle with practiced precision. Aria's balance gave way, and she hit the ground hard.

Heidi winced from the bench, shoulders tensing at the sound of impact.

Beside her, Sylas leaned against the wall, laughing. "I guess she wasn't listening after all."

Pike stepped forward, towering over Aria where she lay crumpled on the floor. His gaze—sharp and unrelenting—locked onto hers. "You need to put it all together," he said. "Balance, awareness, reaction, endurance—they're not separate lessons. If you don't connect them, you'll always be a step behind—and on the floor. But when you learn to move between them, that's when you'll stop falling."

He straightened and turned toward Heidi and Sylas. "On your feet," he barked, motioning for them to join Aria in the open space. "Now we work on reaction. None of you are fast enough—and I intend to fix that."

Pike clapped once, the sound cutting through the air. "Eyes on me," he commanded. "This exercise is simple—block and evade. I'll use this training pole to strike at random, and you'll react without thinking. No hesitation. No overanalyzing. Trust your instincts."

He grabbed a worn wooden training pole leaning against the wall and gave it a swift twirl before settling into position. "Ready?" Without waiting for an answer, he lunged forward, the pole slicing through the air toward Heidi, who barely dodged in time, her breath catching.

"Faster," Pike said sharply. He pivoted toward Aria, sending a quick jab toward her side. She raised her arm to block, but the force of the hit pushed her back a step.

"Good," Pike muttered, already shifting toward Sylas. The next strike from the pole was deflected with ease, but Pike's following feint had Sylas stumbling.

"Don't fall for the bait," Pike growled. "The real attack isn't always obvious." He stepped back, nodding for them to reset. "Again."

For the next two hours, the training hall became a battleground of exhaustion and determination. The rhythmic clack of the wooden pole meeting hastily raised arms mixed with grunts and the heavy thud of bodies striking the floor.

Sweat dripped into Aria's eyes, blurring her vision and stinging until she had to blink it away. Her legs trembled with every movement, her arms hanging heavy as lead. Her ribs ached, but she didn't stop. Even when her muscles screamed for relief, she forced them to move. Somewhere deep within the haze of fatigue, a stubborn resolve kept her upright. *This isn't just training—this is survival,* she told herself, teeth clenched as she deflected another strike.

Pike planted the training pole against the floor, leaning on it just enough to make the wood groan softly under his weight. He surveyed the trio—battered, bruised, and drenched in sweat, their chests rising and falling as they fought for breath. The faint flicker of approval in his eyes was as rare as a warm breeze in Cavandel.

"You're a little worse for wear," he said. "But you've made progress." His voice was steady, cutting through the sound of their labored breathing. "Don't let that fool you into thinking you're ready, though. What you've learned today are just the first steps—steps that will take months of practice to become second nature. Against a seasoned opponent, you won't stand a chance. But if you keep at it, these basics may well keep you alive."

He let the words sink in before continuing. "If you want to excel, you practice every day. What you put in is exactly what you'll get out. There are no shortcuts."

Pike paced in front of them, his gaze shifting between Aria, Heidi, and Sylas. "Aria, your instincts are improving, but you hesitate when you second-guess yourself. Focus on trusting that first reaction. Heidi, you're quick, but you leave openings because you rely too much on speed. Learn to anticipate what comes next. Sylas, you're fluid, but you fall for feints too easily. Don't be so eager to counter before you know the real threat."

He stopped and rested the pole across his shoulders. "You each have strengths—build on them. Fix the weaknesses." He nodded once, then turned and headed for the exit. Without looking back, he said, "Get some rest. Tomorrow, we go again."

He stepped into the dim corridor, his pace steady—then, for the briefest moment, he hesitated. Aria caught the slight flex of his jaw, the shift of his weight as though reconsidering something. Then he was gone, his silhouette swallowed by shadow.

Aria wiped her face with the back of her hand, smearing the sweat but too tired to care. Heidi groaned softly as she stretched out her legs, while Sylas leaned against the wall, his breath finally slowing.

As they gathered their belongings, the scent of sweat and worn leather lingered like a badge of honor—a testament to their endurance. Aria slung her jacket over her shoulder, muscles aching with each step toward the door. Despite the pain, a faint smile tugged at her lips. She wasn't strong yet. She wasn't fast. But her journey had begun.

Heidi nudged her as they walked into the dim corridor beyond the training hall. "So, any regrets?"

"None," Aria replied, her voice steady despite the exhaustion.

Sylas chuckled, his breath still ragged. "Give it until morning. When you can't move, you might reconsider."

Aria smirked, wiping the back of her hand across her forehead. "If we can still stand tomorrow, we didn't train hard enough."

Heidi groaned softly in agreement, but Sylas only shook his head. The three of them made their way into the dim corridor beyond the training hall, their footsteps dragging through the quiet. It would take them a while to reach the District above, but each step felt like progress—one more stride toward being ready for whatever awaited beyond these tunnels.

Location: Cavandel, The Inner District

While Aria trained in the caverns below, honing skills that might one day save her, Hogan sat comfortably in Jaco's Tavern, tucked within the winding streets of the Inner District. Here, the hum of trade and quiet desperation never truly ceased—far enough from the guard towers to feel safe, yet close enough for convenience. Since the Warden's last announcement, Hogan had found no shortage of ways to profit. He spent his nights in luxury—pockets full, conscience light.

The low glow-lamps flickered against the polished wood of the bar, while scents drifted through the air—a tapestry of ale, charred meat, and the quiet murmur of patrons trading stories, deals, and half-truths over heavy mugs. Hogan leaned back in his seat, tipping back the last of his drink before setting the cup down with a satisfied sigh. He'd never had it this good.

A fresh plate sat before him—thick cuts of roasted meat, a portion of warm bread, even a wedge of soft cheese. Real cheese. He couldn't remember the last time he'd eaten anything that wasn't rationed, bartered, or stolen. And now, all it took was a name—one name, a whisper in the right ear, and a handful of Grottos slid into his palm like it belonged there.

"You've been spending a lot these days," the barkeep mused, polishing the inside of a glass without looking up. His voice was casual, but there was something behind it—something just sharp enough to cut.

Hogan smirked, reaching for another piece of bread. "What, a man can't enjoy himself every now and then?"

The barkeep set the glass down with a dull thud. "Depends. Some men work themselves raw for half of what you're tossing around—especially someone so young."

Hogan chuckled, shaking his head. "A bit of good fortune, that's all." He leaned forward conspiratorially, lowering his voice just enough to sound believable. "Got into some business with a merchant. Right place, right time."

The barkeep hummed, unimpressed, his fingers working the rim of a chipped glass. "That so?" he rasped.

Hogan grinned. "Pays to know people."

The barkeep met his gaze then, eyes dark and steady. "That it does."

The silence between them stretched, not quite comfortable. Hogan held his smirk, but something in the barkeep's stare made it harder to maintain.

The man wasn't a fool. He wouldn't push—not outright—but he understood. Deep down, he knew exactly where the money was coming from.

Hogan exhaled slowly and leaned back again, breaking the tension first. "Another round," he said, tossing a few Grottos onto the bar. The barkeep took the coins but said nothing, offering only a slow nod before moving to fill the cup.

Hogan drummed his fingers against the tabletop, his gaze drifting across the room. A few tables over, a pair of men threw dice, their laughter carrying the thin edge of exhaustion. One of them shot a glance his way—brief, but long enough to make Hogan wonder if they, too, had noticed how easily he spent his coin.

The weight of the Grottos in his pocket was reassuring, but something else settled in his chest—an unease he didn't care to name. It pressed just enough to make him shift in his seat, lingering at the edges of his thoughts like a shadow he refused to acknowledge. When the drink was set before him, he reached for it immediately, drowning the feeling before it could take shape.

12

Veils of Deception

Location: Cavandel, The Inner District

The District never truly slept. Even in the dead hours, when the air hung thick and unmoving, it still pulsed with quiet life—the distant trickle of water slipping through cracks, the scuttling of unseen vermin, the occasional groan of rocks shifting overhead.

Drazic Grask stood at the mouth of an alleyway, one boot resting on an overturned crate, listening.

Waiting.

He stood motionless, a barely audible breath slipping past his lips. Scarlet rested coiled at his hip, her familiar weight pressing against his palm as he absently traced the worn leather with his fingers. Waiting had always felt like a dull necessity in a world where action yielded results, but he'd learned patience. Sometimes, it was better to let the prey come to you.

His grip on Scarlet tightened. "This better be worth it."

The words were low, muttered more to himself than to the whip curled in his grasp, but there was truth in them. He had entertained too many desperate men in these tunnels, too many whispering cowards looking to trade information for a few Grottos, protection, or a quick way out of their miserable lives. Most were liars. Those who weren't? He had little use for them once their tongues ran dry.

Drazic had given this meeting the same weight he gave the others—none. He hadn't told the Warden, hadn't considered it necessary. If Lhoris had anything of value, Drazic would be the judge of that. If not? Scarlet hadn't had her fun in a while.

He tapped his foot once, clicking his tongue. If that rat didn't show soon, Scarlet might need something else to keep her entertained. The alley ahead remained empty, shadows pooling at its edges, silent but watching.

Then, faintly, a voice rasped from the darkness. "Sorry to keep you waiting."

Drazic didn't react, nor did he answer. He simply watched.

The darkness shifted. Not just an absence of light, but something moving within it. Quiet footsteps, almost imperceptible against the stone, crept toward the low glow of the brazier.

The figure emerged gradually—not all at once, but with careful, slinking movements. The firelight reached first, licking at the edges of his cloak, revealing a hunched posture and darting eyes that never quite settled. His boots scuffed against the damp earth. He moved like a man who had learned the art of slipping away, but not enough to disappear entirely.

Ahead, Drazic waited, half-hidden in the folds of darkness. His scarred face remained impassive, though his fingers twitched once against Scarlet's coiled grip. The low-burning brazier cast shifting shadows across the uneven stone, flickering gold against the rough texture of the walls. The space between them shrank, yet the silence stretched.

The man stopped just outside the reach of the fire. Not too close. Not far enough to seem unsure. A practiced distance.

"You're late, Lhoris," Drazic said evenly.

Lhoris quickly bobbed his head, his lips curling into a greasy smile. "Apologies, Mr. Grask, truly. You know how it is. Slippery business, this sort of thing."

He glanced over his shoulder, voice dropping to a whisper. "Some things are harder to slip away from than others."

Drazic turned, his sharp gaze sweeping over the newcomer, lingering just long enough to measure his worth. "Convenient," he muttered, though the hint of a smirk played at the corner of his mouth. "Thankfully, a man can learn a lot in the silence. Time has a way of sharpening the blade."

Lhoris flinched slightly, but covered it with a quick chuckle. "Wouldn't dream of wasting your precious time, Mr. Grask. Not when my neck's on the line getting this information."

"Get on with it, then," Drazic said flatly, reaching for the small sack at his belt. He tossed it forward, letting the weight of the Grottos land between them. "So, what have you brought me this time?"

Lhoris bent swiftly, snatching up the pouch before it could even settle, palming the coins with ease. "Ah, always a pleasure doing business with you," he mused, weighing the pouch like a man savoring his winnings at a game he hadn't even finished playing.

He shifted quickly, eager to move the conversation along. "Word is, the Dwellers have something valuable in their possession—something that could speed up their little search for a cure."

Drazic's expression didn't change, but his fingers stilled against Scarlet's handle. "Explain."

Lhoris leaned in slightly. "A book. Don't know the details, but from what I hear, it's important. Important enough that they're guarding it closely. Important enough that it might put them ahead of you."

Drazic let the silence stretch. He didn't trust Lhoris—never would—but the man had no reason to fabricate something like this.

"Where?"

Lhoris hesitated a second too long. "Ah, now that's a tricky thing. Wherever they've got it, it's not sitting on some shelf waiting to be found." He rolled the pouch between his fingers. "I hear they move constantly. A few in the Inner District, some in the Outer. No one's foolish enough to plant their feet in one place for too long."

Drazic's jaw tensed. "That's not what I asked."

Lhoris lifted a hand, grinning. "And I'm giving you all I have." His fingers tightened around the sack of coins. "If I knew the exact spot, I'd tell you. No hesitation. But you've been making them skittish. They know you're looking."

Drazic stepped forward, slow and deliberate. "You always seem to know just enough to get paid, but never enough to be useful."

Lhoris licked his lips. "I do what I can, Mr. Grask. You know how it is."

Drazic's grip on Scarlet tightened. "And you're playing both sides."

Lhoris pressed a hand to his chest in mock offense. "Come now, Mr. Grask. What do you take me for?"

Drazic's gaze didn't hesitate. "A man who would sell his own mother for a few coins."

Lhoris' smirk didn't fade, but something flickered behind his eyes. "Good thing she wouldn't bring much in."

Drazic let the silence stretch. A game of patience, a test to see if Lhoris would fill the void with more half-truths.

Lhoris held his tongue.

Finally, Drazic turned, boots scuffing lightly against the stone. "Keep listening," he said, voice cool. "If you hear anything else, I want to know."

Lhoris gave a quick nod. "Of course. You'll be the first to hear it, Mr. Grask."

Drazic didn't respond. He kept walking. Just before disappearing into the darkness, he spoke without looking back. "Next time, bring me something more useful."

He didn't slow, didn't spare a backward glance. There was no need. He knew the type—men like Lhoris, who survived on half-truths and slippery escapes, feeding off the cracks between power, too spineless to pick a side yet too greedy to walk away from the game. Drazic had let plenty of rats scurry underfoot in his time, but sooner or later, they always ran in the wrong direction.

And when that day came, Lhoris would learn that survival wasn't about slipping through the cracks—it was about knowing when the walls were closing in.

He exhaled slowly, fingers flexing against the worn leather of his whip. The Dwellers were shifting and that meant the Warden would be expecting results. If they were guarding something this closely, it wasn't just important—it was dangerous. And if Lhoris knew even a fraction more than he was letting on, Drazic would find out soon enough. Secrets had a way of surfacing and Drazic had never met a man who could keep one forever.

A moment later, two figures joined him. Drazic didn't glance at them. "Sir?" one of the men inquired.

"He knows more than he's saying," Drazic murmured. "Follow him."

Location: Cavandel, Dweller's Base

The Cantina was thick with the scent of sweat, spilled ale and the distant hum of conversation. Aria, Heidi, and Sylas slipped inside, keeping their heads down. Their goal was simple—get a drink and something in their stomach before heading back to their work.

Aria exhaled slowly, letting her thoughts drift for a moment. That morning, she'd left her grandmother in Jace's care, and though she trusted him, a small part of her ached with guilt. Gran had smiled and told her not to fuss, but the worry was impossible to shake. Every day with her felt like borrowed time, fragile in a way Aria could never ignore.

The Dwellers, for all their hardship, seemed certain of who they were and the fight they were waging, but Aria wasn't sure she had that same conviction. She and her friends had been swept into their world, given work and a cause that still felt like an unfinished puzzle, its edges unclear. But did that make them Dwellers now? Did sharing their food, their home, their burdens mean they truly belonged?

She had tried to convince herself that purpose would come with time, that she'd wake one day and feel it settle in her bones. But every time she looked around, she still felt like an outsider at the edge of things, waiting for someone to tell her where she belonged.

She glanced at Heidi and Sylas, searching their faces for any hint that they felt it too—the unspoken question of whether they truly belonged or were simply playing a part.

"Being a hero," Sylas sighed, stretching his sore arms, "is far less glamorous than the stories make it out to be. No songs, no glory—just endless hard labor and aching muscles." He rolled his shoulders, wincing dramatically. "I swear my arms are going to fall off."

Heidi smirked, taking a slow sip of her drink. "Poor Sylas, doomed to a life of manual labor. Maybe if you complain enough, they'll promote you to something more heroic—like sweeping the floors."

Sylas shot her a wounded look. "Mock all you want, but I'm suffering here."

Aria pulled herself from her thoughts and smirked. "What did they have you doing today?"

"Stacking crates," he huffed. "Heavy ones. Because obviously, I look like a man built for lifting ridiculous amounts of weight."

Heidi snorted. "At least you're doing something useful. I spent the day with Anna—stuck on inventory. It's like they think I'm incapable of actual work. Everyone treats me like a child, and if I hear 'don't touch that' one more time, I'll scream."

"Like a child?" Sylas said dryly.

Heidi didn't rise to the bait; she just exhaled and muttered, "You're not helping."

Aria smiled at her. "I'm sure they'll recognize your brilliance soon enough."

"I hope so." Heidi lifted one shoulder in a half-shrug. "Still, at least they're paying us—and we don't have to break our backs in the mines for a while. That alone makes this better than what we had before."

Aria nodded. Not having to mine meant they had more time to focus on other things—more important things. Like figuring out how to navigate the new world they'd found themselves in.

The exhaustion clung to their bones and even the simple act of sitting down felt like a relief. The first sip of the cool, bitter drink sent a fleeting relief through her, dulling the edge of exhaustion. Heidi sighed in satisfaction and even Sylas leaned back in his chair, momentarily content.

But the moment didn't last.

A burly man, swaying under the weight of too many drinks, wandered close, his eyes clouded but intent. He lingered just long enough to make his presence known before dropping his mug onto their table with a sloppy thud, ale spilling over the rim.

His bleary eyes swept over them, narrowed with something between curiosity and distrust. "New faces around here," he said. "Don't see that too often." He let out a slow chuckle, the sound rough and uneven. "And never so young," he added, swaying as he tried to keep his balance. "When I was your age, I was digging tunnels, not lounging with a fancy drink in my hand."

Aria tensed.

Heidi's fingers curled around the edge of the table, but she said nothing. Sylas shifted uncomfortably, his usual bravado dimming as he eyed the man. "Just having a drink," he said, keeping his tone light but measured.

The man's expression darkened instantly. He slammed his mug down, the impact sending ripples through the spilled ale. "Wasn't talking to you, boy." His words cut through the low murmur of the cantina. "Know your place."

The man sniffed, glancing between them. "Strange times, strange company. Ain't safe to trust just anyone these days." He lifted a shaky hand and took a lazy sip from his mug before adding, "Some folks are saying there are eyes where there shouldn't be."

As the drunk's voice cut through the Cantina, the atmosphere shifted. A few heads turned—some wary, others indifferent. Conversations dulled to hushed murmurs, as if the entire room teetered on the edge of a decision: step in, or pretend nothing was happening.

A group of older miners at a nearby table exchanged murmurs, one of them shaking his head before looking away. Others simply nursed their drinks, pretending not to notice, though they listened all the same.

Aria steadied her breath and pushed back her chair, keeping her movements slow and deliberate. "I think it's time we leave," she said, her gaze fixed on her friends. "We may have overstayed our welcome."

As she began to rise, the man lurched forward, planting a broad hand on the table hard enough to rattle the mugs, his eyes locking onto her with a dangerous glint. "I'm not done talking to you, girl." His tone was low, thick with something more than just ale. "You leave when I say so, little spy."

Heidi tensed, her fingers twitching at her side, but neither she nor Aria spoke. Sylas straightened, jaw tight, hands curled into fists. "Hey, we don't want any trouble—" His voice was steady, though Aria could hear the tension beneath it.

The drunk's eyes swept toward Sylas as he took an unsteady step closer, sizing him up with slow, deliberate scrutiny. A smirk curled at the edge of his lips. "Brave little thing, ain't you? Wonder if you've got the spine to back it up."

Before the situation could spiral further, a gruff old voice cut through the tension.

The miner rose from his seat, his movements slow but firm. Aria's gaze shifted toward him, recognition settling in. It was Guss—the old miner they'd met at the Lift. Back then he'd only offered a brief introduction, but now, seeing the way the other Dwellers straightened at his presence, she understood just how much respect he commanded.

Guss stepped closer, his steady gaze pinning the drunk in place. "Go sleep off your drink, Bram," he said, his tone calm but firm—like a man used to settling disputes before they got out of hand. "And quit stirrin' up trouble."

Bram wavered, his earlier bravado faltering as Guss held his ground. The room seemed to tighten around them, the tension rising. Every gaze stayed fixed on the confrontation, waiting to see if Bram would make a move.

After a tense moment, Bram muttered something under his breath and took a stumbling step back, rubbing his face as if trying to shake off the haze.

Aria exchanged glances with Heidi and Sylas before nodding in gratitude. "Thank you," she said. "Didn't think we'd run into you again."

"Don't worry," he said, waving a hand dismissively. "Bram's bark's worse than his bite—'specially when he's drownin' in ale."

He let his gaze settle on them one last time before adding, "Be careful, though. Trouble's been brewin' and it don't take much to find yourself caught in the middle of it."

***

The ambiance of the lab was thick with the scent of medicine, metal, and something Aria couldn't quite place—like the dampness of a cave threaded with a sharp, mineral tang. The room wasn't just a workspace; it was now a sick ward. Cots lined the back wall, occupied by figures wrapped in blankets, their bodies thin and shivering, their skin marked with faint, glimmering lines of contamination. The signs of Shatterblight were unmistakable.

Aria hesitated at the threshold. She had seen wounds, had even treated bruises and broken skin, but this was something else. This was slow, relentless. The kind of suffering that didn't come from an injury but from the body betraying itself. A different kind of war.

Anna barely looked up from the patient she was tending to, pressing a damp cloth to the young man's forehead. His breath came in shallow, wheezing rasps. The fever had him—another one slipping past the threshold of no return.

Aria stepped forward, drawn toward a frail woman curled on one of the cots. Her breath hitched as she knelt beside her, fingers brushing the woman's hand. The skin was cold, softer than Aria expected. At the touch, the woman stirred, her eyes fluttering open. A murky, unfocused gaze met Aria's—and for a moment, something like recognition passed across her face.

"You came back," the woman murmured, her voice barely a whisper.

Aria swallowed hard. "I—I think you have me confused with someone else."

The woman blinked slowly, her lips parting as if to speak, but her breathing soon grew labored and she drifted back into uneasy sleep. Aria didn't let go of her hand right away.

Behind her, Heidi shifted uncomfortably, gripping the back of a chair. "I don't know how Anna does this every day," she said, her voice quieter than usual. "We can't let this happen to more people. We have to do something."

Anna finally looked up, exhaustion deep in her eyes. "We're trying." Her voice was tight, not unkind, but frayed at the edges. She stood, rubbing a hand over her face before gesturing toward the cluttered table. "Come here. Both of you."

Aria and Heidi stepped over, glancing at the mess of vials, handwritten notes, and partially filled syringes.

"I've tested six different formulas in the last two days," Anna said, tapping a vial filled with an amber-colored liquid. "This one slowed the spread in two patients, but in another..." She exhaled sharply. "It shut down her nervous system entirely."

Aria felt a chill that had nothing to do with the lab's cold air. "So it's a gamble?"

Anna's jaw tightened. "It's always a gamble." She picked up another vial, rolling it between her fingers. "People talk about fighting the Warden, about taking back what's ours, but how are we supposed to do that when we can't even keep our own people alive?"

Silence settled between them, heavy and suffocating.

Aria licked her lips, glancing back at the cots. "How many have we lost?"

Anna didn't answer right away. Instead, she stared at the table, at the careful notes written in her precise script, at the names scratched out in the margins.

"Too many."

The words were quiet, but they landed like a hammer.

Heidi exhaled sharply, arms crossing over her chest. "And the mission? Have we heard anything yet?"

Anna placed the vial down carefully, as if afraid it might shatter in her grip. "No—but we're counting on them. Without that sample, we can't move to the next phase of testing."

Aria didn't like the implication. "So we're still waiting."

Anna nodded. "If they don't bring it back, there is no next step." She trailed off, her gaze drifting to the nearest cot, the unspoken fear settling between them.

A sharp creak interrupted them as the door swung open. The shift in the air was immediate—subtle, but undeniable. The presence of someone who didn't belong in a place like this.

Kegan leaned against the doorway, arms crossed, his smirk barely there but present enough to make the room feel colder. His gaze swept over the patients, the vials, the notes. Aria could see the calculations turning in his mind, assessing, measuring.

"Busy as ever, I see," he murmured.

Anna didn't look up. "Are you here to help, Kegan?"

He chuckled, stepping further inside. "Help? No. I'd be a terrible nurse."

His eyes shifted to Aria, lingering just a second too long. "Just making sure everything's in order."

Heidi tensed beside her, shoulders rigid. She didn't dare meet his gaze.

Anna's reply cut sharp through the room. "Then you've seen enough."

A silence followed, brief but edged. Then Kegan inclined his head, conceding a point none of them had spoken aloud. "Fair enough."

He turned and strolled back toward the door. Before leaving, he glanced over his shoulder. "Hope our little science project pays off," he said. "Would hate to see all this effort go to waste."

Then he was gone, the door clicking shut behind him.

Aria let out a slow breath, her pulse thrumming at the base of her throat. Heidi shook her head, muttering, "I hate that guy."

Anna, however, was already moving, her focus snapping back to the vials and notes. "Forget him. We don't have time to waste. He thinks far more of himself than the rest of us do."

Aria turned back to her patient—the frail woman she had spoken to just minutes ago.

The weight of it settled in her chest, heavier than before. She had come to these people for help, but even they were drowning. And what good was any of it if her grandmother—and everyone else—simply ran out of time?

***

The trio stood outside the heavy wooden door of the training hall, shifting uneasily. Muffled sounds of sparring echoed from within—grunts of exertion, the sharp clap of wood striking flesh, the occasional barked order.

Heidi groaned, rubbing a tender spot on her shoulder. "I'm not a fighter. I'm a thinker. Why do I need to get beaten to a pulp to prove I can be useful? I thought we were just learning the basics. Survival, not... whatever this is."

"Yeah," Sylas muttered, shrugging in defeat. "We're learning the basics all right—basic pain, basic exhaustion, and basically regretting every decision that led us here."

Heidi let out a short laugh, trading a knowing glance with him.

Aria flexed her fingers, managing a faint smile. "At least we're getting better," she offered.

"Tell that to my ribs," Sylas grumbled. "I'm starting to think Pike enjoys watching us suffer."

Before anyone could answer, the door swung open with a low creak. Pike filled the frame, arms crossed, his sharp gaze sweeping over them. He lifted a brow.

"You're late."

Sylas sighed. "And the streak continues."

Pike stepped back and held the door open. "Move."

They slipped past him, his gaze tracking each of them in turn.

Inside, the training hall was lit in clear, steady light, glow-lamps chasing most of the shadows into the corners. Two Dwellers practiced their drills—the sharp crack of wood on wood ringing through the room.

Aria felt their eyes on her. The scrutiny was no longer dismissive, but it wasn't admiration either. Just days ago, those looks had been heavy with doubt. Now, something had shifted. Curiosity, maybe. Or caution.

They still had a long way to go, but at least they weren't complete outsiders anymore.

Pike had been pushing them harder lately, but for the first time, they weren't just struggling to keep up—they were meeting his demands.

Aria squared her shoulders, gripping her wooden training blade. Pike circled her, assessing. Then he lunged. She reacted, parrying his strike, side-stepping—not smoothly, but fast enough. Her movements were sharper now, though still rough around the edges. But this time, when he pressed, she didn't freeze.

Pike grunted in approval. His attacks came faster, forcing her to adjust, testing her reflexes. When he finally knocked the blade from her grip, she stumbled. But instead of hesitating, she lunged to recover it, breathless but determined.

"Better," Pike admitted as she straightened with the blade in hand. "But it still needs work."

Aria nodded, her fingers tightening around the hilt. A week ago, she would have felt frustrated. Defeated. Now, all she felt was resolve.

On the other side of the hall, Heidi and Sylas sparred. Heidi moved with new control, her strikes no longer hesitant or reckless. She wasn't just reacting—she was anticipating. Sylas, despite his endless complaints, no longer relied on instinct alone. He adjusted, adapted, fighting smarter now, using agility to make up for what he lacked in raw strength.

After another round of drills, Pike called them over. He stepped back, crossing his arms as they gathered—sweat-soaked, winded, barely holding their stances.

"You're improving," he said, looking them over. "But don't mistake progress for readiness. The moment you think you're prepared is the moment you begin to fall behind."

Sylas wiped sweat from his forehead. "Motivating as ever."

Pike leveled his gaze at him. "You want encouragement? Earn it."

The trio exchanged tired glances—exhausted, aching, but far from quitting.

"Now," Pike said, tossing a wooden dagger at Heidi. "Time for your favorite drill."

Sylas groaned. "We haven't even touched you once."

"Because we keep charging in like idiots," Heidi muttered. "That's why."

She gestured to Aria, then Sylas. "There are three of us and only one of him. We've got the numbers."

Aria shifted her grip, realization settling in. "So let's use it to our advantage."

"Exactly," Heidi said, narrowing her eyes. "We surround him. At best, he'll only see two of us at a time. If he turns, we keep moving. Whoever's behind him will always have the advantage."

Aria and Sylas exchanged glances, then nodded.

"Sylas, take the back," Aria said. "Make sure he doesn't get a clean escape."

They moved slowly at first, circling Pike. He remained still, arms loose at his sides, watching them. Waiting. The trio tightened their formation, keeping him boxed in, weapons raised. But none of them struck.

Pike chuckled. "What's the plan here? Circle me until I drop from boredom?" He shifted his stance with a smirk. "Let me know when the fight starts, yeah? I've got stew waiting."

"Stay focused," Aria warned. "Don't fall for his taunts."

This time, they didn't charge in blindly. Heidi feinted forward, shifting her stance, trying to draw him off balance. Sylas darted to the side, swinging his blade in a wide arc—a distraction.

For a split second, Pike's focus flickered toward Sylas.

It was all Aria needed. She lunged, but Pike twisted at the last second.

Her wooden blade sliced through air but found nothing.

She retreated quickly, heart pounding, her blade snapping back into guard. The opening she'd reached for still shimmered in her mind. She had been so close. Closer than ever before.

Silence hung between them as the trio closed in again.

Pike exhaled slowly, studying them as if annoyed to find himself a little impressed. Then his smirk deepened. "Close," he acknowledged, his eyes narrowing. "But not close enough."

And just like that, he moved again.

Aria barely had time to react. Heidi ducked. Sylas pivoted to cover her side, while Aria scrambled to block. They weren't in sync—not yet—but they weren't flailing either.

Pike struck hard and fast, exploiting every gap in their defenses. When Heidi left an opening, he swept her legs out from under her. Sylas overextended, and Pike knocked his weapon from his hands. Aria miscalculated a step and found herself cornered.

Seconds later, the match was over.

They lay sprawled on the padded dirt floor, panting.

Pike shook his head. "A fighter who can't see beyond what's in front of him has already lost the battle."

He stepped back, looking them over before nodding. "You're starting to understand. That's a step forward."

Heidi blinked. "What? But we didn't even touch you."

Pike smiled. "The real test wasn't to land a blow." His gaze swept between them. "But to see how long it would take you to start working as a team."

Aria sat on the packed dirt floor, her practice blade resting against her knee. Her breath had steadied, though her muscles still trembled. She turned her hands over, studying the raw patches blooming along her palms.

Pike's words echoed through her mind. *The moment you think you're ready is the moment you begin to fall behind.*

She had moved faster today. She had fought smarter. But it still wasn't enough.

She flexed her fingers as a shadow fell over her.

It was Pike.

"You're improving," he said, his gaze passing over her posture, her hands, the stubborn set of her jaw. "Don't be too hard on yourself."

He glanced toward Heidi and Sylas before looking back at her. "It takes time."

Aria looked up, caught off guard by something like sincerity. She opened her mouth—just a breath away from thanking him.

But Pike's expression snapped back into steel.

"On your feet," he said. "Again."

Location: Cavandel, The Inner District

The guard tower had been mostly rebuilt, but Drazic could still see the scars. It loomed over the bustling market below, one of many such towers scattered through the Inner District, standing like watchful sentinels above the crowd.

The stone was rough in places, the texture wrong where new blocks met old. Fresh mortar clung to the seams, betraying the lines where the Dwellers' explosives had blown the original masonry apart. The repairs looked solid enough, neat even, but Drazic had learned the hard way that solid didn't always mean impenetrable.

His fingers drifted to his side, brushing the coiled leather of Scarlet. "Still feels weak," he muttered. "Like it's waiting to come down again."

The whip, as always, agreed.

Drazic turned as footsteps approached.

A cold wind swept in with his men, carrying the bite of coal smoke from the city below. The older one stepped through first, his usual smirk dulled tonight. His younger partner followed a step behind, gaze flicking toward the unfinished braces still propping up part of the eastern wall.

Drazic said nothing, letting the cold silence work for him—a tool he'd long ago learned to wield.

"We followed Lhoris," the older guard said. "He took the Lift down to the Mining Camp. Went into one of the inns."

Drazic studied them. Still silent.

"We split up," the younger guard added. "I stayed outside." He nodded toward his partner. "He went in."

The older man gave a brief tilt of his head. "He drank like a man with problems to forget. Spent every coin you gave him. Didn't speak to anyone."

Unusual. A silent Lhoris was like a miner without a pickaxe—something wasn't right.

"And after that?" Drazic asked.

"He finished his last drink, got up, and went toward the back rooms. Didn't come out again."

Drazic's grip tightened on Scarlet's handle. "You didn't follow?" The question carried just enough weight to settle in their bones.

"Didn't want to spook him," the older man said. "Figured he was heading to the latrine."

Drazic's gaze shifted to the younger guard, then back to the older. "And?"

"That's the problem," the man replied. "He just disappeared. Never saw him leave. Not through the front, or the back."

"Could've passed out," the younger guard offered quickly. "Maybe rented a room and—"

"Doubt it," the older guard cut in. "Sat close enough to hear him order drinks. Didn't ask for a room."

"Did you see him get a key?" Drazic asked.

"No," the older man replied. "Didn't pay for one either."

Drazic shifted his gaze. His thumb traced along Scarlet's handle, letting the worn texture settle him. "Strange place for a man to disappear," he said finally.

The two guards exchanged a glance but stayed silent.

Drazic straightened, the tower suddenly feeling too narrow. "Keep your eyes on that inn. I don't care how long. Something's not adding up, and I want to know why."

"Yes, sir." They nodded and hurried off, their boots echoing down the spiral stairs.

Alone again, Drazic moved toward the window. Through the narrow slot, the District stretched outward, all glow-lights and shadow.

The Dwellers had been slipping past him for far too long—always one step ahead, always slipping through cracks. But cracks always led somewhere. And he meant to follow them straight to the source.

13

The Silent Hawk's Tale

Location: Cavandel, The Outer District

The early morning air was crisp, the kind of stillness that made every sound sharper, every movement more noticeable. Aria rubbed the sleep from her eyes as she crouched beside the old wooden table where Jace sat, idly turning a coin between his fingers. The soft radiance of the lantern filled the small room, glinting off the scattered lockpicks and metal locks strewn across the table.

"You're getting faster," Jace murmured, slipping the coin into his pocket. "But you're still giving your intentions away. That hesitation will get you caught."

Aria sighed, leaning against the table. "You say that every morning."

Jace smirked. "And every morning, you prove me right."

They had been training like this before most of the District stirred—before Cavandel awakened and duties pulled them in different directions. Jace had insisted that if Aria was going to get involved with the Dwellers, she needed to know how to get out of trouble without drawing a blade.

"Alright, let's see if you're learning," Jace said, leaning back in his chair. He reached into his vest and held up a small brass key. "I'll pocket this, and you try to get it from me."

Aria nodded, watching as he slid the key into his inner vest pocket. He leaned forward, elbows on the table, eyes glinting. "Go."

She reached for it too quickly—too obviously. Jace barely had to shift before he swatted her hand away.

"Pathetic. That was embarrassing for both of us."

Scowling, she tried again, pushing herself to her feet with deliberate slowness. She took a measured breath and circled the table, keeping her steps light. Jace watched her closely, the faintest smile playing at his lips.

She placed a steadying hand on his shoulder, feigning casual balance. "You've been like a father to me, Jace," she said, her voice smooth and deliberate. "And I just wanted to say... thanks for everything."

Jace's smirk deepened. He nodded, humoring her. "Just doing my part."

She lingered beside him, her fingers drifting along the worn grain of the chair's backrest. "I never thought I'd learn anything like this," she admitted.

Jace tilted his head. "It's not that different from anything else you've already learned. Just another way to survive."

Aria huffed a small laugh and shifted her weight, stepping back toward her seat. She lowered herself into it, a puzzled look crossing her face.

"You tricked me," she said flatly, her brows furrowing in disbelief. The pocket where she'd seen him drop the key was empty.

Jace smirked. "Getting better," he murmured. "Not great, but better."

Aria tried not to look too pleased, but Jace leaned back, that familiar smirk returning. "I wonder how much it would go for?" he mused.

Aria narrowed her eyes. "How much would *what* go for?"

Jace lifted his hand, the delicate chain of her necklace dangling between his fingers.

Her breath caught. Her hand flew to her neck, shock and admiration widening her eyes.

"You—"

Jace twirled the necklace once before tossing it back to her. "Misdirection isn't just about hands—it's about attention. People won't notice what you take if their focus is somewhere else. Control where their eyes go, make them believe one thing while you do another. That's the goal."

Before Aria could respond, a faint, uneven shuffling drifted in from the other room. Her stomach tightened at the familiar rhythm of her grandmother's steps—deliberate, careful, slower than before. Jace glanced toward the doorway but said nothing as the old woman emerged, her movements stiff and labored.

"Morning," Aria greeted quickly, forcing lightness into her tone. "Breakfast is ready."

Her grandmother offered a tired smile. "Good. I was starting to think you'd forgotten to feed an old woman."

Jace smirked. "Not much chance of that."

They settled at the table, the usual rhythm of their morning routine returning, though something in the air felt different. Their conversation drifted—Jace teasing Aria about her technique, her grandmother offering quiet remarks about the food, and the kettle rattling softly behind them like it always did. It was familiar, comforting. But beneath it all, Aria could feel the weight of what wasn't being said.

After a long moment, her grandmother finally glanced at her. "And your new friends? How's it going with them?"

Aria set her spoon down, considering. "We're getting closer," she said slowly.

She hesitated, then added, "Anna needs all the help she can get. So far, the samples she's tested... they seem to help in a few cases, but more often than not, they fail. The results are inconsistent at best."

Jace lifted a brow. "Sounds like a bad gamble."

Aria exhaled. "Sometimes it seems to stabilize, but other times—" She shook her head. "It makes it worse. Much worse."

She tapped her fingers lightly against the side of her bowl. "That's why Anna needs the Glowcaps. Without it, she's hitting a wall. It's the key to stabilizing the treatment, to making it safe." Her voice was quieter now, but firm. "A hunting party was sent out to retrieve it. Once they return, we can finally do what needs to be done."

Her grandmother's expression darkened slightly. "As long as you don't get involved with those creatures," she warned. "Screechers are no joke. You've heard the stories."

Jace arched a brow. "Sounds like someone's speaking from experience."

Her grandmother exhaled sharply. "I've seen what they can do, and so have you, Jace. My advice—avoid them at all costs."

"That's the plan," Aria said softly.

Her grandmother started to reply, but a sudden fit of coughing wracked her body, cutting her off.

Aria was out of her chair before she even realized she'd moved, steadying her with a hand against her back. The moment she touched her, she felt it—the unnatural heat radiating from beneath the fabric, the telltale shimmer creeping further up her neck.

Her breath hitched. "Gran...?" she whispered, her voice barely a breath.

Her grandmother inhaled carefully, composing herself, but said nothing.

Aria's voice barely left her throat, caught somewhere between a whisper and a breath. The moment stretched, fragile and unbearable. Her grandmother didn't answer right away—just exhaled slowly, as if even breathing had become an effort.

The air between them thickened, heavy with something unsaid. Aria's fingers hovered just above her grandmother's arm, afraid to touch her again, afraid to confirm what she already knew.

She didn't have to.

The heat pulsed beneath her grandmother's skin, unnatural and wrong, even through the layers of fabric. And there—creeping past the collar of her tunic, faint but unmistakable—the shimmer of Shatterblight, a sickly iridescence that seemed to flicker with every unsteady breath.

No.

Aria's stomach twisted.

"Gran, why didn't you tell me?" The words tumbled out—too soft, barely audible over the uneven rise and fall of her grandmother's breath.

Still, there was no answer. Not at first. Just the slow, deliberate way her grandmother reached for the edge of the table, steadying herself as if the simple act of sitting upright required more strength than she had left.

Jace hadn't spoken, but Aria could feel him watching. The usual amusement was wiped from his face, replaced by something quieter, unreadable.

He knew.

He had probably known long before Aria had even noticed—seen the subtle shifts, the extra pauses in her grandmother's steps, the way she found excuses to sit more often, as if rest were something she needed to ration.

And yet, no one had said a word.

"Gran," Aria tried again, this time barely above a whisper.

Her grandmother sighed, shaking her head as if to brush away the concern, though the movement was weak, almost hollow.

"What would be the point?" she finally said, her voice rasping with exhaustion. "You have enough to worry about."

Aria's hands curled into fists.

That wasn't the point. It wasn't the point at all.

She wanted to argue, to insist, to ask why she hadn't been told—why she hadn't seen it sooner—but what good would that do? What would it change?

Nothing.

No one had to say it, but they had all hoped the illness would spread somewhere else—to a hand, a leg, anywhere less vital. Somewhere that wasn't *this*.

Aria swallowed hard, willing herself not to cry. Not yet.

"How long?" she asked, her voice unsteady.

Her grandmother didn't need to answer, her silence spoke loud enough. Before Aria could continue, a voice called from outside.

"Aria! You coming?"

Sylas.

She froze, her hands curling tightly against the table.

Jace shifted beside her, the quiet scrape of his chair breaking the silence. He didn't say anything—didn't need to. She could feel the weight of his gaze, sharp as ever, but softer somehow.

Her grandmother exhaled slowly. "Go on, Aria. You shouldn't be late."

Aria shook her head. "I can't leave you like this. Not today."

Her grandmother reached across the table, covering Aria's hand with her own. Her grip was warm—too warm—but steady.

"Fire only helps if you use it in the right place, child. Staying here won't stop this. If you want to help, you need to be where the cure is."

Aria's breath caught in her throat. "Then I'll take you to Anna."

Her grandmother's expression softened—sad, knowing. She squeezed Aria's hand gently.

"You said it yourself—the cure isn't certain, and it could make things worse." She coughed, her voice quiet but firm. "And I'm too old to make that journey for a gamble that might do me more harm than good."

"But—"

"No, Aria." Her grandmother shook her head, her grip tightening just slightly. "I've made my peace. Now you need to focus on what you *can* change."

Jace, silent until now, finally spoke. His voice wasn't teasing, wasn't distant. Just steady. "She's right."

Aria opened her mouth in protest, but nothing came.

Only tears.

The room held still for a long moment, the weight of unspoken things pressing down on all of them.

Eventually, Jace exhaled, slow and even. "Come on, Aria." His voice was kind, but firm. "I'll see to her."

Aria hesitated, gripping the worn edge of the table as if anchoring herself to something solid, something certain. If she let go—if she stood up—it would mean accepting something she wasn't ready to face.

Her fingers loosened their grip, slowly, unwillingly.

Through the tears, she forced herself to rise, each movement feeling like a quiet betrayal. Pushing the chair back. Steadying herself. Taking a step away from the table. It all felt too real, too soon.

The weight in her chest tightened as she reached the door. She hesitated, fingers brushing the frame, every part of her screaming to stay—to sit back down, to pretend she still had time.

She inhaled sharply, straightened her shoulders, and stepped outside.

No one spoke at first.

Sylas stood motionless, rubbing the back of his neck, his usual easy confidence nowhere to be found. His gaze flickered toward the ground, then to the house behind her, then away again. If he had a joke to fill the silence, he kept it to himself.

Heidi shifted, unfolding her arms. Her expression was unreadable at first, then softened. "Is... she alright?" she asked quietly.

Aria's chest tightened. She managed a small nod, though it barely felt like the truth.

Heidi let out a slow breath. "It'll be okay, Aria."

A promise Aria wanted to believe.

She nodded again, the motion thin and automatic, more habit than conviction.

Sylas exhaled softly, his voice barely above a murmur. "Come on."

It wasn't rushed, it wasn't impatient. Just a reminder.

Aria swallowed hard and took a step forward, then another. Each movement stretched the space between her and the fragile warmth of home, pulling her farther from where she still wanted to be.

Her grandmother's presence lingered just behind the door. If she turned around now, she could still go back. Still sit with her. Still steal another moment.

But moments weren't enough.

She kept walking, even as something inside her begged her to stop. *There was still time.*

There had to be.

Location: Cavandel, Dweller's Base

"Easy now," a healer murmured from somewhere deeper in the infirmary. "Deep breaths."

Aria moved toward the voice, the glow-lamps revealing rows of cots and the pale, restless figures lying beneath thin blankets. A coughing fit broke out near the far wall, sharp enough to turn every head.

She wrung out a cloth in warm water, watching ripples distort her reflection before placing it gently over a fevered brow. The man beneath it stirred but didn't wake. Around her, murmured voices wove through the steady rhythm of footsteps, the rustle of fabric, the occasional clink of glass.

Across the room, two assistants hurried past, their whispered exchange folding into the low hum of activity. A woman carried a tray of fresh bandages to one of the far cots, while another carefully measured a dose of tonic, the amber liquid catching the glow-lamp's warm light.

The space vibrated with movement—figures weaving between stations, hands working fast but precise. Nearby, someone muttered a count of supplies under their breath while another offered quick instructions over the quiet din.

Her fingers lingered in the basin, warmth leeching away as her mind circled back to Gran.

Time with her was slipping like sand through Aria's fingers—impossible to hold, impossible to reclaim. How much longer did they have? How many more mornings, more quiet conversations?

She exhaled slowly, forcing her focus back to the task at hand. Waiting was its own kind of agony. The cure was close, but saving Gran still felt hopelessly out of reach. And the entire infirmary felt caught in the same breath—everyone waiting for the hunting party, the only hope they had left.

Across from her, Heidi folded strips of gauze, her fingers quick but not careless. Sylas sorted finished poultices into neat stacks, his usual restlessness replaced by a focus that bordered on quiet tension.

At the far table, Anna worked without pause, her hands moving from vial to parchment to pestle with the practiced efficiency of someone too busy to acknowledge exhaustion. Around her, assistants moved in an unspoken rhythm—one grinding fresh herbs, another transferring liquid to delicate glass vials, while flipping through a worn medical ledger.

Anna reached for a pinch of crushed violet powder, hesitated, then set it aside with a frown. A spoon scraped against ceramic. A chair leg scuffed against stone. Then—nothing.

The silence thickened, pressing in from all sides. Every movement seemed to slow, as if caught in the pull of waiting.

Then, at last—footsteps. Soft but deliberate.

Every gaze snapped toward the entrance as Sebastian stepped inside. Hope flickered, thin as a thread. Anna's hand hovered over her work, caught between motion and hesitation. She did not look up, but when she spoke, her voice was measured, almost careful.

"Any word?"

Sebastian exhaled, his gaze sweeping the room—assessing, hesitating, before landing on Anna. He shook his head, slow and deliberate, the weight of his words heavy before they even left his lips.

"Prepare the cots," he murmured. "They're bringing in the wounded."

For a moment, no one moved. The words settled over them, sinking deep, heavier than the air itself. Then, like a taut wire snapping, the room erupted into action.

Anna straightened, pushing aside the vial she had been holding. "Clear the back rows," she ordered, already stepping away from the table. "We need space for the worst of them."

Heidi moved first, sweeping past Aria to strip the nearest cot of its blankets. Sylas followed, dragging a crate of supplies closer to the center of the room. The shift was immediate—tension transmuted into movement, urgency sharpening every step.

Aria forced herself into motion. She stacked fresh linens, pressed bandages into waiting arms, but her mind snagged on the unspoken—the weight beneath Sebastian's words. The mission had gone wrong and the cost had been steep.

The first sounds reached them—a low murmur, the uneven scrape of boots against stone. Then came voices, sharp with urgency, overlapping, too many at once. The entrance darkened as figures appeared, moving toward them.

A stretcher passed through the doorway, carried by two Dwellers whose faces were drawn with exhaustion. The man they bore was barely conscious, his breathing shallow, his tunic slick with dark patches that clung to his ribs. A faint groan escaped him as they eased him onto a cot.

Anna was already there, assessing, issuing clipped instructions. Heidi pressed a cloth to his side, her hands steady as she worked with focused determination. Sylas moved to the next arrival—a woman cradling her arm protectively, her expression tight with agony.

Aria stood frozen for half a breath, then forced herself forward. She grabbed a roll of bandages, hands moving on instinct even as her mind struggled to process the wreckage before her.

Another stretcher passed. Another familiar face. The weight of it settled in her chest, tightening like a fist.

"Aria!" Anna's voice snapped her back. "Over here. Now."

She moved, but the sight of the next arrival rooted her in place. A choked murmur rose from the cot, barely audible beneath the shuffle of movement. "There were too many," the voice rasped. "We never stood a chance."

The words threaded through the infirmary, each one heavier than the last. Aria's hands clenched around the bandages in her grip. She glanced at Sebastian, and saw the grim set of his jaw.

He already knew.

Anna knelt beside the first survivor, pressing two fingers lightly to his pulse. His breathing was unsteady, his skin clammy beneath the flickering glow-lamps. She hesitated, as if a question had formed on her lips, but she didn't ask it—not yet.

The man swallowed hard, blinking slowly. His lips parted as if to say something, but then he only exhaled, his gaze slipping toward the ceiling. Whatever answer he might have given was lost to exhaustion.

A silence settled, colder than before.

Then, from the tunnels beyond, came the echo of pounding footsteps. Fast. Uneven. A voice cut through the murmurs in the infirmary, rough with something deeper than anger.

"Where is he? Where's Calder?"

The entrance darkened as a broad-shouldered man stormed in, breath ragged, his clothes still dusted with the grit of the tunnels. Urgent, teetering on reckless—Aria recognized him at once. Bram. The drunk from the Cantina. The man who had nearly started a fight with them.

But now, there was no slurred speech, no unsteady swagger—only raw desperation as his eyes swept the room and landed on the figure sprawled across the cot.

"Calder!"

He barreled forward before anyone could stop him, his shoulder catching Aria hard enough to send her stumbling back. He dropped to his knees beside the cot, gripping Calder's limp arm, his breath ragged. "Cal? Come on, look at me."

"You're not helping," Sebastian said, his voice sharp and steady. "Step back." He didn't wait for Bram to argue. "Let them work, or you'll only make it worse." His tone left no room for debate. "If you want to help him, stay out of the way."

Bram's chest rose and fell like a man barely keeping himself from breaking something. His hands curled into fists, but he didn't argue. He didn't move either.

Aria steadied herself, pushing aside the sting of the shove and without hesitation, moved back toward the cot.

"We need to keep the pressure on," she said, her voice firm, even. She knelt, pressing a fresh cloth to Calder's side, her hands steady despite the tightness in her throat.

Bram watched, his fingers flexing once against Calder's arm before falling still. His gaze drifted to Aria, lingering just a moment. Then his jaw tightened, and he stepped back, the fight draining out of him. His shoulders sagged, tension unspooling into weary acceptance.

Aria's throat tightened. Somewhere beyond the infirmary, the sound of more footsteps echoed through the corridors, bringing the rest of the wounded—and, perhaps, the full truth of what had happened.

Another figure followed, half-walking, half-dragged, his boots catching on uneven patches, scraping with a dull, hollow sound. His left leg buckled, forcing the man beside him to bear more of his weight.

The last survivor.

A murmur rippled through the infirmary, the kind that didn't form into words, just the collective sigh of exhaustion and grief.

No one asked if more were coming. No one called out for another name. There would be no more.

Bram exhaled, a quiet, shuddering sound. His knuckles were white where his fists tightened at his sides. His gaze moved from Calder to the others being settled into cots. The fight was over, but no victory had come with it.

Sweat and the acrid scent of iron mingled with the sharp, bitter aroma of crushed herbs.

Somewhere nearby, a basin clattered as it was hastily moved, the sound stark against the hush that had fallen. Footsteps shuffled, measured but hurried, as whispered conversations bled into one another.

None of it felt real.

Aria held her hand firmly against Calder's side, feeling the weak rhythm of his breath beneath her fingertips. She could sense the shift in the air—something that had been fraying for days was now unraveling, slipping beyond their grasp.

She didn't look up at Bram, but she felt his eyes on her. He wasn't pressing her for answers or demanding reassurance. He was just watching. Waiting.

At the far end of the infirmary, Sebastian stood with his arms crossed, his shoulders rigid. He hadn't moved since the first wounded arrived. He didn't have to. The weight of the failure settled on him, unseen but unmistakable. His jaw tightened, though his expression remained still.

A survivor stirred, his breath catching in a ragged rasp that barely made it past his swollen lips. His voice was little more than a whisper. "It wasn't enough."

No one responded. The words needed no answer. The truth had settled in the room, thick as the uncertainty around them. Aria swallowed against the silence. She thought of the others—the ones who hadn't returned. Their names hadn't been spoken, but they were there, filling the spaces left empty, woven into every breath still taken.

Across the room, a woman knelt beside another cot, pressing damp cloths against a man's fevered brow. The man's fingers twitched, but his eyes remained closed. His breathing was slow, uneven.

Further down, another assistant moved between cots, her hands sure but trembling at the edges. Aria could see the exhaustion in her steps, the way her shoulders sagged under the weight of knowing what had become of the mission.

Anna moved then, slow and deliberate, setting down a bundle of linen she had been clutching without thought. She exhaled, rubbing her temples, then turned to the room at large. "We'll do what we can tonight," she murmured. "After that... we'll see where we stand."

Sebastian nodded once, a sharp movement barely visible. His jaw was tight, his thoughts already leagues ahead. Aria knew whatever came next wouldn't come from grief, but from purpose—the kind that hardened men into something unyielding.

Aria's hand trembled. Her thoughts narrowed to a single, brutal truth. They'd failed. Failed the mission. Failed the chance at a cure.

So many lives risked... for nothing.

How many more would suffer now, because they'd returned empty-handed? The weight of consequence pressed against her shoulders like something solid.

Her grandmother's pale, weary face surged to the front of her mind. Aria exhaled slowly, fighting to steady the tremor rising inside her.

Had she promised too much?

Had she let herself believe—against all reason—that they would succeed, that she could save her? If the cure was lost, what else remained? What hope could she offer now?

14

The Fall of Hope

Location: Cavandel, Dweller's Base

A dull hum filled the room, the kind that clung to the walls after too many hours without sleep. The study felt smaller than usual, the quiet pressing in from every side. Papers lay scattered across Sebastian's desk—maps shoved aside, notes half-smudged, corners curled where someone had brushed past in a hurry. No one bothered to straighten them. No one dared to move.

Sebastian sat at the center of it all, fingers steepled, gaze fixed on nothing. The stillness around him felt heavy enough to crack.

Anna stood closest to him, one hand braced against the desk, the other hovering near a stack of reports she hadn't yet found the strength to open. The light caught the strain in her posture, a taut line running from her shoulders to her jaw.

Across the room, Guss rested in the old chair by the wall—the only one besides Sebastian's. Its legs creaked beneath him as he shifted, the sound soft but certain. His hands folded over the head of his cane as he watched the room with the weary stillness of someone who had seen too much to be startled anymore.

Pike leaned against a bookshelf near the window overlooking the corridor, arms crossed, the shadows sharpening the hard angles of his face. He didn't speak. He didn't need to. The tension rolling off him spoke for itself.

Kegan stood near the map board with his hands clasped behind his back, posture straight, expression unreadable. His gaze moved slowly across the room—Sebastian at the desk, Anna at his side, Pike in the shadows, Guss in the old chair—taking in every stillness, every tightened jaw, every breath held a moment too long. He wasn't waiting for someone to speak. He was watching for the moment the silence cracked.

The hum deepened. The room held its breath.

Anna exhaled sharply, her voice clipped, measured. "Three didn't return," she said, staring at the scattered papers as if she could carve the truth into them. "Lars, Dain, and Petra. Elric and Calder are badly injured. They'll need a lot of help." She swallowed, her throat working around the words. "Two more with minor wounds—Jane and Harlan. They'll recover, but Harlan won't be mobile anytime soon."

No one spoke.

Then Anna lifted her gaze, her eyes cold. "We sent them down there during mating season. Without a real plan." Her voice didn't rise, but the weight of it landed like a blow. "What did we expect?"

The silence tightened.

From his place near the map board, Kegan shifted—not forward, not toward a chair, but just enough to make his presence felt. His hands remained clasped behind his back as he spoke, voice smooth and composed. "We all made the call," he said, each word carefully even. "And we're all paying for it. But we'll recover. We always do."

He let the stillness breathe before continuing, tone threading the careful line between reason and inevitability. "No one forced them down there. No one forced any of us to fight. We chose this—because we had to. And we knew the risks."

Anna's fingers curled into fists. Her voice, when it came, was quieter but honed to a razor edge. "Tell that to their families, Kegan."

Kegan met her stare without flinching. "And what would you have me say?" His tone didn't shift. "That we give up? That their loss means we stop fighting for the cure?"

Anna let out a sharp breath, shaking her head. It wasn't amusement—it was disbelief, raw and unfiltered. "Fighting for the cure? That's rich." She straightened, arms crossing over her chest. "Tell me, Kegan—how many times have you actually *helped* in the infirmary?"

The question slipped between them like a blade. Anna didn't elaborate, didn't press. She didn't need to.

Kegan didn't answer.

Anna let the silence stretch before tilting her head slightly. "I thought so," she murmured. Her voice was quiet, edged with something cutting. "So don't pretend it's about them."

For the first time, something flickered across Kegan's expression—there and gone before anyone could name it. But when he spoke, his voice was as smooth as ever. He exhaled, shaking his head slightly. "Believe what you want, Anna. But waiting won't stop the Shatterblight."

He let the words settle, then straightened with slow, deliberate ease. "We have two choices," he said, no urgency in his voice, only certainty. "We try to fix this now—and yes, we may lose a few people. Or we do nothing, and we watch Shatterblight take us all, one by one."

Silence reclaimed the room, heavy and unmoving.

Pike shifted near the narrow window, uncrossing his arms as his gaze cut toward Sebastian. "You ask them to go back down there," he said quietly, "and they will. They won't hesitate. That's the kind of men they are."

Sebastian turned to Guss, the only man in the room whose silence carried more weight than words.

The old man adjusted his grip on his cane, breath slow. "Aye. But that don't mean we should," he murmured. His voice was soft, worn, but steady. "Make sure it's the right call."

Sebastian's fingers brushed the corner of a map, tracing its worn crease without really seeing it. He turned the choice over one last time, feeling it settle, heavy and final. Then he drew in a slow breath and straightened, his hands coming together on the table.

"No."

Kegan went still.

Sebastian shook his head, more certain now. "Not like this. We don't have the manpower. We don't have the supplies. If we go down now, we're just throwing bodies at something we have no way of beating—not yet. We wait. We prepare."

Anna's shoulders eased, the breath she released almost too soft to hear. Across the room, even Guss gave a small nod. Kegan exhaled, slow and controlled, as if conceding the point.

It was decided.

Sebastian's mouth had barely opened to dismiss them when Kegan shifted—not his posture, but his presence, a quiet ripple that threaded its way into the room.

"Then why don't we ask them?" he said, gesturing toward the door.

Sebastian's brow furrowed.

Kegan leaned forward, just enough to be noticed. "The ones waiting outside," he said. "The ones who lost friends. Some who might have Shatterblight creeping through their own families." His voice was patient, almost generous. "Let them decide."

The words drifted through the room like dust—weightless at first, then settling in the cracks.

Sebastian didn't answer. Pike shifted near the window, jaw tight. Anna didn't move at all, but Sebastian felt her brace, the air around her sharpening.

Kegan pressed on, smooth and steady. "They deserve a say in their own future, don't they?"

Silence coiled.

Sebastian's gaze shifted briefly toward Kegan before settling on Guss.

The old man met his eyes, weary but steady, and gave a single, deliberate nod.

Only then did Sebastian look back to Kegan.

Sebastian drew a slow breath, the decision settling. "Fine."

Kegan leaned back, slow as settling sand. But there was a glint in his eye—one Sebastian didn't like.

Sebastian pushed back from the table, standing. "We'll take it to the people."

Kegan smiled.

The room didn't breathe again until he did.

***

The Cantina was packed.

Bodies filled every inch of space—miners, healers, scavengers, fighters—all pressed together in tense anticipation. The low murmur of voices drifted between the clatter of mugs and the occasional scrape of a chair, but no one was really talking. Not like they normally would. There was no laughter, no idle chatter about the day's work.

The air was too thick. Too charged.

Aria sat near the back with Heidi and Sylas, hands clasped tightly in her lap, her foot bouncing beneath the table. She wasn't the only one restless. People shifted in their seats, eyes fixed on the entrance. Some leaned against the walls, arms crossed, brows furrowed. Others clutched drinks they hadn't touched in minutes.

They were all waiting.

Then, the door swung open.

The sound in the room died at once, every gaze snapping toward the entrance.

Sebastian walked in first, his presence commanding without pressing on the room around him. Guss followed, steady in his pace, cane tapping softly against the floor. Pike came next, expression unreadable, shoulders tense beneath the weight of so many eyes. Anna slipped in after him, her gaze sharp, already taking stock of everything.

Kegan arrived last. While the others moved with purpose, his steps were looser, more fluid, as though he were adjusting himself to the room before it even settled.

They didn't need to ask for attention. They already had it.

Sebastian stepped forward, taking in the faces before him—the expectant eyes, the worry, the exhaustion. He let the silence stretch a breath before speaking, his voice steady, carrying the weight of everything they'd endured.

"I won't waste words. You all know why we're here."

His gaze swept across the packed crowd, hundreds of faces turned toward him in unbroken silence. His tone stayed steady, but something solemn threaded through it.

"First, I want to tell you how proud I am of you."

A murmur rippled through the crowd—small, but real. A few people straightened, as if the words held something they needed.

Sebastian continued.

"What we've built here—it isn't just survival. It isn't just resistance. It's a future. And that's because of you. Every one of you has fought for something bigger than yourselves."

Aria swallowed hard. Around her, she saw faces soften, shoulders lift, hands unclench.

"But we've paid for it."

His voice lowered, the words settling over the room.

"We've paid in sweat, tears, and sacrifice."

Silence gathered once more.

"We suffered a severe blow down there." His voice didn't waver, but the weight of it settled just the same. "Lars, Dain, Petra—" he paused, letting the names hang. "And to those who knew them... to those who stood beside them—" his gaze shifted toward a cluster near the back, "you have my deepest respect."

Someone sniffed quietly. A woman near the center bowed her head, gripping the hand of the man beside her.

Sebastian gave them a moment.

Then he exhaled and straightened.

"But their loss wasn't just a tragedy. It was a reminder. Proof that the Warden will never stop trying to snuff us out. Proof that even now, even after everything, he still tightens his grip."

A low murmur stirred at the mention of the Warden.

Sebastian's voice rose.

"We are forced into darkness while he sits above us. He eats while we starve. He breathes clean air while we choke on dust. And even now, as our people suffer, as sickness spreads, he does nothing."

He let his gaze sweep the room, giving the words room to settle. "That's why we need the cure. Without it, the rest of Cavandel won't stand with us—not against him."

Muttered agreement rumbled through the crowd. Some nodded. Others tightened their grips on their mugs.

Sebastian let the tension settle for a breath before continuing.

"But you acted."

The words hit the room like a spark. Murmurs died. A shift ran through the crowd, the air pulling taut.

Sebastian nodded, his voice firm and clear.

"You did something. You're the reason we still have a chance against this plague. You fought for this. You suffered for this."

A few people murmured in agreement, the tension softening into something quieter—pride.

Sebastian exhaled. "And we thank you for it."

He let the words sit, let them settle with the people who had given so much.

Then his expression sharpened.

"But as you know, everything comes at a cost."

A hush fell over the Cantina.

Near the front, a man straightened. A woman shifted her weight, arms crossed tight.

Sebastian's hands rested at his sides.

"We can't ask you to go back down there, knowing the dangers."

Silence stretched.

The glow-lamps flickered overhead. The crowded room seemed to shrink, Sebastian's words pressing into every corner.

Aria glanced at Heidi and Sylas. The tension pressed against her ribs—thick, unrelenting. They were all waiting.

Sebastian's voice cut through the silence.

"So we won't ask you," he said, steady, unwavering. "But we'll let you decide."

A stir passed through the crowd. Someone whispered. A chair scraped. A man near the back folded his arms, expression unreadable.

Then a voice—calm but firm—cut through the tension.

"And if we don't go back?"

An older miner, his face lined by years in the tunnels, leaned forward with his hands clasped over the table. "What happens if we don't?"

Sebastian met his gaze. "We prepare. We hold onto what we have. We focus on keeping our people safe."

Aria swallowed. *Safe.* The word rattled inside her, hollow and useless. If they waited, her grandmother wouldn't live long enough to see that safety.

A younger woman stood. "Safe from what?" Her voice carried through the room without hesitation. "The Warden isn't just going to let us sit here and wait."

"And what if we do go?" a voice drawled from somewhere near the middle—smooth, edged with quiet self-interest. Heads turned, revealing Lhoris leaning back in his seat, gaze fixed on Sebastian. He lifted his chin slightly, fingers tracing the rim of his cup. "Pride's all well and good," he murmured, "but pride alone won't feed empty bellies."

Sebastian narrowed his eyes, weighing the intent behind the words. Then he nodded once. "We'll make it worth the risk. A thousand Grottos to each volunteer. Paid upfront."

A ripple of quiet surprise traveled through the Cantina. Brief murmurs of disbelief rose and fell just as quickly. Lhoris tilted his head, evaluating the offer against some private scale, a faint smile curling at the corner of his mouth.

"Make it two," he said softly—almost lazily. "And you'll have your first volunteer."

The offer hung suspended in the air. Then the room stirred—low murmurs rising at the thought of two months' wages in advance.

"He's right," a man near the front said, frustration bleeding into his voice. "We can't leave it undone. The Screechers will still be there come mining season. Why wait?"

From the back, someone added, "And more of us will be sick."

Aria turned toward the voice. A woman stood near the far wall, arms crossed, face unreadable. But her words carried. "We don't have a cure. Not yet. And without those Glowcaps, it means nothing."

A heavy pause followed.

Then another voice—sharper, weary, frayed with anger. "And how many more are we willing to lose for it?"

This time the words hit harder. A thick-shouldered miner glared from the corner, jaw tight. "We barely made it out last time. If we go back, we might as well dig our own graves."

Aria's fingers curled in her lap. Every point made sense—waiting was safer. Smarter. But waiting had a cost too.

Anna's voice cut through the rising tension—calm, firm, steady. "Then we wait."

Heads turned toward her as she crossed her arms.

"Like we always do. We wait until mining season—when the Rocknids aren't mating, when they're less aggressive." She swept her gaze across the room. "That's how we've always done it. Why should this time be any different?"

A shift ran through the crowd—soft, uncertain, but spreading.

It was exactly what Kegan had been waiting for.

He leaned forward slightly, posture easy, eyes sharp.

"No one's blind to the risk," he said, voice steady, deliberate. "But ask yourselves—what's more dangerous? Facing it now? Or waiting until the Warden decides for us?"

A pause settled, heavy and listening.

"Because he will," Kegan added. "And when he does, it won't be on our terms."

He let the words settle before sweeping his gaze over the room. "The Warden knows we're close. He feels it. That's why he's coming down harder than ever."

His voice dipped lower, threading through the silence.

"You've seen it yourselves. The new patrols. The way Drazic's men watch us. He's not just tightening his grip—he's getting ready to crush us."

A few people shifted, uneasy.

"If we wait, we give him time to do it."

A murmur of agreement swept through the room—quiet, uncertain, but growing. Kegan could feel the shift.

Then he pushed a little further.

"And let's not forget what we're fighting for." His tone softened just enough to draw people in. "It's not just the mines. Or the cure. It's Cavandel itself."

The room stilled.

Aria felt the shift deep in her gut, unease curling tight. He wasn't just persuasive—he made his argument feel inevitable.

"The cure is more than survival," Kegan continued. "It's proof. Proof that we can stand on our own. Proof that we don't need the Warden's scraps to live."

Another ripple of murmurs.

A man near the back, arms folded, called out, "What are you saying, Kegan? That we go back no matter what?"

Kegan's smile was small and knowing.

"I'm saying we already know the answer."

The words landed softly, but the weight of them settled over the room like a closing door.

No shouting. No frenzied calls for action. Just silence.

A few glances exchanged. A flicker of realization passing from person to person.

Then, slowly, a man near the front exhaled and nodded. "We should go."

A murmur followed—not loud, not overwhelming, but steady as others joined in.

Kegan said nothing. He didn't need to. He had already won.

***

Anna watched in silence as Sebastian adjusted the strap of his armor, his movements steady and efficient. The worn leather creaked under his touch, filling the quiet space between them. He tightened a buckle, checked the blade at his side. Routine motions. He'd done them a hundred times before.

But tonight, it felt different.

"How many volunteered?" she asked, her voice calm, measured—though she knew he heard what she wasn't saying.

Sebastian kept his hands occupied, fastening the last strap with practiced precision. "About thirty."

Anna's arms tightened around herself, fingers curling against her sleeves, pulling the fabric taut. "That many, willing to risk their lives..." She shook her head, releasing a thin breath. "I can't decide if that makes me proud or terrified."

Sebastian finally looked up, his sharp gaze softening as he took in the tension in her shoulders, the set of her jaw. He stepped forward, reaching for her hand, his fingers warm as they brushed over hers before he rested his forehead against hers.

He didn't say anything.

He didn't need to.

Anna closed her eyes, her breath catching for a moment before she let herself lean into him, her palms settling lightly against his chest. His heartbeat was steady beneath her hands.

"Promise me." Her voice was barely above a whisper.

Sebastian pulled back just enough to meet her eyes, his grip tightening. "I'll come back to you," he murmured, his voice low, steady.

It wasn't a guarantee. They both knew that. But for now, she let herself believe it.

He gave her hand a final squeeze before stepping away, the warmth between them fading as he turned toward the waiting volunteers. Anna stayed where she was, watching as he walked away, the flickering glow-lamps casting his shadow long against the stone. She didn't move, didn't say anything, only listened—for his footsteps, for the promise she had to believe he would keep.

Sebastian moved through the gathered volunteers, nodding to each of them in turn. His hand landed on a shoulder here, a clasp on an arm there, offering quiet words of encouragement. He checked a man's armor straps, nudged a blade at another's hip to ensure it was secure. This wasn't ceremony—he was one of them and they needed to know that.

Pike watched from a few steps away, arms crossed, expression unreadable. He didn't interrupt, didn't call out, just observed as Sebastian moved from one fighter to the next, carrying himself like a man who had already made his decision.

When Sebastian turned to check the fit of a younger volunteer's bracer, Pike finally pushed off the wall and stepped forward.

"With all due respect," he grumbled, voice even, "what do you think you're doing?"

Sebastian barely glanced at him, adjusting the strap of a man's shoulder guard before patting it once. "Making sure we're ready," he said evenly.

Pike exhaled slowly, tilting his head just slightly. "Is that what you call it?"

Sebastian finally faced him fully, brow raised. "Is there a problem, Pike?" he asked, tone sharp but controlled.

"Yeah." Pike folded his arms, his stance firm. "Because from where I'm standing, it looks like you're about to walk into the Abyss with us." He let the words settle for a moment before adding, "Risking your life won't bring those men back."

Sebastian's jaw tightened. Pike didn't have to name them. They both knew who he meant.

"I can't ask my men to risk their lives while I do nothing." Sebastian's voice was level, but there was steel beneath it. "That would make me no better than the Warden."

Pike let out a slow breath, shaking his head. "You're not sending them, Sebastian. They're volunteering." He gestured toward the room. "Each one of them had a choice—to go or to stay. Many are staying, but these ones?" he exhaled, rubbing the back of his neck. "They're *choosing* to go."

His gaze shifted toward the side of the room where Aria and Heidi were fastening the last of their gear. His mouth pulled into a thin line before he muttered, "Much to my displeasure."

Aria's hands paused over the strap of her pack.

She turned, one brow raised, meeting Pike's pointed look. Her grip tightened around the strap and for a moment, she wasn't sure if she wanted to scowl at him or smirk.

She settled for neither, adjusting the buckle a little harder than necessary before glancing over at Heidi, who was smothering a grin.

Sebastian ignored the exchange, still watching Pike, still weighing the choice. His fingers flexed at his sides before he spoke.

"So what would you have me do?"

Pike didn't hesitate. "Stay."

Sebastian's expression didn't shift, but Pike pressed on. "I know you feel like you have to be in the thick of it. That's who you are. But this isn't about proving yourself. You matter too much to be wasted on a single fight."

Sebastian started to shake his head, but movement at the edge of his vision stopped him. Some of the volunteers were nodding—small, subtle gestures. A few traded glances, quiet understanding passing between them. They weren't just following orders. They believed Pike was right.

Sebastian adjusted the strap across his chest, shoulder rolling once beneath the weight, but doubt still held.

Pike lowered his voice, gaze sharp. "If something happens to you, who are these men supposed to come back to?" He paused. "Kegan?"

Sebastian stilled.

"I'm not a leader," Pike said, quieter but steady. "I can keep them alive, I can lead them into danger, but I don't have your vision. And if Kegan has the reins, we're finished."

The truth of it settled between them, heavy and inescapable.

Sebastian looked past Pike at the gathered fighters—men who had stepped forward by choice, not command. A few still watched him, steady and expectant, waiting for him to acknowledge what they already understood.

He rolled his shoulders again, slower this time, as if letting the weight shift. Then, finally, he nodded. Not in agreement, but in resignation.

"You take them, then."

Pike nodded once. "I'll bring them back."

Sebastian didn't respond right away. Instead, he reached for Pike's forearm, gripping it firmly for a breath before releasing it.

No argument. No wasted words.

Sebastian turned away, stepping back toward the others as Pike faced the gathered volunteers, his expression set.

"We leave at first bell."

The murmurs of conversation shifted, sharpening with purpose. The decision had been made.

Pike set his stance before turning his gaze onto the trio.

"And you three."

His tone carried the unmistakable weight of an exasperated guardian catching troublemakers in the act. His eyes swept over them, lingering just long enough to make it clear that whatever came next wouldn't be a lecture—but it wasn't going to be a compliment either.

"I suppose I shouldn't be surprised." He let the words settle as he crossed his arms. "Brave of you to volunteer, I'll give you that. But bravery and good judgment aren't always the same thing."

Aria tensed but said nothing, waiting.

Pike dragged a hand down his face, clearly restraining whatever else he wanted to say. "You've been training for just over three weeks. Three. Weeks." He let the words hang before continuing, his voice flat. "This isn't a sparring match with blunted weapons. This is the Abyss. Screechers. Collapsing tunnels. Things that don't care how determined you are." His voice remained level, but there was an edge to it. "You're far from ready. And down there, if you can't hold your own, you're not just putting yourselves at risk. You're putting the entire team in danger."

Sylas let out a quiet huff, shifting his stance. "Well, if I'd known volunteering came with this much enthusiasm, I would've signed up twice."

Pike's gaze landed on him—unimpressed.

Heidi smirked, then immediately pressed her lips together when Pike's eyes narrowed.

"This is no time for games," Pike warned. His voice carried the weight of someone who'd already seen too many overconfident men dragged back in pieces.

Aria lifted her chin, keeping her voice even. "We know the risks."

Pike didn't budge. "Knowing the risks and being able to handle them are two different things."

Aria's grip on her pack tightened, but she held his stare.

The last team had gone down with ten. Ten. And it still hadn't been enough—not for what they faced, not for what they needed. Even the survivors admitted they'd been outmatched. So how could they call for volunteers, talk about strength in numbers, and now try to cut those numbers again?

She drew a slow breath, choosing her words. "You asked for volunteers, so we're volunteering."

Pike's expression didn't change, but something in his stance shifted—weight settling, guard lowering just a fraction.

Aria squared her shoulders. "Last time, they weren't out-skilled. They were outnumbered. They said it themselves. They needed more hands."

She hesitated, then pressed on. "And now you have more... but you're cutting numbers again. Doesn't that put us right back where we were?"

She glanced at Heidi and Sylas before looking back at Pike. "We want to help. We know it's dangerous, but we came here for a reason. Let us prove we can do more than just stand back and watch."

Heidi adjusted the strap on her shoulder, gaze steady. Sylas just gave a slow shrug, like the matter had already been settled. Silence settled over them, tense but controlled.

Pike rubbed his jaw once before finally nodding.

"Alright," he said, giving them a once-over, his gaze lingering on Aria a moment longer. "Stay close. Follow my orders. Exactly."

Then, under his breath: "I'd better not live to regret this."

The room had settled into something quieter, a tension that no longer buzzed with uncertainty but pressed heavier, more defined. The rustling of final preparations continued—packs adjusted, weapons checked. There were whispered exchanges between those who had chosen to go—but it was subdued, sharpened by the reality of what lay ahead.

Pike stood at the center, his gaze sweeping over them, assessing, measuring. They were ready—or as ready as they could be. Now it was his job to make sure they understood what that meant.

"Alright. Listen up."

His voice carried, steady and deliberate, cutting through the space with a weight that made even those in the back straighten. "We know what's waiting for us down there and we know what's at stake."

Aria shifted slightly, fingers flexing at her sides. She had known this moment was coming, but now that it was here, the weight of it settled differently.

"This time, we do it right." Pike announced.

No cheers followed, no one moved to fill the space he left open. Good. They understood.

He adjusted his stance. "We stay together at all times. We cover each other's backs. No one moves alone."

Heidi exhaled slowly. She had been steady throughout the argument, but now, standing among the others, she braced herself, feeling the full scope of what they had signed up for.

A few nods, quiet murmurs of understanding, the scrape of a belt being tightened.

"We move smart. We stay unseen. We get what we came for, and we bring it back."

His gaze settled for a fleeting moment on the edges of the group, where weapons had been checked and rechecked. He knew what they were expecting, what some of them were hoping for.

Sylas adjusted the strap on his pack, fingers moving with an ease that didn't match the tension in his jaw. He wasn't the type to dwell on fear, but even he had fallen quiet now, his usual sarcasm absent.

"This isn't a show of strength. It's a mission. We get the job done and we come back alive."

Silence. No hesitation.

Pike gave a slow nod. "Good."

His posture remained firm, voice steady. "Remember, no one strays. No one plays the hero. We work as a unit, or we don't work at all."

There was nothing else to say. No final words that could make the task ahead any easier. He turned, glancing once toward the doors leading out of the hall.

"Rest up. We move at first bell."

The room shifted—not in a rush of movement, but in quiet, focused resolve. The sound of packs being lifted, steel sliding into place, murmured words exchanged between those who knew this could be the last time they spoke.

No grand declarations. No illusions. Just the understanding that the time for questions was over.

Now, they followed through.

15

Buried in Shadow

Location: Cavandel, Dweller's Base

The massive reinforced doors groaned as they slid shut behind them, the finality of the sound echoing through the chamber. Aria felt the weight of it settle in her chest. There was no turning back now. The air beyond the doors to the Abyss was colder, untouched, thick with stillness. Ahead, the tunnel stretched into darkness, a passage known only to the Dwellers, carved deep to circumvent the Warden's control.

Pike let the silence linger before speaking. "You all know the plan. It's a four-hour trek. We don't stop unless we have to. Keep your pace steady and don't fall behind." He shifted his lance into a more comfortable grip, fingers adjusting the leather wrapping along its shaft. His gaze moved over the group, pausing on each face as if already weighing their endurance. "Anyone planning on twisting an ankle, do it now."

Sylas squinted into the darkness ahead, tightening his grip on his lance. "I don't care what anyone says—that Lift and I had something special. I think I owe it an apology."

Pike didn't spare him a glance. "That Lift gets you noticed. This route keeps us alive."

Sylas didn't argue.

They pressed forward, glow-torches sparking to life and casting steady, pale light along the tunnel walls. Shadows stretched with each step, warping against the rough stone. The air thickened with the scent of damp earth, tinged faintly with old metal. Lances were held close, angled carefully to avoid scraping the narrow walls. Most carried knives or short swords, but those were a last resort. Against a Screecher, distance was survival.

Pike's voice cut through the shuffle of boots on stone. "Mind your footing in the narrows. The ground gets loose, and some of these ledges don't give second chances." He didn't slow, but the weight behind his words made it clear he wasn't exaggerating. "If you slip, don't expect anyone to go diving after you. Keep your weight balanced, step where I step, and don't let the dark mess with your head."

No one argued. They understood what it meant to move through the dark.

"Let's go," Pike said and without another word, he stepped into the passage. One by one, they followed.

The descent was slow and methodical—every step measured, every sound amplified by the silence pressing in around them. The glow-torches cast shifting halos of warm light against the rough stone, illuminating the narrow passage just enough to guide their way. Beyond the reach of the light, the dark stretched endlessly, swallowing sound and sight alike.

The air grew colder as they moved deeper, the damp stone walls pressing close, forcing them into single file when the path narrowed. In places, they had to crouch, the ceiling lowering just enough to scrape against the taller men's heads. The deeper they went, the more the tunnels felt like something closing in around them.

Old mining remnants littered the path—rusted tools, broken rope, and half-collapsed tunnels that told their own silent stories. Aria's fingers brushed a length of twisted iron as she passed, its surface worn smooth by time.

How many had taken this path before... and how many never made it out?

Pike moved steadily ahead, his steps sure and unbothered, as if he'd walked this path a hundred times before. He didn't look back—he trusted the others to keep up. They followed in near silence, their footfalls muffled by the packed dirt, the occasional clink of a lance against armor the only sound breaking the quiet.

Sylas shifted his grip, glancing up at the uneven ceiling. "I feel like we're being watched?"

Pike didn't turn, but his voice carried back through the tunnel. "Less talking. More walking."

The tunnel narrowed for several more steps—then abruptly widened.

Aria slowed as the passage spilled into a cavern so vast it swallowed their lights whole. The ceiling vanished into darkness. The floor dropped away in uneven shelves of rock, some steady, others crumbling toward a bottomless pit below.

Pike lifted a hand, signaling the group to tighten formation.

A low rumble shivered through the stone. Not loud, but deep—felt more than heard. Aria's breath hitched as the vibration trembled up her boots.

Heidi leaned in, voice barely above a whisper. "What was that?"

Pike kept moving along the narrow ledge, eyes forward. "Just the cavern reminding us we don't belong," he cautioned. "Stay sharp."

The stone shifted again.

Loose gravel skittered across the ledge—then the ground gave way beneath someone.

Jared stumbled sideways, his boot sliding over a patch of unstable rock. A shout tore from him as the shelf collapsed under his weight, pitching him forward into the abyss.

Pike moved faster than thought. His arm snapped out, fingers locking around Jared's forearm just as the man's weight yanked him toward the edge. His boots skidded across the dirt, the pull nearly dragging him off balance, but he planted himself hard and held.

"Hold still," Pike ground out, muscles bunching as he kept Jared from dropping into the void below.

For a moment, nothing moved. Then, two others rushed forward, grabbing Jared's other arm and hauling him back onto solid ground. He collapsed onto his knees, breathing hard, his face pale beneath the flickering torchlight.

Aria stared past them, trying to see what had almost swallowed him. She edged closer, carefully this time, and found nothing—just a yawning chasm where the ledge simply ended. The drop vanished into darkness. There was no telling how far it went, only that if Jared had fallen, there would've been no way back up.

Pike didn't lecture. He didn't need to. He just gave Jared a once-over, checking that he was steady before stepping past him, eyes sweeping the ground ahead. "We move carefully from here."

***

From there, the group pressed on without further incident. Eventually, the tunnel widened enough for a brief stop, and Pike lifted a hand, signaling them to halt. Boots slowed. Quiet murmurs passed through the group as they adjusted gear, stretched stiff limbs, and rationed what little water they carried.

"We're an hour out," Pike said, resting his lance against his shoulder. His voice was steady, measured, filling the space like something tangible. "Drink. Rest your legs. Won't be stopping again until we reach the Cave." He let them settle, gave them those few stolen moments to breathe, then added, "But stay sharp. Don't get too comfortable."

The words settled over them, quiet but firm, and the group shifted in a slow, deliberate way. A few cast quick glances toward the darkness beyond the torchlight, as if reminded that the tunnels around them were far from empty.

Sylas exhaled, adjusting the strap of his pack before glancing at Pike.

"So this cave we're heading to," he said, tilting his head. "Is that where the Glowcaps are?"

Pike met his gaze, a faint crease forming between his brows. "Last team would've found them if they were that close." He reached into his pack and tossed a strip of dried meat to one of the younger men. "It's only the holdout. From there, we go deeper."

One of the Dwellers looked up at Sylas's question but didn't comment—only tugged a buckle into place before setting his pack aside.

Pike continued, "We camp there during mining season. Safest place in the tunnels. Narrow entrance, defensible, enough room for a team without getting boxed in." His gaze tracked the path ahead. "We make it there, we can breathe."

Sylas took in his words. Then, after a moment, "Ever seen one before?" He paused. "A Screecher, I mean."

Pike gave him a slow, pointed look. "Anxious to see death, are we?"

Sylas shrugged. "Just asking."

Pike let a long breath slip free, the kind that carried more than it said. "Whatever you imagine, it's worse."

Sylas nodded once, swallowing whatever follow-up he'd been forming. The warning settled in, and his gaze drifted toward the dark ahead, as if searching for a shape he wasn't sure he wanted to see.

Lhoris, a miner farther down the line, spoke instead. "Fast ain't enough," he warned. His voice was rough but steady. "You don't hear them coming. You don't see them—until it's too late." He paused, jaw tightening. "Only warning you'll get... are the eyes."

Heidi's grip tightened around her lance. "You mean the glow?"

The man nodded. "Aye. Bright purple. Like Crythium." He hesitated. "But if it blinks—" He tapped the shaft of his weapon. "Run."

He looked past them, as if seeing the scene play out again in the dark. "First time I saw one, I didn't even know it was there. Thought the tunnel was empty. Then I saw it shift—not fast, not at first. Just moving where nothing should've been."

His lance clicked lightly against his boot. "It got Old Pete before anyone understood what was happening."

The air seemed to chill. "We ran," he added quietly. "It didn't."

The space around them felt smaller, closer.

He met Heidi's eyes. "Hope you're faster than Old Pete."

She didn't answer, though the small, uneven rise of her shoulders gave her away.

Another miner crouched near his pack, carving thin slices from a strip of cured meat. Without looking up, he said, "And steel won't save you if you swing wrong. That'll just anger it. Don't forget to keep your distance."

A younger man lifted his lance, tapping the long shaft. "That's why we use these."

Lhoris gave a humorless huff. "Distance is nice. Until you run out." His gaze swept the group's weapons. "Crythium blades would help more." His expression darkened slightly. "Not that many of us get our hands on those."

A scoff rose from the back. "Some of us do."

Aria glanced at Pike, then a few others. Only now did she notice it—their lances. Same build as the Warden's guards, their blades unlit to preserve the power capsules inside.

An older miner followed her look. "Would be nice if everyone had one."

Pike didn't comment.

The older miner's voice lowered. "And remember—never trust a quiet tunnel. You see one Screecher, chances are you don't see the second."

Sylas frowned. "What does that mean?"

"It means," the man replied, "if you're staring at one, you're already in the other's shadow."

A few paces away, Aria spoke, her voice dry. "Are you trying to terrify her, or is this just your natural charm?"

Lhoris laughed. "If this scares her, she's not ready for what's ahead."

Pike slung his lance back into place. "Enough." His tone was flat, final.

He let the silence settle, then nodded once. "Break's over. We move."

***

After four grueling hours, they arrived.

The cave loomed ahead, its entrance jagged and shrouded in darkness, barely wide enough for two people to slip through at once. The rock face around it was uneven, pitted with timeworn hollows and deep fissures that seemed to swallow the light whole.

Lightmoths drifted lazily through the damp air, their wings scattering flecks of gold across the cavern's shadows.

Mud gripped their boots with each step. The scent of wet stone and something stale lingered at the back of Aria's throat, thick and unmoving, as if the cave itself had been holding its breath.

She exhaled slowly, stretching her back to ease the dull throb in her muscles. The weight of her lance had long since settled into her bones, an ache pulsing in time with her heartbeat. Sweat cooled on her skin, though she barely noticed. More than the exhaustion, more than the stiffness in her limbs, was the feeling she couldn't shake.

Reaching their destination should have brought relief. Instead, unease curled in her chest, winding tight around her ribs.

The cave was supposed to be safe. Pike had called it a holdout, the only shelter down here worth the name. But standing at its threshold, staring into a darkness the torchlight couldn't touch, she felt only one thing.

Watched.

Pike raised a hand, signaling a halt. His gaze swept the entrance before settling on the men. "Standard sweep."

The Dwellers moved without hesitation, their motions sharp, confident. One stepped forward and struck a torch alight—not a glow-torch, but real fire, the kind that sent living things skittering from its reach.

Another crouched, knife in hand, skimming his fingers across the mud in search of tracks. The wet earth gave easily under his touch, leaving deep imprints. The soft squelch of shifting boots filled the silence as they worked, a quiet rhythm of movement and breath.

As they moved, Pike's hand shifted on his lance. A flick of his fingers, a press of the mechanism near the grip and the weapon hummed to life. The tip of the Crythium blade shivered, a deep purple light pulsing along its edge, casting thin, eerie reflections along the stone. One by one, a few others followed, the glow of empowered metal spreading among them like a slow-burning ember. The air thickened, charged with the faint hum of energy.

Sylas hovered near the back, gripping his blade too tightly. His usual restlessness was gone. He leaned slightly forward. "So, uh, what happens if something's inside?"

"We take it out," Pike said, his tone flat.

The group pressed in closer, forming a loose perimeter. Torchlight flickered against the rock, stretching their shadows into thin, spindly things. A few men took position near the entrance, watching, listening, fingers curled around the hilts of their weapons. The purple glow of the lances mixed with the firelight, sending warped reflections flickering across the uneven stone.

Pike took a step forward—then stopped.

Something pale stood out against the dark rock. At first, it seemed like nothing—just a smear of discoloration along the stone. But when he crouched, tilting the torch for a better view, the texture became unmistakable.

Not a stain.

Shed skin.

A long, curling strip of it, dry and brittle at the edges but still thick and leathery near the center, clinging to the rock like a discarded husk. More pieces lay scattered near the entrance, caught in the uneven cracks beneath their feet, some half-sunken into the mud.

Heidi took a step closer, grip firm on her lance. She lowered the tip and prodded the husk carefully, watching the way it gave beneath the pressure. It flaked in some places, but the center resisted.

"What the heck is that?" she asked.

Pike didn't hesitate. He glanced at her, then back at the skin. "Screecher." His tone was level, but something in the way he said it made the word feel heavier. "Must have molted here."

Aria exchanged a glance with Heidi. Uncertainty flickering between them.

Heidi cleared her throat. "I thought this was supposed to be the safest place down here."

"It is," Pike said.

He scanned the entrance, his expression unreadable in the shifting firelight. "Looks like a big one. Stay back."

Heidi's stance tensed. "How big?" she whispered.

Pike remained crouched, shaking some of the damp residue from his fingers. "Bigger than we'd like."

A hush settled over them. The fire crackled softly, the only sound in the thick, waiting silence.

Then—

A deep, guttural snort echoed from inside the cave, followed by the heavy scrape of something hard against stone.

A large horn burst from the cave, jagged and thick, catching the torchlight in a dull gleam. For a split second, it was all they could see—an eerie silhouette emerging from the dark. Then the rest of it followed.

The boar exploded into view, its muscular bulk barreling forward with startling speed. Gnarled tusks jutted from its maw, curved and wicked. Its hide was matted with mud, its eyes wide with panic, nostrils flaring as it charged straight through their ranks.

Mud splattered in its wake, a chaotic spray that sent men stumbling aside with curses on their lips.

Heidi flinched back, her breath catching in her throat.

The beast didn't stop. It tore past them, wild-eyed, disoriented, its breath coming in ragged huffs. Within seconds, it was gone, hooves hammering into the tunnels beyond, the sound fading into silence.

Pike didn't lower his lance. His grip remained firm, the Crythium tip still pulsing faintly. His gaze stayed fixed on the cave's entrance, unreadable.

Without a word, he gestured sharply. Stay vigilant.

They adjusted their stances, eyes scanning the tunnel's mouth for movement. No one spoke. No one needed to. The cave yawned before them, thick with damp air and the weight of something unseen. If the Screecher was still inside, it wasn't moving—not yet.

Pike took point, stepping forward with care. One by one, they followed him in, their lances gleaming as they pushed into the waiting darkness.

***

The cave was empty.

They swept every crevice, every shadowed pocket of stone, their lances casting thin violet halos as they moved with practiced precision. No sign of Screechers. No fresh tracks beyond the patch of molted skin outside. No movement but their own.

And yet, the unease lingered.

The space felt wrong. Too still. The kind of silence that stretched too thin, pressing in from all sides as if the rock itself were listening. Even the men—seasoned Dwellers used to the depths—moved with hushed caution as they set up camp.

Bedrolls were spread out against the smoothest parts of the cavern floor. Packs were dropped with minimal sound.

Pike stood near the entrance, gaze sweeping the tunnel beyond before turning back to them. "Five-man shifts on watch," he ordered, voice low. "We rotate every few hours."

A few nodded in quiet acknowledgment.

"Get the fire going," Pike continued. "We need to eat."

The men moved to obey, feeding coal, tar, and kindling into the growing blaze. Pike's gaze lingered on the flames a heartbeat too long before he pulled it away, the heat brushing against an old welt he preferred not to remember. The quiet crackle settled into the space between thought and silence. Soon, the scent of cooking meat mingled with the damp earth, grounding them in something familiar.

Shadows flickered along the cave walls, twisting in the firelight, giving the illusion of movement where there was none.

They sat in subdued clusters, eating in silence or speaking only in whispers. Conversations never lasted long—just a few words traded before falling away into wary quiet. Even Sylas, who usually filled the space with nervous chatter, said little.

One by one, they turned in for the night.

Aria lay on her bedroll, staring at the uneven ceiling above, listening to the shifting sounds of the cave. She tried to focus on the warmth of the fire, the distant murmur of the men still awake, the familiar weight of her lance beside her. But beyond that, in the far-off dark, she heard them.

A screech. High, sharp, distant—but not distant enough.

Then another.

And then something else. A choked squeal, guttural and short-lived. Her breath caught. Was it the horned boar meeting its end? She strained her ears, waiting, but the sound was gone. Only silence remained.

The cave might have been empty, but outside, something hunted.

She clenched her jaw and forced her eyes shut. Sleep would not come easily tonight.

And when it did, it brought no comfort.

In her dreams, the fire had gone out and the Screechers were already inside.

***

Aria woke to the scent of bitter tea and roasted meat.

For a moment, she didn't remember where she was. The rough stone beneath her bedroll, the dim flicker of firelight against the cavern walls—it all felt distant, blurred by exhaustion. Her body ached with the kind of heaviness that came from restless sleep, and her mind lagged behind as she blinked herself into awareness.

The low murmur of voices stirred around her. Boots scuffed against stone. Weapons shifted against belts. The others were already moving.

She pushed herself upright, the cool air licking at her skin where the blanket had fallen away. Nearby, Heidi and Sylas were stirring as well, groggy, blinking against the ever-present gloom.

Most of the men had already eaten. Some stood near the fire, adjusting their gear. Others lingered by the entrance, waiting.

Aria reached for her pack with one hand, and a strip of meat with the other, chewing as she pulled on her boots. Heidi was already eating, quick and efficient, while Sylas took a few gulps from a canteen before slinging his pack over his shoulder. The tea was strong, bitter, still hot from the fire. Aria swallowed a mouthful, chasing away the last of the haze clinging to her thoughts.

The hunting party gathered near the entrance. Pike stood at the front, his gaze sweeping over them before he spoke.

"We head out soon," he said. "Stay sharp. No unnecessary noise." His eyes swept over them, ensuring every word landed before continuing.

"Our best odds of finding the Glowcaps are to break into teams, but for our safety we'll stay together."

A ripple of nods followed, some firm, others slower, more thoughtful.

"As you know," he said, "we avoid these things for a reason." His voice carried easily through the hush. "So no one plays the hero."

His eyes moved across the gathered hunters.

"We head down to the pass, about twenty minutes in. It's wide enough, with solid footing. Hopefully, the Glowcaps are there."

He paused, something like respect in his eyes. "If not, Rylin, Petra, Vance, Orin, Hale, and Des," he called out. "You're our fastest, so you're on scout duty. Go in, find a patch and report back. Then we move as one." He gave each of them a sharp nod. "Stealth is key. Do not engage."

The six nodded.

Then his tone sharpened. "If something goes wrong—if you lose sight of each other or get cut off—fall back here. No running blind, and do not engage."

Another round of nods. No hesitation.

The weight of his words settled over them. No one spoke, but the message was clear.

Pike adjusted his grip on his lance. "Move out."

The hunting party fell into formation.

Aria tightened her hold on her weapon, falling into step beside Heidi. The plan was solid. They had numbers, experience and strategy. But plans didn't always matter. Not against something like this.

She exhaled slowly, pushing the thought aside.

One step at a time.

***

The tunnel stretched dark and endless ahead, illuminated only by the flickering glow of their torches. The group moved in near silence, their footsteps muffled against damp stone, each step a small reminder they hadn't been completely swallowed by the deep.

Odd scents wafted through the air, cool and damp, carrying the distant, rhythmic drip of water somewhere beyond the reach of their light. Shadows stretched long against the uneven walls, twisting and warping with each movement of the glow-torches, making the cavern seem deeper than it was.

Somewhere in the distance, a faint skitter echoed—a sharp, fleeting sound that came and went so quickly that Aria wasn't sure she had heard it at all. She tensed, fingers tightening around the shaft of her lance, waiting for someone else to react, but no one called a halt. Just another sound in the deep. Just the tunnels breathing around them.

Near the back of the formation, Lhoris shifted uncomfortably, his stomach twisting. His bladder was making demands. He had been holding it for too long now, trying to ignore the discomfort, but the need was becoming unbearable. He exhaled slowly, casting a glance ahead. Pike wasn't stopping anytime soon. The others were focused, their gazes set forward, their movements steady. If he veered off now—just for a moment—no one would even notice.

Careful not to draw attention, he slowed his pace, letting a few steps open between him and the man in front of him, just enough that the last glow-torch barely reached him. Then, keeping his movements smooth, he stepped away from the path, slipping behind a jagged outcropping of stone. The shadows swallowed him whole.

Relief came quickly, tension draining from his shoulders. He sighed, shaking out his free hand and stretching his fingers against the damp rock beside him. The stone was slick beneath his touch, cold and uneven, traced with the faint veins of Crythium that ran like frozen lightning through the cavern walls. He let his head tilt back slightly, exhaling a slow, measured breath. "See?" he muttered under his breath, barely above a whisper. "No big deal."

That was when he saw it. Just a few feet away, nestled deep in the rockface, a thick, uncut vein of Crythium pulsed faintly beneath the surface, its violet light muted but unmistakable. It wasn't like the thin, stubborn traces found in the mines above, the ones that took hours of back-breaking work just to free a handful's worth of raw ore. This was thick, rich, untouched. He could already see where the edges met, could already imagine the weight of a piece in his palm.

His breath caught in his throat.

Six months. Maybe seven.

That was how much this was worth. That was how much time he could shave off the endless grind, how much labor he could skip if he just took what was sitting right in front of him. His fingers twitched toward his belt, his mind racing—the coin he'd already blown through making the vein shine even brighter.

A slow grin crept across his face.

He'd found it.

Not them.

Not the group.

Him.

And there was no reason anyone else needed to know. Not yet. Not ever.

Lhoris reached for his chisel, palming the handle as he dropped into a crouch, barely aware of the wet press of stone beneath his knee.

With this—after getting paid just to show up—

He wouldn't be stupid about it—he'd be quick.

The tool bit into the rock with a soft crack, dust sifting down as he worked, careful, steady. The Crythium's glow reflected faintly in his eyes, flickering with each precise stroke of his chisel. He adjusted his grip, shifting his weight, working at the edges of the stone until he felt it begin to loosen.

His pulse thrummed in his ears.

It was almost free. A few more strikes. A little more pressure—

The shard came loose.

Cool in his palm, heavier than he expected, it gleamed in the dim light, smooth and perfect. He ran his fingers over the surface, feeling the fine ridges where the stone had fractured, feeling the weight of something that could change everything.

Still grinning, he stood and stepped out from behind the rock, brushing dirt from his knee as he adjusted the pouch at his hip. His fingers lingered on the weight of it, his pulse still humming with excitement.

Lhoris' boots scuffed against stone as he moved back toward the path, rounding the outcrop with a satisfied ease.

Then he stopped.

The tunnel stretched ahead, empty.

The flickering glow of torches had vanished down the path, their light swallowed by the deep. The sound of footsteps, once steady and rhythmic, was gone. No quiet murmurs. No shifting armor. Nothing but silence.

His grin faltered.

His stomach twisted.

How long was he there?

The excitement drained from his limbs, replaced by a cold, creeping unease. He pulled the pouch tighter against his hip, fingers fumbling with the cord as he secured it, his pulse hammering against his ribs. His free hand tightened around his lance, the familiar grip grounding him. It was fine. No big deal. Just catch up.

He stepped forward, his boots scuffing against the stone, each footfall disturbingly loud in the stillness. The air felt different now—thicker, pressing against his ears, his lungs. It wasn't just the absence of sound. It was the feeling that something else was there.

Then—

A sound.

Soft. Faint. A whisper of movement against the stone, too slow to be falling debris, too deliberate to be water dripping from the cavern ceiling.

Lhoris stilled.

The silence stretched, thin and unnatural.

Then he heard it again.

A slow, deliberate scrape—claws against rock.

His breath caught in his throat.

His muscles locked, stiff with the kind of tension that made even breathing feel dangerous. The edges of his vision blurred as his senses sharpened to the darkness beyond. Slowly, carefully, he turned his head.

Glowing eyes stared back.

Nestled within the shadows, a shape unfolded. It uncoiled in slow, deliberate movements, arms shifting, the unnatural smoothness of its form making Lhoris' skin crawl. It rose to its full height—towering a head and half again above any man. The light from his torch barely touched it, tracing only a silhouette that was too long, too still, too aware.

The air around him seemed to shrink.

His grip tightened on the lance, his knuckles aching from the pressure. *Too close. Too close.*

He took a careful step back, pressing himself against the cavern wall, his breath sharp and uneven. His heartbeat slammed against his ribs, urging him to run, to bolt, but instinct held him in place.

The Screecher tilted its head, eyes wide.

Then blinked.

For a long moment, it stayed perfectly still. Then, slowly, it withdrew—one slithering motion, then another.

It was leaving.

Lhoris' breath shuddered out, sharp and ragged.

It wasn't attacking.

Did it fear the torch? Had it decided he wasn't worth the fight?

A shaky, nervous laugh tried to claw its way up his throat, but he swallowed it back. His fingers loosened around his lance, the tension in his shoulders easing. The cold wall pressed against his back, grounding him.

Safe.

He was now safe.

Then—

Something shifted above him. A whisper of movement. A scrape of claws as the air stirred. By the time realization set in, it was already too late.

16

The Darkest Hour

Location: Cavandel, The Abyss

The cavern stretched wide before them, jagged and open, just as Pike had described. The space swallowed their torchlight, leaving only broken glints along the damp stone. It gave them one advantage the tunnels never could—room to move.

Pike raised a hand. "Fan out. Search the area." The command was quiet, but it carried, sharp and certain.

The group moved quickly, spreading along the wall just inside the cavern's mouth, forming a loose arc that left the center open. Boots scuffed over stone, weapons shifted, but no one spoke. They all knew the plan.

Here and there, someone knelt to examine the ground—patches of lichen, faintly luminous under their torches, or the pale, knotted stems of mushrooms half-buried in the damp. A few Glowcaps clung low to the stone, small and unopened, their caps still tight and dull. Not in bloom. Not what they needed.

Pike stood near the center, grip firm. The Crythium edge pulsed faintly in the dim, catching the low light like an ember on the verge of burning brighter. He cast a glance toward the waiting scouts.

"Go," he whispered.

Six figures peeled away from the group, vanishing into the tunnels beyond.

And then, they waited.

The pass had never felt so quiet.

The moment the scouts disappeared, the group settled into stillness. No one spoke. No one moved more than necessary. There was only the damp hush of the cavern, the slow burn of their torches casting flickering light along the walls.

Somewhere in the distance, there was movement. A faint, rhythmic shifting—not close, but not far enough to ignore.

Aria exhaled slowly, tightening her grip on her lance. She'd thought the waiting would be easier. But standing here, with nothing to do but listen to the dark breathe against the stone, was worse than anything she'd imagined. In a fight, at least there was direction. Movement. Something to answer. But this—this was different.

A few feet away, Sylas shifted where he stood, trying to keep the restlessness from showing. His fingers tapped once against the shaft of his weapon, then stilled, as if realizing the sound carried too easily.

His breath stayed shallow. It had all seemed simpler at first. Just a hunt. Just another adventure. But standing here, with the dark pressing close and the tunnels yawning before them, he couldn't shake the question—was any of this worth it?

Heidi stood near him, still as stone, her expression unreadable in the dim light. Aria studied her stance—the tight shoulders, the steady grip on the lance—and tried to decide if that tension was real or if she was only seeing her own nerves reflected back at her. Heidi had been confident at the Dwellers' base, excited even.

Here, though, the cavern pressed in differently.

Maybe it wasn't Heidi who was wavering.

Maybe it was her.

A quiet thought edged in—was this a mistake?

Somewhere beyond their torches, a noise echoed. A scrape against stone. A breath of movement that felt like it was just on the edge of their range.

No one reacted outwardly, but the tension pulled tighter.

Pike stood motionless at the front, his Crythium lance gleaming faintly in the dark. If he was worried, he didn't show it.

Ten minutes had never felt so long.

Suddenly, a sound broke the silence.

Distant at first, but sharp—shouting, the unmistakable rhythm of boots pounding against stone.

The hunting party snapped to attention. Lances shifted in their grips, feet adjusted on solid ground. Aria's pulse kicked against her ribs as she turned toward the tunnel's mouth, eyes narrowing into the dark.

The shouts grew louder. Urgent. The sound of running.

Then—movement.

Five figures burst from the tunnel, their torches bobbing wildly with their strides. Their breaths came in ragged gasps, eyes wide, weapons clutched in too-tight grips.

Aria barely had a second to register their faces before a thought cut through the chaos—one of them was missing.

Then the tunnel behind them erupted.

The creature came fast. Too fast for something that large.

The first thing Aria saw was the gleam of its blackened carapace, slick and ridged, moving with unnatural fluidity as it surged forward. It didn't crawl, didn't lurch like the smaller creature she had imagined. It flowed—smooth , efficient, terrifyingly precise.

And then—it screeched.

A sound so sharp, so raw and unnatural it felt like it had been carved straight into the air itself. Only then did she understand the name—Screech-er. The sound ripped through Aria's skull, rattling her bones, making her legs weaken beneath her. She clenched her teeth against the overwhelming urge to flinch, to drop her weapon, to run.

It was the first time she had seen a Rocknid, and it was worse than she had ever imagined.

She had expected it to be huge—but standing this close, it felt impossibly large. It dwarfed them, capable of snatching a man off his feet with little effort. Even the tallest fighters barely reached its midsection.

Its elongated body, all slick muscle and blackened plating, moved with a terrifying efficiency, every motion disturbingly smooth. The armored plating along its back gleamed like wet obsidian, jutting in sharp, uneven ridges where its exoskeleton met pale, sinewy flesh, a grotesque fusion of armor and raw muscle.

Its arms were long and sinewy, almost disturbingly human in shape, but ending in curved, serrated claws meant for rending flesh from bone.

And its face—its mouth was wrong.

She had expected mandibles, something insect-like, something foreign. But this—this was worse. A jagged mockery of a maw, stretching far too wide, its lipless grin revealing rows of sharp, jagged teeth that gleamed wet in the torchlight. Its jaw flexed slightly as it studied them, its throat pulsing with the remnants of its ear-splitting cry.

The eyes were the worst part. A piercing, lidless purple—too large for its face—swept over the gathered hunters with an unsettling patience. Calculating. Watching.

And then—it lunged.

The nearest Dweller hurled himself aside as the Screecher's claws tore through the space he'd occupied a heartbeat before. The creature's arm, thick as a man's torso, slammed into the stone wall, a deep crack spidering through the rock. Chunks broke free, crashing to the ground in a sharp, echoing clatter.

The ground shuddered beneath them. Dust and debris kicked up from the force, scattering across the cavern floor. The flickering glow of their torches shook, casting wild shadows across the pass, twisting the Screecher's already unnatural form into something even more monstrous.

Someone shouted an order, but Aria didn't hear it because the creature was already moving.

"Fall back!" Pike's voice cut through the chaos, sharp and commanding.

The hunters reacted instantly, shifting into position, weapons raised, preparing to retreat. It had picked its target. One of the Dwellers—Neil—had barely escaped its first lunge, but the Screecher wasn't done. It turned on him again, massive arms slamming against the ground as it surged forward, jaws parting just enough to reveal those rows of jagged teeth.

Neil scrambled back, spear raised. The creature struck. Stone shattered. Dust exploded into the air, swallowing the moment whole.

A figure rushed forward, movement quick and decisive. A Crythium lance flashed in the torchlight—a clean, sharp strike.

The creature recoiled, a piercing shriek rattling through the cavern. Not retreating—just enraged.

A blur of motion—its tail lashed out, sudden and brutal. The strike sent the man hurtling backward, lifting him off the ground and flinging him across the pass before he crumpled to a stop.

Aria's breath caught. Then she moved toward the man. Her body reacted before her mind had time to think. She lunged forward, feet pounding against the rock, her breath coming fast and shallow. The world had narrowed to a single point—him, lying still on the cavern floor.

She had to get to him. Had to—

"Fall back! Now!" Pike shouted. "It's an alpha!" His voice snapped through the haze, stopping her cold. The sound echoed off the damp cavern walls, multiplying until it seemed to come from everywhere at once.

Aria barely managed to halt her momentum, feet skidding over stone slick with cave moss. She stopped just short of the fallen man, breath tight in her chest. The Screecher had already shifted, its sharp, lidless eyes snapping to its next prey. In the wavering torchlight, they gleamed like polished bone.

The retreat unraveled in an instant.

It moved too fast, too ruthlessly, cutting off their escape like a predator herding prey. One of the hunters—Devran—was half a step too slow, his boot catching on an unseen ridge in the stone.

A sudden impact. The creature swung with frightening precision, its armored plates clicking against each other with each fluid motion, a sound like knives being sharpened.

Pike didn't hesitate.

The Rocknid had left an opening and he took it. The torchlight caught his face—jaw set, eyes hard with determination. He lunged, his Crythium lance flashing in the dim light. The glowing metallic tip traced an arc of pale purple light through the darkness. The strike landed, slipping deep between the armored ridges of the creature's torso.

The Rocknid reeled, its entire form recoiling from the force of the blow. The impact sent tremors through the ground, loose pebbles skittering across the stone.

For the first time, it reeled back, injured. Its confident predatory grace faltered, replaced by something jerky and uncertain.

Then—it retaliated.

Its tail lashed out in a blur, catching Pike full-force. The air itself seemed to shudder.

Pike had no time to react. The impact struck him hard, sending him backward. He hit the ground with a jarring thud, the breath knocked from his lungs. The sound of his armor scraping against stone set Aria's teeth on edge. For a moment, he struggled, fighting against the disorientation, before forcing himself to roll onto his hands and knees.

Aria's pulse pounded, each beat echoing in her ears like distant war drums. She had reached the unconscious Dweller—Sivaz.

The Screecher heaved, its movements growing sharper, more erratic. Steam rose from its hide in the cool cave air, carrying with it a smell like hot metal and something else—something organic and wrong. It lashed out in sweeping strikes, forcing the hunters back. Their boots scraped against stone as they retreated, trying to maintain formation even as they gave ground.

Pike planted a foot beneath him, forcing himself upright. His hands trembled—from pain or adrenaline, Aria couldn't tell. The creature noticed. Its head snapped toward him with terrible focus, pupils contracting to pinpoints in its pale eyes.

It turned, body coiling—ready to strike again. The torchlight caught its armored plates, turning them to liquid shadow.

Someone moved first.

A hunter—one of the Dwellers—threw himself between them, weapon raised. His face was a mask of grim determination. A clash of movement, a sharp sound lost in the chaos. The torchlight wavered, casting wild shadows that made it impossible to track what happened next.

Aria barely had time to process before she saw it. Sivaz—the unconscious Dweller's lance. It lay just beyond her reach, the blade still pulsing faintly with Crythium's glow—a steady heartbeat of purple light against the stone. Something deep in her chest answered that rhythm and instinct overtook thought.

She dropped her rudimentary weapon and dove for it.

She picked up the Crythium lance. Her fingers closed around the shaft, the solid weight grounding her, setting something firm in her chest. The metal was warm against her palm, almost alive.

The hunters pressed forward now.

They weren't retreating. Not anymore. Their boots found purchase on the stone, stance widening, weapons leveled. The air grew thick with purpose. They aimed for the weak point in the creature's armor, forcing it back. Each strike was calculated, precise. They moved like parts of a single machine, each fighter covering the others' blind spots.

And this time—they weren't letting up.

The creature faltered, but it wasn't finished. Something changed in its stance—a gathering of tension, like a spring being wound too tight.

Its pale, lidless eyes darted between the hunters surrounding it. There was an intelligence in that gaze that made Aria's stomach twist.

The Screecher let out a deafening sound, eerie and shrilled, then barreled toward them. The hunters moved to intercept, weapons ready.

As they did, a new sound cut through the cavern—a high-pitched reply, too thin to belong to the alpha. Then more followed, a scatter of sharp cries swelling into a chorus from the dark.

The sound scraped against Aria's nerves like fingernails on glass. It seemed to come from everywhere and nowhere, bouncing off the cavern walls until direction became meaningless.

The sound was followed by a blur of movement. A shout cut short as one of the hunters was yanked into the shadows, followed by another.

Gone.

The cavern seemed to shrink around them, the darkness pressing in like a physical weight. Each breath grew thick with the smell of fear—sweat and metal and something else, something primal that made Aria's hands shake. For the first time, true panic set in. It spread through the group like a poison, visible in widened eyes and shortened breath.

The alpha was no longer the only threat.

Aria barely had time to think before she was moving again, positioning herself between Pike and the alpha. Four others flanked her, lances raised. The formation was instinctive, born from countless drills and bitter experience. Her muscles remembered even when her mind threatened to freeze.

Behind them, Heidi and Sylas rushed to the wounded, dropping to their knees beside them. Their hands moved quickly, pressing down on wounds, working fast, their faces pale in the shifting glow of the torches. Two Dwellers stood guard around them, weapons raised, eyes sharp.

The fight wasn't over. It was only getting worse. The darkness beyond their torchlight seemed alive now, writhing with possibilities. Every shadow could hide another set of those glowing eyes.

Pike pressed a hand to his ribs, gritting his teeth against the deep, bruising ache, but he forced himself to move. His spear lay nearby, half-buried in the gritty cave soil, its Crythium tip still glowing faintly. He staggered toward it, fingers closing around the familiar grip. Steady. Solid. The weapon hummed with energy.

The hunters had tightened formation. Their movements were sharper, more deliberate. The alpha, though faltering, was still dangerous. Its stance remained firm, its pale eyes darting between them, assessing, calculating.

Then, slowly, it settled on Pike.

There was something almost contemplative in its gaze.

Did it single out Pike as the one in charge, the greatest threat?

Or was there something colder behind that focus—something that had nothing to do with rank at all?

It inhaled sharply, body coiling, muscles bunching beneath its slick hide. The sound was like steel being drawn from a sheath. Aria saw it—the moment before the lunge. Time seemed to crystallize, every detail sharp and bright as broken glass.

A blur of black carapace and ridged plating surged forward. The sheer weight of it sent mud and dirt scattering as it closed the distance. The air cracked with the force of its movement.

Pike had just regained his footing when the creature surged forward. It moved fast—maw wide open, ready to swallow him whole. The inside of its mouth was the color of old bruises, lined with rows of teeth that curved like hooks.

Pike stood his ground. Grip steady. Stance firm. His face was set in lines of granite, but his eyes were alive with cold fire.

At the last possible second, Pike planted the lance, bracing its butt against the stone. Then he sidestepped—just as the creature's massive jaws snapped shut where he'd been. The alpha's momentum drove it forward, and the lance punched into its skull, sinking deep as its jaws clamped down.

A piercing shriek split the cavern, deep and grating like metal against stone. The sound drove needles into Aria's ears.

A final spasm, limbs jerking, claws scraping uselessly against rock—each movement accompanied by a sound like breaking pottery.

Then stillness.

A heavy silence settled over the pass, broken only by the rapid breathing of the survivors.

Aria's breath came fast, her chest rising and falling in sharp, uneven pulls, but she barely noticed. The lance in her hands felt impossibly heavy. Around her, the other hunters remained frozen, weapons raised, waiting—expecting it to move again. But it didn't.

Then she saw them. The glowing eyes in the dark. Watching. Waiting. But not attacking.

For a long moment, no one spoke. No one moved. The torchlight flickered, making the eyes seem to dance in the darkness. Aria's muscles burned, but she didn't dare shift.

Then, one by one, the eyes disappeared.

Pike exhaled, shoulders rising and falling. A thin sheen of sweat made his face gleam in the torchlight. Then, without a word, he turned to the others. His voice was steady, though Aria could hear the exhaustion beneath it. "Stand guard. See to the wounded. Stay vigilant and start extracting those venom sacs. Take some tissue samples as well."

The hunters moved without hesitation, falling into practiced roles. Some formed a perimeter while others approached the fallen creature with tools that glinted in the low light.

Weapons remained raised as they worked. There was no relief. No celebration. Every shift in the dark carried weight, stirring a sense of unease that none of them dared voice.

The venom was secured and carefully stored in crystalline vials that pulsed with a sickly phosphorescence. Now they had to protect it at all costs.

The dark seemed to watch them as they began the long journey home—silent, patient, hungry for another chance.

Location: Cavandel, Dweller's Base

The journey back was no easier than the descent.

From the pass, they had retraced their path, pushing through the winding tunnels until the cave came into sight once more. By the time they reached it, exhaustion had settled deep in their limbs, rest offering little beyond a brief pause. The night had been quiet—uneasy. Even as their bodies gave in to fatigue, no one truly slept.

As soon as they were able, they set out again.

The path was just as treacherous for their ascent. Loose rock, narrow passes, unseen ledges waiting to claim missteps. Their pace was measured, their senses sharp. Even battered and worn, no one could afford carelessness. The tunnels were never empty. Even now, they could feel it—the hush of unseen things beyond the edges of torchlight, the lingering awareness of something just out of sight.

When the heavy reinforced doors of the Dwellers' base came into view, the tension in Aria's chest finally loosened.

They had made it.

The weight of exhaustion didn't lift, but something else settled in its place—relief. Not the kind that erased pain or softened the ache of loss, but the kind that came with reaching solid ground after too long on unsteady footing.

Pike stepped ahead and struck the metal twice with the butt of his lance. He paused, then added three more. The sound rang sharp against the stone. A moment passed. Then another. Mechanisms groaned from the other side, gears ground as locks disengaged and the doors parted.

The first few faces that appeared in the light were wary, searching. Then—recognition.

The shift came swiftly, like a breath held too long and finally exhaled. Murmurs swelled into movement, figures stepping forward, hands clasping arms, claps landing firm against shoulders. Some faces broke into relieved grins, others lingered with quiet nods, their gazes tracking over the battered group as if measuring what had been lost and what had been won.

Someone peeled away, vanishing down the corridor. Word would reach Sebastian soon.

By the time they stepped fully inside, the tunnels ahead were already alive with movement.

It wasn't long before footsteps echoed down the passage, urgent but steady. Sebastian, Anna, and Kegan emerged from the corridor, their silhouettes sharpening in the glow.

Sebastian's sharp gaze traveled over them, taking in the bruises, the torn gear, the sheer exhaustion in their stances. He didn't hesitate—just clapped a hand on Pike's shoulder, the pressure firm, solid.

"You brought them home," he murmured. No ceremony. No wasted words. Just that. Pike inclined his head, the closest thing to relief either of them would allow in a place like this.

Anna barely spared them a glance before moving through the group, her hands quick but careful as she steadied the wounded, assessed their injuries. There was something unspoken in her expression—something caught between gratitude and quiet relief.

By then, more had gathered. Words carried low, hands reached out to steady those barely standing. A few offered nods, murmured quiet praise. Others clasped forearms in a way that needed no translation.

Aria barely noticed any of it. They were home and for now, it was enough.

The initial rush of their return had settled, but its weight still lingered in the air. The wounded were led away first—hands guiding them toward the infirmary, quiet reassurances murmured beneath the hum of voices. Others remained, caught in small clusters, speaking in low tones, exchanging grips of forearms and half-smiles edged with exhaustion.

Eventually, most of them drifted toward the Cantina.

The space was already filling by the time Aria stepped through the archway. The scent of charred meat and spiced broth clung to the air, but more than hunger, there was a pull toward something else—the need to talk, to listen, to make sense of the losses and victories that had brought them back.

She was barely two steps in when Pike's voice stopped her.

"Aria."

She turned to find him beside her. His expression was unreadable, but there was something different in the way he regarded her now. Not just as another member of the group.

He gestured toward the lance still clutched in her hand. "You fought well." His tone was even, but not dismissive. If anything, there was weight behind the words, something measured. "You stepped up when it mattered."

Aria didn't know what to say to that. She hadn't fought for recognition. She'd fought because there'd been no other choice.

Pike watched her a moment longer before nodding toward the weapon. "Sivaz sends his thanks. Said you should keep it."

Her grip tightened around the shaft. The weight felt different now. Not heavier. Just different.

She met Pike's gaze, searching for something in his expression. A test, maybe. A challenge. But there was none. Just quiet certainty.

"It'll have to stay down here until you really need it," he said, measuring each word. "Can't let the Warden's men see you with it."

Aria gave a small, knowing nod.

Pike didn't say anything else. Just inclined his head slightly before stepping past her, moving toward the rest of the group.

Aria exhaled, then followed.

From behind her came a familiar voice. "Back in one piece, I see." Kegan drawled.

He stood just off to the side, arms crossed, his usual smirk firmly in place. He took a slow glance over them, gaze lingering on the bruises, the torn gear, the exhaustion etched into their faces. "Barely."

Sylas shot him a glare. "Yeah. Shame you missed it."

Kegan tilted his head slightly, amusement flickering in his expression. "Looks like you had it covered," he said dryly.

He let the words settle for a moment, the corner of his mouth twitching—just enough to suggest he wasn't entirely convinced. Then, with a slow smirk, he added, "I can't wait to see what else you get up to."

His tone was light, almost casual, but something in the way he said it made it clear—he'd be watching.

Aria didn't answer.

Kegan didn't press—just gave them all one last slow, knowing glance before turning on his heel and strolling off.

The Cantina had settled into something quieter now. Voices wove together in overlapping stories, some spoken with reverence, others punctuated by rough chuckles—a release, a grasp at something lighter after too much dark.

Sylas, already half-seated at a nearby bench, caught her eye and smirked. "Look at you. Came back with a hero's weapon and everything."

Aria leaned her new lance against the table next to theirs. "Yeah," she said with a smirk, "but Pike says I can't leave the base with it."

Sylas raised a brow. "Why not?"

"Because the city guards would definitely see it," Heidi sighed, shaking her head. "Try to keep up, Sylas." Her tone was mocking, but light.

Sylas huffed. "That's too bad. If only it was a bit shorter, you could just—" He made a vague motion, miming tucking it away.

Heidi snorted. "If it was shorter, it wouldn't be a lance, genius."

The words had barely left her mouth before she froze.

Then blinked.

Then sat up straighter. "That's—actually a brilliant idea."

She turned to Sylas, eyes wide with realization. "Sylas, you are a genius."

Aria frowned. "What?"

Sylas, sensing something, straightened as well. "I am?" he recovered quickly, nodding like he understood. "I mean... obviously."

Heidi ignored him, extending a hand. "Let me see that."

Aria hesitated, then passed the lance over. Heidi turned it slowly, her fingers running along the shaft, eyes narrowed in thought.

"No," Aria said dryly. "You're not using it for parts in your next—invention."

Heidi shook her head, still studying the weapon. "No, not quite." She turned it once more, brows furrowed as she tested the balance. "I need to talk to Sebastian. And scavenge a few parts, but—"

She kept turning the lance over, her mind already elsewhere. "Give me a few days—"

Aria shrugged, but didn't argue.

The conversations that followed were short, edged with exhaustion, but real.

Aria studied Heidi, puzzled by the intensity in her expression as she examined the weapon. The mission was over. They'd gone in search of Glowcaps and returned with venom—something far more valuable.

But she knew.

The fight wasn't over. Not yet.

17

Echoes of Resistance

Location: Cavandel, The Stratum

The guards posted outside the Power Facility, one of the Administrative Hall's more tightly secured chambers, straightened as the Warden passed, their nods clipped and controlled. He moved on without acknowledging them.

Trailing a step behind him, his assistant, Nibs, moved with far less precision. His strides were quick but uneven, as if he couldn't quite decide whether to keep pace or stay a respectful distance back.

His wiry frame was half-swallowed by a coat too large for him, the sleeves perpetually threatening to slip past his wrists.

The clipboard tucked under his arm wobbled with every hurried motion. Pages rustled as he skimmed his own notes, muttering just loud enough to seem like he was talking to himself—but not so loud that the Warden wouldn't hear.

"—adjustments holding steady, no critical deviations, though the secondary conduits ran a fraction hotter last cycle—not a problem, not yet, but something to note—" He flipped a page, barely pausing for breath. "If you asked me, Warden, and I know you didn't, but if you did, I'd say it's worth keeping an eye on. Not that it's urgent, obviously. Just... noted."

His words spilled out in hurried fragments, his mouth chasing after thoughts that refused to slow.

The Warden walked on, unbothered.

Nibs nearly collided with him when they stopped.

The chamber pulsed with the sound of machinery, a deep, steady hum that resonated through the metal grates beneath their feet. The heat was tangible, rolling off the massive structure that dominated the room.

The Crythium Core loomed before them, an enormous sphere of interlocking plates, reinforced pipes, and thick cables that coiled into the walls like veins feeding the city itself. It rested on four massive metal pillars, its bulk suspended above the grated floor, leaving just enough space for engineers to work beneath its looming structure.

At its front, a thick pane of glass pulsed with a fluorescent glow.

Behind it, lodged deep in the heart of the machine, sat the reason Cavandel existed at all—Crythium. A jagged mass of it, rich and volatile, radiating a deep violet light that pulsed in slow, rhythmic beats, as if breathing.

Around them, workers moved with silent urgency. Tools clanked, voices murmured in clipped exchanges, sweat glistened under the industrial lamps bolted into the ceiling. These men knew their tasks well, tending to the Core with methodical precision.

The chief engineer stopped a few paces from them. He was a broad-shouldered man, arms dusted with residue, his uniform smudged with oil. His gaze darted toward the Warden—brief, measured—before settling on the gauge strapped to his wrist.

"It's holding." His voice was even, but there was weight behind it. "We've adjusted output thresholds in anticipation of the increased demand during the festival."

Nibs, already flipping to a fresh page in his notes, gave a sharp nod. "Good, good—adjusted, thresholds accounted for—" He tapped the clipboard with his knuckle. "And stability? We don't want any surprises, not with the Stratum full of nobles and—" He hesitated. "Other important people."

The engineer barely spared him a glance. "Nothing's redlining."

Nibs clicked his tongue, shifting his stance. "Which means?"

The engineer exhaled, adjusting his grip on the gauge. "Which means you'll have your power for Founders Day."

Nibs nodded quickly, jotting something down. "Excellent, excellent. No concerns, no deviations, everything within operational—"

The Warden cast him a glance.

Nibs cleared his throat. "I mean—good. That's very good."

He snapped his clipboard shut and stepped aside.

The Warden studied the engineer for a long moment, unreadable as the Core's glow pulsed against the glass. The deep hum of the machinery filled the space between them, steady and unbroken, a mechanical heartbeat that dictated Cavandel's survival.

At last, he spoke. "I expect that to remain the case."

The words weren't a threat. Not quite.

The engineer nodded. "We'll keep monitoring."

The Warden didn't answer immediately. Just watched, as if measuring whether his words carried the weight they needed to.

Then, without another glance, he turned and strode forward, his coat shifting in the wake of his movement. Nibs hesitated only a second before hurrying after him, notes in hand, already flipping to the next matter on the li st.

The Core hummed behind them, its glow stretching long shadows against the walls.

The Warden moved through the corridor with purpose, his coat sweeping behind him as he walked. The inner walkways of the Administrative Hall stretched ahead—broad passages of reinforced steel.

They left the inner offices and followed the corridor toward the Administrative Hall's tram station. Tracks wound through the Stratum's vast interior, threading through adjoining halls and slipping in and out of buildings through reinforced arches.

A tram waited on the line, its polished frame catching the lamplight. Smaller than the civilian units, built for efficiency and comfort, it rested with a quiet hum behind the open gate. The operator straightened as the Warden approached. He stepped aboard without hesitation.

Nibs scrambled in after him, adjusting his grip on his clipboard as the car picked up speed once more. "Well, that went smoothly," he muttered, flipping through his notes. "No system collapses, no catastrophic failures—always a good sign, wouldn't you say?"

The Warden said nothing.

The tram carried them forward, weaving through the secured corridors that connected the different wings of the Stratum. Overhead lamps flickered in rhythmic intervals, their pale glow cutting through the dim tunnels. The hum of the track beneath them was steady, a constant undercurrent to the controlled world that existed above the city.

Nibs tapped his pen absently against his clipboard. "Now, just for the record—not that I need to remind you, Warden—but this is, of course, strictly routine. The research team is well-funded, well-monitored and well-aware of expectations." He hesitated, shifting slightly. "Though, in the highly improbable event that anything is amiss, it would be useful to establish, ah... just how amiss that particular thing is."

The Warden's gaze remained fixed ahead.

The tram picked up speed, carrying them closer to the West Wing.

The silence expanded in the space between them until even Nibs seemed reluctant to fill it. He shifted restlessly in his seat, fingers tapping a nervous rhythm against the clipboard, eyes darting periodically toward the Warden before settling back on the blurred walls racing past. The soft pulse of overhead lights seemed to quicken, marking the distance with a muted, relentless rhythm.

Here, in the quieter reaches of the Stratum, the air felt different—not colder exactly, but sharper somehow, stripped of the usual murmur of voices, and steady hum of human activity. The tram slowed slightly, taking a curve with ease, the sound of metal on metal briefly rising before fading once more into the steady hush of the tunnel.

Nibs cleared his throat, hesitated, then thought better of speaking. Instead, he fidgeted, shifting the clipboard from one hand to the other as though uncertain what exactly awaited them, despite all his careful notes and meticulous schedules.

The Warden didn't shift in his seat. His expression was unreadable, gaze fixed steadily toward the faint glow at the end of the tunnel—the West Wing, an area less traveled and more closely guarded than most.

As the tram slowed, the Warden's grip tightened slightly, his knuckles whitening against the armrest. It shuddered softly as it came to a halt. For a moment, neither man moved. Then, with a faint hiss, the doors slid open. Without hesitation, the Warden stepped out into the sterile passageway beyond. Nibs hurried after him, clipboard held tight against his chest, footsteps echoing quietly.

They passed through a succession of offices, each one colder and more precise than the last. Clerks hunched over ledgers beneath the glare of white lamps; the scratch of pens halted as the Warden entered, then resumed only after he'd gone. The scent of oil and ink hung in the stillness. Nibs caught glimpses through glass partitions—high shelves, stacks of papers, indistinct silhouettes moving behind frosted panes—but no one met his eyes.

The air changed subtly as they advanced, taking on a heavy quality that seemed to press against his skin. Nibs' pulse quickened as he caught sight of the single reinforced door ahead, marked with symbols of caution. Whatever lay ahead was known only to a select few.

They entered and the doors locked behind them with a heavy, resonant thud. Nibs felt a chill run along his spine, as the mechanism sealed them off from everything familiar.

The chamber beyond was expansive and meticulously ordered. Bright, clinical lights illuminated a network of containment units crafted of reinforced glass, standing neatly in rows atop grated flooring lined with embedded pipes. Within each unit, shadowy shapes shifted restlessly—large, insectile forms moving in agitated patterns behind thick, transparent barriers.

Rocknids.

Nibs felt his throat tighten, his fingers gripping the clipboard until his knuckles whitened. Each glass enclosure was meticulously fitted with brass gauges and slowly rotating clockwork dials, ticking quietly with mechanical precision.

Footsteps approached sharply. A figure emerged—tall, professional, the collar of his lab coat high and pristine. The lead scientist's expression was neutral, controlled.

"We've been expecting you," he said, directing his gaze squarely to the Warden, his eyes flicking to Nibs for only the briefest moment.

"Report," the Warden instructed simply.

The scientist nodded once, succinct. "Containment is stable. We've implemented your latest directive on toxin dispersion and are tracking its efficiency. Mortality rates within isolated samples indicate potential for rapid extermination." He paused, choosing his next words with careful precision. "Given current progress, we anticipate soon achieving the capacity to eliminate large swaths of Rocknid populations efficiently, should conditions remain optimal."

Eliminate large swaths. The scientist's tone was clinical, removed, but Nibs felt an uneasy chill at the thought.

The Warden moved slowly past the nearest enclosure, observing its occupant with detached scrutiny.

"Careful, sir," the scientist cautioned quietly, taking a cautious step forward. "Though subdued, they can still be unpredictable."

Inside, a Rocknid shifted sluggishly, its normally sharp, restless movements dulled, slowed. The creature seemed diminished, its usual predatory strength stripped away.

His gaze sharpened as he watched the subdued movements of the creature, thoughts quietly weaving through his mind. For years, Rocknids had plagued Cavandel, lurking in shadowed tunnels, striking swiftly and without warning. He recalled countless reports—miners lost, tunnels sealed, precious time wasted. The threat hung constantly over production, a grim inevitability, an enemy hidden beneath their very feet.

But now, the possibility stretched before him clearly—eradication. Not simply containment, not cautious defense. Absolute, final eradication. A future free from their threat, tunnels secure, miners unburdened by fear. Production lines flowing uninterrupted, workers delving deeper into unexplored veins of Crythium without hesitation.

Cavandel would rise, prosperous and unchallenged, its strength multiplied many times over. And at the center of it all would stand the Warden himself, the architect of their safety, the man who tamed the untamable.

A fleeting satisfaction traced the edge of his thoughts, cold and clinical yet undeniable in its appeal.

The Warden let the thought settle, final and unquestioned. "Good. Continue as planned." His voice was calm, decisive. Then, without another word, he turned, coat flaring slightly and strode back toward the doors. Nibs lingered only a second before scrambling after him, nearly tripping over his own feet in his haste to keep up as the massive doors sealed shut behind them.

The last leg of the journey brought Thaddeus and Nibs to the Lift station. The massive structure loomed ahead, its iron framework stretching high into the cavern, reinforced with thick chains and gears.

The main platform rested in its dock, secured by interlocking metal braces, while the surrounding walkways bustled with movement—guards stationed at key points, workers tending to the machinery that powered the Stratum's only passage downward.

As they approached, Drazic was already at work. He stood near the platform's edge, giving low, precise commands to a cluster of guards. His movements were sharp, decisive, one hand cutting through the air as he directed them, the other resting against his belt where Scarlet hung coiled at his hip.

The guards nodded in clipped motions before peeling away, their boots striking hard against the metal as they moved to carry out his orders.

Nibs lingered a step behind as Thaddeus approached.

Drazic, without looking, shifted his weight, his hand brushing the coil of Scarlet as if shedding the last conversation before turning to greet the next. His gaze passed over them, slow, unreadable, before settling on the Warden.

Thaddeus's voice was low, even. "Mr. Grask."

Drazic's mouth tilted slightly. "Warden."

His gaze moved briefly to Nibs, offering nothing more than a nod.

Nibs, perhaps taking the silence as an invitation—or maybe just unwilling to let it stretch—cleared his throat and hurried to fill it.

"The Warden wanted to check on the final festival preparations," he said, voice quick, words tumbling over each other. "The procession, the vendors, the—uh—the musicians, of course, but also the ale situation—" He gestured vaguely, as if that explained everything. "Everything's coming together nicely, I'm sure, but it never hurts to check, does it?"

Drazic didn't blink.

Nibs swallowed. "Right. Of course."

Thaddeus exhaled. "I take it that preparations are underway, Mr. Grask?"

Drazic let the question settle before exhaling, unhurried. "Everything's on schedule, Warden."

Thaddeus adjusted the cuff of his sleeve. "The streets," he said after a moment. "Did you hear about the flooding near the east quarter? Some of the merchants are claiming their stalls took water damage. That won't affect the procession route, will it?"

Drazic studied him, considering. "Already handled, Warden. We redirected foot traffic and reinforced the worst of it. So there shouldn't be any delays."

Thaddeus gave a slow nod. "Very good." He cleared his throat. "And the ale?" he hesitated briefly, then added, "Last year, some of the merchants thought we were running low."

Drazic gave a short, knowing exhale. "I'm not surprised." Then, with a slight shake of his head he added, "We weren't."

Thaddeus exhaled, glancing aside. "No, of course not," he said quickly. "Still. A perception issue, if nothing else."

Drazic inclined his head slightly. "Maybe. But it's easy to complain about ale when it's on someone else's coin."

Thaddeus tapped his sleeve once. "And Rosfort had the gall to claim that the boar was overcooked."

Drazic, despite himself, offered a small, deferential nod. "Well, we can't please everyone, Warden."

Thaddeus let out a slow breath. "No. No, of course not."

A moment passed before he shifted his weight. "And, the music?"

Drazic's tone remained measured. "Do you have a particular request, Warden?"

Thaddeus hesitated. "What kind of music do you suppose the prince enjoys?"

Drazic took a brief moment before answering. "Difficult to say... But I'm sure the musicians can adjust as needed."

Thaddeus ignored that. "We shouldn't assume, of course. But do you think we ought to... restrain them from playing anything too—" He searched for the word. "Rambunctious?"

Drazic's expression remained unreadable, but his voice was as steady as ever. "I'll make sure they keep it civilized."

Thaddeus gave a single nod. "Good."

Drazic let the silence settle for a breath before exhaling. "Anything else, Warden?"

Thaddeus straightened. "Very good, very good. Keep up the good work."

He turned and strode away.

Nibs, scrambling after him, echoed the words under his breath. "Yes, keep up the good work."

Drazic watched them go, his expression unreadable—except for the slight crease in his brow, as if wondering what in the depths that was all about.

Location: Cavandel, Dweller's Base

The strike came fast.

Aria barely caught it in time. She shifted her weight, pivoting to deflect the blow, but the impact still rattled up her arm. Too slow. Too rigid. She corrected, adjusting her stance just as Pike pressed forward again, forcing her onto the defensive.

She tried to read him—tried to anticipate—but he wasn't giving her anything. No hesitation. No wasted movement. Just relentless, calculated strikes, each one pressing her closer to the edge of the sparring ring.

A feint. A sudden shift.

Aria swung too late.

Pike knocked her weapon aside and drove forward, catching her off balance. She twisted, bracing for the fall, but the padded floor met her hard. The impact sent a jolt through her arms as she caught herself.

Pike stepped back. "Again."

Aria exhaled sharply, pushing herself upright. She rolled her shoulders, resetting her grip on the wooden lance. This time, she didn't wait for him to move first.

She lunged.

A clash of wood. A step, a pivot, a counterstrike—she met him this time, the force of the impact vibrating through her grip. He adjusted easily, shifting to break her momentum, but she didn't let him. She forced him back. Just a step. Just enough.

Something flickered behind his eyes—not surprise, but acknowledgment. Then, just as quickly, he reset.

The next exchange was faster. Harder. Aria matched him as best she could, but he was still stronger, still quicker. A wrong step sent her skidding and before she could recover, Pike had her again

He tilted his head. "Better," he said. Then, after a breath: "Much better."

He hesitated, as if weighing whether to say more. "You can't always count on someone to pull you out when the fire closes in," he added quietly. "Learn to stand before it swallows you."

Aria lay still for a moment, her pulse thrumming in her ears.

Not enough.

That was how it had always felt.

In the beginning, every fall had been a failure. Every misstep, a reminder of how much further she had to go. But now, the sting of losing wasn't what lingered.

It was the weight of why she kept getting back up.

At first, it had been for her grandmother. For the cure. For the small, personal fight that had mattered more than anything else. But the more she trained, the more she fought, the more she saw—she realized it had become more than just that.

It was for all of Cavandel.

The city she had once dreamed of leaving, now a place she couldn't walk away from. Not while it suffered. Not while it decayed under the weight of the Warden's rule.

It was for the Dwellers who had stood at the gates, waiting, counting, hoping to see a familiar face return from the depths. It was for the ones who would never get the chance to fight at all.

And somewhere in the back of her mind, she thought of the book.

The worn pages, the careful script, the way her grandmother had always turned to it with reverence. She had followed its words like a map, like a promise—never realizing where they would lead her.

She thought of the surface and realized she hadn't thought of it at all. Not for days. Not since before the hunt.

Once, it had been an obsession—the unknown sky, the stories of open air, the world beyond Cavandel. But here, now, that longing felt distant. Small.

Because no matter what existed beyond this city, this was where she was needed.

She rose to her full height, knees steady beneath her, grip firm around the lance.

Pike watched her, unreadable.

She squared her stance. "Again."

Aria was ready this time.

Pike moved in fast, but she saw it—the shift in his footing just before he struck. Instead of blocking outright, she pivoted, redirecting his momentum just enough to throw him off-balance. He caught himself before stumbling, but it was a near thing.

A near thing was still a victory.

She stepped back, grip steady on her lance.

From the doorway, Heidi let out a low whistle.

Pike turned his head slightly, but Aria didn't miss the way his gaze lingered on her just a moment longer. Then, with a small nod, he said, "You're getting there."

It wasn't praise. Not exactly. But from him, it might as well have been.

Aria exhaled, steadying herself as Pike stepped back, flexing his fingers as he uncoiled the tension from them. "We'll go again tomorrow."

He turned toward the exit, only to find Heidi still standing there, arms crossed, a huge grin plastered across her face.

Pike eyed her. "Haven't seen you in two days."

Heidi rocked back on her heels. "Sorry. Been a little busy."

Pike gave a low humph, brushing past her without another word.

The moment he disappeared, Heidi turned back to Aria, her grin widening.

"You really whooped him."

Aria wiped the back of her hand across her forehead. "Don't know about that," she murmured.

Heidi scoffed. "Well, I do."

Aria shook her head, a quiet laugh slipping out. "Maybe a little."

Heidi's own laugh rose in answer, gentle and unforced, and for a moment neither of them spoke. They simply stood there, looking at each other, sharing something silent yet understood.

Then, Heidi's voice softened. "How are you doing?"

Aria took a breath, flexing her fingers before resting the lance against her shoulder. "Hanging in there." She met Heidi's gaze. "And you?"

Heidi hesitated, her gaze lingering on Aria for a moment before she shrugged. "I don't know... every time I close my eyes, it feels like I'm back down there." She forced a smirk. "Remind me to never do anything like that again."

Aria studied her lifelong friend, something unreadable in her expression. Then, she nodded. "I'm sorry."

Heidi shrugged again, but there was no real dismissal to it. Just acceptance.

Aria let the silence settle before she tilted her head. "Where's Sylas?"

Heidi's lips twitched. "I think he's smitten with Anna."

Aria blinked. "What?"

"He spends all his time in the lab now," Heidi said, amusement coloring her voice. "Thinks he's some kind of scientist. But I know he's just trying to impress her."

Aria let out a quiet breath of a laugh. "He better hope Sebastian doesn't find out."

That set both of them off, their laughter soft and brief before fading back into the moment.

Heidi nudged her playfully. "Anyway, come on. I can't wait to show you this." She led Aria toward the benches.

Heidi sat down, stretching her legs out in front of her. "Honestly, this thing would've been impossible without Sebastian's help."

Aria quirked a brow. "Really?"

Heidi's eyes widened. "Have you seen his machine shop? That place is insane. He's got parts for everything and tools I didn't even know existed." She shook her head, still impressed. "Give me enough time and the right pieces, and I could probably build anything."

She sat up, flashing Aria a grin. "Which is why you're gonna love what I'm doing with your lance."

***

The scent of antiseptic and crushed herbs lingered in the air as Aria and Heidi stepped inside. The lab was alive with movement, voices low but constant, weaving through the clink of glass and the scratch of ink against parchment.

Anna stood at the heart of it all, the weight of Aria's grandmother's book balanced in her hands, its pages worn from years of careful study. She moved through the space with quiet purpose, her gaze sharp as she checked over each workstation, pausing only long enough to observe, to correct, to ensure that no mistake went unnoticed.

Each of her assistants was working on a different test sample. Some measured powders in careful increments, others stirred solutions over low heat, watching intently for signs of change. The cure was close—but close wasn't enough. Every minor adjustment, every alteration in technique, might be the difference between failure and the answer they needed.

Against the far wall, a handful of patients rested on cots, their breathing uneven. One stirred, rolling onto his side, coughing into the crook of his arm before going still again.

Aria swallowed. The weight of their presence was impossible to ignore.

Anna finished reviewing one station, nodding slightly before stepping toward the next. Her gaze settled on Sylas, who was hunched over a small glass vial, carefully swirling its contents. The liquid inside was dark, its viscosity wrong, refusing to blend the way it should.

"How's your sample coming?" she asked, her voice quiet but firm.

Sylas didn't look up immediately. He gave the vial another turn in his hands, watching the way the liquid pulled apart before exhaling sharply. "The extract isn't binding," he murmured. "Separates the second I stop stirring."

Anna pressed her lips together, flipping through the pages of the book, her thumb skimming across a familiar passage. "Try increasing the heat," she said. "Not much—just enough to keep the suspension stable."

Sylas gave a small nod, already adjusting the burner beneath his vial.

Anna lingered only a moment longer before moving on, but the tension settled across her shoulders like a weight she refused to acknowledge. There was no outward frustration, no visible strain, but it was there—in the way she held the book a little tighter, in the way her gaze flickered, however briefly, toward the patients before snapping back to the work in front of her.

Heidi stood beside Aria, arms crossed as she studied the array of flasks and powders. "How close are we?"

Anna didn't answer right away. She skimmed a few more notes, eyes narrowing before she let out a slow breath. "Close," she said softly.

The conversation moved on in low, precise threads, details traded in careful tones, each instruction carrying the weight of someone who understood exactly what hung in the balance.

At first, Aria didn't notice the figure at the doorway. He wasn't meant to be noticed.

Kegan leaned against the frame, listening. Watching. His presence didn't announce itself; he offered no quip, no comment, made no attempt to join the conversation. He was simply there, absorbing what he could, his eyes drifting over the work, taking in the pages of notes, the murmured exchanges, the steady glow caught in the glass vials.

He didn't linger long.

By the time Aria felt the prickle at the back of her neck, he was already gone.

She turned sharply, her pulse kicking up for a reason she couldn't quite name. But when her gaze swept toward the doorway, it was empty.

The work continued around them, undisturbed. The murmurs remained steady, the quiet urgency of the lab unchanged.

And yet, something inside her warned that Kegan had seen exactly what he came for.

18

The Dark Gambit

Location: Cavandel, Dweller's Base

The small workshop held no sense of time, but Aria knew the hour had grown late. The glow-lamps burned lower, and the steady hum of voices had quieted to a murmur. Those still awake moved with a sense of finality, finishing tasks before retreating to their quarters.

Anna had worked them to the bone before finally shooing them out of the lab, muttering about needing peace to finish her calculations. Instead of resting, they had turned their attention to the lance, determined to make progress before the night was through. They had been at it for some time now, the work slow and meticulous, each adjustment bringing them closer—but not close enough.

Heidi hunched over the workbench, unwavering, her sleeves shoved past her elbows, eyes sharp with concentration as she studied the mechanism before her. If exhaustion had crept in, she ignored it entirely. Heidi muttered something under her breath, twisting a bolt into place. "Tension's not distributing right." She sat back slightly, frowning at the mechanism. "Something's still off."

Sylas, slumped against a chair with his head resting in his palm, gave a lazy wave of his other hand. "You've said that for the past hour."

She ignored him, adjusting the compression mechanism with steady hands.

Aria pressed down on the shortened shaft as Heidi made another tweak. With a sharp clank, the lance extended about a foot before jerking to a halt, the movement stiff and unsteady.

Heidi swore under her breath, tightening a bolt before exhaling sharply and dragging a hand through her hair. "Right now, it compresses fine, but the tension spring isn't resetting properly. It won't extend all the way unless you manually adjust it."

She let out a short, frustrated sigh. "I need a stronger release mechanism. And probably a better locking pin—something that can withstand repeated stress without jamming."

Aria wiped a smudge of oil from her palm. "Maybe the coil needs more tension?"

"I thought of that," Heidi said, already reaching for a screwdriver. "But if I tighten it too much, it'll resist unfolding entirely."

Sylas let his head tip back against the chair. "And you're sure this thing won't randomly snap open and impale someone in a crowded market?"

Aria gave him a flat look. "You do realize I'm the one carrying it, right?"

Heidi rolled her eyes. "There's a safety latch. You have to twist the handle like this first"—she demonstrated the motion with a quick turn of her wrist—"before you press the release. It won't extend otherwise."

Sylas lifted a hand in mock surrender. "Right. Because everything always works exactly as planned."

Heidi regarded him with a slow, measured look—one that conveyed, with effortless precision, just how little she thought of his remark.

Aria exhaled before pushing off the workbench. "We should wrap up soon," she said, glancing toward the entrance. "I need to check on Gran."

Heidi barely looked up, still turning the mechanism between her fingers, testing the weight of it. "Don't let us keep you," she murmured, her tone light with understanding. "We'll finish up here soon—go on. We'll see you in the morning."

Sylas groaned, letting his head roll to the side. "What about me?" he sighed dramatically. "If you're staying, that means I have to stay."

Heidi smirked, shifting a gear between her fingers as if considering it. "Go ahead, Sylas. I'm sure I can manage without you," she said, her voice dripping with sarcasm.

Sylas rubbed a hand over his face, shaking his head. "Right... and let you take all the credit?"

Aria shook her head, lifting a hand in farewell as she slipped toward the hidden exit at the back of the workshop. It had taken her weeks to memorize the twisting tunnels that led out from the Dwellers' base without passing through Marielle's Inn, but now, it was second nature.

She pressed through the narrow gap, stepping into the concealed passageway, where the air was cooler, laced with the faint scent of damp stone. The walls brushed her fingertips, rough beneath her touch, and somewhere in the distance, the soft drip of water echoed through the tunnels.

A few minutes later, she emerged into the Mining Camp, the scent of rock dust and iron filling her lungs.

Location: Cavandel, The Mines

Outside the Dwellers' stronghold, the world widened. The scent of smelted iron bled into rock dust and the damp, mineral-laced air of the mines. The shift was subtle but distinct, a reminder that she was stepping beyond the place where she had spent most of her recent nights.

The Mining Camp stretched around her, its low-built structures clustered together against the rock face. Lanterns flickered behind canvas flaps and workers moved between shelters, some just coming off shift, others gathering in quiet groups.

She kept her pace steady, watching without lingering. City guards patrolled the pathways, their presence a quiet weight in the air. A handful of men strung up cloth banners between wooden beams, their colors dulled beneath the lights. Nearby, an older worker inspected the decorations with a frown.

"More of this nonsense already," he muttered, voice carrying just enough to invite disagreement. "Whole festival's still days off and they're already wasting time on this."

A younger man laughed, shaking dust from his sleeves. "Don't worry, Harren, no one's forcing you to celebrate."

The older worker scoffed but said nothing more. Aria moved past them, their voices trailing into the shuffle of boots over packed dirt.

Beyond the camp, the Lift loomed, its massive framework rising into the dark. The Lift's machinery churned steadily, its deep, rhythmic hum woven into the city's breath.

A handful of people waited near the boarding platform, some sitting idly, others speaking in hushed tones. A merchant counted his inventory, pausing to shift a barrel before muttering something under his breath.

A pair of guards stood near the controls, their posture lax but their presence enough to remind everyone who controlled the passage upward. Another pair lingered farther back, speaking in hushed tones, their watchful eyes sweeping over the waiting passengers.

Aria stepped onto the platform as the Lift operator called for passengers.

The great metal construct shuddered, as it lurched upward. Below, the Mining Camp shrank, its lights dimming to scattered embers before vanishing into shadow.

Darkness swallowed everything but the brief gleam of embedded shaft lights, flickering past in steady intervals. The ascent was familiar, but tonight, the movement of the Lift felt deliberate, its rhythm weighted. The increased patrols gnawed at her awareness, another sign of a city tightening its grip. Above and below, layers of metal and stone stretched endlessly, gears shifting, voices rising and fading like echoes in the deep.

The darkness finally relented.

As the Lift eased to a halt, the District emerged, its lights pushing back the lingering shadows.

The railcar station was quieter at this hour. The few passengers waiting stood apart from one another, their conversations muted. Aria took a seat by the window as the car rumbled to life, the tracks vibrating beneath her.

She could see the remnants of the day's festival preparations—streets bearing the quiet imprint of celebration. The stalls, now shuttered for the night, bore traces of the day's activity—crates stacked beside awnings, the scent of spices lingering in the still air, and stray festival ribbons still tied to poles, fluttering faintly in the stillness.

Broad streets lined with merchant stalls stretched before her, the buildings taller, their glow-lamps casting golden light onto polished stone.

Through the glass, she watched the last stretch of the Inner District—festival lanterns strung across streets, unlit but waiting.

As the railcar carried her forward, the glow-lamps grew sparser, the polished storefronts giving way to dim lanterns and simpler façades.

Then, the Outer District.

The shift was gradual—buildings stood lower, the streets emptier. Where the Inner District was lined with polished storefronts, the Outer District bore the weight of necessity. Here, the festival had yet to truly take hold.

The railcar screeched softly as it eased to a stop, its motion fading into the quiet of the platform.

Aria stepped off, the familiar scent of home settling around her—coal smoke, damp stone, and a faint trace of something fried lingering in the air.

She walked the narrow streets without hurry, the weight of the day pressing into her steps.

At the end of the lane, her grandmother's home stood in quiet patience, its shutters closed against the night. The sight of it, unchanged, was both a relief and a reminder of everything she carried with her.

Inside, the air was still. A single lantern sat on the small table, its light stretching in soft amber across the walls, making the space feel smaller, warmer.

Aria set down her things without a sound, slipping past the main room to where her grandmother slept. She paused in the doorway, her gaze settling on the gentle rise and fall of the blankets, the quiet rhythm of breath beneath them.

Something inside her eased. Not fully, but enough.

She did not speak, did not wake her. Instead, she sank onto the small chair by the hearth, pulling her knees close as she watched the last embers settle into the quiet glow of dying warmth.

Outside, the city stirred—its breath a hush of distant footsteps and the soft murmur of voices behind shuttered windows.

Inside, she let the quiet settle around her, if only for a little while.

Location: Cavandel, The Outer District

Morning stretched quiet and unhurried, the soft glow of Cavandel's artificial daylight filtering through the shutters in narrow bands. It painted the small room in gold and shadow, shifting with the flicker of the bedside lamp.

Aria worked the comb carefully through her grandmother's hair, slow and methodical, easing out the knots that had formed overnight. The strands, once thick and dark, were finer now, silver tracing through them like delicate veins in stone.

Her grandmother sat with the quiet stillness of age—hands resting lightly in her lap, breath steady. She had always liked the quiet rhythm of a comb working through her hair, the way it eased her into wakefulness. Even now, when her body grew weary too quickly and lifting a comb herself felt like more effort than it was worth, she still welcomed it.

Aria combed through another section, careful not to tug.

"Careful hands, just like your mother's. More patient than mine ever were," her grandmother murmured.

Aria paused, the comb hesitating in her grip. A mention of her mother—her grandmother rarely spoke of her without purpose. Something was coming. She made a quiet sound in response, neither agreement nor denial and continued. A long moment passed, the hush between them comfortable. Then, just as Aria reached the last of the tangles, her grandmother spoke again, her voice soft, almost idle.

"The festival will be here soon." Her grandmother's tone was light, conversational. "The streets must be filled with decorations already."

The comb stilled for only a second before continuing its path.

"I suppose."

Her grandmother hummed. "You used to love seeing them go up. Always asked me when the lanterns would be hung."

Aria finished the last stroke and set the comb aside, reaching for a ribbon to gather the strands neatly. "The festival's still days off," she said, as though that alone excused her lack of thought.

"Yes," her grandmother agreed. "But it will come quickly. It always does."

Aria said nothing.

She tied the ribbon with practiced ease, letting the ends trail softly over her grandmother's shoulder.

"You used to love Founders Day," her grandmother mused. "When you were small, you'd race out the door before I could even fasten the buttons on your dress."

She let the memory settle between them, her smile thinning with a hint of curiosity. "And this year? I imagine a few young men have asked if they'll see you at the festival."

Aria exhaled and leaned back. "I have far more important things to worry about," she said, dismissive. "And besides, I was just a child back then."

She could almost see it—lanterns strung between balconies, the scent of spiced pastries drifting through the streets, laughter echoing between the stone walls. The giddy rush of weaving through crowds, Sylas chasing her, Heidi placing bets on which couple would make fools of themselves first. She had loved it once, hadn't she?

Her grandmother's words cut through the memory, drawing Aria back to the present. "And are these things more important than your own future? Than finding someone to share your heart with?" Her tone stayed gentle, but the plea beneath it was unmistakable. "It isn't selfish to want something beyond survival, Aria."

She knew what was coming before the words even formed.

Her grandmother reached for her hand, holding it tenderly, her touch gentle but steady. "You've grown so much, Aria. But not so much that you should turn away from life entirely."

Aria lowered her gaze.

The weight of the moment pressed against her ribs, an ache she had not invited.

"I'm not turning away from anything," she said, quieter than she intended.

Her grandmother's fingers lingered over hers, a warmth that was both familiar and fleeting. She had always been there—the reason Founders Day had never felt lonely. The thought of walking through the streets without her felt—wrong.

"This is the first year I won't be there." She paused, her grip on Aria's hand tightening slightly. "I wish I could, but..." The words drifted off, unfinished.

Aria swallowed.

That was what made it different, wasn't it? Not just that she had outgrown the festival, not just that there were more important things to do.

It was that this year, the person who had made it feel like home wouldn't be beside her, watching the lanterns glow against the cavern walls, laughing at the songs drifting through the streets.

It wouldn't be the same.

And if it wouldn't be the same, then what was the point?

She hesitated too long. Her grandmother saw it. Gently, she curled Aria's fingers into a loose fist. "You don't have to go for yourself," she said calmly, "but maybe go for me."

Aria looked up then, something twisting in her chest.

The warmth of the room, the hush of morning—it felt too soft to hold the weight of the words.

Her grandmother smiled, faint but steady. "One night, Aria. That's all."

Aria didn't answer. Couldn't. Maybe because part of her wanted to say yes. Maybe because she wasn't sure if she belonged there anymore. Instead, she nodded, just enough to be seen and let her grandmother press a kiss to her knuckles before releasing her hand.

***

By late morning, Aria had prepared breakfast, ensured her grandmother took her medicine and seen her off to rest. The house had settled into a quiet lull, the kind that came after a morning spent in careful routine—measured, familiar, steady.

She had just taken up her needle by the window, the fabric stretched across her lap, when the knock came. Sharp and rhythmic, followed by the unmistakable clatter of Sylas setting something down too forcefully.

"Aria," Heidi's voice carried through the wood, bright and unbothered. "Let us in before he drops anything else."

Aria sighed, tying off the last stitch in her fabric. She considered leaving them to struggle—just to see how long Sylas would wrestle with whatever he'd dragged to her doorstep. But she pushed up from her seat and un-latched the door, stepping back just as Heidi swept inside, arms laden with flour-dusted cloth and bundles of colorful ribbons.

Sylas followed, a wooden crate wedged against his hip, his movements betraying his strength despite his casual demeanor. "Morning," he said, as if he hadn't just declared war on her doorstep.

Aria folded her arms across her chest, eyebrow arched. "You know, I'm starting to think you two just like making a mess of my house."

"Not true." Heidi set her things on the table, already unwrapping a bundle of spiced sticks that filled the air with their warm aroma. "We like making a mess of your house and eating all your food."

Sylas nudged the crate onto the floor with a dull thud. "And borrowing your things. Let's not forget that part." His eyes sparkled with mischief.

Aria gave him a withering look, but he only grinned, undeterred.

For years, festival preparations at Aria's home had been their tradition—a day of baking, decorating and arguing over outfits. It was their way of marking the season, a ritual built from friendship and the quiet understanding of children who had lost their parents to the mines.

What had begun as an escape from the crowded streets leading up to Founders Day had become something sacred—an unspoken bond, a rare piece of stability in a world that offered little of it. Now, it was expected.

Even if Aria had outgrown the festival's charm, even if part of her yearned to keep her distance this year, Heidi and Sylas had never been ones to take no for an answer.

Heidi was already unrolling a length of fabric, her eyes lighting up as she held it against her torso, the color bringing out the amber flecks in her gaze. "I found the perfect color," she declared with theatrical pride, swaying from side to side as if modeling the fabric. "You both should be honored to witness this moment."

Sylas leaned against the counter, arms lazily crossed, the very picture of nonchalance. "Truly, a privilege," he said.

Heidi ignored him, holding up a different strip of fabric, this one darker, more subdued. "What about you, Aria? Something dark, maybe? You do love to brood."

Aria exhaled, shoulders dropping slightly. "I do not brood. And besides, I already have something from last year."

The quiet stretched, heavier than expected, like a breath held too long.

She had expected a quip, a sharp remark—something, anything—but instead, the room went entirely too still.

Heidi and Sylas exchanged a look, the kind that passed between conspirators. Then, Heidi took a slow, deliberate sip from her tea.

Aria frowned, suspicion creeping in. "What?"

Sylas exhaled, a half-smile playing at his lips. "Well... have you tried it on?"

She narrowed her eyes. "Of course I have."

Sylas did not look convinced. "This year, or last?" There was a weight to his amusement now, a smug undercurrent that immediately put her on guard.

Heidi set down her cup with exaggerated delicacy, the muted clank against the table punctuating the moment. "No offense, but, um... it's been a year, Aria."

Aria scoffed. "So?"

Heidi raised her eyebrows. "Well, you don't exactly look the same. You have more—" She gestured vaguely but knowingly at Aria, her meaning clear in its implication.

Neither of them spoke, but Aria felt heat creep up her neck, blooming across her cheeks in a bright crimson flush that betrayed her.

Then—Heidi made an entirely unhelpful gesture toward the back room. "Go on then, let's see."

Aria stared, incredulous. "You're not serious."

Sylas smiled, all teeth and challenge. "Oh, we are."

Aria muttered under her breath and turned sharply on her heel. Fine. She'd prove them wrong and wipe those smug looks from their faces.

Not even two minutes later, regret settled in like a stone in her stomach.

The dress had fit perfectly last year. Now the seams tugged uncomfortably at her shoulders, and the skirt, which should have flowed easily around her legs, felt like a trap closing in.

She muttered silently under her breath, twisting and testing the fit. The seam pulled taut—dangerously so, threatening to split with each movement.

Absolutely not.

She was about to wrench the whole thing off when a voice carried from the other room, far too amused for her liking.

"You're being awfully quiet in there."

Aria scowled at the closed door. "I'm fine."

Heidi laughed, the sound light and knowing. "If you have to say that, then you're definitely not fine."

Aria glared at the old mirror as though it had personally betrayed her, showing truths she wasn't ready to face. "It still fits," she turned and called through the door.

Sylas snorted. "And by *fits*, you mean?"

She considered making something up, even storming out in the cursed thing just to prove them wrong.

But then she imagined Sylas' expression—the slow, insufferable grin, the barely-restrained laughter that would follow her for weeks.

No. She wouldn't give him the satisfaction.

Scowling, she tugged the dress off, threw on a more comfortable tunic and stalked back into the living room, empty-handed and defiant.

Sylas took one look at her empty hands and let out a low whistle. "You're making this too easy."

Heidi pressed a hand over her mouth, eyes bright with painfully contained amusement that danced behind her fingers.

Aria set her hands on the table with enough force to make the flour shift in small clouds. "Not a word."

Sylas opened his mouth, challenge written across his features.

She narrowed her eyes, a silent warning.

He closed his mouth, but the victory gleamed in his eyes nonetheless.

Heidi cleared her throat, smoothing out a ribbon that didn't really need smoothing. "Well," she said, entirely too pleased, "I suppose that means we're going dress shopping."

Aria groaned, dragging a hand down her face in defeat.

Sylas clapped her on the back as he passed, his touch warm and familiar. "Look at it this way," he said. "Now you don't have any excuses left not to go."

***

The tailor's shop was one of the quieter ones, tucked between a perfumery and a bookbinder's stall. It carried the clean scent of freshly pressed fabric, with lavender sachets nestled between bolts of fine fabric.

Aria stood stiffly as the tailor draped a length of fabric against her, muttering about adjustments.

Heidi, however, was positively thriving. "This one," she said, pressing a deeper shade of blue into Aria's hands. "It'll look perfect with—"

"Whatever mask you force on me," Aria said in a dry, level voice.

"Yes," Heidi agreed, her smile brief but genuine.

Sylas lounged near the entrance, studying the array of masks on display. "This one," he mused, lifting an intricate silver piece with cutout filigree. "For the brooding heroine aesthetic."

Aria ignored him.

The tailor fastened a pin at her waist, stepping back to examine the fit. "Lovely," she remarked. "A fine choice."

Aria shifted, vaguely uncomfortable.

Heidi beamed. Sylas looked as if he were about to unleash something devastatingly sarcastic but, mercifully, kept it to himself.

"I hope you enjoy the festival," the tailor added, adjusting a sleeve.

Aria's mouth pressed into a line.

She wasn't sure enjoy was the word.

But she was going.

And apparently, she'd be wearing something that fit.

***

Overnight, the streets had transformed. What had been a slow, creeping buildup—the occasional banner strung between buildings, the murmured anticipation of merchants—had fully bloomed into something impossible to ignore.

Aria moved through the Inner District with her friends, their pace steady but unhurried, absorbing the transformation around them. Glow-lamps traced the avenues, casting warmth onto stone façades. Overhead, paper lanterns swayed, stirring with each passing step. Vendors had expanded their stalls, pushing closer into the streets, their displays richer, more extravagant than usual.

Crates of fresh produce sat beneath cloth awnings, fruit—fresh from the Stratum, polished to a near-shine. Stands selling fine fabrics and delicate embroidery unfurled their wares like offerings, bolts of fine linen and brocade draped over wooden frames. Perfume merchants fanned small glass bottles beneath the noses of passing customers, the scent of crushed florals and spice curling into the air.

The festival had yet to arrive, but the city was already breathing as if it had.

Ahead, a group of children dashed between the stalls, their laughter sharp against the low murmur of conversation. A woman with flour-dusted hands bartered over the price of imported sugar, her voice rising in mild protest as the vendor waved a dismissive hand. A cluster of men leaned against a railing, discussing which tavern would have the best stock of festival ale.

The city hummed with anticipation, the air thick with movement, voices, light. Yet Aria remained untouched by it. She wove through the crowd, her steps light but detached, watching the city move around her like an observer rather than a participant.

She had walked these streets her entire life, knew their patterns, their rhythms. But today, they felt different. Not because they had changed—but because she had.

She turned a corner and nearly collided with a miner hauling a sack over his shoulder. He muttered something under his breath, shifting the load, but it was the look he cast toward the festival stalls that caught her attention.

Disdain.

Disinterest.

She followed his gaze to a vendor arranging delicate silver trinkets onto a velvet cloth. A woman—dressed in the fine-cut linen of a wealthier merchant's wife—picked one up, turning it over in her hand before smiling at the craftsmanship. She didn't spare a glance at the miner beside her.

Aria exhaled slowly.

The contrast had always been there—the divide between those who kept Cavandel running and those who thrived from its labor. But on festival days, it sharpened.

A little girl, no older than six, tugged at her father's sleeve, pointing toward a table of painted festival masks. He hesitated only a moment before kneeling, lifting a simple wooden one for her to inspect.

Nearby, a pair of young men, dressed in the rich fabrics of the Inner District, debated over two nearly identical masks of intricate gold filigree.

The father set the wooden mask down. Shook his head. Took his daughter's hand and led her away.

The young men laughed as they made their purchase.

Aria's stomach twisted.

Further down, a group of miners gathered outside a metalworking shop, their voices edged with quiet irritation. "All this coin wasted on nonsense," one grumbled, rubbing a hand over his jaw. "Food, ale, decorations—it'll be gone in a night."

"And we'll still be here when it's over," another said. "Still underpaid, still overworked."

A third let out a short laugh, humorless. "At least we'll get a free drink out of it."

The first man didn't laugh. "Not free," he grumbled, shaking his head. "Nothing ever is."

Aria kept walking.

Their voices faded behind her, lost beneath the sound of a street musician testing the strings of his lyre.

The city was dressed for celebration. But beneath the finery, its bones remained unchanged. That was the Cavandel she knew. And now, standing here, wrapped in the hum of festival anticipation, she felt the distance between the two worlds like a fault line. A seam waiting to split. All of it was just a brief distraction, before work resumed the next morning.

She adjusted the strap of the parcel she carried, fingers curling briefly around the edge.

She had a dress now. A mask.

She had everything required of her.

Yet for all the city's laughter and light, she had never felt further from it.

***

The house had long since settled into silence.

Aria sat on the edge of her bed, feet planted firmly against the worn wooden floor, the fabric of the dress pooling across her lap like spilled ink. She traced a hand over its folds, feeling the unfamiliar weight of it, the softness that belonged to someone else.

It was finely made. Not extravagant, not cut from the impossibly delicate linens of the Inner District, but well-crafted, with careful stitching along the seams and a drape meant to flatter. She supposed it was beautiful.

But it did not feel like it belonged to her.

The mask lay beside it, its carved lines catching the lamplight, turning its painted filigree into sharp, glinting curves. It was meant to conceal, but right now, it only felt like something that would make her stand out.

Her fingers hovered over the fabric once more, hesitating, before she turned her gaze elsewhere.

The city outside was alive with anticipation. She had seen it in the stalls, in the streets, in the glow-lamps casting warm halos over festival banners. She had felt it in the way people spoke, their voices edged with a kind of excitement she could not share.

She had walked through it all, an observer rather than a participant.

And yet.

Her grandmother's words stayed with her. The quiet way she had spoken, the way her fingers had curled gently around Aria's hand.

You don't have to go for yourself. But maybe go for me.

Her heart ached.

She had already made peace with the fact that the festival would not feel the same this year. That there would be no guiding hand at her side, no knowing smile cast her way as the first lanterns were lit. Her grandmother would not be there. And that should have been reason enough to stay home.

But even now, sitting here, she couldn't shake the weight of her grandmother's voice, the spark in Heidi at the mention of their traditions, or the quiet understanding in Sylas beneath his teasing.

She exhaled, setting the delicate dress back in its place. Just one night. She did not belong in it. She no longer would. But she could wear it.

For them.

For one night.

19

A Light in the Darkness

Location: Cavandel, The Stratum

Founders Day traced its origins to a single strike of a shovel. Steel met stone and the earth split open, exhaling dust and promise. From that first breach, a city had been born—not in light, but in darkness, carved from bedrock by hands that sought fortune beneath their feet. Cavandel had not been built; it had been unearthed. And so, every year, the people would remember.

To the citizens of Cavandel, Founders Day was more than a festival. It was a triumph, a testament to endurance and ambition, to the power of those who had shaped the city from the raw marrow of the earth. It was the one day when the past was honored, the present embraced, and the future celebrated with open arms.

On that day, the mines would fall silent, the forges would cool, and the endless rhythm of toil would give way to something greater. Streets would transform beneath fluttering banners of gold and crimson, lanterns would cast the city in amber glow, and music would spill from every corner, filling the cavernous air with melody and laughter.

The morning would begin with the Grand Procession, a spectacle of color and revelry that drew the entire city into its wake. It was the one day when residents of the Stratum would step down from their polished corridors and mingle with the crowds of the District, their paths converging in a rare harmony.

The procession itself would start in the Outer District, where the streets swelled with families, traders, and miners, then wind its way inward toward the heart of Cavandel, its songs rising against the stone like echoes from another age.

By the time it reached the Inner District, thousands would move as one through the city's carved arteries, voices layered in a single, swelling chorus. Perched upon the great platform, the Warden would deliver his proclamations of unity and prosperity, each word rolling through the streets with the weight of prophecy.

Then ale would flow, tapped from casks as tall as a man, a gift to the people in celebration of their labor, their sacrifice, and their unyielding strength. Feasts would stretch across the squares, tables groaning beneath food from the farthest reaches of the Stratum and beyond—exotic fruits, roasted meats, delicacies most would never taste beyond this one sacred day.

As night deepened, the city would gather for the Silent Tribute. For a breath, a heartbeat, a moment suspended in time, all would go still as they honored the forgotten pioneers whose torches had been snuffed out in darkness, and all those who had been lost to the mines since.

Then the music would return, drums would thunder, and the festival would carry on, untamed and unrelenting, until the final embers of celebration faded into dawn.

Founders Day was more than memory carved in stone, more than revelry painted in gold and crimson. It was a promise. A tradition. A legend.

And for some—those who glimpsed the shadows between the lanterns' light—it was, perhaps, also a lie.

***

The Warden's receiving chamber embodied a calculated grandeur, with rich wood gleaming under lamplight, polished brass catching every flicker, and heavy velvet drapes softening the harsh edges of a city carved from unyielding stone.

Along the back wall, an intricate relief of Cavandel had been meticulously etched into dark stone, its veins of Crythium capturing and refracting light, a silent testament to the wealth that had shaped the city from its deepest reaches. Every element served its purpose—not indulgence, but strategy—measured and deliberate, like the man who presided within it. Warden Thaddeus Blackthorne.

Prince Gideon Everhart sat across from the Warden at the long table, the hearth's dancing glow casting amber light over crystal and steel. His delegation remained nearby, silent yet vigilant, their presence a constant reminder that even in these secretive exchanges, he was never truly alone.

A glass of dark amber liquor rested between his fingers, its surface barely disturbed as he rotated it with deliberate ease. His keen gaze swept across the room with quiet assessment, noting the symbols of authority woven seamlessly into its design.

The Warden, his uniform immaculate, without a single wrinkle, carried himself with the assurance of a man accustomed to absolute control. His own glass remained untouched before him, his posture unwavering, his gaze steady and penetrating. The intermittent firelight accentuated the sharp lines of his face, revealing nothing of the thoughts behind his composed expression.

The silence stretched taut between them before the Warden finally broke it. "Your Highness, I trust your journey was smooth."

Gideon took a measured sip of his drink, allowing the warmth to settle in his throat before answering. "Uneventful—for the most part. But we were well received."

The Warden offered a brief, economical nod. "Given the significance of the occasion, I imagine Your Highness would find it beneficial to have some insight into what awaits him tomorrow."

Gideon acknowledged this with a slight incline of his head. "Absolutely. I assume the festival holds significance beyond mere celebration."

The Warden exhaled softly, his gaze never wavering. "It is a day of remembrance as much as revelry. The city honors the first strike of the spade—the moment Cavandel was carved from the earth. Every drumbeat echoes that first motion, every step in the procession marks the path that built this place." His fingers tapped almost imperceptibly against his glass. "For a day, the city belongs to its people, free from duty, free from responsibilities."

He allowed the words to settle before continuing. "You and your party will be provided with suitable clothing to better blend into the crowd for the procession. I trust Your Majesty and his guests will excuse our prudence on the matter, but it is of the utmost importance that you go unnoticed."

Gideon turned his glass slowly, contemplating its contents. "A reasonable precaution," he said.

However, he knew better. The Warden had framed it as a gesture of concern, but Gideon recognized control when he encountered it. How often had he heard similar words spoken in the palace halls, meant not to protect but to constrain?

The Warden inclined his head slightly. "Such precautions are not taken lightly, nor without due consideration for Your Highness' well-being, which is why I cannot overstate the importance of remaining only as honored observers."

Gideon exhaled, leaning back slightly. "And here I thought I would finally have a little adventure," he said with a mischievous glint in his eyes.

The Warden's penetrating gaze remained steady, unreadable. "Cavandel does not lend itself to anonymity, not even in celebration. A stranger, no matter how well concealed, remains a stranger."

Gideon considered the Warden's words, running a thumb deliberately along the rim of his glass. "I see..."

He traced the rim again, slower this time, watching the Warden carefully. The words were measured, calculated—too calculated. He had heard court advisors speak thus, meticulously crafting a version of truth that best served their own interests. The festival, it seemed, was not as straightforward as the Warden wanted him to believe.

The Warden inclined his head slightly. "Which is why you and your party will be returned to the Stratum after my speech. By then, Your Highness will have seen all that is necessary—the city's traditions, its people united in festivity, and the prosperity that Founders Day represents."

Gideon's gaze lifted, direct and unwavering. "Does the festival end with your speech, then?"

"Not exactly, Your Highness," the Warden said evenly. "But the procession and speech are the important parts. The rest of the festival is for the people." He paused momentarily, then added, "By then, it will have taken on a different spirit—one less suited for royal guests."

Gideon gave a thoughtful hum, swirling the last of his drink in the glass. "Can't be that bad, can it, Warden?"

He set his glass down with deliberate care. "The others may leave, but I came here to see the people as they truly are. So I must insist on staying—until I am satisfied." He allowed the silence to stretch between them. "But I shall remain an observer, as you wish."

It was a small defiance, but a defiance nonetheless. He was used to being guided, managed, held in place by careful words and convenient reasoning. But here, he was not in his father's halls. He had been granted passage into Cavandel, and this time he would not accept half-measures.

The Warden, for the first time that evening, hesitated. A long silence stretched between them as he weighed his response, carefully constructing an exit. "Your Highness—"

"I insist," Gideon said with a tone of finality. The words were quiet but carried the full weight of command.

The Warden held his gaze for a moment longer before inclining his head

Location: Cavandel, The Outer District

The dress was beautiful—too beautiful and that was the problem.

Aria stood before the mirror, fingers grazing the fabric at her waist, tracing the careful embroidery that wound like vines along the edges. It was finer than anything she usually wore, rich and elegant, dyed a deep blue that caught and held the lamplight.

It suited the occasion but it did not suit her.

She tilted her head, studying her reflection, searching for some version of herself in the way the fabric clung and flowed. But all she saw was a girl playing a part—a girl shaped for a world of dancing and masks, not for the dust and grit that had toughened her hands and hardened her heart.

Outside, the city pulsed with fevered life. Laughter and distant music filtered through the window, voices rising and falling like waves against stone. The scent of roasted nuts drifted in, warm and spiced, curling through the air as if the world beyond her door had no room for anything but celebration.

Founders Day.

A day of unity, of remembering where they came from. A day to forget the cracks in Cavandel's foundation, if only for a little while.

How many even had the chance to celebrate? The ones laid up in the infirmary, lungs wasting away from Shatterblight—were they meant to lift a glass in unity? Or the ones dragged from their homes just days ago, accused of being Dwellers with no proof, their families left with nothing but hollow questions and deafening silence?

And yet, the ale would flow freely today. Some would drink with gratitude, reveling in the moment, but others—others would drink just to push it all down, to forget that by tomorrow, nothing would have changed.

"Aria?"

Her grandmother's voice cut through the quiet, gentle but expectant.

"Let me see you, sweetheart."

For a moment, she hesitated. Then, sighing softly, she reached for the mask resting beside her—silver, delicate, shaped to fit the angles of her face. She didn't put it on yet. Just held it between her fingers like something fragile and uncertain.

Then she stepped out of her room.

Her grandmother sat in the old chair by the hearth, a knitted shawl draped over her shoulders, hands folded in her lap. The fire burned low, casting a soft glow over her lined face as she looked up. At first, she said nothing at all. Then, slowly, a smile spread across her face—quiet, almost awed.

"Oh," she murmured. "I've never seen you look so beautiful."

Aria smiled, but it didn't reach her eyes.

Because as her grandmother spoke, she saw it—the creeping veins of Shatterblight, faint but unmistakable, curling like ink just above the collar of her dress. A slow, merciless spread.

Her throat tightened. How could she celebrate while her grandmother faded before her? When every precious second felt stolen, slipping away like sand?

She stepped closer, letting her grandmother smooth the fabric at her side, adjusting a fold at the sleeve. A small gesture, precise and careful, as if she were memorizing the moment through her fingertips.

"You look just like your mother," she said softly.

Aria lowered her gaze, saying nothing, and picked up the small mirror on the table.

A tiny glass jar rested beside it, filled with fine silver powder. She dipped her fingers in, pressing it beneath her eyes, tracing the embellishments along her cheekbones. Each movement was practiced, familiar. But as she caught her own reflection, something about it felt different. Foreign.

Her grandmother watched her in silence before finally speaking. "Thank you," she said softly.

Aria glanced at her through the mirror. "For what?" she whispered, her voice unsteady.

"For going," her grandmother answered, her tone gentle, faintly mournful. "For giving me this gift."

A gift.

Aria's throat tightened. A fleeting thought passed through her—the only gift she wished to give, the only one that truly mattered, was the cure that still remained elusive.

She turned from the mirror and leaned down, pressing a gentle kiss to her grandmother's forehead. "Jace should be here soon," she whispered, offering what little reassurance she could.

Before the thought could settle, the door burst open.

"Aria!"

The voice came first, followed by the whirlwind of Sylas and Heidi. The room, so quiet a moment ago, filled instantly with their presence—Heidi grinning as she leaned against the doorframe, Sylas sweeping an exaggerated bow before her.

Sylas had dressed for the occasion, though in his own way—his deep green tunic had been freshly pressed, but the sleeves were rolled up as if he had already grown tired of formality. A patterned sash, slightly askew, hung at his waist and his mask—bronze, shaped with sharp angles and a sly curve at the mouth—was tilted just enough to give him a perpetually amused expression.

Heidi, by contrast, had made an effort to look polished, though the practical touches remained. Her deep red dress carried slits along the sides for ease of movement, paired with sturdy boots that had seen their share of work. A leather cuff circled her wrist, and her mask, dark and understated, rested in her unruly curls like an afterthought.

Aria's grandmother placed a hand over her chest with a sigh. "Storming in like that—are you trying to send an old woman to her grave?"

Sylas straightened, adopting a look of exaggerated innocence. "Perish the thought. We'd never," he said, his grin far too broad to be convincing.

Heidi just cleared her throat and offered a sheepish, "Sorry."

Aria let out a slow breath. The moment had slipped away like water through her fingers, leaving only the quiet weight of what came next.

The mask was still in her hands, but soon she would have to wear it.

It was time.

***

The streets pulsed with life, transformed into something unrecognizable beneath the glow of countless lanterns. Music wove through the air, a melody of strings and drums that thrummed beneath Aria's feet as she walked.

Everywhere she looked, color bloomed—masks of deep crimson and gold, banners twisting above the crowds, the warm spill of torchlight reflecting off polished stone. The scent of roasted meat and sweet pastries curled through the air, mingling with the tang of burning oil from the lanterns overhead.

Aria, Heidi, and Sylas moved through the throng, their pace dictated by the tide of bodies pressing forward. Laughter rang out from every direction, the hum of conversation blending with the music in a symphony of celebration.

Figures twirled in the open spaces between stalls, masked revelers locking hands in impromptu dances. The city felt alive in a way it never did beneath the weight of daily labor—unburdened, untamed.

Heidi nudged Aria with her elbow. "You're scowling," she teased, her voice barely cutting through the din.

Aria adjusted the mask on her face before speaking, "I'm wearing a mask," she said defensively.

"I can still tell," Heidi shot back without hesitation.

Sylas only laughed, spinning on his heel as he let the music carry him, weaving through the revelers with effortless ease. For a fleeting moment, he became part of the celebration itself, his movements light, untethered.

Aria watched him, something unreadable settling in her chest. Only days ago, he had been facing down Screechers in the Abyss, the weight of survival pressing against his every breath. And now—he was here, letting it all go, losing himself in the joy of a moment he knew would not last. Was that what the city was doing? Choosing to put it all aside, even if only for a night? Choosing, despite everything, to be happy?

They passed a row of vendors peddling sugared nuts and spiced cider, their voices rising in playful competition. A symphony of aromas danced in the space between them, redolent of warm pastries, spiced fruit, and roasted meat. Sylas slowed his pace, glancing between the stalls before slipping away into the crowd. Aria barely had time to notice before he returned, weaving through the throng with three pastries wrapped in parchment.

"Here," he said, pressing one into her hands before passing the other to Heidi. "It'll help you lighten up."

Aria took the pastry but hesitated, glancing down at it for a long moment. *Could she do the same?* Could she make that choice—to set aside the weight of everything, if only for tonight? The city had chosen. Sylas had chosen. And here she was, standing on the edge of it, uncertain.

She sighed. "I'm trying."

Sylas huffed a quiet laugh. "Well, try harder," he shouted, disappearing into the shifting tide of bodies, swallowed by the current of music and laughter.

Only then did she take a bite. The crisp, buttery layers melted on her tongue, the sweetness lingering. Warmth spread through her chest, as if the weight she carried had momentarily eased. Without thinking, she gave a small smile.

"Come on," Heidi said, grabbing Aria's wrist and pulling her into the flow of the procession. "We have the whole night ahead of us."

Aria let herself be led forward. The crowd thickened as they neared the heart of the city, where the Warden would soon address the gathered masses.

The revelry swelled around them, music rising, voices lifting, the city itself caught in the rhythm of Founders Day.

For a moment, even Aria almost believed in it.

The procession carried them forward, the streets narrowing as they neared the city square. The revelry pressed in from all sides—music swelling, voices lifting, the rhythmic beat of drums reverberating through the stone beneath their feet.

As they emerged into the square, the heart of Cavandel unfolded before them. A grand platform had been raised at the center, its edges lined with banners of deep crimson and gold. Torches flanked the structure, their flames casting long, flickering shadows against the polished stone. Beyond it, th e official band played, the deep hum of strings and the sharp call of horns filling the air with melodies older than memory.

To the right of the square, open spaces had been marked for the festival's upcoming games—barrels stacked high, a ring of weighted lances driven into the ground and the long stretch of mud-pits waiting for their competitors. The anticipation was tangible, an electric undercurrent threading through the crowd as masked faces lifted toward the stage.

Behind the Warden, a row of wealthy merchants and dignitaries sat in stately silence, their masked faces unreadable as they observed the gathered masses. Draped in rich fabrics and adorned with subtle emblems of their status, they watched—not as participants, but as those who held the pulse of the city within their grasp.

Then, the music faded. One final note hung in the air before dissolving into silence.

The Warden stood maskless on the platform before them, a figure of un-wavering strength against the lanternlight. The silence that stretched across the square was not forced. It was given.

The people of Cavandel waited as their leader prepared to speak. The Warden stepped forward, his silhouette carved in sharp relief against the lights. With a measured gesture, he set his hands upon the voice amplifier, and for a moment all of Cavandel seemed to hold its breath.

Then, he spoke.

"We were not given this city. We built it. With our hands, our sweat, our will. The first of us carved through stone, not knowing if the earth would swallow them whole. And yet, they pressed forward. They dug and they built and they endured. Because that is who we are."

The crowd listened, rapt.

"Every tunnel, every forge, every street that winds through Cavandel exists because of the labor of its people. Not one of us stands alone. Strength is not measured in the effort of the individual, but in what we accomplish together. Alone, we are stone—unyielding, but fixed in place. Together, we are the foundation upon which all else stands."

A ripple of movement passed through the crowd, subtle but present. Shoulders straightened. Chins lifted.

"That is why we celebrate. Not because the work is easy, but because we choose to do it anyway. Because each year, we stand here—stronger than the last. Tonight, we mark not just what we've built, but what still lies ahead. The depths yet to be carved, the future yet to be shaped. The legacy that is ours to claim."

He extended a hand toward the crowd, palm open, as if grasping the very spirit of the city itself.

"To Cavandel! To its people. To the strength of our unity!"

A roar of approval erupted, voices rising in thunderous applause. The city trembled beneath the weight of its own heartbeat, as the sound swelled into the cavernous air above.

The festival carried on, but the words remained, a vow sealed by the roar of the crowd. Applause thundered through the square, rolling over the masked faces like a tide. Then, as if on cue, the first resounding clang of a mallet striking a cask echoed through the space.

A second strike followed. Then a third.

The festival shifted like a living thing, the reverence of the speech giving way to renewed revelry. At the edges of the square, massive barrels had been hoisted onto raised platforms, their aged wood dark with years of use. The first cask burst open, spilling golden ale into waiting mugs, a symbol of the Warden's generosity—a gift to the people.

A cheer rippled outward as attendants worked swiftly, filling cups and passing them into eager hands. The scent of fermented grain mingled with the lingering smoke of torches, and soon the square was alive with laughter and the dull clank of mugs striking tabletops.

Then, the music began.

The official band struck up a lively tune, the deep hum of strings and the sharp trill of pipes lifting into the cavernous expanse. The shift was effortless—seamless. As the first notes filled the air, masked revelers took to the open spaces, stepping into dance, hands clasping, bodies swaying in time with the rhythm.

At the heart of it all, the Warden descended from the platform, his guards forming a silent barrier around him while his dignitaries followed in his wake. He did not linger to watch the festivities unfold. Instead, he moved with purpose, slipping out of the square's firelit glow and toward the passage that would carry him back to the Stratum, where he would observe the celebration from above.

The night had only just begun.

The festival pulsed on, alive with music and motion. The band played a lively tune, its notes weaving through the square as dancers spun and laughter rang beneath the glow of lanterns. Mugs sloshed with spiced ale, raised in exuberant cheer, the scent of roasted meat thick in the air. The city, for this night, belonged not to labor or toil but to revelry.

Then, a sudden burst of drumming cut through the merriment—a rapid, rolling rhythm that sent a hush rippling through the crowd. The dancers slowed, masked faces turning toward the grand platform once more.

A man stepped forward, his silhouette framed by the flickering torch-light. Cloaked in a deep crimson coat adorned with gold trim, the Master of

Ceremonies lifted both arms wide, basking in the moment before his voice rang out, rich and theatrical.

"Good people of Cavandel!" he boomed, his voice swelling in the square's natural acoustics. "You have feasted, you have danced, and you have drunk your fill—but what is Founders Day without a test of might, wit, and balance?"

A cheer erupted from the crowd.

"Tonight, champions shall rise, challengers shall fall, and Cavandel will bear witness to feats worthy of legend! So I ask you now—who among you has the strength to endure, the skill to triumph, and the courage to compete?"

The crowd roared in response, voices swelling with excitement.

The Master of Ceremonies turned, gesturing toward the first event.

"We begin with a battle of raw strength and unity! Gather your allies, for the Tug of War begins now!"

A surge of energy swept through the square as eager competitors rushed toward the marked space, where thick ropes lay coiled, waiting.

The festival games had begun.

Excitement crackled through the square as the first competitors gathered, the thick ropes uncoiled and stretched across the designated space. Two dozen people stood on either side, hands gripping the coarse fibers, feet digging into the packed earth. The festival lights gleamed off their masks, sweat already forming on determined brows.

Heidi's eyes lit up as she turned to Sylas. "Come on, let's go."

Sylas took a slow sip of his drink, then another, before exhaling with exaggerated relief. "Heidi," he said, lifting his mug. "Look at me. I'm not built for that." Then, as if to prove his point, he tipped his head back and downed the rest of his ale.

Heidi huffed but wasted no time slipping into the growing crowd of volunteers. Aria watched as she flexed her fingers before wrapping them around the rope, her stance already one of unwavering determination.

The Master of Ceremonies strode forward, raising his arms for silence.

"Strength is not measured in words," he declared, his voice carrying over the eager murmurs. "It is proven—in the grip of the rope, in the dig of your heels, in the fire of your will!"

A cheer rose, competitors bracing themselves. The thick rope stretched taut, muscles coiling in anticipation.

"On my mark!" the Master of Ceremonies bellowed.

There was a moment of silence.

Then—"Pull!"

The struggle erupted instantly.

The rope jolted, bodies wrenching back as the battle for ground began. Feet slid against the packed earth, heels dug trenches in the dirt. Faces contorted beneath masks, teeth gritted as each side fought for control. The line marking the center quivered, shifting inches one way—then the other.

Heidi's side surged backward, forcing the opposing team onto their heels. A roar of encouragement came from the crowd, boots scraping the ground as they strained to hold the advantage.

But then—a shift.

The other team rallied, their collective force yanking the rope with renewed strength. The momentum swung violently in their favor. One step. Another. Then another. The tension in the rope sang like a bowstring before—

A sudden, final pull.

Heidi's side collapsed into a tangled heap, a chorus of laughter and groans rising as the crowd burst into cheers.

Heidi pushed herself up, breathless but grinning. "Next year," she declared, dusting herself off.

The Master of Ceremonies stepped forward, gesturing grandly. "A noble effort! But the night is still young, and the games have only just begun!"

As the winning team celebrated, the festival pulse quickened once more.

20

Whispers in the Dark

Location: Cavandel, The Inner District

The festival unfolded before Gideon like a living thing, untamed and unrestrained. He had expected revelry, had imagined something akin to the celebrations of the surface—formal affairs where nobility drank fine wine beneath silk-draped pavilions, where every shared drink was a carefully veiled exchange of power, where music existed only as a backdrop to whispered negotiations.

But this—this was something else entirely.

Laughter and music swelled through the cavernous city, voices rising uninhibited, bodies moving with wild abandon. The people of Cavandel did not merely celebrate; they threw themselves into it, drinking deep of the moment as if the night itself was something to be conquered.

Gideon stood at the edges of the square, half-masked and unnoticed, watching as the festival games unfolded.

The Mug Run had been the first to catch his attention—a test of agility and balance, where contestants dashed through an obstacle-laden course while carrying brimming mugs of ale. It had been pure chaos—men and women slipping on scattered hay, stumbling over uneven stones, ale sloshing over the rims of their cups as the crowd howled with laughter. One man had reached the finish with barely a sip spilled, lifting his mug high in triumph. Another arrived soaked, his mask askew, and gave a theatrical shrug at his own defeat before downing the remainder of his drink to the spectators' delight.

Other games followed—tests of strength, speed, endurance, each met with the same unrelenting enthusiasm.

Gideon had seen a woman hoist a barrel over her shoulder and carry it across the square, feet pounding against stone as the crowd roared encouragement. He had watched as teams of men and women locked arms in an intricate dance of balance and coordination, weaving through shifting planks in a challenge that seemed more ritual than game.

And yet, it was not the games themselves that held his attention. It was the people.

They cheered for strangers. They laughed, cursed, and clapped one another on the back, no matter the outcome. There was no cold detachment here, no calculated maneuvering for favor. They celebrated each other.

Something in that stirred him.

He had told the Warden he would remain an observer. That his role here was just to watch, to learn. And yet—as he stood on the fringes, a part of him itched to step forward.

Then came the final game of the evening.

A long, shallow pit of churned mud stretched before the crowd, a barrel balanced across it like a bridge between worlds. Two contestants at a time would step onto the wood, with a simple task—outlast the other. No shoving. No striking. Only balance, only endurance. The loser would plunge into the mud. The winner would walk away clean.

The crowd surged forward, eager for the spectacle.

Gideon exhaled slowly.

Perhaps it was time to do more than just watch.

***

The first two contenders stepped onto the barrel, arms spread wide as they found their footing. A hush fell over the crowd, anticipation thick in the air. Then, with a signal from the Master of Ceremonies, the game was on.

Aria watched with arms crossed and a faint smile, while her friends cheered.

She knew this game well. She could already pick out the victor before either contestant had fully steadied themselves. The man on the left stood too rigid, his feet planted too wide.

The crowd cheered as the two competitors shifted their weight, eyes locked, muscles tensed. The wood creaked beneath them, the barrel rocking precariously as they adjusted, each trying to outlast the other.

The man on the left leaned too far forward, corrected too late and—with a yelp—toppled backward into the mud. The crowd erupted in cheers and laughter as the victor stepped off, boots clean, while the loser sputtered and wiped muck from his mask.

And so the rounds continued.

Each match brought new cheers, new wagers, new strategies, and new missteps. Some contestants fought fiercely, toes gripping the slick wood, bodies tensed against every shift. Others toppled almost immediately, laughing as they accepted their fate. And now and then, both would plunge into the mud together, swallowed by the crowd's delighted roar.

Aria had always loved this game.

It wasn't about strength or speed, but control. A keen awareness of weight, of movement, of the smallest shift that could send someone tumbling. Last year, she'd stepped onto that barrel and walked away the victor.

Now, as she watched another competitor crash into the pit, her heart pulled toward it, aching for the familiar thrill of the challenge.

Then, just as quickly, she forced the feeling down.

"You're thinking about it. Aren't you?" Heidi asked, nudging her.

Aria shook her head. "I'm not."

"You're on a three-year winning streak. You're not just going to break it, are you?" Heidi pressed.

Aria huffed, grasping at the first excuse she could find. "I'm in a dress."

Heidi arched a brow. "That didn't stop you last year."

Aria opened her mouth, then closed it.

Another match ended. The victor hopped down to a chorus of cheers as the Master of Ceremonies stepped forward, his voice booming over the noise.

"Who dares step forward next?"

Heidi turned to Aria, grinning. "Go on, then."

Aria hesitated. Her mind said no, but her heart had already made the choice.

With a sigh, she stepped forward, exhaling sharply.

One last time, she thought to herself. *One last time.*

Last year, she hadn't hesitated. She had climbed on without a second thought. Had let herself enjoy it. Had felt, for that fleeting moment, untouchable.

The crowd roared, voices rising in excitement as Aria approached the edge of the pit, but she barely heard them. Her focus lay elsewhere.

She glanced down at her dress. Too long. Too impractical.

With a practiced motion, she gathered the fabric at her sides, twisting it into a loose knot at her hip. It wasn't perfect, but it would do—enough to keep the material from tangling around her legs, enough to let her move the way she needed to.

Satisfied, she took her place at the barrel's edge, the wood shifting beneath her weight as she found her footing.

The mud pit stretched below, dark and glistening, ready to claim whoever faltered first. Each inhalation brought a tide of damp earth and smoke, the warmth of the festival pressing in from all sides. Voices rose in anticipation, cheers blending with laughter, but Aria heard none of it. Her world narrowed to the curve of the barrel beneath her feet, the rhythm of her breath, the familiar pull of balance and counterbalance.

She rolled her shoulders, loosening the tension in her limbs, then lifted her gaze to meet her opponent's.

Across from her, her opponent climbed on—his posture steady, shoulders squared. Taller than most, broad in the way that suggested strength, but she knew better than to assume strength alone could win this game. Strength was nothing without control.

The Master of Ceremonies raised a hand.

"Steady your feet—"

Aria adjusted her stance.

"Find your balance—"

Her opponent did the same.

"Let the battle begin!"

The barrel lurched beneath them.

Aria shifted immediately, knees bending, weight adjusting with the roll of the wood. Her opponent moved as well, but she caught it—the slight delay, the fraction of hesitation as he read the motion beneath him instead of feeling it.

He was strong. He was steady. But he wasn't practiced.

She let him settle into false confidence, let him think he had control. And then, she moved.

It was subtle—a shift of weight, a tilt of her ankle, just enough to send the balance spiraling in a way he wouldn't expect.

He adjusted too late. His body stiffened.

A mistake.

The moment he tried to correct, she shifted again—faster this time, sharper. The barrel spun beneath them as he teetered toward the point of no return.

It was over before he knew it.

His arms flailed in a desperate attempt to counter the fall and for a moment, it almost looked like he might save himself—then gravity took hold.

He crashed into the mud with a spectacular splash, arms still reaching, boots kicking up a wave of filth as he went under.

The crowd erupted in laughter and cheers, the energy crackling through the square.

Aria exhaled, stepping off the barrel with ease, her boots untouched by even a drop of mud. The familiar rush of victory surged through her, leaving her breathless, weightless.

Then—movement from the pit.

Her opponent pushed himself up, mud dripping from his clothes, his mask knocked slightly to the side. He wiped a hand across his face, blinking through the grime.

And for the first time, Aria actually looked at him.

She had never seen him before.

Even covered in mud, he carried himself differently. His features were half-shadowed by torchlight, his expression unreadable.

But then, to her surprise—he grinned.

***

Prince Gideon Everhart—Master of the city of Cavandel, and heir to the throne of Valmere—stood covered in mud.

It dripped from his hair, slithered down the back of his neck and clung to his arms in thick, wet clumps. The laughter of the crowd still rang in his ears, echoing through the square like the beating of a drum.

And, despite himself, he grinned.

He hadn't expected to fall. That, in itself, was humbling. But more than that, he hadn't expected—her.

His opponent, the young woman standing dry and victorious on the other side of the pit, had bested him effortlessly. Not through brute force, not even through sheer endurance, but through something far deadlier. Control. She had read him in an instant, anticipated his every movement and

315

dismantled him before he even had the chance to find his footing.

Gideon pushed his hair back, feeling the weight of the mud slicked through it. How long had it been since he had lost at something so completely?

From the sidelines, masked spectators clapped him on the back as he waded out of the pit, their laughter good-natured, their energy infectious. Here, failure was not a disgrace but a spectacle, a thing to be celebrated just as much as victory. It was a stark contrast to the surface, where every loss carried weight, where every misstep could mean ruin.

But it was not the crowd that held his attention.

It was her.

She stood with ease in her blue dress, her boots still spotless, her silver mask betraying nothing. But there was something in the way she held herself—assured, unshaken, unmoved by the spectacle of his defeat. She hadn't won through mere chance. She had won because she was better at it.

And for some reason, that made Gideon laugh. Still grinning, he flicked a glob of mud from his sleeve and met her gaze.

Who was she?

He promised himself he would find out soon enough. Mud clung stubbornly to his clothes as he moved through the festival square, slipping past the well-meaning hands of his guards.

"Your Majesty, at least let us—"

"I'm fine," Gideon muttered, shaking off an insistent towel that had been thrust toward his face.

Another guard, looking pained at his casual dismissal, held out a fresh cloak as if warding off disaster. "Sire, your attire—"

Gideon shot him a look. "Unless you plan to wring me out like laundry, I suggest you stop fussing and go find me a change of clothes."

He pressed forward, paying no mind to their quiet protests as he wove through the revelers, gaze sweeping the shifting crowd. The young woman had disappeared into it like mist.

She had left with two others—a short-haired girl with quiet confidence in her step, dressed in red, and a boy whose mask sat slightly askew, as if it had been tugged at one too many times.

It didn't take long to spot them.

The trio lingered near a food stall. The boy spoke with his hands, drawing laughter from the short-haired girl. Beside them stood the other—his victor—calm, unreadable, unshaken.

Gideon adjusted his mask, still streaked with dried mud. He wasn't about to slink off just because he'd lost; if anything, he found himself even more intrigued.

He had barely taken two steps before the boy slid into his path, planting himself squarely between Gideon and his target. The boy crossed his arms, weight balanced just so—not a challenge, but a clear message all the same.

"Well, well," he drawled, tilting his head. "If it isn't Mr. Mudslide himself."

The short-haired girl pressed a hand to her mouth to stifle a laugh. The other, the one in the silver mask and blue dress, said nothing, she simply watched—unreadable as ever.

Gideon didn't bother acknowledging the remark.

"Where I come from," he said, voice light, "the defeated is allowed to buy his victor a drink."

The young man let out an exaggerated sigh. "And where I come from," he said, "we usually just let the loser marinate in his own failure."

Red Dress huffed a laugh, but Silver Mask just exhaled—not quite a laugh, not quite disapproval.

Then came the pause, long and drawn out. The young man stared at Gideon and Gideon stared back. Neither moved and neither blinked.

The festival sounds faded to the background—music, laughter, the shuffling of feet—and yet, the two of them remained locked in a silent, unspoken standoff.

Finally, Gideon spoke, hand extended. "Gideon Everhart. Pleasure to meet you."

Another moment of silence.

Then—the girl in red sighed.

Stepping in smoothly, her tone even and deliberate, she gestured to herself. "I'm Heidi," she said. She tilted her head toward the young man beside her. "This is my little brother, Sylas. As you can see, he can be a bit much." Sylas did not move. Instead, his expression darkened as he glared at Gideon.

"And this—" Heidi hesitated, her gaze darting toward her friend in the silver mask and blue dress, "is Aria."

Gideon smiled and immediately committed the name to memory.

He barely had a chance to speak before Sylas cut in again. "Sorry to break it to you," he said, rocking back on his heels, "but we don't do second chances."

Gideon arched a brow but said nothing.

Heidi exhaled, rubbing her temples. "Sylas..."

"What?" Sylas gestured toward Gideon. "I'm just telling it like it is."

"Sylas," Heidi repeated, sharper this time. She cast a glance toward Aria, then grabbed his sleeve. "Come with me."

Sylas twisted away. "Why?"

"Because I want a drink," Heidi said flatly.

"There's ale right here," Sylas said, pointing to the nearby food stand.

"Well, now I want a drink over there."

She didn't wait for a response, steering him toward another section of the festival with a force that left little room for argument. Sylas threw one last glance over his shoulder, narrowing his eyes at Gideon before disappearing into the crowd.

And just like that, they were alone.

The music still played, voices still rang through the square, but the space between them was quiet—a pocket of stillness amid the revelry.

Aria didn't speak, but took a seat at a small table beside the food stand.

Gideon tilted his head, studying her as she sat. She hadn't laughed at Sylas's jabs, nor had she intervened. She'd simply observed, the same way she had during their match—measuring, assessing, revealing nothing.

A slow smirk tugged at his lips as he stepped closer. "Do you always let him do the talking for you?"

Aria exhaled, a hint of amusement flickering across her face. Then—for the first time, she spoke.

"Only when he's entertaining."

Her voice was smooth, edged with quiet confidence. A simple reply. Yet somehow, it still felt like a victory.

Gideon allowed her words to settle, turning them over in his mind. *Only when he's entertaining.* A deflection, but not a dismissal.

He raised an eyebrow. "And I wasn't?"

Aria paused, as if considering. "Well, you were—something." She held his gaze just long enough for her meaning to blur between compliment and provocation.

A laugh caught in his throat, unexpected and genuine.

Gideon studied her for a long moment—*Aria.*

The name felt familiar now, as if it had always belonged to her, carved into stone like the city itself. She hadn't moved, she simply regarded him with that same measured restraint, but there was something new in the way she sat. Not quite ease, but not rejection, either.

She was sharp. Not in the way Sylas was, all loud bravado and reckless jabs, but in a quieter, more deliberate way. Precise. Controlled. Unshaken.

Gideon shifted uncomfortably, the weight of half-dried mud still clinging to his clothes. He gestured to the chair opposite her. "May I?"

Aria responded with nothing more than a curt nod, her eyes revealing nothing.

"You sure did a number on me," he said, easing into the chair with deliberate casualness. He ran a finger along the edge of his mud-caked sleeve. "I'd like to think I left a lasting impression as well."

Aria's gaze traveled slowly from the mud splattered across his clothing to the dark smears streaking down his mask. A smile—so slight it might have been imagined—touched her lips.

"Oh, you did."

There was no mistaking her tone this time—she was teasing him.

For a moment, the festival around them blurred—the music, the laughter, the flickering lanterns above—until there was only her and the space between them.

He had spent his whole life surrounded by women who knew the weight of a glance, who smiled with purpose, who wove their words like silk to guide conversations exactly where they wanted. Aria wasn't like that. She was careful, but not calculating. Guarded, but not dishonest.

His gaze drifted, tracing the details of her that had eluded him in the firelight of the match.

Delicate yet self-assured. The dress—deep blue, elegant in a way that felt almost at odds with the woman who had just sent him into the mud—clung to her form before spilling into soft folds at her waist.

Dark hair framed her face, a few strands slipping loose from where they had been pinned back. Beneath the smooth edges of her mask, her hazel eyes held a quiet intensity, shadowed by thought. And then there were her lips—full, lightly painted, parted just slightly as if she were on the verge of speaking yet chose not to.

"Do you really not give second chances?" Gideon asked.

Aria considered him for a moment, "There's always next year."

Gideon exhaled slowly, as if the weight of it pressed too heavily against his chest. "An entire year," he protested, voice rich with disbelief. "Such a cruel thing to ask of a heart still reeling from defeat."

Aria snorted.

The sound was soft but undeniable, slipping out before she could catch it. "Where I'm from, that kind of poetry seldom works?" she said, mirroring his earlier comment.

Gideon blinked, momentarily thrown.

Then his lips curled. "Skilled with her feet and with her words."

Aria's expression didn't shift, her gaze remained steady, unreadable. The festival buzzed around them—music, voices, children darting between stalls—but here, in the space between them, something else lingered.

Gideon let his gaze wander, taking in the way the lanternlight played over the fabric of her dress. The deep blue suited her—not just in color, but in contrast. Elegant, yet strong. Fitted, yet not fragile.

"You wear it well." His voice dipped lower, quieter.

Aria's fingers brushed the fabric at her side—a small, fleeting movement, as if she'd only just remembered it was there.

For the first time, she looked away.

But then she looked back.

"It's just a dress," she murmured, even and controlled, though something in her expression gave her away.

Gideon watched her carefully, intrigued. She hadn't dismissed the compliment outright—only distanced herself from it.

"A fine one, all the same," he said, finally meeting her gaze.

She didn't respond, but he felt the shift in the air between them. He let the silence stretch, then added, "And I still owe you that drink." The thought of an unsettled debt, even one so trivial, needled at him like a splinter beneath the skin.

Aria gave a curt smile. "It's quite alright," she said slyly. "Watching you struggle in the mud was payment enough."

Gideon placed a hand over his chest in mock offense, drawing out the gesture just enough to be ridiculous.

It worked—Aria smiled.

He let the moment linger, then tilted his head. "Surely there's..." He hesitated, his eyes softening as he chose his words. "Something I can do for you?"

The words landed heavier than he likely intended.

Something he could do for her?

There was nothing. No favor, no gift, no grand gesture could give her what she truly wanted. What she truly needed.

Her fingers curled at her sides. If there was anything at all, it would be a cure. A life not measured in dwindling days. A future where her grandmother was still there, still smiling, still—

She swallowed hard, forcing the thought down.

But Gideon had already noticed the shift.

His playful ease faded just slightly, his gaze sharpening—not unkind, not prying, but aware. "I'm sorry. Was it something I said?"

Aria hesitated. "No," she said eventually. "It just—" She exhaled. "It doesn't matter."

The moment lingered, but instead of pressing, Gideon adjusted. "I envy you, you know?"

Aria said nothing at first. Her gaze rested on him, steady, unreadable, brows lifting just slightly in quiet surprise.

Gideon exhaled, glancing toward where her friends had vanished into the crowd. "You seem close. Loyal." He hesitated, as if tasting the words before committing to them. "That's rare."

"We are," she said softly, but there was weight behind it. A certainty he didn't possess—the bond itself something foreign to him, or perhaps it was her unwavering confidence in it that felt so distant.

"I can tell," he murmured.

She didn't reply this time, only lowered her gaze slightly. A thought unspoken, a truth she wasn't ready to give voice to.

The silence between them stretched, but Gideon let it breathe.

Then, almost absently, "It's hard to find friendships like that in the—" He caught himself. A pause, brief but sharp. He smoothed over the slip before it had time to settle. "I never had that growing up."

This time, she didn't look away.

Her hazel eyes studied him, quiet and considering, peeling back layers he hadn't meant to reveal. Then, at last she said, voice gentle, "I'm sorry."

"It's alright," he said, his tone deliberately lighter, as if brushing away dust from an old book. "My life has its own set of—advantages."

That earned him something small—not quite a smile, but the shadow of one, barely touching the corner of her mouth.

Still, curiosity pulled at him. "Have you always been this close?"

For the first time, Aria truly smiled. Deep. Genuine. Not out of amusement, not out of politeness, but something real that transformed her face.

"Yeah," she murmured softly, warmth threading through her voice. "I'd do anything for them."

The moment settled. The smile faded, just slightly, as her brows furrowed, reality settling back in.

"In Cavandel, you don't get very far without people who will stand beside you," she muttered.

Gideon let his gaze sweep over the square, at the laughter and music woven into the night. "There must be a lot of that down here," he mused softly. "I see it everywhere tonight—in the way people look at each other, in the way they hold on."

A soft, humorless breath of laughter escaped her. "Is that what you see?" The question carried an edge.

Gideon tilted his head slightly, intrigued by the shift in her voice. "Perhaps I'm seeing Cavandel through the wrong eyes," he said, tone gentle. "What do you see?" he asked.

Aria held his gaze for a long moment. *Was he from the Stratum?* The son of some wealthy merchant, tucked away in polished halls above the city? Someone who had only ever seen Cavandel from a place of comfort? Something unreadable passed through her eyes—not quite hesitation, not quite caution, but something close. A calculation, weighing risk against trust.

Then, at last, she spoke.

And this time, she told him the truth.

She gestured vaguely toward the city, to the lantern-lit streets, the towering stone buildings carved from the earth itself. "What you see tonight is just a façade Gideon. In Cavandel, you work, you survive, you keep your head down when it matters and lift it when it doesn't. And on nights like this, you pretend it's enough."

Her voice was even, but there was something beneath it—something older than her years, something worn but not broken. Gideon fell silent, watching her, absorbing the weight of what she hadn't said.

Then, she turned her attention back to him. "Are you from the Stratum then?" It was an innocent enough question, but Gideon felt the weight of it.

For a heartbeat, he considered the truth, but the Warden's warning echoed in the back of his mind—*for your safety, it is of the utmost importance that you go unnoticed.*

Instead, he offered her a measured smile. "Something like that," he said, finally.

Aria's expression didn't shift, but he could sense her weighing the response, filing it away.

"Something like that," she echoed, her voice almost inaudible.

Gideon only shrugged, letting the answer settle, offering nothing more.

Her eyes lingered on him a moment longer before she exhaled and turned her gaze back toward the festival. The silence between them felt different now—not awkward, not cold, but charged with something unspoken.

For the first time, Gideon wondered if she would be the one to unravel him first.

The lanterns swayed above them, casting dancing shadows across the table. Around them, the festival continued unabated—laughter mingling with music, bodies weaving through the crowded square as the night deepened. For a moment, it was almost possible to believe they were just two people enjoying Founders Day like everyone else.

Movement at the edge of Aria's vision caught her attention. Three men in dark clothing approached, moving with the deliberate grace of those accustomed to navigating crowds while remaining unnoticed. Their masks were simple, unadorned, but there was nothing simple about the way they carried themselves.

One of them—taller than the others, with shoulders like carved stone—stepped closer to Gideon. He bent, handed him a change of clothing, then whispered something in Gideon's ear, his voice too low for Aria to catch beneath the festival's din.

Gideon's expression shifted instantly, the easy charm giving way to something colder, more controlled. He nodded once, a sharp, precise movement, before the man melted back into the shadows.

"Friends of yours?" Aria whispered, curiosity threading through her voice.

Gideon hesitated, his fingers drumming once against the table before stilling. "Just close companions," he said softly, his tone deliberately light. "Nothing to worry about."

Aria regarded him for a moment, studying him. "They seem to be enjoying the festival," she said dryly.

Gideon smirked but said nothing.

Then, without warning, he rose.

The motion was swift, abrupt—so much so that Aria flinched before she could stop herself. His chair scraped back and suddenly, the space between them felt wider, the air charged with something unspoken.

"Remain here," he said softly.

It wasn't a request.

The quiet weight of his words settled over her, pressing against her like an unseen force. For a breath, she felt as though she couldn't rise even if she wanted to. There was no trace of teasing now, no lingering smirk—just quiet authority, effortless and absolute.

He adjusted the bundle of clothing in his grip. "I need to change," he said, voice measured but brisk. "I'll be back in a moment."

And just like that, he turned and disappeared into the crowd.

***

Hogan stood at the edge of the crowd, his eyes fixed on Aria and that man. The festival raged around him—laughter, music, the rhythmic stomp of dancers—but he heard none of it. His focus was locked on her.

The sight of them together made his blood simmer. He clenched his fists so tightly that his nails bit into his palms, but he barely noticed the pain. It was nothing compared to the ache in his chest.

He watched as Aria tilted her head back in laughter, at something the man said. The sound carried across the space between them, each note like a thorn digging deeper into his heart. He had never been close enough to make her laugh like that, had never dared to try.

But I could have been, he thought bitterly. We could have been.

The weight of the Grottos in his pocket seemed to mock him now. He had been so proud of his new wealth, accumulated through whispered reports to the Warden. Each coin had felt like a step closer to proving himself, to becoming someone she could admire.

Today was supposed to be different. He had rehearsed his approach a hundred times, walking the streets of the city at night when the darkness gave him courage. He would approach her during Founders Day, casual but confident. He would finally speak to her.

He had been approaching, steps heavy with purpose, rehearsing the words he would say. He would apologize. She would see that he had changed. That he had something to offer now.

But just as he neared, just as he opened his mouth to speak—that man—the interloper cut in.

Now, he could only watch as Aria sat across from him, her posture relaxed, her head tilting ever so slightly as she listened.

Hogan's jaw tightened as he remembered Aria's match. She had been magnificent, a warrior woman claiming victory with fierce grace. He had cheered for her then, his chest tight with admiration and yearning.

Now here she was, fawning over the very same man.

Disgusting.

A tremor ran through him, heat pooling in his chest, creeping up his throat. His jaw locked tight, his breath flaring sharp through his nose. He forced it down.

Then—something dark and cold settled in the pit of Hogan's stomach as he watched them talking, their conversation flowing with an ease he would never experience. The coldness spread through him, hardening his resolve.

She never even noticed him. Never spared him a passing glance...

Hogan made himself a promise.

The next time he saw Aria, he would turn her in.

Not today, the festival made that impossible, but tomorrow—tomorrow was another day.

Hogan turned away, his features hardened with resolve. Five hundred Grottos richer. That's what he'd be the next time their paths crossed.

As he slipped through the crowd, a single tear flowing, the noise of the festival dimmed beneath the thunder of his heartbeat. She had made her choice. By the time he reached the edge of the celebration, he had made his.

21

A Spark Rekindled

Location: Cavandel, The Inner District

The moment Gideon disappeared into the crowd, Heidi materialized at Aria's side, her eyes bright with barely contained excitement. She practically vibrated with anticipation as she slid into the recently vacated chair.

She leaned close, a knowing smirk painted across her face. "Alright, spill it," she demanded, her tone light but expectant. Aria felt heat creep up her neck. She quickly busied herself adjusting the sleeves of her dress.

"Spill what?" she said casually.

Heidi propped her chin on her hand, studying her like a puzzle that had almost, but not quite, come together. "You know what," she accused with a grin.

Aria feigned confusion, but she could already feel her defenses crumbling under her friend's eager scrutiny. Heidi leaned forward, angling herself into Aria's line of sight. "You owe me," she said, incredulity written across her features, though her tone remained playful. "Or should I have left Sylas here as your third wheel?"

Sylas, who had just pulled up a chair beside Aria, let out a scoff. "What's that supposed to mean?"

Aria sighed deeply, shoulders slumping in resignation. Her hand fell away from her sleeve as she recognized the futility of deflection. Heidi was relentless when she wanted something and Sylas, if nothing else, would make sure she suffered through it.

"So," Heidi continued, practically bouncing with giddiness. Her words spilled out fast, tumbling over each other like ale poured out too quickly. "What did he say? Exact words please. Also, how old is he? Is he from the Inner? Did he ask you to dance later? What'd he think of your dress?"

Each question tumbled into the next without pause, then finally she said, "I need to know everything."

Heat spread across Aria's face, the weight of Heidi's eager attention pressing in from all sides. The barrage of questions had left her flushed and overwhelmed, with nowhere to run.

"Well?" Heidi prompted, impatience threading through her posture.

Aria thought of her conversation with Gideon. His gaze had carried something unsettling—awareness, perhaps, or recognition of something she herself couldn't name. She swallowed, fighting to keep her voice steady. "He just wanted to talk," she finally offered, her voice barely above a whisper.

Heidi narrowed her eyes slightly. "And?" Her tone made it clear she wasn't buying such a simple explanation.

"And... he asked about you guys," Aria conceded. She knew this small offering wouldn't satisfy Heidi's hunger, but she hoped it would postpone the inevitable.

Sylas perked up instantly, his earlier disdain forgotten. "What'd you say about us?"

Heidi shot him a glance, making it clear he was missing the point, then turned back to Aria. "And?"

"Then he asked about Cavandel," Aria said slowly, frowning in thought. "Almost like—" She trailed off, remembering the peculiar way he'd phrased his questions. The way he deflected. "I think he's from the Stratum."

That caught Heidi's attention. Her voice lost some of its playfulness, curiosity giving way to something more cautious. "Why do you say that?"

Aria lowered her voice. "I don't know," she muttered. "He just spoke like he didn't know what it was like down here." The memory of their conversation stirred something in her chest. "Before I could find out more, three men came and—"

Aria hesitated, the memory still tangled. She gave her head a small shake, as if trying to clear a fog she couldn't name. When no clarity followed, she exhaled sharply, her fingers tightening at her side as if pushing the confusion away.

Heidi paused, mulling it over. "Yeah, we saw them." Her brow tightened for an instant before her expression brightened. "But if he's really from the Stratum, that's even better." A slow grin spread as the thought settled. "And he's cute," she added, almost conspiratorial.

Aria felt the heat in her face spread instantly, coloring her cheeks crimson. She ducked her head, but not before Heidi caught the reaction. Denial was pointless.

Heidi's grin deepened at Aria's silence. "So you did notice?" she said slowly. Heidi leaned closer, her voice dropping conspiratorially. "Okay. So—what's next?" she asked, her voice low and eager. "We need a plan. I absolutely cannot let you mess this up."

Sylas groaned, throwing his hands up in exasperation. "What's so special about this guy anyway? He lost the Barrel Bout, remember? Please don't tell me you're planning on becoming Mrs. Mudslide?" he sighed, pulling both hands slowly down the sides of his face.

If Aria thought she couldn't blush any harder, she was wrong. Heat radiated from her face as she wished desperately for the ground to open up and swallow her whole. The words hit their mark effortlessly, leaving her momentarily speechless. Sylas leaned back, smug, while Heidi fought to suppress a laugh. Her gaze fixed on a point beyond Aria's shoulder. "Okay—" her voice suddenly dropped to an urgent whisper, her fingers digging into Aria's arm. "Here he comes..."

Aria's heartbeat stuttered as Heidi released her arm. She glanced at Sylas, her gaze a silent warning—do not say or do anything to mess this up.

Gideon returned, freshly changed, balancing a tray of ale in one hand as he stepped back into view. The richer fabric of his new outfit still marked him as an outsider, yet something about him had shifted. The easy charm he carried before had softened into something quieter, more composed.

He approached the table with a measured stride, setting the tray down. Without a word, he passed a tankard to Heidi first, who took it with a knowing smile. Then to Sylas, who accepted but gave Gideon a long, skeptical look, as if trying to decipher what he was scheming.

Finally, he held the last one out to Aria. She hesitated for a fraction of a second before taking it, her fingers brushing the cool metal as she met his gaze briefly. She gave him a small nod in thanks, the gesture subtle but deliberate.

Gideon glanced down at himself, then spread his arms slightly. "Well? What do you think?"

Aria studied him, taking in the fresh clothes. "Not bad," she said, the words half-lost behind her tankard. She still wasn't sure what to make of him. But curiosity, for now, had outpaced caution.

He smirked. "No thanks to you, but I'll take that as a compliment."

Aria gave a small chuckle at his efforts before taking a sip of her drink. Gideon let the moment settle before lifting his chin slightly. "Did I miss anything?"

Aria considered him for a moment before answering. "Not much." She let the words linger, then added, "We've just been waiting for you."

He lifted his ale for a slow drink, a faint smirk tugging at his mouth. "For a moment, I thought you'd take the opportunity to escape me."

Heidi, watching from the sidelines, nodded knowingly at Aria and winked. "And yet he still returned."

Gideon let out a quiet breath, amused. "That I did."

Aria gestured toward Heidi and Sylas, her drink still in hand. "Well," she said dryly, "as these two will tell you, I'm not the type to run and hide."

Gideon leaned in slightly, his gaze intent. "What type are you, then?"

Before she could answer, Sylas cut in. He spoke in a low, muttered voice. "She's the type that can whoop your—"

Heidi squeezed his hand hard, making him wince. "Ouch. Okay—okay."

Gideon's smirk lingered. He folded his arms with an easy confidence, taking a stance of unshaken patience, like a man who knew he would get his answer—eventually. "Well?"

She didn't answer right away, letting the question settle between them before giving him a small, knowing smile. "The kind that doesn't make it easy for strangers."

He let out a soft chuckle. "I see I'm not winning any favors tonight."

The sounds of the festival continued around them, but then a new melody threaded through the night air, a single solemn note from the official band rising above the din. It wasn't immediate, but gradually, laughter softened, voices lowered and movements slowed as people turned toward the square. The Song of Tribute had begun.

The tradition was as old as Cavandel itself, a moment of quiet reflection for those lost to the mines. It was a silent acknowledgment of sacrifice, a reminder that their city—no matter how much it flourished—was built on the backs of those who never made it out.

Aria straightened, her fingers tightening slightly around her drink before she set it down. Her expression didn't shift, but there was something in the way she exhaled, something steadier, more intentional. Around them, others took notice, some standing a little straighter, others tilting their heads toward the music, in quiet tribute.

Gideon, still standing, observed it all. The shift was subtle, but undeniable. Not a forced silence, but something ingrained, something understood without words. Even those who continued to speak did so in softer tones, a natural reverence settling over them.

Heidi nudged Sylas gently. "Let's go closer," she murmured. Sylas hesitated for a second, then nodded, and the two began weaving through the crowd.

Aria watched them go, then moved to follow. Gideon lingered for an instant, then fell into step beside her as the four of them moved toward the tribute.

As they walked, the melody deepened, each note carrying through the streets, weaving through the hush that had overtaken the festival. Aria's expression remained neutral, but her fingers brushed briefly over the pendant at her throat—a fleeting gesture before her hand dropped away.

Gideon took in every detail—the bowed heads, the quiet, the way people instinctively turned toward the music. When he finally spoke, his voice was low, measured. "It's beautiful," he said.

Aria glanced at him, something unreadable flickering behind her eyes. "It is."

The response hung between them and Gideon took it in, his gaze returning to the gathering. The music carried on, threading through the hush like something ancient, something that had existed long before either of them had stepped into this moment.

Gideon nodded toward Heidi and Sylas as they wove through the crowd, his voice quieter. "This must be really important to them."

Aria's fingers tensed slightly before she released a breath. Her voice was quieter now. "They've lost much to the mines. More than most."

Gideon studied her, then nodded slightly. "And you—is there someone you're remembering tonight?"

Aria hesitated. The question struck something fragile, buried deep beneath the surface. A chill curled through her and before she realized it, she had wrapped her arms around herself, as if bracing against a weight only she could feel. She thought of her parents—memories of them vague and scattered, slipping through her mind like fragments of a half-forgotten dream. And then her grandmother—frail, fading. Would she stand here next year, mourning her too?

She swallowed hard against the tightness in her throat, steadying her breath, but the ache in her chest remained. Her eyes stung, and though she did not wipe them away, she was quietly relieved that the mask hid the silent tears slipping free, vanishing into the fabric below.

Gideon said nothing at first, he only watched her, absorbing the weight of what she hadn't said. In the dim glow of the lanterns, he caught the faint glimmer in her eyes—a flicker of something raw and unguarded. Something he hadn't seen before. Just as he turned to look away, a single tear slipped free. It caught the light like a lone star falling through the night sky, slipping from beneath her mask and trailing like a whisper of silver before disappearing.

For the first time, his heart ached in a way he hadn't expected. He had seen grief before, ornate and rehearsed in the court, worn like a veil to suit the moment, but this was different. This was real. Raw. And it unsettled something deep within him.

He wanted to reach for her, to offer something—comfort, closeness, a gesture that said—I see you. But he held back. That kind of closeness came with weight he hadn't earned—not yet.

Gideon didn't move. He simply stood there, helpless against the weight of her sorrow.

She was so different from the women of court, the ones who spoke in careful pleasantries and measured smiles. Ones like Charlotte, poised and practiced, every emotion painted to perfection. And then he looked at Aria again, standing here in quiet sorrow, guarded but unafraid to feel.

Something shifted in him then, though he couldn't yet name what it was.

***

A hush still lingered over the square, the weight of the tribute settling into the bones of the city. But slowly, the energy of the festival began to stir once more. The solemn melody faded, replaced by the rhythmic tapping of a cane against wood.

The Master of Ceremonies had returned.

Standing atop the platform, he raised his arms wide, a broad grin cutting through the somber air. "My friends. Fine people of Cavandel," he called, his voice rich with theatrical flourish. "Tonight, we remember those who came before us, those who built this great city with their sweat, their hands, and yes, their sacrifices. And because of them, we stand here today—strong, proud, and unyielding. Let us honor them not only with our silence, but with our joy, with our laughter, and with the bonds we forge on this night!"

For a moment, the square remained suspended in quiet reflection, heads nodding in solemn approval. Then, slowly, conversation began to rise again, a murmur at first, building like coals reigniting beneath ash. A few clapped in acknowledgment of the words spoken, others exchanged glances before allowing small smiles to return. The weight of remembrance lingered, but the city, as it always had, pressed forward.

The Master of Ceremonies swept his cane toward the musicians and with that single motion, the somber air dissolved. The first bright, playful notes of the next song rang out—a melody that sent the square humming with renewed life.

"And now," he declared, "let us continue this grand tradition with a dance! Young and old alike, this is your moment. The Matchmakers' Dance begins!"

The response was immediate. Laughter and excitement rippled through the crowd as people moved eagerly toward the open space of the square. Some reached for their partners without hesitation, while others hesitated, scanning the gathering for a familiar face—or perhaps, for someone new.

A young miner approached Heidi, offering a hand with a shy but hopeful grin. She barely hesitated before taking it, beaming as she let herself be led toward the dance.

Sylas lingered near the edge of the square, tapping his foot to the music but making no move to step forward. He watched the dancers with an expression torn between interest and apprehension, as if the thought of asking someone was just a bit too much effort.

Gideon and Aria remained where they stood, watching as the first dance unfolded. The music wove through the air, the rhythm easy and inviting.

Gideon glanced sideways at Aria, smirking. "You've bested me once already. I hope you'll allow me the chance to redeem myself before the evening ends."

Aria turned to him, one brow lifting with quiet amusement. "Redemption often comes at a cost," she said coolly, a faint smile tugging at her lips.

The song came to an end and the dancers parted with breathless laughter. Heidi returned, flushed with excitement and immediately turned to Sylas. "You owe me a dance from last year," she announced, grinning.

Sylas groaned, rubbing the back of his neck. "I'm sure you're just making that up."

"Not a chance," Heidi shot back, already pulling him toward the square. He let out a dramatic sigh but didn't resist.

Gideon turned back to Aria, amusement still tugging at his lips. "I know you're not the kind to run or hide, but do you dance?"

Aria hesitated.

The square buzzed with movement and laughter around them, yet for a moment, it all felt distant. She had danced the Matchmakers' Dance before—many times. Yet, somehow, this felt different. She wasn't sure why, only that the weight of the moment pressed heavier than it had in years past.

Her fingers curled slightly at her sides, as if debating the decision. Then, finally, she exhaled and reached for his hand.

His fingers closed around hers, warm and steady, as he led her toward the dance.

***

The music shifted, settling into a slower, lilting melody that wound through the air like a lingering warmth. Around them, couples stepped into place, moving in fluid, measured steps that carried them into the rhythm of the dance.

Gideon led without hesitation. His hand was firm yet careful at her waist, guiding her with the natural ease of someone accustomed to leading. Aria followed, though not without effort at first. Her movements were stiff, her body tense in the space between them. It had been a long time since she had danced with someone she did not know, someone whose presence unsettled something beneath her ribs.

But as the music wove through the square, her steps became surer, the hesitation fading like the last remnants of a breath. She let herself move with him, the tension in her limbs easing as the rhythm carried them forward.

"I was right," Gideon said, his voice low, threaded with amusement. "You *are* good with your feet."

Aria said nothing. She dropped her gaze for a brief moment, steadying herself before looking back at him. They moved in measured steps, the lanternlight casting shifting shadows across the sharp line of his cheekbone, the curve of his jaw, the hint of something unreadable behind his mask.

Who was he beneath it all? Who was this stranger wrapped in mystery, stepping into her world as if he had always belonged? There was an ease to him, an unspoken confidence that made it seem as though he fit anywhere he chose to stand. And something about that—about him—drew her in, held her gaze longer than it should have.

His voice dropped lower, the rich timbre threading through the space between them. "Tell me—" he said softly, "is my redemption in sight?"

The sound of Gideon's voice left a flutter in the pit of her stomach, a hollow feeling she hadn't anticipated. She concealed it, tilting her head just so, letting a strand of hair fall across her cheek. Her lips curved into the faintest hint of a smile, eyes never leaving his.

"Maybe," she said, the word hanging in the air between them. She let the moment stretch thin, watching uncertainty flicker across his features before she added, "You're getting there." The last words carried just enough warmth to keep him guessing.

For a time, they danced without speaking, the conversation slipping away, leaving only the quiet pull of movement between them. The air carried the faint warmth of burning oil and the distant sweetness of festival spices, the glow of festival lights casting golden hues across the square. Laughter and murmured conversations swelled and faded in the background, but Aria hardly noticed.

She let herself sink into the moment, just this once. Her grandmother's words drifted through her mind, soft but insistent—*And are these things more important than your own future, than finding someone to share your heart with? It's not selfish to want something beyond survival, Aria.*

For now, the fortress of careful distance she had built around herself seemed to crack, hairline fractures spreading with each turn of the dance. Their steps carried them beneath strings of golden light, and when his hand tightened almost imperceptibly at her waist, she didn't stiffen or pull away. They didn't need to say what this was. It wasn't a promise, but it was close. A possibility, blooming quietly in the dark.

She would unravel this feeling later. It would need to be contained, examined, and likely set aside. She would remember who she was, who he might be, and all the reasons why this should be extinguished.

But not yet.

The music held them, suspended in a moment that belonged to neither caution nor consequence. For now, there was only this—his breath close enough to feel, the rhythm binding them together and the strange, quiet tension of allowing herself this moment.

***

The music slowed, the final notes fading into the hum of conversation and scattered laughter. The dance had ended, yet neither of them moved. Aria's pulse was steady now, her breathing even, but the warmth of Gideon's hand still lingered, a presence she couldn't quite shake.

He didn't step away. He remained close, his gaze contemplative beneath the mask.

The space between them was filled with the distant sounds of revelry, the laughter of festival-goers, the distant hum of voices entwining with the soft strains of music—but for a breath, it felt like the square had shrunk to just the two of them. Something in the silence felt unfinished—not a conclusion, but a door cracked open.

Then, finally, he leaned in just slightly, his voice dipping low, inviting. "Walk with me."

He didn't frame it as a request or command—just a step forward, offered freely. And somehow, she took it.

He slipped away from the main square, weaving through the mingling crowd. Aria hesitated only a moment before trailing after him, drawn forward by something she couldn't quite name. The weight of eyes on them prickled at the nape of her neck, not from the festival-goers, who were far too occupied in their own merriment, but something else, something unseen.

Gideon recognized the feeling intimately. His guards were near. He couldn't see them, but they were always there, lurking in the crowd, watching over him in silent vigilance. He let the breath leave him and turned away.

They reached a quieter stretch along the edge of the square, where lanternlight cast long shadows across the stone. The night air was cooler here, tugging gently at the hem of Aria's dress, whispering across her skin. Gideon stopped beneath a narrow archway veiled in shadow, the distant glow of the festivities tracing the curve of his shoulder and catching along the line of his j aw.

They stood in silence for a moment, the distant sounds of music and laughter drifting toward them, muted by the hush beneath the archway.

Gideon stole a glance at her, and for a moment, forgot everything else. She wasn't like the women of court. There was no performance to her. Just quiet strength and a silence that somehow said more. And tonight, in the lanternlight, she was quietly radiant.

He turned slightly, his eyes catching the low, golden glow from across the square.

"You dance well," he said, a faint smile tugging at the corners of his mouth.

Aria shifted, glancing down before looking back at him. "And, you managed to keep up this time," she whispered, her voice softer now, touched with a hint of teasing. "I'm impressed..."

He smiled, slow and genuine. "I've been waiting all evening to hear you say that."

She lowered her gaze, but the smile remained. "I guess it's been a successful evening, then?"

"So far," he whispered, the words low and easy, as though he wasn't quite ready to let the night end. He watched her a moment longer. "Truth is, I wasn't quite sure what to expect," he added.

Aria looked up at that, a hint of curiosity softening her expression. For a breath, she said nothing. His words unsettled the careful balance she usually held. And in some wordless way, she'd felt the same—unsure, reluctant and now, unexpectedly at ease in his company.

"Neither did I. But... I'm glad," she muttered.

She didn't finish the thought. Instead, her gaze dropped to the space between them. Her fingers curled loosely at her sides, uncertain, almost like she didn't trust them not to reach for something they shouldn't. A breath passed and she shifted her weight slightly, not stepping back, but not quite leaning in either. Just... holding still, caught somewhere, between retreat and wanting to stay.

Gideon watched her a moment longer. The silence between them wasn't uncomfortable, just full, like it carried something neither of them knew how to name.

"Will I see you again?" he asked, the words quiet, not pressing, just wondering.

Aria blinked, caught off guard by the sudden shift. She hadn't thought about what came after this, hadn't allowed herself to.

She searched what little she could see of his face. The question carried more weight than it should have, settling somewhere deep within her chest. "I—I don't know," she whispered slowly.

Gideon let his gaze settle on her, weighing her silence. After a breath, he spoke again, his voice gentler. "If this is the last time we see each other, then I hope you'll let me see you. The real you," he muttered.

Aria froze. The words landed like a stone in her stomach. "The real me?" she repeated, her voice low, uncertain.

"Yes," he breathed softly. "The one behind the mask."

She swallowed, staring at him in stunned silence. "You don't—we don't—" Her breath caught and she looked away quickly, as if the weight of his question had struck somewhere unguarded.

Gideon studied her reaction, something unspoken flickering behind his eyes. "We don't what?" His voice softened, uncertain, almost pleading.

"We don't do it like that, down here," she murmured, hesitation fraying her words.

"I don't understand," Gideon murmured, a slight frown forming across his brows. "Surely, you don't spend your entire life behind a mask?"

A flicker of doubt stirred in her chest.

Any man from the District would already know this, wouldn't he?

"You truly don't know?" Aria asked, her gaze narrowing.

"No," he admitted softly, a trace of impatience seeping into his tone.

She regarded him for a long moment. "In Cavandel, we don't exchange masks unless—" She hesitated, the words catching just before they could form, like saying them out loud might shift something neither of them could undo.

"Unless what?" he pressed, his voice low, steady.

Heat rose to her cheeks before she could stop it. Her eyes dropped, posture stiffening—not in retreat, but as if bracing for something she couldn't name.

"Unless, I was certain of your intentions," she whispered softly. "It's a promise." She glanced away, almost as if the words were too heavy, too exposed.

Understanding flickered in Gideon's eyes, but it didn't settle cleanly. It landed uneven, like a stone shifting underfoot. Removing her mask wasn't some passing gesture, not in this world. It was something more. A declaration. Not a vow, but something close. An offering of trust and permission to begin.

He should have known. Should have seen it in the way she stilled, the way she didn't meet his gaze. How easily she could hold herself in silence, like she'd been taught that offering too much could cost everything.

And yet, he'd asked anyway.

His mask felt heavier now. Not just the physical curve of it, but what it meant, what it protected. Who it separated him from.

What would it mean to remove it?

He was a prince. The next in line for the throne. He had been sent here to see Cavandel, to observe quietly, to blend in—not become part of it. And now he stood beneath a dark archway with a girl who didn't know who he was, asking her, however unknowingly, for something sacred.

If she took hers off, if she gave him that piece of trust—what would he owe her in return?

He felt a slow tension coil in his chest. All those women in court, dressed in silk and trained in smiles, hadn't managed to touch him, not the way this girl did with just a glance. She didn't know who he was. She didn't care. And that made her dangerous.

Would he bring her back with him to the surface? Would she even want to go? Would he declare her to the court, the queen, the king? Let them see the girl from the caverns below, who had never stepped into sunlight?

What would they say?

No title. No pedigree. No reason, except the way she had looked at him without calculation. The way she'd said "I don't know," like it was the most honest thing in the world.

A part of him, the part trained by years of strategy and silence, told him this was reckless—foolish even. That no good could come of it.

But something quieter rose beneath it. Not strategy. Not duty. Just a want he hadn't let himself feel in years. That maybe, just maybe, he didn't want a girl who was trained to be chosen. Maybe he wanted the one who didn't know who he was and wouldn't have cared even if she did. Because for the first time in a long time, he wanted to be seen—not as a future king, not as a prize to be won—but just as he was. And she had already done that.

He looked at her, still as stone, gaze downturned, as if waiting for something inevitable.

Was this truly a door he could open? A threshold he was ready to stand on, knowing what it might lead to? And yet, the stillness in her posture, the way she braced herself, unmoving, struck him all over again.

He hadn't meant to ask for her trust. But now that he understood what it meant, he knew one thing clearly—if she ever gave it, it wouldn't be on a whim. It would be a choice. A beginning.

The decision hadn't been made in words. It had settled into him slowly, unbearably, somewhere between what he feared, what he wanted and something deeper still.

He reached up, undoing the ties of his own mask without hesitation. Once it was free, he took it and pressed it into her hand, his fingers brushing against hers for the briefest moment. The black fabric came away easily, revealing the sharp lines of his face and the startling clarity in his eyes.

The ease with which he did it sent Aria reeling. Did he not understand what he had just done? What he was asking of her?

She took a step back, the curve of her spine meeting the cold stone wall behind her. It felt as though she'd been trapped between the weight of his decision and the stone at her back—no path forward, no safe retreat, only the question hanging in the air between them.

Instinctively, her hand rose to her mask, pressing it closer against her face as though sheer pressure might hold it in place, might shield her from what came next. The gesture felt as reflexive as breathing, as if protecting it meant protecting something far deeper.

"What are you doing?" she hissed, the words tumbling out too fast, too thin. Panic slipped into her voice before she could catch it, while her other hand gripped the edge of the wall behind her, as if anchoring herself might keep her from unraveling.

Gideon met her gaze. "Revealing my intentions. Letting you see who I really am. No pretenses," he said, the words steady, unwavering. Something softened in his expression, a weariness that hadn't been there before. "I've spent my whole life behind masks of one kind or another." His voice lowered. "I don't want that here. Not with you. With you, I want to be seen and accepted, for who I really am."

She glanced around, panic sparking behind her eyes. She leaned closer, her voice dropping to a sharp whisper. "Put it back on."

Gideon didn't move. "I will not," he said flatly.

"You don't understand," she said, breath catching, her hand still pressed hard against her own mask. "Someone might see you."

"I know," he said. His voice was low, steady. "I do want someone to see me. And I want it to be you."

Her breath caught again—not from fear this time, but from the slow, dawning realization of what he was offering. And what it might mean.

A quiet war waged inside her, one half urging retreat, the other anchoring her in place, unwilling to surrender whatever was blooming between them. Above them, paper lanterns swayed in the night breeze, casting shifting shadows across his unmasked face. The distant sound of festival drums pulsed like a second heartbeat beneath their words.

He had removed his mask so easily, as though his whole life has been leading to this moment.

Did he even know what he was giving away? Her fingers curled around the edges of hers. She studied his face, searching for something—remorse, understanding, anything to suggest he knew the weight of what he was o-ffering so easily.

He was from the Stratum. She was sure of it. She could feel it in the way he spoke, in the ease of his confidence. The son of some merchant, maybe—someone with connections, with reach. And she—she was not even from the Inner District. A Dustborn from the Outer, with miner's blood, carrying the grime of the tunnels below.

Could something like this even work? Would he whisk her away? Take her to the heights of the Stratum, a world of polished voices and untouchable names? Would she follow? Could she leave Heidi and Sylas behind? Could she walk away from everything she'd known for the comfort of something that didn't feel like it was meant for her?

And what of Gran? Her illness was spreading. Shatterblight had already taken root and she needed constant care. Would he see her as a burden? Someone to be cast aside?

"I'm a Dustborn from the Outer District," Aria said finally, "I have nothing to offer."

Gideon studied her carefully. "A Dust—" He cut himself off, unable to finish the sentence. Did she truly not see it? The way she held herself, even now, with every reason to run, and none to hope? She carried her pain like it was something earned, something she owed the world to bear in silence.

"You're stronger than any woman I've ever met," he said evenly, his voice low. "And you don't even realize it."

Aria didn't acknowledge his words, not really. Her voice trembled as it left her. "My grandmother is sick. And she's getting worse."

Gideon didn't look away, he knew she was just deflecting. The shift in his gaze was subtle but immediate. Concern, quiet and real, softened the edges of his expression.

He thought back to earlier that evening, to the shadow that had lingered behind her smile, the way she'd looked away when the music turned softer. Had this been the weight she carried all along?

"I'm sorry," he said, and he meant it.

There was a pause, then he added. "She must mean a great deal to you."

Aria felt the sting behind her eyes before the tears could form. Her voice was quiet, shaped by something close to reverence. "She's everything to me."

A breath escaped her—too dry to be a laugh. "I'm only here tonight because of her," Aria whispered. "She wanted me to come."

The scent of poured ale and roasted meat lingered in the festival air around them. A burst of laughter erupted from somewhere in the distance, reminding her how close they stood to being discovered. Yet she couldn't bring herself to step away.

Gideon's gaze didn't waver. "Then I'm forever in her debt," he murmured, with a low, easy grace. His eyes held no mischief, only a calm that met her where she stood. A quiet kind of promise, even if he hadn't spoken one aloud.

Aria opened her mouth, then closed it. Her fingers curled at her sides, grasping for something, anything, to hold the moment at bay. A gust of cool night air swept through the narrow passage, carrying with it a reminder of her friends.

"Sylas won't approve," she muttered, clinging to the excuse even as it left her lips. "You saw the way he looked at you, like you were trouble."

Gideon gave a quiet laugh. "I like him already." He paused for a brief moment, then his expression sobered. "His caution is warranted. He cares for you," Gideon said softly, "I would be the same in his position." His eyes held hers, revealing a quiet sincerity beneath his earlier confidence. "But I hope to prove myself worthy of his trust. As well as yours."

She didn't return the smile. His words had been too earnest, too genuine. It made her chest ache. Because he wasn't retreating. Because every excuse she'd offered—Gran, Sylas, the difference between them—none of it had mattered.

And now, there was nowhere left to hide.

She swallowed, the words rough in her throat. "Down here," she said softly, "it's not done lightly. It's a promise." She held his gaze.

Gideon gave her a smirk, attempting to ease the tension. "You're not trying to run, are you?"

"I'm not running," she said softly. "I just need to be sure you understand."

He didn't flinch. "I do," he promised, his voice low, sincere. "And I don't regret it."

Beyond them, festival lights flickered in the distance, casting a golden glow over the square, but in this moment, everything else had dimmed, the edges of sound dulled. The stone wall at her back firm, a stark contrast to her tangled thoughts. She should have walked away. She should have left him standing there. A man who clearly didn't belong in her world and yet here he stood, unflinching, undoing her piece by piece.

But she didn't leave.

She took a deep breath, then slowly, she lifted her mask, letting it slide free. Her hand hovered for a moment—then she offered it to him.

The motion felt like a promise, not a forever, but a real beginning.

They stood in silence, the weight of what passed between them hanging like spun glass. Fragile. Sacred. Then, before she could speak, before she could gather her thoughts into armor—Gideon reached forward, hesitant, careful and let his thumb trace the line of her cheek down to the point of her c hin.

Aria shivered. His touch was barely there, but it marked her in ways she couldn't explain, like a promise written directly on her skin.

The walls she had carefully constructed slowly began to crumble.

For the first time in longer than she could remember, she wasn't thinking of tomorrow's burdens or yesterday's losses. There was only this moment, this breath, this revelation, and the quiet understanding that nothing would be the same again. She wasn't giving herself away. Not entirely. But she was giving him something real, something no one else had earned.

"You're beautiful," he began, then exhaled, his voice quieter. "Like the morning sun breaking through the darkness."

Her breath caught.

The Sun.

Her stomach twisted. No one in Cavandel spoke of the Sun—not like that. Not unless they'd seen it.

Her eyes snapped to his, sharp with realization. "You're not from the Stratum, are you," she said, her voice quiet but certain. "You're from the surface."

Something shifted in his face. A hesitation. A calculation. And in that shift, she saw it—confirmation.

"I—" He caught himself, but it was too late.

"You kept that from me."

He hesitated, then exhaled. "I had little choice," he said, his voice lower now, nearly lost in the sound of distant laughter and the hush of lanterns swaying above.

Aria stepped back. Just a breath. But it felt like a chasm. "Who are you, Gideon? And why are you here?"

Gideon didn't answer right away. His gaze didn't waver, but something in it shifted, as though weighing what could be spoken. "Come back with me."

Her heart gave a strange stutter. "What?"

"To the surface." His voice was steady. "Come with me."

For a brief, reckless moment, she wanted to say yes. Once, she might have—would have chased the promise of sky, of sea, of light. But now—

Now, Cavandel was on the edge of something fragile, something vital. The Dwellers were close to the cure. They needed her. She couldn't leave. Not yet.

Her voice was quiet but firm. "I can't." She looked at him and the regret that surfaced was real. "I want to. Really, I do. But I can't."

Gideon's jaw tightened, but he gave a slow nod, as if some part of him had expected it. Even so, something unspoken lingered in his eyes. An ache, a refusal to let go.

"Then I'll come back for you," he said firmly.

It was a promise and yet not quite. There was uncertainty tangled in it, like a thread pulled too thin. Her expression shifted—longing, fear, a fragile hope she didn't trust herself to name.

She opened her mouth, then closed it. Her fingers twitched at her sides like they didn't know what to hold onto. "Don't say that," she whispered. "Not if you don't mean it."

"I mean it," he said, the words quiet but sure. "I'll come back. I swear it."

She looked at him then, really looked, as if she could read the truth straight from his face. But whatever answer she was searching for, she couldn't find it, or it wasn't clear enough. After a moment, her gaze shifted, the question fading from her lips before it ever formed.

She glanced down at the mask in her hand—his mask. Her fingers toyed with the edges, tracing its lines without really seeing them. It felt like holding a piece of another world, one she'd only ever imagined in stolen pages and quiet dreams. Her pulse fluttered. The question rose, unsteady, curling in her chest like something too fragile to name.

Instead, her voice came quieter. Different. "What's it like?" she whispered.

Gideon blinked, unsure. "What do you mean?"

She hesitated, then gave him the smallest of smiles. Almost sad. "The Sun. The lantern in the sky," she whispered.

Her voice trembled on the last word, the way it had the first time she read it in the book. A world she had only known through whispers and pages—until now.

Gideon's mouth curved, the beginnings of a smile tugging at one corner. "Lantern, huh?" he said, a quiet laugh in his voice. "That's... not exactly wrong. Just makes it sound a lot smaller—and a lot less terrifying."

Aria's face flushed. "That's what the book called it," she muttered, suddenly unsure. "I didn't—I don't know how else to describe it."

The amusement in his eyes softened. "Hey," he whispered gently, "I'm not mocking. It's just... it's kind of beautiful, the way you said it."

He let out a breath, something between a laugh and a sigh. "It's nothing like these lights," he said, glancing at the golden glow of the square. "It's warmer. Wilder. You can't look at it—you feel it. In your bones, in your blood. Like the world is waking up just to see you standing there."

The words tangled with memory—her fingers once tracing an old illustration of the Sun suspended above a vast blue ocean, of trees curling into the sky like something imagined. Fanciful things. Impossible things. And yet here he was, speaking of them like they were real.

"I would like to see it one day," she said, her voice low and contemplative.

Gideon placed a hand gently on her shoulder, his touch warm and grounding. "You can. You'll see it. I promise."

But she thought she heard hesitation woven through those words. Something passed over Aria's face—longing, uncertainty, a fragile hope she was afraid to name. Her breath caught in her throat. She wanted to believe him, but down here, hope was a luxury she'd learned to live without.

Aria didn't speak. She only held his gaze, the weight of everything unsaid stretching between them like the space of an entire world.

He stepped back slightly, but his eyes stayed on hers. "Will you meet me again?" he asked.

She hesitated, but only for a moment. "I'd like that," she answered softly.

Gideon smiled, deep and quiet, relief washing over him. "Two nights from now. At the ninth hour. Meet me at this very spot."

Aria nodded. "The ninth hour. I'll be here," she murmured.

And when she said it, part of her wished she already was.

She stood there a moment longer, listening to the fading footsteps in the square, the hush that always followed music and the weight of his promise still lingering in her chest.

She didn't move. Not yet. Because part of her—a quiet, impossible part—was already imagining what it would be like to see the Sun. Not in stories. Not in dreams. But beside him. And just like that, the moment passed—not like something lost, but like something waiting to return.

***

The festival still roared behind them, but as Aria walked beside Heidi and Sylas, the noise transformed. The cheerful melodies and laughter faded, replaced by the hollow echo of her own heartbeat. The weight of the mask in her hand seemed to grow with each step. The material was cool against her fingertips, its edges unfamiliar. Gideon's mask. Or rather, the mask that had been his. Now hers.

He had promised to return.

The words still lingered, weightless yet unshakable, as they parted ways. He hadn't lingered much after that, nor had she asked him to. No assurances, no grand gestures—just that quiet promise before the three men from earlier had whisked him away.

Heidi's mouth had parted, her eyes widening as she took in the empty space where Aria's mask should have been. Sylas had frozen mid-step, his usual smirk replaced with something unreadable before a short, dry laugh escaped him—like he didn't quite believe what he was seeing. The silence that followed had been louder than any festival cheer.

Aria kept her gaze forward, though she could feel Heidi's eyes on her, sharp and assessing. The cool night air carried traces of ale and spiced wine, scents of a celebration she no longer felt part of. Sylas, for once, was silent, but it wouldn't last.

It didn't.

"I still can't believe you did that," Heidi said, breathless with disbelief. "You actually—" She cut herself off, as if saying it aloud would somehow make it more real, more dangerous.

Aria's shoulders tensed beneath her thin cloak, her fingers tracing the unfamiliar ridges of Gideon's mask—so different from the one she had worn earlier. The mask she had just given away, breaking one of the oldest traditions in Cavandel.

Sylas exhaled sharply, crossing his arms. "So, do we call you Mrs. Mudslide, now?"

"It's not marriage, Sylas." Aria retorted.

Sylas scoffed, the sound escaping on the edge of a breath. "Not yet," he muttered, more to himself than to her.

Aria said nothing, gripping the mask a little tighter, her knuckles whitening. A flush crept up her neck, not just from embarrassment but from something deeper—defiance, perhaps, or something else.

Heidi shook her head. "Aria, he's from the surface. We don't even know him." She hesitated, then added more softly, "How do we know if we'll ever even see him again?"

"He said he'll come back," Aria murmured, her voice steadier than she felt.

Sylas snorted. "And you believe him? What if he doesn't come back?" He gestured upward as he said, "How is this even supposed to work if he's all the way up there," then let his hand fall to their surroundings. "And we're all the way down here."

Aria's grip on the mask tightened, her fingernails digging crescent moons into her palms. The thought had already crept into her mind, unbidden. What if Gideon never returned? What if this was just another passing moment, one that only she would hold onto? She had given him her mask—had broken tradition for him—and now she was left with the weight of it, the uncertainty of what came next.

Heidi exhaled, then reached out, her arm settling around Aria's shoulders in a quiet show of support. "I just don't want to see you get hurt," she said softly. "I know you, Aria. And I know you wouldn't have done this lightly."

She hesitated, then gave Aria's arm a gentle squeeze. "Just... be sure. Be sure this isn't because he's from the surface."

Aria's breath hitched. Was that true? Was it because he was from the surface? Was it the mystery of him—the way he didn't belong—that made her reckless? Had she only wanted an escape, something or someone—that felt like a way out?

In the distance, a ceremonial bell tolled, signaling the festival's final hour. The deep chime reverberated through the emptying streets, a sound that had always marked the end of Founders Day. Aria ran her thumb across the foreign mask's surface once more—slowly, deliberately. This wasn't like the years before, when the bell had meant nothing more than another festival fading into memory.

Gideon's mask was in her hands now, just as hers was in his. A silent exchange. A promise neither of them had spoken aloud. This time, the night felt different. Whatever came next, she had made her choice.

22

Rays of Revolution

Location: Cavandel, The Outer District

The scent of fresh bread filled the small kitchen, warm and rich, mingling with the faint smoke of the dying embers in the hearth. Aria moved between the stove and table with effortless familiarity, her hands busy but her mind elsewhere. A melody slipped past her lips—soft at first, then rising into a quiet whistle. The tune carried on, unbidden, shaped by a lightness in her chest she hadn't felt in a long time.

Had she paused to consider it, she might have recognized how rare such moments had become. Had she glimpsed herself in a mirror, the faint smile playing at her lips might have startled her.

Earlier that morning, she had woken before the city stirred, a rare occurrence after Founders Day. The lingering scent of smoke and festival ale still clung to her, but it was the mask on the bed beside her that held her attention.

Gideon's mask.

She had reached for it before she could think better of it, running her fingers over its unfamiliar edges. It wasn't hers. It never should have been hers. And yet, here it was. Proof of what had transpired the night before. Proof of what she had done.

She had sat there for a long while, staring at the mask in her hands, turning it over as if its weight might somehow reveal an answer. She had told herself not to think of him. She had promised herself she wouldn't. But in the quiet solitude of morning, with only the mask and her own thoughts, it was impossible to ignore the shift that had taken place within her.

A promise had been made—not spoken, but understood. He had said he would return. And she had believed him.

Now, standing in the kitchen, humming a song she hadn't realized she was singing, she forced herself to shake the thoughts away. There was breakfast to make. Things to do. The day would move forward as it always did.

Her grandmother had been standing in the doorway for some time now, watching her with quiet amazement. Aria, lost in her thoughts, hadn't even noticed.

There was something different about her this morning—something lighter, something at ease.

A knowing glint sparked in the older woman's eyes, but instead of prying just yet, she decided to have a little fun.

"Well, well," she said slowly. "Who is this bright-eyed stranger cooking in my kitchen, and what have you done with my Aria?"

Aria huffed, tossing a glance over her shoulder. "Morning, Gran," she said, the warmth in her own voice catching her off guard. She hadn't meant to sound so light, but the morning had settled into her bones in a way that felt safe. Failing to smother the cheer beneath it, she added, "I have no idea what you're talking about."

She turned back to the stove, slicing a piece of bread before adding, "Am I not allowed to sing now?"

Her grandmother pressed a hand to her chest as if steadying herself. "By all means, sing away," she said, "I just need a moment to recover from the shock." With an exaggerated sigh, she eased into a chair. "I just never thought I'd see the day."

Aria shot her a warning look, though amusement danced in her eyes.

"One more word and it's the extra-spicy mushrooms for you," she cautioned. "We all know how much you enjoy those."

Her grandmother sighed dramatically, shaking her head. "Now I know for certain—for my sweet, kind-hearted Aria would never be so cruel."

Settling back in her chair, she gave a mischievous glint. "But, if this is to be my fate, at least I'll know my last moments were spent witnessing a miracle."

Aria laughed as she slid into the seat across from her, playful exasperation written across her face. "I expected this kind of behavior from Sylas, Gran, but certainly not from you," she said, her tone light with affection.

The kitchen fell into an unusual silence as they ate. Aria focused on her plate, determined to keep her thoughts in order, but she could feel her grandmother's eyes on her—watchful, amused, waiting.

She kept her posture relaxed, took measured bites and willed herself to remain unaffected. It worked at first, but as the silence stretched, her mind wandered—steel blue eyes, warm hands, the weight of a promise left unspoken.

Heat crept up her neck, betraying her.

Her grandmother set down her cup with a quiet clink, tilting her head. "Are you feeling well, dear?" Her lips curved into a knowing smile, amusement dancing in her eyes. "You look a little flushed," she said lightly. "I do hope you're not coming down with something."

She let the teasing linger for a moment longer before her expression softened. "I haven't seen you like this in a long time, Aria." Her voice was quieter now, more thoughtful. "Your mother looked like that once." She stirred her tea absently, lost in memory. "Years ago," she said, her voice laced with nostalgia. "She met your father at the festival. I remember the way she smiled when she spoke of him, the way she carried herself as if the whole world had shifted beneath her feet. And now, here you are. My Aria, the result of that match."

She exhaled, a warm but wistful smile touching her lips. "Thank you for going," she said softly. "Seeing you happy—truly happy—is the best gift you could have given me."

Aria lowered her gaze, her fingers tracing the rim of her cup. "Gran..." she murmured.

Her grandmother tilted her head, studying her. "So, who is he? Is it someone I know? Is he from the Inner?"

Aria hesitated, uncertainty flickering across her face. Misreading the look for embarrassment, her grandmother gave a reassuring smile. "It's perfectly fine if he's from the Outer, dear," she whispered reassuringly. "I grew up here, and so did your parents—we didn't turn out too bad, did we?"

Aria hesitated, turning the cup between her hands. How much should she reveal? The truth sat heavy on her tongue, demanding to be spoken, yet she hesitated, as if saying it aloud would make it more real.

Finally, she exhaled, lifting her gaze to meet her grandmother's. "That's the thing, Gran," Aria said slowly, "He's not from the Outer, or the Inner, or even the Stratum."

She swallowed hard, just before the words escaped her.

"He's from the surface."

Her grandmother blinked once, then again, the weight of the words settling between them. After a long moment, she set her cup down carefully and murmured, "Oh dear..."

Location: Cavandel, Dweller's Base

The underground lab was a clutter of scattered notes, half-empty vials, and the sharp bite of antiseptic. Anna barely glanced up as Aria, Heidi, and Sylas stepped inside. Her gaze stayed fixed on the flask before her, intent on the delicate process unfolding within it. Focus sharpened her features, each movement precise as she worked.

"Look who finally decided to show up," Anna muttered, swirling the liquid in its glass. "Didn't think I'd see any of you today. Figured you'd be nursing headaches and regretting poor choices."

Sylas smirked, casting a sideways glance at Aria. "Some of us are."

Aria shot him a warning look, one that made it clear now was not the time.

Anna remained focused, her mind already moving to the next step. "We don't have time to waste. Aria, help with the patients—keep them cool and stable. If you notice anything, even the smallest change, we need to know."

Aria nodded and moved to a nearby cot where a young nurse was tending to a feverish man. The nurse passed her a damp cloth without a word, and she laid it gently against the patient's forehead, watching his chest rise and fall in labored breaths.

Anna didn't pause. "Heidi, we need more solutions. Prep eight vials, and please be precise. We can't afford mistakes."

Without hesitation, Heidi moved to the supply station and gathered the necessary materials. She set to work quickly, measuring out the Crythium powder, her brow furrowed in concentration.

"Sylas, go through your samples again. If there's anything we overlooked, I need to know."

Sylas moved to a cluttered workstation and sifted through the rows of labeled vials. He muttered to himself as he inspected each one, occasionally lifting a vial toward the light to study its contents more closely.

Anna moved through the lab, scanning the steady hum of activity around her. Lab assistants worked swiftly at their stations—grinding ingredients, recording observations, and preparing materials. She wandered over to Sylas' station, glancing at the samples he had laid out.

"Anything promising?"

"Complete failures over here," Sylas said, tapping a row of vials. "These are my last samples. Nineteen milliliters each. These four stayed purple—no good."

Anna nodded. "Yes. I can see that."

He gestured to the remaining three, his tone shifting ever so slightly, an undercurrent of frustration beneath his usual lightheartedness. "These made it past the next stage. They went clear for a few hours but then failed. See?" He pointed. "They all turned black."

Anna studied the vials, her brow knitting as he continued. "This one was mixed at eighty-nine degrees. This one here"—he tapped the vial—"at ninety-two. And the last one," he said, "at eighty-one."

Anna frown deepened as she continued to study the vials. Then, after a pause, she asked, "Sylas, are you colorblind?"

Sylas blinked. "I don't think so. Why?"

She pointed at the last vial, her voice even but carrying the weight of something far more pressing. "That one isn't black. It's gray."

Sylas leaned in, narrowing his eyes at the vial. He stared at it for a long moment, his expression shifting ever so slightly before he let out a short, nervous laugh. "Well, look at that... I guess it is."

Anna straightened, her mind already racing ahead. "Get your notes," she said, urgency threading through her voice. "I need to know exactly what you did on that last sample."

The next few hours dissolved into measured movements and hushed calculations, the silence broken only by quills scratching against parchment and the delicate clink of glass. Time stretched and compressed as they worked—testing, adjusting, refining.

Vial after vial was prepared, each one meticulously cataloged, their colors shifting in slow increments. Sylas's original sample had turned clear at first, before darkening to a failed gray. Using this as a foundation, they altered ratios, stabilizers, and dilution levels in precise increments.

Each new attempt followed the same painstaking pattern. The liquid remained clear at first, but then, with the deliberation of a held breath, it began to transform—each successive iteration settling into progressively lighter shades of gray.

Then—finally—a sample remained clear. Unchanged.

At first, no one dared to hope. They had seen this before.

Anna marked the time with a quick stroke of ink, setting the vial aside. Minutes blurred into hours, yet the liquid refused to darken. It remained as it was—unchanged, untouched by the slow decay that had claimed every previous attempt.

The others forced themselves to work, their hands performing familiar motions while their attention repeatedly gravitated to the single vial sitting beneath the lamplight.

Finally, Anna held it up. Still clear. Still unwavering.

Her breath left her in a slow, measured exhale. A quiet certainty settled over her, as if the moment had been waiting for her to claim it.

She turned the vial slowly between her fingers, watching the lamplight catch on its surface. The liquid remained unchanged, its clarity unyielding. Her breath left her in a slow, measured exhale. Steady. Certain.

"This, is it," she murmured, the weight of the words settling over the room. No one spoke. Then Heidi jolted into motion, already moving for the door. "I'll get Sebastian."

Anna nodded absently, her focus transfixed on the vial, fingers tightening around the glass as if it might dissolve between heartbeats.

Minutes passed in a slow crawl. The others moved around the lab, restless with anticipation, but the vial remained unchanged.

Then, at last, footsteps echoed in the corridor. A shadow fell across the threshold. Sebastian stepped inside, his gaze sweeping the room before locking onto Anna with fierce intensity. Kegan followed just behind, his expression carefully neutral as he took in the scene.

Sebastian's voice cut through the tension, calm yet edged with something sharper. "Tell me."

Anna didn't hesitate. "We've had a breakthrough," she said evenly.

A hush fell over the lab, every eye drawn to the vial in her hands. But its weight was not in glass and liquid. It was in the fragile thread of hope it carried.

Her gaze drifted to the rows of occupied cots. The still forms beneath thin blankets. Some with days remaining. Others, mere hours.

Sebastian exhaled, tension easing from his stance, though his focus remained sharp.

Kegan's gaze lingered on the vial, his smirk slow to form. His attention drifted briefly to the patients, then back to Anna, calculating. Measuring. "So," he murmured, voice smooth, unreadable. "Is this the miracle we've been waiting for?"

Anna stood resolute. "We're about to find out." She turned to the others, her grip firm around the vial. She met their expectant gazes with a single, determined nod. "It's time."

Location: Cavandel, The Stratum

High above Aria and her companions—beyond the crowded District that divided the city—Gideon sat in the Stratum, near the center of a quiet room, arms loosely crossed as he regarded the man before him. Warden Thaddeus Blackthorne sat behind his heavy wooden desk, his expression schooled into something unreadable. He had the look of a man who had spent too many years holding power in a place that demanded control at every turn. His gaze settled briefly on the documents stacked beside him before returning to Gideon.

"Crythium production remains steady. The latest projections indicate a three percent increase by the end of the next cycle. Given recent optimizations, we expect output to continue rising—barring any unforeseen disruptions."

Gideon nodded slightly, absorbing the words before responding. "My father will be pleased."

The Warden continued, his tone as even as his gaze. "Of course, there are still variables to consider. If certain—obstacles can be eliminated, we may see an even greater yield in the future."

Gideon gave a slight nod, letting the words settle. "Progress is always welcome," he said, "provided the methods do not create more problems than they solve." He understood well enough that the Warden was speaking carefully, withholding more than he revealed.

The Warden studied him with a measured, calculating gaze. "Of course, Your Highness," he said offhandedly. He went on, "Naturally, prosperity depends on more than production alone. Some provisions are more difficult to sustain underground. Take fruit, for example, an essential resource that requires careful management to maintain. The quality we receive often suffers during the journey. Fresh citrus and unblemished apples would do wonders for morale among the workers. A necessary consideration."

Gideon caught the subtle request. "Rest assured, Warden, my father greatly values Cavandel's contribution to the kingdom. I'll personally review the transportation protocols for perishables. Perhaps faster conveyances or improved preservation methods are needed. The workers deserve better than spoiled fruit after their labor. I'll ensure my report addresses these quality concerns directly."

The Warden's shoulders relaxed almost imperceptibly. He inclined his head with measured gratitude. "Your attentiveness is appreciated, Your Highness. Such matters may at first seem trivial, but they can significantly impact morale."

A brief silence settled between them, filled with unspoken calculations. The Warden's fingers traced an invisible pattern on his desk before he ventured into more delicate territory.

"Naturally, His Majesty is not one to speak idly," he said, his tone growing more cautious. "But I have often wondered—does he still look upon Cavandel with the same confidence as before?"

Drawing a slow breath, he continued. "One must always be mindful of how one's work is perceived. Has His Majesty expressed any specific concerns about our operations or management here in Cavandel? I would be remiss not to ensure his expectations are met."

A fleeting moment passed, deliberate, but not prolonged.

"Cavandel has always served the crown well," Gideon said evenly. "And my father values results over reassurances. If he had concerns about Cavandel, I doubt he would leave them unspoken."

The Warden nodded slowly, a hint of relief crossing his features. "Your words are reassuring, Your Highness. The crown's confidence is our highest priority." He paused, then shifted his approach. "I also trust that nothing during the festivities was found wanting?" His voice was smooth, unreadable.

Gideon held the Warden's gaze, his expression steady. He gave a slight nod, brows lifting just enough to suggest genuine approval. "It was quite impressive," he said at last, then added, "and informative."

The Warden nodded, folding his hands atop his desk. "I'm pleased to hear that," he said. "Yes, very pleased." A faint smile tugged at the corner of his mouth—controlled, fleeting, almost satisfied.

"And now that Your Highness has seen Cavandel at its finest, I imagine your delegation will be quite eager to return home."

His tone left no room for doubt, the weight of his words pressing the conversation toward its inevitable conclusion.

Gideon studied him, noting the ease with which he extended the suggestion. The Warden was careful not to overstep, but his meaning was clear. The festival was over. The time for observation had passed. Whatever he wished to keep hidden beneath Cavandel's glittering mask, he preferred it remain unseen.

Unfortunately for him, Gideon had no intention of leaving. Not yet.

"The festival was only part of the picture," Gideon said, his voice cool and deliberate. "It showed me the people at their best. But to truly understand them, one must also see them in different circumstances." He let the words settle before adding, "You can learn much about a city by witnessing both its triumphs and its struggles."

The Warden leaned back slightly, considering this. "I assure you, Your Highness, Cavandel is exactly as you have seen it. Our city thrives, our people endure, and our traditions remain strong. There is little more to observe—nothing, I imagine, that would warrant further distraction from Your Highness's valuable time."

Gideon gave a slow nod, feigning thoughtfulness. Behind his carefully composed expression, Aria's face flashed in his mind—her eyes behind the intricately carved mask they had exchanged during the festival. He remembered how easily she had bested him in the challenge, her unexpected laugh, and the impossible weight she seemed to carry behind that smile.

"Even so, I would prefer to stay a while longer," he said, his voice revealing nothing of his true thoughts. "To gain a more complete perspective." He gestured with one hand. "Most of the delegation will return to the capital on the morrow, but I will remain with a small contingent of my guards."

The Warden's fingers drummed once against the desk before stilling. "If that is your wish, Your Highness."

It was a measured shift—deference dictated by necessity, not preference. The Warden did not have the authority to deny him, though Gideon could sense the displeasure beneath his carefully composed exterior.

"I'm grateful for your hospitality," Gideon said smoothly.

Thaddeus studied him for a fraction longer than necessary before dipping his chin in acknowledgment. "Of course, Your Highness. My only concern is your comfort. The Stratum is not like the surface. It may grow tiresome after prolonged exposure."

Gideon offered a measured smile, then glanced down at his glass, letting it turn once in his hand. The amber liquor caught the light, swirling quietly as he studied it for a moment. Then, without another word, he finished it in a single, unhurried swallow.

"I appreciate your concern, Warden," he said, tone even. "Truly. But rest assured—I'm a little more durable than I appear. And besides, I've grown rather fond of Cavandel's more... unique charms."

The Warden's expression remained unreadable, but something in the way he regarded Gideon had shifted, as if he were reassessing his expectations.

If he suspected Gideon's reasoning for staying was anything other than what he claimed, he did not voice it.

Finally, the Warden pushed back his chair and stood. "I will ensure that your continued stay is well accommodated, Your Highness."

Gideon rose to his feet with unhurried grace. "Much appreciated, Warden."

As he turned to leave, he felt the Warden's gaze linger on him, watchful, calculating. Yes, the man would be keeping an eye on him. But that was of little consequence. For now, Gideon had bought himself time—and that was all he needed.

Location: Cavandel, The Outer District

Later that evening, deep in the Outer District of Cavandel, in the quiet warmth of her home, Aria sat at the table beside the hearth. A row of iron locks lay before her, their worn surfaces catching the amber glimmer of the nearby lamp. Its light pooled gently across the rough stone walls, casting soft shadows that shifted with the fire.

The scent of stew and fresh bread still lingered in the air, softened beneath the sharper traces of dried herbs and the faint metallic lift of iron and oil rising from the locks spread across the table.

Supper had been quiet but comfortable, the kind of meal that filled the space between words rather than requiring them. Now, the bowls sat rinsed and stacked near the basin, and her grandmother had long since been coaxed off to bed.

The slender pick rested between Aria's fingers, its familiar weight steadying her as she eased it into the first mechanism. Across from her, Jace leaned back in his chair, arms folded, his gaze steady despite the relaxed angle of his posture.

The first lock clicked open within the span of a breath. She barely paused before moving to the next. Another click. Then another. Her movements were fluid, deliberate, precise.

Jace watched in silence, his only reaction the faint arch of a brow.

Aria smirked, setting the last lock down with a soft, confident thud.

"Impressive," Jace said at last. "When we started, you struggled with a single lock. Now you're clearing a row without a second thought. You're getting faster. Sharper."

"I have a good teacher," Aria replied, her smile touched with genuine warmth.

Jace made a noncommittal sound, reaching for the nearest lock. He turned it over between his fingers, clicked it shut and set it back down in front of her. "Good. Now open this one again."

She reached for her pick, but he was faster. With an easy motion, he plucked it from her fingers and leaned back, spinning the slender piece of metal between his knuckles before setting it on his side of the table.

Aria blinked. "Without the pick?"

He nodded, lifting a brow and tilting his head—a silent challenge.

She frowned, turning the lock over in her hands. "That's impossible."

Jace arched a brow. "Is it?"

Her jaw tightened, but she didn't argue. Instead, she kept her expression carefully neutral as she reached up to her hair, remembering the hairpin tucked there. If he wanted to make things difficult, fine. She'd find another way. But as her fingers searched for the pin, they found only empty space where it should have been.

Her stomach sank.

Jace leaned back, twirling something between his fingers. A thin glint of metal caught the light. "Looking for this?"

She barely stopped herself from scowling.

He must have swiped it earlier, and she hadn't even noticed. Her backup plan was gone.

How was she supposed to get it open?

She set her jaw, running through the problem again. No pick. No pin.

No obvious way out.

Then she exhaled, shifting her approach.

She tilted her head, a slow smirk forming. "You're the expert, aren't you?"

Her gaze held his. "So go on—show me how it's done without a pick."

Then, with a lazy sort of elegance, she extended her hand.

"So hand those over," she said smoothly. "Wouldn't want you to be tempted."

Jace's eyes narrowed, a flicker of suspicion behind his otherwise unreadable expression. "Lock first," he said, voice dry. "Then we'll discuss the tools."

Her smirk faltered—just for a moment. With a casual shrug, she slid the lock across the table.

Jace didn't rise to challenges often, but when he did, there was no walking it back. He reached forward and took the lock with one hand, at the same time, he slid her lockpick and hairpin back across the table with the other.

He turned the lock over in his hands, thumb brushing the mechanism as if weighing the odds. For a moment, it seemed like he might try. Aria leaned forward slightly, her tools now safely back in her possession, anticipation flickering in her eyes.

He'd asked her to open it. He hadn't said how.

But then he set the lock back down, unopened.

"Nice try," he said. "But no. I won't open it for you."

Her smirk faded.

He tapped the table between them.

"That was good." Jace said, his tone softening slightly. "Quick thinking—using me to solve your problem."

There was no criticism in his voice, only observation.

"Improvisation. Adaptation. Always looking for the path of least resistance. It's a useful instinct," he said softly, "You won't always have a lockpick or a hairpin." He met her gaze then—deliberate, steady—as if trying to press the thought into place, to leave no room for doubt.

"But you'll always have your mind."

Aria's brow furrowed, her thoughts a tangle. "But I didn't get it open," she said quietly.

Jace leaned forward, resting his forearms on the table. A hint of approval warmed his usually guarded expression. "Some problems require a different kind of key, Aria." His gaze held hers. "And you used all the ones at your disposal. You saw the challenge for what it was, not what it appeared to be."

He picked up one of the locks, turning it between his fingers. "You did what I would've. And although it didn't work on me, that's not to say it won't work on someone less... well, you know."

There was something like respect in his eyes now. "Trust your instincts—and remember, it's not only what you know, but what you feel."

Aria held his gaze, the corner of her mouth tugging upward. Not a smile, exactly, but something close. She gave a slight nod but said nothing, the quiet between them holding more weight than words could manage.

Without another word, Jace gathered the locks into the worn leather pouch, the metal pieces clinking softly against each other. "There isn't much more I can teach you," he announced softly, pulling the drawstring tight. "Keep practicing. Keep refining your skills. The difference between good and great isn't knowledge. It's precision."

As he was about to rise from his chair, a soft cough echoed from down the hall, barely audible but enough to draw Aria's attention. Her gaze drifted instinctively to the shelf above the hearth, where her grandmother's medicine sat, the amber bottle catching the dim light. The tincture had been keeping the worst symptoms at bay, but little more.

Jace followed her line of sight. "Word's spreading about the breakthrough," he said quietly.

Aria's fingers traced an absent pattern on the tabletop. "Yeah... we think we've found it," she said. "But it needs testing first. Anna's working with a few patients now to make sure there are no side effects."

Jace nodded, his expression grave. "Smart." He tapped his fingers thoughtfully against the table, a habit she'd noticed when he was considering something carefully. "How long before we know?"

"I should have a sample in a day or two, once we confirm it works." Her voice was steady, but her fingers had stilled against the wood, betraying her restraint. "If it works," she murmured.

The words hung between them, weighted with cautious hope. She hadn't mentioned it during supper, couldn't bear to offer her grandmother another promise that might crumble. Too many of those had already passed between them.

Jace regarded her in the silence. Aria's shoulders curled forward, as if she were physically carrying the weight of her grandmother's illness, the Dwellers' expectations, and now this fragile possibility of hope. So much weight for shoulders so small.

Finally he said, "Thorough testing might help with the skeptics." He leaned forward slightly. "People are divided. Some are desperate enough to believe anything; others think it's just another false promise." He paused. "There's even talk about how the Warden will react when he finds out."

Jace leaned back in his chair, studying her. "If this cure really works, it changes everything." His voice dropped lower. "It's exactly what the Dwellers need to secure the people's support."

He rose from his chair and glanced toward the hall where her grandmother rested. "My advice? Get the cure, then get out before things get worse. The Warden won't let this stand. He can't afford to." His eyes held hers, the intensity of his gaze leaving no room for misunderstanding. "When power shifts, those caught in between rarely fare well, Aria. Some locks, once opened, can never be closed again."

Jace gathered his coat and moved toward the door. "Think about it," he said and then he was gone, the door closing softly behind him.

Aria considered his words carefully, her thoughts turning to those he had asked her to leave behind.

Pike, who had shaped her from a complete novice into what she now was—something much more. All the others who had fought beside her to secure the venom, those who had risked their lives without hesitation, and Anna, who had given everything in search of the cure.

How could she just abandon them?

A flicker of uncertainty crossed her face, quickly replaced by stubborn determination. Yet something had shifted. Jace's warning echoed deep within her, casting a shadow over a decision that had once seemed so clear.

23

Clash of Light and Shadow

Location: Cavandel, Dweller's Base

Sebastian's workshop was a shrine of chaos. Stripped wires hung like vines from the rafters, and the floor looked as though someone had swept the clutter into half-formed piles before losing interest altogether.

In the middle of it all, hunched over a metal casing clamped in a vice, Heidi muttered something about torque ratios and jabbed a screwdriver where it probably shouldn't have gone. The lamp above her head buzzed with a tired flicker, casting her in a golden haze.

Aria lingered in the doorway a moment longer than she needed to, watching. Smiling, despite herself. There was something oddly steady about Heidi's unflinching tenacity, the way she poured herself into things without ever asking to be noticed. An orphan who had every reason to close off, who'd had so much taken from her—yet all she ever seemed to do was give. To Sylas, to the Dwellers—to her.

"You know," Aria said, stepping inside, "most people sleep when the day's over."

Heidi startled just enough for the screwdriver to slip. It clattered to the floor, bounced once, then disappeared beneath a shelf crowded with metal scraps.

Aria crouched, spotted the tool wedged between a gear and what looked suspiciously like part of an old teapot, and fished it out. She set it on the edge of the table beside Heidi's elbow without a word.

"Thanks," Heidi muttered, still not meeting her eyes. "Most people don't have half a week to rewire a Crythium conduit by hand."

"Is that what you call talking to yourself and threatening innocent screws?" Aria asked, her smile returning.

"They weren't innocent," Heidi said flatly. "They knew exactly what they did."

Aria leaned against the edge of the table, watching Heidi adjust a coil with focused care, her fingers steady, exact. Every movement had purpose, measured and deliberate. For a few moments, neither of them spoke. The workshop hummed softly around them, metal cooling, wires settling, and something ticking in the corner like a heartbeat trying to remember its rhythm.

"Have you heard from Sylas?" Aria asked quietly.

"Yeah," Heidi said, still working. "He's with Anna in the infirmary. A few of the patients had minor reactions—flushed skin, lightheadedness—but it passed. Seems like it's working."

She hesitated, then looked up at Aria, the edge of her mouth tugging into something small and proud. "My little brother. Saving the world."

Aria's smile deepened. "I'm proud of him too," she murmured softly.

Were they really this close to the cure?

Had all that they'd done—every risk, every loss—actually been enough? The thought pressed at her ribs, equal parts wonder and disbelief. For so long, hope had felt like a story someone else was telling. But now—

Heidi reached for another tool, but paused halfway. Her gaze lingered on the empty corner of the room where Sylas used to sit, fiddling with scraps just to be near the workbench.

"It's weird, not having him underfoot," she murmured. "He's always been right there, asking questions, pretending not to care about the answers.

Now he's off doing something that actually matters." She gave a small shrug. "I mean, it's good. Just quiet."

Heidi's fingers hovered over the half-tightened coil. She gave a shrug, eyes still on the empty corner of the room. "But life goes on, I suppose."

Aria didn't say anything. She just gave her a look, quiet and steady, full of sympathy and understanding. Not pity. Not surprise. Just a kind of shared knowing that didn't need to be spoken aloud.

A soft click broke the stillness.

Heidi blinked, startled, then looked down at the lance. The coil settled, then slid into place with a crisp, seamless fit. The stabilizer hummed softly. No sparks. No resistance. Just smooth, functional alignment. Exactly as she'd designed it, though she hadn't dared to believe it would actually work.

"Huh," she said. "That wasn't supposed to happen."

Aria tilted her head. "Not supposed to happen, good, or not supposed to happen, bad?"

Heidi leaned back, wiping her hands on her already-streaked shirt, eyes still fixed on the device like it might change its mind. She reached for the grip and pressed a hidden catch. The lance folded down in two clean motions, compacting into a length no longer than Aria's forearm. A faint click. No jamming. No lag.

"Well. Would you look at that," she said quietly. "Something in this place actually cooperated."

Aria stepped in closer, her hand drawn almost unconsciously toward the device. She ran her fingertips along the smooth casing, marveling at how something so powerful could feel so refined, like a whisper held together by tension.

"You really did it," she murmured.

Her fingers hovered near the grip, as if pressing too firmly might undo whatever fragile balance had settled there. Then she stepped back, not because she wanted to, but because the weight of the moment felt like it needed space.

Heidi watched her for a moment, then gave a small nod and gestured toward the weapon. "Go on. Try it," she said with a smile.

Aria stepped forward and reached for it, her fingers wrapping carefully around the grip. It was lighter than she expected—but not weak. The weight was balanced, centered, with just enough pull to remind her it was real. She lifted it slowly, testing the heft, the feel of it in her palm. The casing was smooth but not slippery, the grip wrapped in fine-leathered coil for traction. No edges. No clutter. Just precision.

She found the cleverly hidden mechanism near the handle and pressed it. With a soft click-hiss, the device extended. The head slid free with a smooth metallic whisper, unfolding into a slender arc of Crythium-infused alloy, tapering to a narrow, aerodynamic point. Aria turned it gently in her hands, then pressed the mechanism again. It folded down with the same clean motion, collapsing to its compact form with barely a sound.

She extended it again. Retracted. Again. Each time smoother than the last.

Heidi watched in silence, arms crossed, a small smile tugging at her mouth like she couldn't quite stop it. Pride radiated off her—quiet, unshakable, like the device in Aria's hands was some small piece of her come alive.

Aria gave the lance a slow test swing, easing it from one hand to the other. It moved cleanly through the air, responsive but stable.

Heidi arched an eyebrow. "Is that all you can do?"

Aria grinned and in a fluid motion, spun the lance into a full stance, extended it and swept it in a tight arc. Her footwork followed instinctively, the swing low and controlled, then high with a practiced turn of her wrist. The Crythium edge hummed faintly in motion, catching the lamplight in quick flickers.

"I'll need to practice with the trigger while moving," she said, catching her breath as she came to a stop. "But it's... it's perfect." The word drifted from her lips, faint and almost reverent.

Aria stared at the lance in her hands, her expression shifting from focus to something quieter—almost wonder. She retracted it one last time and looked at Heidi, her voice soft.

"Thank you, Heidi."

The silence that followed wasn't awkward, just full. A quiet exchange that didn't need words to be understood. Aria allowed the moment to settle before speaking again.

"I know it's been hard for you. And I know you didn't have to do any of this. Not the lance, not the cure, none of it. You risked more than I can even name. I don't know what to say, except—thank you."

Heidi shrugged and reached for a tool, adjusting something that didn't really need fixing. "Wait till you get the tally sheet," she said with the hint of a smile.

Aria blinked. "The what?"

"You know," Heidi said, smirking. "The absurdly long list of favors you now owe me. It starts with dinner and ends with a replacement for my last three soldering tips."

Aria laughed—quiet and warm—and then, without thinking, stepped in and wrapped her arms around Heidi in a tight hug. "Deal," she promised gently.

Heidi froze. Arms locked. Shoulders stiff.

"Okay," she muttered. "This is happening..."

Aria smiled against her shoulder, unable to help herself.

When she finally stepped back, Heidi looked flustered, like she needed to rearrange the entire room to recover. She turned away, fiddling with a loose wire on the bench, saying nothing, but Aria didn't need her to.

The weight of the device rested solidly in her hand, compact, elegant and real.

In Cavandel, you don't get very far without people who will stand beside you.

She'd told Gideon that once. And here was Heidi, awkward, brilliant, relentless Heidi, proving it all over again without ever needing to say a word.

Aria looked down at the device, the Crythium core still faintly humming at its center.

Cavandel was shifting. Being reshaped into something new.

But so was she. And whatever came next, she wouldn't be facing it alone.

***

They left the workshop at a brisk pace, the collapsible lance held securely in Aria's satchel. Shadows stretched ahead as the corridor narrowed toward the infirmary. The stone walls caught the flicker of embedded glow-lamps that cast thin pools of wavering light along the floor. Pipes ran low along the ceiling, humming gently, their warmth brushing across Aria's skin as they moved beneath.

A pair of Dwellers passed in the opposite direction, nodding silently. One carried a tray of vials, the other a tattered ledger, their conversation little more than a murmur as they disappeared around a bend.

The infirmary buzzed with quiet urgency, the space saturated with the scents of medicinal herbs and cautious hope. Anna moved with measured precision between the cots, her eyes sharp as she checked each patient's vitals. The soft light of the glow-lamps cast her shadow against the table as she made notations on her chart, her expression carefully neutral despite the weight of what they all awaited.

Sylas hovered nearby, passing vials and instruments to her with an attentiveness that would have been unimaginable weeks ago. His usual irreverence had given way to something more focused, more purposeful. He glanced up as footsteps approached. Aria and Heidi appeared in the doorway, their faces etched with equal parts exhaustion and anticipation.

"Any change?" Heidi asked, her voice barely above a whisper.

Anna didn't look up immediately, finishing her examination of a miner whose crystallized veins had stabilized after days of creeping spread. When she finally straightened, there was something in her eyes that hadn't been there before—a cautious light, carefully contained but unmistakable.

"The first three patients have shown marked improvement," she said, her voice steady but unable to completely mask her excitement. "Temperature normalized and the crystallization appears to have halted. No new spread in over twenty-four hours."

Aria stepped forward, her heart thundering against her ribs. "It's working?"

"It appears so," Anna replied, allowing herself a small smile. "We still need more time to be certain of long-term effects, but—" She gestured to the patients. "See for yourself."

Aria moved closer to the nearest cot. The man lying there was awake, his eyes clear for the first time in days. The telltale shimmer of Shatterblight that had crept up his neck just yesterday remained, but it had not advanced. The angry purple veins seemed faded, frozen in place, as though something had finally managed to halt the disease's relentless crawl. He blinked slowly, then managed the faintest nod, as though seeing her there anchored him somehow.

For a breath, Aria couldn't move. The stillness of his gaze, the way the disease had stopped just short of his throat, left her suspended between relief and disbelief. She had imagined this moment so many times before. Her grandmother, stable, her people no longer fading one by one—but the reality was quieter than she'd pictured, no trumpets, no fanfare, just this slow unraveling of dread.

Maybe hope didn't come crashing in; maybe it crept in like morning light, uncertain but steady, illuminating everything it touched. Her fingers drifted toward her satchel, where the lance lay hidden, as if part of her still didn't trust the stillness, still braced for everything to fall apart again.

Anna returned to her workstation, methodically filling a small vial with the clear solution they had worked so tirelessly to perfect. When she turned back to the group, the vial caught the glow-light, its contents shimmering with a quiet promise.

She looked up and gave the smallest nod. "Come here."

Aria stepped forward, her breath caught somewhere in her chest. Anna waited for her to cross the room, then pressed the vial into her hand with a careful firmness.

"You've earned it," she said, her voice steady despite the weight between them. "The dosage is precise—three drops, twice daily. If it holds, the progression will stop."

Aria stared at the small vial, its weight so slight in her hand yet heavier than anything she'd ever carried. "Thank you," she whispered, the words inadequate for the gratitude swelling in her chest.

"Don't thank me," Anna replied. "This belongs to all of us." She glanced at Sylas, who stood a little straighter under her gaze. "Your friend here was instrumental in the final breakthrough."

Sylas's cheeks colored slightly, but he couldn't quite hide his pride. Heidi caught it too, a flicker of recognition softening her usual reserve.

He exhaled softly, rubbing the back of his neck. "Just doing my part," he said, his voice quieter than usual.

Aria glanced at Heidi then, and a small smile touched her lips. Heidi returned it, brief but real.

Anna watched them both for a moment, then said quietly, "Get going. There isn't much time." She looked to Aria next, her voice low but firm. "Take Sylas with you. If your grandmother has a bad reaction, he'll know what to do."

Sylas nodded without hesitation, already stepping toward the door. "Got it."

Aria closed her fingers around the vial, feeling its cool surface press against her palm. After so much searching, so much sacrifice, it was finally here—real and tangible. Hope, contained in glass and crystal.

She slipped the vial carefully into her satchel and turned to follow the others, her steps light despite the weight of what she carried. For the first time in what felt like years, the path ahead didn't feel carved from desperation—it felt chosen.

Around her, the hum of the infirmary, the soft light of the glow-lamps, even the quiet rhythm of Sylas's footsteps beside her, all seemed to pulse with the same quiet truth. Something had changed. Not everything was broken.

Not anymore.

Location: Cavandel, The Stratum

The tram rattled along its narrow track, on its way to the West Wing of the Stratum. It hummed swiftly through the corridors. Drazic sat rigidly, arms folded across his chest, boots planted firm against the floor. His imposing military coat with its gleaming brass buttons, and gold-fringed epaulets contrasted sharply with the sterile surroundings. Beside him, the Warden sat unmoving, his gloved hands folded neatly in his lap, the high collar of his black leather coat framing a face etched with cold calculation beneath his distinctive top hat.

The tram dipped slightly as it turned into an upward slope, the hum of its engine deepening. The tunnel swallowed them whole. Outside, the walls blurred—metal, shadow, and the occasional flash of lights.

Drazic angled his head toward the Warden, raising his voice slightly to cut through the noise. "The prince went down into the District. Brought two of his own."

The Warden didn't respond at first.

"We're keeping an eye on them," Drazic added.

Still nothing. Just the faintest shift of the Warden's gloved fingers.

"So far, all seems well."

A slight tilt of the Warden's head. His gaze stayed fixed on the blur outside. "Keep me posted," he said—not sharply, but with a finality that ended the subject.

Drazic shifted, tension running through his shoulders, the golden embellishments on his brown leather coat catching what little light filtered through the tunnel. "Then there's the other matter. The Dwellers."

That earned the Warden's attention. His fingers stilled. His head turned just enough, his sharp gaze cutting through the dimness.

"We've found them," Drazic said. "One of my informants got us close. Disappeared after that, but not before we had him followed."

He leaned forward slightly, voice steady but tight. "Led us to one of the inns in the Mining Camp. Slipped into the back rooms and never came out. No street exit. No alley. Just gone."

The Warden didn't speak.

"We kept watching. Quiet surveillance. No obvious tells, not at first. But Scarlet and I asked around—discreetly. Just enough pressure to make people talk. A few names came up. A few places. Most of them dead ends, noise, or distractions. But this one kept surfacing."

He let the words settle before adding, "Marielle's Inn, I think it's called."

The Warden's hand stilled.

"They're in there. Planning, nesting. Building something. And they're doing it right under our feet," Drazic grumbled.

The silence stretched, but the Warden said nothing.

He pressed on, choosing his words carefully, watching the Warden from the corner of his eye, gauging his reaction. "There's something else. Rumors are spreading—quietly, but quickly."

He paused, waiting for some indication that the Warden was ready to hear it. None came.

"People are saying the Dwellers have found it—a cure for Shatterblight."

That got the Warden's attention. His eyes narrowed, lips parting silently. A breath unsheathed like a blade.

Drazic nodded once, careful not to rush the words. "We haven't confirmed it yet. But the talk is out there. If people start to believe it—really believe it—"

He stopped short. The Warden didn't look at him, didn't move. Just that same measured stillness, as though listening to something far quieter than

Drazic's voice.

Drazic's gaze lingered on him a moment longer, then dropped. "They'll rally behind whoever gives them a reason. Doesn't matter who it is. Doesn't matter what it costs."

He straightened slightly, forcing himself not to look away. "We can crush them now, well before they weaponize it. Before it becomes a banner to march behind."

Drazic's jaw tightened further. He refused to drop his gaze. "I've drawn up the plans. Two full units. First light. We seal the building off, sweep the lower levels, and cut off the alleys. No warning. No room to run."

He looked at the Warden directly. "The men are set. The city needs to see what happens to those who forget their place. A clean strike. Loud enough to be remembered."

He let the air hang heavy between them. "We'll put an end to it. Once and for all."

The Warden's voice came slower this time, dry and measured beneath the shadow of his hat brim. "You really wish to move now? While Prince Gideon's still down there. Watching and asking questions." He shook his head faintly. "I won't hand him a massacre wrapped in smoke and ashes."

Thaddeus turned back toward the blur of the tunnel. "No. Not yet."

Drazic froze, momentum buckling in his chest. But he said nothing.

The Warden kept his gaze forward. "That spoiled brat is not to be trusted," he said. "Too curious. Too shrewd. I won't have him returning to the surface with stories of corpses in the alleys and fire in the streets."

The pause grew dense, almost suffocating. Drazic's jaw flexed. "Every moment we wait is another they spend widening their reach. We may not get another window like this."

The tram began to slow. The tunnel opened into a wider chamber—metal columns, stacked crates, distant silhouettes of waiting guards. The platform lights strobed briefly as the car glided to a stop.

The Warden rose without a word. Drazic stood a moment later, falling into step behind him as the doors hissed open. Boots hit metal. The air here was colder, heavier. Neither man spoke as they crossed the platform.

The Warden looked at Drazic then, gaze sharp beneath the smooth calm. "Increase searches. Especially those taking the Lift. Apprehend any who might be distributing this... cure. Detain them quietly, away from prying eyes."

His voice lingered as they moved forward into the chill of the chamber, footsteps echoing into silence. "We'll deal with them properly once the prince is gone."

He let the silence stretch into something cold and final.

"Then we burn out the rot," he murmured, low and deliberate, as though testing the taste of it.

Drazic's jaw clenched, a muscle twitching beneath the weathered skin. He gave a curt nod, but his eyes betrayed him, that familiar fire of impatience barely contained. His fingers flexed at his sides, brushing against the worn leather of his belt.

"Understood," he said evenly, his voice low and graveled. "And if they start to get out of hand?"

The Warden didn't break stride, his gaze fixed ahead as they moved deeper into the shadows. "Then you'll be there to stop them. Mr. Grask. Quietly." His emphasis on the last word carried weight beyond its syllables. "The prince may be watching, but he can't be everywhere at once."

Drazic absorbed this, the tension in his shoulders easing fractionally. Not permission for his raid, but not complete restraint either. A compromise he could work with. He fell back into step behind the Warden, their shadows stretching thin in the dimness ahead.

Location: Cavandel, The Mines

Aria, Heidi, and Sylas left the Dwellers' base quickly, ducking out beneath Marielle's Inn and emerging into a world transformed. Aria's heart drummed frantically, her palm damp against her satchel where the small glass vial rested securely inside. She forced herself to remain calm, breathing deeply as they moved forward. Beside her, Heidi and Sylas walked stiffly, their eyes darting nervously at the scene unfolding before them.

The street had changed dramatically in their brief time underground. The air felt heavy with tension—a metallic taste that coated Aria's tongue with each shallow breath.

Guards had filled the narrow lanes, their armor creaking faintly with each movement, the sharp smell of polish, and leather cutting through the usual scent of damp stone and coal dust.

They clustered around frightened miners, voices sharp and accusing as they demanded information, connections to the Dwellers, anything suspicious. Someone cried out as two guards dragged a protesting man away toward an armored wagon. Heidi flinched, reaching instinctively for Aria's sleeve.

"Keep your heads down," Sylas murmured. "We're almost there." His voice was barely audible over the rising tension.

Aria gave the smallest nod, the movement barely more than a twitch. She swallowed hard, tamping down the sick twist of fear in her gut. Being caught aiding the Dwellers wasn't just a crime—it was a disappearance. No trial. Just vanishing footsteps in the night and doors that never opened again. Her grip tightened around the satchel strap until her knuckles whitened, as if sheer force could anchor it to her body, could keep it from being torn away like so many others.

The vial felt impossibly heavy despite its small size, weighted by the hope and desperation she carried for her grandmother. She allowed herself a moment of fragile hope, picturing the warmth returning to her grandmother's eyes. She couldn't lose that now, not after coming this far.

They joined the end of a long, sluggish line at the Lift. The crowd stretched down the street, a shuffling column of miners, workers and wary-eyed citizens pressed shoulder to shoulder. Voices murmured low around them, tension clinging to every breath. A few people were turned away. Others were pulled aside by guards and not seen again. Each step forward was a quiet surrender to whatever lay ahead.

Under the watchful eyes of the guards, the massive platform made Aria feel even smaller than usual. Her pulse quickened as they stepped aboard and the structure shuddered beneath them. Just past the threshold, a Lift operator sat behind a thick iron console, taking payments one by one. When Aria reached him, she dug into her pouch and pulled out two Grottos—clean, stamped, still warm from her hand.

The operator didn't speak. He took the coins slowly, his gaze lingering on her face just a little too long. She held it, steady, her expression unreadable. A flick of his eyes to her companions, then back to her. Something calculating moved behind his blank stare.

Then he nodded, motioning her through with a grunt. Only after she stepped past him did she allow her breath to ease out. The Lift groaned as gears locked and disengaged overhead, beginning its slow, grinding ascent toward the District above.

Guards stood at intervals around the platform's edge, silent and watchful, their weapons slung over shoulders or held casually in gloved hands. No one spoke. Every sound—from the scrape of boots to the jostle of straps and the faint hiss of breath—was swallowed by the dense press of bodies. There was no emptiness now, only the suffocating stillness of too many people packed too tightly, each one trying not to be noticed.

The Mining Camp fell away beneath their feet, a patchwork of ramshackle structures, eternally dim under perpetual dust clouds.

Each grinding turn of the mechanisms overhead sent tremors through the platform, vibrating through Aria's boots and up her spine. The air grew thinner, tighter, carrying with it the scent of oil and rust. Sweaty bodies pressed too close, the collective heat and fear filling what little space remained. Aria kept her eyes on the rising wall of stone and struts outside, anything to avoid looking at the guards.

Heidi stood frozen beside her, breathing shallow, one hand compulsively smoothing her collar in the nervous habit she'd had since childhood. Sylas didn't speak, but his hand drifted unconsciously near the satchel slung across his chest. They all felt it—the noose tightening.

They rose for minutes. Long, quiet, aching minutes.

At the top, just visible now through the opening gates, unfamiliar shapes shifted into view—figures standing in formation, unmoving, unreadable.

Then, finally, the Lift slowed. A jolt ran through the platform as the locking clamps engaged.

Aria forced her breathing to steady, feeling Heidi trembling slightly beside her. Sylas shifted his weight subtly, readying himself for whatever might come next.

As the metal gates screeched open, a ripple moved through the crowd—small at first, barely noticeable, until the tension shifted. Murmurs broke out ahead. Then came the sharp bark of a command. A guard stepped forward, grabbing the nearest man by the shoulder and demanding he empty his bag.

They were searching people. Line by line.

Aria's stomach turned to ice. They weren't safe. Not yet. Her breath caught in her throat as she scanned the guards, watching how they moved with purpose, pulling passengers aside and rifling through their satchels. No hesitation. No mercy.

She glanced at Heidi and Sylas. Heidi looked ready to collapse, her eyes wide and glassy. "They're searching everyone," she whispered, leaning close.

Sylas shifted nervously beside Aria. "What do we do?"

"Stay calm," she whispered evenly, deliberately keeping her gaze forward. She tightened her grip on the satchel and forced her mind to focus. She had to think—had to be sharp. Jace's lessons came flooding back. Every flick of the wrist, every misdirection, every breath spent waiting for the right moment.

She glanced up the line. Two more passengers ahead.

Now.

She shifted slightly, letting the bulk of the crowd shield her from view. One arm across her chest, the other dipping into her satchel. Her fingers found the vial—cool glass, small as a knuckle and heavy with everything she couldn't afford to lose.

One breath. Just one.

She palmed the vial against her heated skin while pretending to massage her shoulder. The liquid inside made no sound as she moved, but she could feel its presence, heavier than it should be, as though the hopes it carried added physical mass.

She could still see Jace demonstrating the move, his calloused hands surprisingly graceful as they made small treasures disappear. She brushed the inner cuff of her sleeve—Jace's addition. Just in case. With a subtle twist of her wrist, she slid the vial into the specially sewn compartment, securing it against her forearm.

A nearby guard shifted. Aria looked up, blinked dully like she was half asleep. The guard's gaze moved on.

Her pulse did not.

"Keep it moving," a voice commanded and suddenly they were at the front of the line. The guard stepped toward Heidi and Sylas first. "Pockets out. Bags open," he barked sharply, roughly patting Heidi down, then Sylas, who looked away, jaw clenched tight. Aria's heart hammered in her chest, her fingers tightening around the satchel strap as the guard moved toward her.

He was an older man, with a face mapped by fine creases around eyes that looked like they'd seen too much to care anymore.

"Arms out," he grumbled.

His brown leather uniform rustled as he began searching her—brisk hands checking her coat pockets, then its lining. Resignation lined his mouth, but his hands moved with the quiet precision of someone who'd done this a hundred times before.

Aria noted the slight stiffness in his left shoulder—an old injury per-haps—and the way he favored his right side. She stood still, not stiff but loose, pliable. She extended her arms, keeping her elbows slightly bent—not enough to look suspicious, but enough to prevent the vial from shifting in its hidden pocket.

His hands patted down her sides, checked her inner pockets, then moved toward her sleeves. As his fingers approached the hidden vial, Aria subtly shifted her weight to her left foot, creating a slight movement that drew his attention to her opposite side.

She knew the trick wasn't to disappear, but to give him nothing to notice. *Create a space for their eyes to follow and their hands will trail behind.*

The guard ran his hands along her arms. Her muscles stayed loose, her stance casual. As his fingers neared the cuff where the vial lay hidden against her wrist, she dipped her shoulder just slightly—just enough to shift his grip past it without him noticing. He moved on.

"Turn around," he instructed with a huff.

Aria complied, using the pivot to adjust her sleeve position once more. She kept her breathing even, her expression neutral—neither too relaxed nor too tense. The guard checked her back pockets, then stepped away. Aria didn't flinch. Her breath slowed. She let her eyes glaze, playing the part of someone already exhausted by the day.

Then he reached for her satchel.

His hand slid inside, rummaging through its folds. She shifted again, just a fraction. Fabric rustled as his hand closed around something solid. Her heartbeat was thunder now, but her fingers stayed relaxed at her side.

The lance.

He pulled it free, still retracted, frowning as he turned it slowly in his gloved hands. "What's this, then?" he asked, suspicion sharpening his voice.

Aria kept her voice calm, face carefully blank. "Picked it up earlier. Just one of my tools."

The guard's eyes narrowed, skeptical, but he soon shrugged, thrusting it roughly back at her. "Move along."

A taller guard stood just beyond, watching the exchange in silence, his expression unreadable. He wore a streaked gray ponytail and mismatched gloves—one black, one brown. His eyes swept over them without expression.

Heidi exhaled shakily as they stepped forward, Sylas nudging them to keep moving. For a fleeting moment, relief spilled through Aria, warm and dizzying.

They'd made it.

Then came the familiar voice, sharp and unmistakable, cutting through the relief like ice down her spine. "Them! Right there!"

Aria's breath caught.

She spun, ice splintering through her veins as Hogan emerged from the crowd, arm outstretched, finger pointed straight at her. Fury contorted his features, eyes burning with cold triumph. "Dwellers!" he shouted. "Three of them!"

Everything blurred into motion. Guards turned sharply toward them, weapons raised. Aria grabbed Heidi's arm, shouting for her to run. Sylas stumbled forward, his breathing ragged with panic.

They bolted. Guards shouted. Chaos erupted as the crowd split apart in a panic. Bodies collided. A child wailed. A man cursed. Someone screamed. The guards' voices cut through the chaos like blades.

Five steps. That was all Aria managed. Then Hogan slammed into her and the world tipped sideways.

Time slowed. Hard stone bit into her palms. Her satchel jerked sideways, the strap cutting across her chest. Every sound dulled, distant, as though she'd plunged underwater. She twisted, lungs straining for air, and saw Hogan's face above her, triumph etched into every line.

She struggled desperately beneath him, gasping, heart hammering wildly. Above her, guards closed in, seizing her wrists and dragging Hogan aside.

"No!" Heidi cried from somewhere nearby, her voice breaking. Aria twisted, searching for her through the blur of bodies, but found only Hogan's bitter gaze staring down at her.

"Got you now," he growled softly, face contorted with hatred.

The guard with the mismatched gloves and gray ponytail seized Aria and yanked her to her feet. She lashed out, twisting hard against his hold. One elbow caught his side, but it barely slowed him.

Another pair of arms hauled hers behind her back, gripping tight. She thrashed once more before he barked for rope. They bound her wrists, the coarse fiber biting into her skin as she fought against it, breath ragged and chest heaving.

Hogan stepped back, watching, satisfaction curdled on his face like spoiled milk.

But then she heard Heidi cry out again—closer this time. Aria twisted in the guard's grip just in time to see two more guards wrestle Sylas to the ground, while Heidi was dragged back by her cloak, her face streaked with tears and panic.

The sight hollowed her. This was her doing. She had pulled them into this—into her fight, her risk, her cause. And now they were paying for it.

The guard with the mismatched glove shoved Aria forward with another rough yank, twisting her arm up high. She cried out in pain. Hogan stepped in with a scowl. "Hey—easy," he snapped. "She's already tied."

The guard barely glanced at him before swinging a sharp backhand that caught Hogan across the face. He stumbled, crashing to the ground, stunned. "Take him too," the guard muttered to another, tilting his head towards Hogan. "He might know more than he says."

"What? I'm not with them!" Hogan shouted, scrambling to his feet. "I'm not—"

A boot pushed him back down. "Didn't ask," the guard said flatly.

Another called out, shouting for citizens to clear the way as they dragged her forward through the frightened crowd. People recoiled as she passed, some turning their faces, others watching with wide, fearful eyes. Murmurs followed her—disbelief, pity, or silent, judgmental fear. A few children clung to their parents. A man whispered something that made a woman recoil. No one dared intervene.

Aria clenched her fists behind her back, relief surging faintly when she felt the tiny shape of the vial, secure and hidden, pressing against her palm.

They hadn't taken it. Not yet.

Would they find it?

Panic clawed at her throat. She had come so far, risked everything, just to get this vial to her grandmother. And now she was being hauled away while her grandmother lay waiting, breath shallow, eyes dimming by the hour.

She blinked hard, trying to push the image away—but it burned into her vision—her grandmother's frail hand trembling, her whisper of a smile fading as the sickness overtook her. Aria bit down on the inside of her cheek until she tasted copper. She couldn't fail her. Not now.

Then her thoughts snapped to Hogan. Anger surged like wildfire, each step away from the Lift feeding its flames. Her body trembled with it, not just fear alone, but with fury sharpened by betrayal. She wanted to scream at him, to tear free of the ropes and make him pay.

How dare he?

He'd struck her now, here, where it hurt most. Not because he was loyal to the guards, or because he believed in anything—but because hurting her made him feel like he mattered.

She didn't speak. Her jaw locked tight, her glare like steel. He wouldn't even look at her now.

The coward.

As they marched her away, Aria straightened her back, chin rising d-efiantly despite the rage and terror boiling in her chest. They might have her, but she still held the cure. And if she got the chance—any chance—she would see it through. No matter what it took.

She closed her eyes briefly, the image of her grandmother's weary smile returning not as comfort, but as a vow. She would not fail her. Not now. Not ever.

24

The Heart of Darkness

Location: Cavandel, The Inner District

The ninth hour came quietly. Had Gideon arrived sooner—say, the seventh—he might have heard it. The distant shouts, the thunder of boots, the panicked churn of a crowd breaking open somewhere near the Lift station. Had he followed the echoes through the winding streets, he might have heard her, seen her—dragged through the crowd, shoulders wrenched back, wrists bound, cloak trailing through the dirt.

But he hadn't.

He'd come when he said he would.

Now the square was empty.

The remnants of the festival had long since been swept away. The lanterns were gone, the banners stripped down, leaving only faint discolorations where they'd hung. No laughter. No dancers. Just a city returned to stillness, bare and watchful.

Gideon stood beneath the narrow archway where they had last spoken, wrapped in the same layered attire he wore to pass unnoticed through the Districts—rugged boots planted shoulder-width apart, leather pauldrons darkened from wear, his belted tunic gathered neatly beneath a weathered travel cloak. The fabric shifted in the slow drag of air, the cloak's hem brushing lightly against the stone behind him. It was clothing meant for movement, for slipping between places without drawing attention, but now, standing still, it felt like armor that no longer served its purpose.

He glanced toward the edges of the square, where shadows once trembled with color and music. Now, the silence pressed in like stone.

She wasn't there.

He had sent his guards to search the surrounding blocks—first with discretion, then with more direction. They'd returned empty-handed. No sightings. No leads. Not even a whisper.

He told himself she was delayed. That something had come up. That she'd meant to come.

But the ninth hour passed. Then the tenth.

Still, she didn't come.

He stayed anyway, pacing once or twice before settling again beneath the archway, the soft creak of leather shifting as he moved. The city around him seemed to breathe differently now—slower, colder. Even the sounds felt altered, as if the stone itself had grown tired of waiting.

The eleventh hour passed and the square remained still.

He thought of how she'd looked the last time they were here—the softness in her voice when she'd agreed to meet, like the promise was too fragile to hold but too precious to let go. He'd seen it in her eyes. The wanting. The fear.

And maybe that's all it had been. A moment. A flicker of trust that wasn't meant to last.

He tried to bury the thought, but it wouldn't stay buried.

Maybe it had been a mistake.

Maybe he'd imagined more than there was.

He was a prince. He had duties, responsibilities. He should be back already—not lingering in the outer edges of a place he didn't belong and never would—dressed like a common traveler, waiting on a girl who barely knew his name.

He shifted, cloak rustling as he turned his back to the arch.

He would leave Cavandel. It was time. Whatever spark had pulled him here in the first place—it was gone. Maybe it had never been real to begin with. And it had left him standing in the dark, alone.

That should have been enough.

He told himself it would fade. That he'd return home, forget her face and call it what it was—a mistake he should've known better than to make.

And still, something in him refused to let go.

***

Aria and her companions were dragged to the guard tower—a massive structure of iron and stone, built straight into the cavern wall like a ribcage bolted to the city itself. Pipes ran through its frame like veins, hissing faintly with pressure. Nothing about it felt designed for comfort—only containment.

The walls seemed to hum with the weight of too many voices that had once echoed there. The guards hauled them down a narrow corridor and wrenched open a heavy iron door. Without pause or care, they were tossed unceremoniously into the cramped cell.

Aria wrinkled her nose against the stench—rust, sweat, and something sour, like fear that had steeped too long in stone. A sharp whiff of mildew and bile hit the back of her throat, making her gag before she could stifle it.

Damp walls pressed in from every side, rough, and cold against her back. The flickering glow-lamp in the corridor cast crooked bars of shadow across the floor, its light catching on the grime-blackened walls of the cell. Somewhere above, water dripped steadily, echoing in the silence like a slow, deliberate clock.

A guard sat slouched just beyond the bars, his chair tilted back against the wall. He twirled a small knife between his fingers, eyes half-lidded but never fully closing. Every so often, his gaze moved toward the cell, not with interest, but with the lazy menace of someone who enjoyed the quiet before the cruelty.

Beside him sat a metal crate filled with confiscated belongings—satchels, belts, half-broken tools, and a few glints of dulled jewelry. He'd likely already picked through it, eyeing each piece not by its worth to the owner, but by what it might fetch from the right buyer.

They were packed in tight—too many bodies crammed into too little space, each breath shared and stale. Heidi sat with her knees drawn to her chest, face buried in her arms. Sylas leaned against the wall beside her, his breathing steady but shallow, gaze fixed on the ground.

An ache pressed hard against Aria's ribs—not for herself, but for them. They were here because of her. Caged and silent, in a place that reeked of despair, and she had led them straight into it.

Hogan crouched near the door, arms folded, head down. He hadn't spoken since they were thrown in, but Aria could feel his presence like smoke in her lungs.

Serves him right, she thought bitterly. He'd lit the fire, thinking he'd be safe from the flame—only to get burned by it like the rest of them. He hadn't even earned his coin. And now he sat there, sulking like a victim. She didn't speak to him. She didn't trust herself to. But there was no use now. The damage was done. And worse than her anger was the way he wouldn't even look at her.

Coward.

Her jaw clenched so tight her teeth ached. She turned away from him, unwilling to waste another thought.

She let her gaze drift to the others. They were all citizens—strangers, mostly. Tired faces. Hollowed eyes. One man sat alone in the far corner, watching Hogan with a stare that didn't waver. An elderly woman rocked gently against the wall, her fingers tracing invisible patterns in the air as she hummed a broken melody that seemed to belong to another time, another life.

Aria shifted, her shoulders aching from where they'd pinned her. The ropes were gone, but the memory of them remained, carved deep into her skin. Her wrists still pulsed with it—bruised, burning. Her chest hadn't eased since their capture—tight as wire strung beneath her ribs. Her eyes darted toward the cage by the bars—her satchel was in there somewhere. She'd need it.

Heidi hadn't moved. She still sat curled in on herself, face hidden, shoulders drawn tight as if trying to disappear. Aria hesitated, then pushed off the wall and made her way to her.

She crouched beside her friend, unsure of what to say. Words felt useless here, swallowed up by stone and silence. So she didn't speak. She simply reached out and laid a hand gently on Heidi's back.

For a moment, Heidi didn't respond. Then she let out a trembling breath—not quite a sob, but close—and leaned slightly toward Aria, just enough to close the space between them.

It wasn't much. But it was enough.

"I'm sorry," Aria whispered. "I never should've dragged you into this."

"You didn't," Heidi murmured, voice small. "It was our choice."

The quiet held.

Sylas stepped forward, his voice quiet but strained. His fingers wrapped around the cold iron bars, knuckles whitening as he gripped them.

"There's been a mistake," he said to the guard. "We're not who you're looking for."

The guard didn't respond. The knife kept spinning between his fingers.

Sylas's grip tightened. He glanced back at Heidi, then leaned closer to the barrier between them. "Look at her," he said, his voice rising just slightly. "She shouldn't be in here. She hasn't done anything."

Still nothing. Not even a flicker of interest.

"At least tell us why we're here," Sylas pressed, voice tight. "That's not too much to ask, is it?"

The guard gave a long, exaggerated yawn and leaned his head back against the wall.

Sylas's shoulders tensed beneath his thin shirt. His fingers curled and uncurled at his sides, the knuckles straining with each clench. When he spoke again, his voice cut through the silence—flat and brittle, as though something inside him had finally cracked.

"We're stuck in here."

Around the cell, a few heads turned. A woman let out a shaky breath and looked away. The man in the corner who'd been watching Hogan narrowed his eyes, his jaw tightening. An older prisoner shifted, muttering something inaudible as he pulled his knees closer to his chest.

Aria looked up at the sound of his voice. Beside her, Heidi shifted—just slightly.

Sylas turned from the bars and began pacing a short line along the wall. His jaw was tight, fists clenched.

"Sylas—" Aria started, but he cut her off with a sharp wave of his hand, not even turning to look at her.

His pacing slowed, eyes fixed on Hogan—still crouched near the cell door, still not looking at anyone. Sylas took a few steps toward him, slow and deliberate.

"You don't even have the guts to say anything, do you?" Sylas hissed. "You did this."

Hogan flinched but didn't rise. He shrank further into the shadows, eyes fixed on the floor.

Sylas stopped just short of him. For a moment, he only stared.

"You coward," he hissed, voice low but cutting. The words didn't rise—but they struck like a stone. He turned away sharply, fists clenched and pressed his palms against the wall, shoulders tight, as if holding back the urge to strike it.

"No one's coming," he said finally, lower this time, but it carried just the same.

Silence returned—thicker now, heavier.

Aria didn't try to break it. She just stayed where she was, hand still resting lightly on Heidi's back. The ache behind her ribs refused to fade. She wanted to believe he was wrong, but who would come for them?

The Dwellers had their own problems—always had. And now that they had the cure for Shatterblight, would they even care what happened to a few prisoners?

Gideon's face flickered through her mind, unbidden.

Had he waited for her? Had he stood at the edge of the square, wondering why she never came?

He barely knew her, barely knew this city.

And what could one man even do?

Her chest constricted. It wasn't just fear—it was the slow, sinking weight of knowing Sylas might be right—that no one was coming.

Just then, the sound of boots echoed in the corridor beyond the cell. Two guards appeared—hulking figures in layered leather armor, their boots heavy against the stone. The first wore a cloak with a frayed hem, and mismatched gloves—one black, the other brown. His gray ponytail was tucked neatly over his shoulder.

Aria recognized him immediately.

The other carried a long-bladed lance crackling faintly with violet light. He stopped at the desk to murmur something to the guard twirling the knife, who answered with a grunt but didn't look up.

The first guard—Ponytail—stepped forward, keys clinking as he approached the cell door. "Up," he barked. "Stratum wants another batch."

"What does that mean?" Sylas asked, his voice sharp. "Where are you taking us?"

Ponytail turned toward him, his face hard—expression unreadable but edged with something darker. "Shut it, boy," he said, voice low, dangerous. "We ask the questions here."

He stepped closer, one gloved hand pressing to the bar, the black-gloved finger of the other aimed squarely at Sylas. "You'll speak when I say so. Got it?"

Sylas stared back at him, unflinching. His jaw worked, like he was biting down hard on whatever he'd been about to say. But his eyes burned—hot, defiant, unbroken. Slowly, he took a step back. There was fear in it, just enough to make his throat tighten, but he masked it behind clenched teeth and steady eyes. His gaze flicked to Heidi for a moment, but he said nothing. The wrong move might give them an excuse and he wasn't going to hand it to t hem.

Ponytail pointed at a cluster of prisoners—two strangers, then Heidi, Sylas, and finally Hogan. One of the guards pulled a length of segmented iron from his belt—thin, interlocking cuffs that snapped shut with a twist. "Hands out," he barked, and one by one the prisoners obeyed, sticking their arms through the bars. The restraints clicked into place with a cold, mechanical finality. Heidi winced, her breath hitching—but she didn't resist. Sylas's jaw clenched. Hogan offered no protest, just turned his hands over without a word.

"Don't want anyone slipping into the cracks," one of the guards muttered, checking the tension on the cuffs.

Aria surged forward. "Take me too," she said quickly. "I'm with them."

The guard shoved her back with a sneer, eyes narrowing. "Eager to be tossed over the wall of the Stratum, are we?"

He slammed the cell door behind the chosen group and, without a word, motioned to his companion. Together they headed down the hallway, dragging the prisoners behind them.

Aria's hands gripped the bars until her knuckles turned white, her breath coming in shallow bursts.

Tossed over the wall of the Stratum.

The words wouldn't leave her. Her stomach twisted. Her mind raced, cataloging every possible route, every potential ally, every tool she could twist to her advantage.

She watched Heidi's slight form disappear down the corridor—dragged away by armored guards. The two strangers followed stiffly behind Sylas.

Hogan shuffled at the back, his head bowed, as if trying to shrink away from what he'd done.

She'd gotten them into this and now they were gone—maybe for good. Taken into whatever waited for them in the Stratum.

She would find them. Not because she had a plan, but because no one else would. Because she'd led them into this—and now it was on her to get them out.

Whatever it took.

***

Aria gripped the iron bars, her gaze fixed on the guard slouched in his chair, flipping two battered coins between his fingers. The knife he'd been twirling earlier now lay forgotten on the table beside him, its dull edge catching the light with each pass of the coins. Every so often, he muttered something under his breath—half a conversation with no one. Something about dried meat, or a bet gone wrong. Then silence again, broken only by the soft clink of metal in his palm.

Just beyond him sat the crate of confiscated belongings—including her satchel. She shifted, jaw clenched.

There had to be a way out.

The guard hadn't moved in what felt like ages. He wasn't sharp, but he wasn't asleep either—and that was enough to keep them trapped. Her lockpick was still in her boot, right where it belonged, but even the thought of reaching for it felt useless with him sitting so close. One wrong move and he'd raise the alarm before she even made it to the door.

Her eyes swept the cell, taking in every crack in the stone, every rusted bolt, every face slumped against the walls. Nothing useful. No loose bars. No tools. No more options. She glanced back at the guard, hoping for some lapse in attention, some flicker of distraction. But he just kept flipping those coins, lips twitching as he whispered to himself.

A harsh, rattling cough tore through the stillness.

Aria turned. In the far corner, the old woman had curled tighter into herself, her breath wheezing shallow and uneven. Her skin held a pale gray cast, lips dry and cracked. One trembling hand clutched at her chest.

Aria hesitated, but only for a moment. What kind of threat could a woman like this possibly pose? She was sick, frail, barely conscious—and yet they'd locked her up like the rest of them. Just another life trapped in the darkness. Maybe that was all it took now—being slow to stand, or coughing at the wrong moment. The kind of offense that didn't need a charge. Just a uniform and an empty cell.

And still, no one had helped her.

Aria crossed the cell and crouched beside her, resting a hand gently on her arm.

"You need to lie back," she murmured. "Slow your breathing."

The woman gave a faint, dry laugh. "Breathing's never been the problem, girl. It's what comes after."

Heat pulsed beneath Aria's fingers as the woman's pulse fluttered weakly. The signs were all there—the tremor, the pallor, the fever behind her eyes.

The early stages of Shatterblight?

She leaned in closer, watching the faint rise and fall of the woman's breath, the too-smooth sheen beneath her skin. Her fingers brushed lightly along the wrist, then hovered at the base of the throat—searching, not quite knowing what she hoped to find.

The woman shifted under her touch. Then, with a faint grunt, she tugged her sleeve higher, exposing the inside of her arm.

"This what you're looking for?" she asked, voice low but steady. "It's all right. I'm not ashamed. I'm an old woman with little left to lose."

Aria's chest tightened. The shimmer was unmistakable—sickly lavender, faint as breath, glimmering just beneath the skin.

The woman caught her look and smiled, almost amused.

"Don't feel sorry for me, girl," she said softly. "I've had a good, long life."

Aria's breath caught.

A good, long life?

Was that even possible down here—trapped in these mines, working for scraps, only to die nameless in a cell full of strangers?

Her hand dropped into her lap. She looked down slowly at her arm, at the vial pressing lightly beneath the seam of her sleeve.

Would it be enough to share?

She'd fought for this cure. Nearly died for it. Risked everything. And now—

She swallowed, throat raw.

If she used it now, there might not be enough left. She didn't know when—or even if—she'd ever get another. Not with the Warden hunting the Dwellers like animals. If she wasted it here—

Her fingers trembled as she drew back her sleeve.

She'd seen what Shatterblight could do. It had hollowed out her grandmother, stealing life piece by piece, slow and cruel. She couldn't bear to watch that happen again. Not this time.

This cure wasn't just for Gran anymore. It was for everyone the Warden deemed disposable—left to wither behind metal bars while the city looked away. If the cure was hope, then she would be its keeper. Even if it cost more than she could afford to give.

The woman blinked, then frowned slightly as Aria lifted her sleeve, revealing the slender glass vial tucked against the inside.

"What is it?" she asked, voice barely above a whisper.

The thick, amber-colored liquid shimmered faintly in the light.

"Something to help carry the weight," Aria said softly. "Open your mouth."

The older woman blinked, confused, but obeyed. Aria didn't dare use all of it. She tilted the vial just enough for a few shimmering beads to fall onto the woman's tongue. Enough to slow the climb. Enough to buy her some time.

She coughed again, but the spasm softened.

"Thank you," she rasped.

Aria turned slightly, sleeve already tugged back down, the vial hidden once more. She didn't answer.

But when she looked again, the woman's face had begun to soften. The tightness around her eyes had eased and for the first time, she looked almost at rest. Aria reached up and gently wiped the sweat from her brow, fingers steady now.

"I'm going to get you out of here," she said quietly, with a calm confidence that left no room for doubt.

A voice behind her cut through the quiet.

"Don't make promises you can't keep, girl."

Aria turned. The male prisoner was tall and lean, with a miner's shoulders and hollow cheeks. He stood near the far wall, arms crossed, watching her with a look that wasn't quite disdain. Just weary disbelief, like he'd watched too many would-be saviors promise hope, only to vanish into the stone.

He held her gaze a moment longer, then looked away.

Aria stayed crouched beside the older woman, listening to the quiet rasp of her breathing.

She could feel the weight of eyes on her—seven of them left, including her. Enough to move quietly—if they moved smart. Most had said nothing. The hollow-face man who challenged her had fallen back into brooding silence, though his gaze never fully left her.

She didn't move—just shifted slightly where she knelt, angling her head to glance across the room. The guard was still planted in his chair, flipping the same two coins, lips twitching in his half-muttered conversation. Idle, but alert.

Without standing, Aria motioned for the others to come closer. It took a moment, but one by one they inched toward her.

The movement caught the guard's eye.

"Hey!" he barked, sitting forward in his chair. "What's all that shuffling?"

Aria steadied herself, angling her body slightly as she nodded toward the older woman. "She stopped coughing," she said, just loud enough for the guard to hear. "We thought maybe she'd stopped breathing."

The guard frowned, squinting toward the cell. "If she's dead, leave her be. If she's not, keep it to yourself." With a low grunt, he sank back into his chair and resumed flipping the coins.

Hollow-face lingered a moment longer. His jaw tightened at the guard's words, a flicker of something unreadable passing through his gaze. Then he stepped forward—arms crossed, stance easing, resolve settling in his shoulders.

Aria leaned in, eyes scanning the group. "I think I can get us out," she whispered.

That drew looks—wide eyes, sudden stillness.

She raised a hand gently, signaling for them to stay calm, to keep quiet.

"How?" someone whispered.

"I can pick the lock," Aria said softly, patting her boot. "But not while he's here," she added, tilting her head toward the guard.

Hollow-face grunted. "You'll be waiting a while, then," he said, his voice low. "He only leaves at shift change, or when he hauls us out to do our business."

Another voice, one of the younger prisoners—barely older than she was—spoke up. "Does anyone need to go?"

Blank stares. A few head shakes. No one moved.

"Someone has to go," another voice whispered.

A wiry man raised his hand halfway, eyes narrowed. "What's the plan, then?"

Aria looked to the door, to the lock, and then to the guard again. "If he leaves, even for a few minutes, I can open it. I have the tools. But we need him away from that chair." She leaned in, voice steady. "We wait till he's gone.

Then we act. Quickly. Quietly."

The wiry man spoke again. "And if you can't—"

"Then we're no better off," Aria said calmly, cutting him off mid-sentence.

A moment passed. Then the young man spoke up again. "I'll do it," he whispered.

Aria blinked, caught off guard—not just by the words, but by the quiet steadiness behind them. Then her eyes dropped, catching a faint tremble in his hands. He was scared. Of course he was. Yet, he was stepping up anyway.

Something stirred in her chest. Pride, maybe. Or hope.

She gave him a single, sharp nod, her expression unreadable to the others, but steady all the same.

"What's your name?" she asked quietly.

He hesitated, then swallowed. "Ansel."

Aria nodded once more. "All right, Ansel."

"Just say it," he continued, steadier this time. "Whatever you need."

Before Aria could answer, the guard called out again, voice dripping with disinterest. "So what's the verdict? The old bat dead yet?"

Ansel straightened slightly, his voice stronger than before. "No, sir," he called back. "She's still breathing. Just real sick is all. We're trying to make her comfortable."

"Yeah?" the guard snorted. "Then do it faster. And maybe worry more about what's coming for you."

Ansel didn't respond but his jaw clenched, and Aria felt the flicker of pride all over again.

She leaned in closer, voice low. "Fake it. Say you need to use the privy. Once he takes you out, I'll pick the lock. We'll wait just beyond the entrance. When he comes back, we jump him."

The boy gave a tight nod, his throat bobbing as he swallowed.

He took a steadying breath, stood, then stepped forward toward the bars.

"Hey," he called. "I, uh... I really need to go."

The guard groaned. The coins stopped flipping as he sat forward. "Now?" he asked, tone somewhere between boredom and disdain. "Can't you just hold it?"

"I've been holding it all day," Ansel replied, shifting his weight with just enough desperation in his voice to sound convincing. He glanced over his shoulder, curling his arms across his stomach like he was bracing against a cramp.

The guard sighed dramatically, muttering something under his breath. "Every single time," he grumbled.

He stood, pocketing his knife as he shuffled toward the cell door. He reached for the key looped through the ring at his belt.

"Back up," he barked, motioning to the prisoners. "All of you."

Aria held her breath as they all moved back. Nothing sudden. Nothing that might raise suspicion. She stayed near the back of the group, her fingers twitching in anticipation.

The guard approached, pausing at the bars. His eyes swept across the cell, lingering for a moment too long on the old woman. He shrugged, then jerked his chin at the boy. "Hands."

Ansel stepped forward and held out his arms. The guard clicked the shackles around his wrists—tight and final. He unlocked the cell with a lazy clatter, the iron door slowly swinging open on creaking hinges. He gave the boy a nudge with the back of his hand.

"Move."

Ansel stepped out, but before the guard ushered him forward, he looked back—just once—at the others behind the bars. His gaze darted to Aria, then to the sick woman still slumped in the corner. No words, just a quiet acknowledgment.

The guard swung the door shut with a hollow clang, and relocked it with a bored twist of the key. The metal rasped in the silence.

Aria waited, heart pounding, until the sound of their boots faded down the corridor. Only then did she move—quietly, quickly. She dropped to a crouch beside the cell door, fingers already reaching for her tools.

The lock waited, still and quiet.

Her fingers brushed the picks tucked into the lining of her boot and she drew them out carefully, barely breathing.

She took a deeper breath, steadying herself.

"We've got five, maybe ten minutes tops," someone whispered behind her.

The tension in the cell thickened. No one moved. Even the coughs were swallowed.

Aria set the picks to the lock.

The first turn gave her nothing. Just a soft scrape.

She adjusted her grip and tried again, counting quietly in her head—one, two, three—anything to stay focused.

A minute passed. Maybe two. Her knees ached from crouching. The air in the cell seemed to press in tighter, like it knew they were running out of time.

The metal groaned faintly as she shifted the picks again. Another click. Still wrong. Still not enough.

Behind her, someone exhaled too sharply. There was a brief shuffle of feet as a prisoner shifted his weight.

She tried to block them out. To block everything out.

Each click felt too loud, each shift of the tool like it might snap. She leaned in closer, her brow tightening, the picks slipping slightly in her grip.

Sweat prickled at her hairline.

She wiped her forehead with the back of her wrist, trying to blink away the sting from her eyes. Her hands had started to tremble. Something was wrong—it wasn't catching. Aria's jaw clenched. The mechanism felt off—rusted, jammed, or worse.

Someone behind her whispered accusingly, "I thought you knew what you were doing..."

She didn't answer.

Another voice came, more urgent, "We're running out of time. They won't be long."

"Quiet," Aria snapped, harsher than she had intended. "Just let me—" Her voice caught. She swallowed it down and focused.

She paused, the picks still trembling between her fingers. This wasn't what she'd trained on with Jace. This mechanism was older, stickier, the pins too soft. She closed her eyes, breathing slow.

Not what you know, but what you feel.

That's what he'd always said. She tilted the pick slightly, adjusted the angle of pressure and let the tension bar settle deeper. Just enough. Then—

Click.

Then another.

The bolt slid open with a soft clunk, barely audible. Aria opened her eyes. The door creaked as it eased open. A hush swept through the cell.

"She did it," someone whispered, half in disbelief.

Aria motioned for silence. A few prisoners stepped forward, moving carefully in the hush. One squeezed her shoulder in passing; another gave a silent nod, eyes wide.

Aria didn't respond. She turned toward the crate beside the guard's desk and crossed to it without hesitation. Her satchel lay near the top. She checked it quickly, fingers brushing over the familiar weight of her lance. Fastening the collapsed weapon to her side, she slung the satchel over her shoulder and snapped the buckles into place.

The guard's lance lay propped against his desk. Hollow-face stepped over and lifted it carefully, his grip uncertain at first. He turned it once, then again, the weight drawing a quiet nod. "Left his lance behind," he muttered. "Not the brightest move."

The others joined her, rifling through the crate for anything they could use—broken metal rods, a length of chain, a wooden broom.

"Not much," someone mumbled. "Better than nothing, though."

Aria motioned toward the door.

Four prisoners followed her, creeping toward the threshold. The sick woman remained slumped in the corner of the cell, while one of the quieter men knelt beside her, offering support.

"We wait until he's just inside," Aria whispered to the group. "Then we move. No noise. No mistakes."

25

Shadows Lifted

Location: Cavandel, The Inner District

They crouched by the door, breaths held, hearts pounding. Every creak in the hallway could've been them—guard and prisoner. Every footfall might've been a trick of the silence, or the end of it. Aria kept her voice low. "Stay close to the wall. Let them enter first."

The others nodded, their makeshift weapons gripped tight, eyes fixed on the door. The man at the back of the cell shifted his weight, murmuring softly to the old woman. She gave the faintest nod, her head sagging forward again.

The silence stretched, then fractured. Footsteps echoed down the corridor, measured, controlled, and closing fast. Aria braced herself against the wall, eyes locked on the handle. She counted each step. Four. Five. Six.

The key rattled in the lock, sharp and deliberate—a sound that sliced through the stillness. The door creaked open by inches, slow and cautious, as if reluctant to reveal what waited inside. The boy stepped in first, posture tight. The guard followed, muttering something under his breath—about the smell, or the wait, or both.

Aria moved first, lunging forward the instant the opening was wide enough. She grabbed the arm that held the keyring and twisted hard. The others surged forward in the same breath. Ansel slammed his shoulder into the guard's chest while the wiry man kicked his legs out from behind. They swarmed him—swift and silent, giving him no time to call out.

The guard crumpled beneath them with a stifled grunt, out cold before his body met the floor.

Aria crouched over him, snatching the ring of keys and his knife. She glanced at the others, clipped and focused. "Get him in the cell."

They dragged him inside.

The quiet prisoner who cared for the old woman helped shift the guard to the far corner, movements steady, expression grim.

Hollow-face stepped forward and stood over the unconscious guard, jaw tight. He held the guard's lance stiffly, both hands too close together, clearly unfamiliar with its weight. His foot shifted slightly, as if preparing to strike.

Aria caught his arm. "Don't," she said, quiet but firm.

He tensed beneath her grip. "After what they've done?" he muttered, voice low. "Would he do the same for us?"

"Then be better than him," Aria said. Her voice was calm, but her grip didn't loosen. Hollow-face didn't pull away. His eyes stayed on the guard a moment longer, then dropped.

"He's down," she added, voice flat. "That's enough."

The old woman shifted slightly, watching them with tired eyes that had seen too much already.

Aria dropped to one knee beside the guard. From the crate, she pulled a length of rope and bound his wrists and ankles tight. Someone passed her an old rag, and she tied it firmly over his mouth.

"If he wakes up, he won't be calling for help," she said.

The rest were breathing hard, some crouched, some standing with fists still clenched. One flexed his fingers, shaking out the tension. Another leaned against the wall, panting.

Aria glanced back. The old woman was trying to rise, her limbs slow, unsteady. "Help her," she said firmly, already turning toward the door. "She goes with us."

The quiet prisoner moved without hesitation, slipping an arm under her shoulder. Together, they steadied her upright.

"We need to move." Aria's voice was steady, despite the hammering in her chest. "Before someone checks on him—or the next shift comes through."

No one argued. Freedom lay ahead—but only if they moved now.

The hallway beyond the cell room was narrow and dim, lit by flickering glow-lights suspended from the ceiling. Aria paused at the threshold, still and steady, her breath tight in her chest.

The stale air carried a hint of chemicals, barely masking something older and mustier beneath. The others clustered behind her, tense, uncertain. With a quick twist of her wrist, she extended her lance—metal segments unfolding with a sleek, mechanical whisper.

No one spoke, but more than one pair of eyes widened. Whatever they had expected, it hadn't been that.

Aria said nothing, only gripped the lance tighter and stepped into the corridor, each movement measured. Her focus narrowed to the path ahead. Every corner, every sound.

Without warning her mind drifted to Heidi and Sylas.

Were they okay?

She pushed the thought aside, letting the familiar cold clarity of survival take over. She would find them. She had to find them.

Behind her, the others followed in tight formation. Hollow-face took the rear, the guard's lance held awkwardly in his hands as he glanced over his shoulder. The quiet prisoner helped the old woman forward, step by step, her breath shallow but steady. Ansel kept touching the raw skin on his wrists where the restraints had been, fingers scratching an anxious rhythm against the marks.

They reached a junction where the corridor split, one path ending at a locked stairwell, the other curving deeper into the tower's second floor. To their right, tucked behind a grated panel, the Ascender sat idle, its platform locked in place, the control panel dark.

"Too exposed," Aria murmured. She moved on without hesitation. "We take the stairs."

She halted, listening. No voices—only the intermittent hiss of a steam vent overhead and the low, pulsing hum of pressure valves somewhere below.

She held up the ring of keys, her thumb moving deliberately over the rusted metal. Half were worn smooth. None were clearly marked.

She picked one, slid it into the lock. Nothing.

Behind her, someone shifted. Another muttered under their breath. They were all too exposed in the corridor—too many shadows, not enough cover.

A second key stuck halfway. She pulled it back and tried a third.

Still locked.

From behind her, someone exhaled a little too loudly, just as the old woman's cough returned, low and ragged.

Fourth key. It slid in. She turned it—

Click.

The bolt slipped free. She pushed the door open just enough to glimpse the stairs waiting on the other side.

"Down," she whispered.

They moved as one, careful not to let the stairs betray them. Over-head, the lights flickered—plunging them into darkness for a heart-stopping moment before sputtering back to life. A step gave slightly beneath Aria's weight, the metal worn thin with rust and years of use.

Halfway down, a noise echoed from above—low voices, a sharp scrape of metal, and the measured rhythm of footsteps passing somewhere beyond the hallway above.

Aria stiffened, one hand braced against the wall, her eyes snapping to the others. A flicker of alarm passed between them.

"What was that?" Hollow-face murmured.

They pressed to the side of the stairwell, backs against the wall, weapons close. The old woman breathed heavily, head bowed. Ansel held his breath entirely.

The voices faded, footsteps trailing away with them.

Aria exhaled, low and controlled. "Keep going," she said, her voice just above a whisper. "We're not clear yet."

The stairwell spiraled downward into dim light, every step sounding too loud in the silence, each scrape of stone sending thin echoes up the shaft. Aria led the way, lance raised, its violet glow spilling restless shadows that chased themselves across the walls. Behind her, the prisoners followed close, the old woman's cough a brittle rasp against the hush.

Then came another sound—bootfalls, urgent and uneven, climbing from below. Aria raised her hand, halting the others against the wall.

A figure burst into view from around the bend—a soldier, no older than Aria, his lance braced in white-knuckled hands. He froze at the sight of them, breath rattling through his teeth. "D-Don't move!" he barked, but the crack in his voice betrayed him.

Aria's grip tightened as he stepped closer, but she held steady, the hum of her lance a quiet thread in the silence.

"Think carefully before you swing that," she said, her voice calm, even, carrying more weight than his bluster. "No one needs to get hurt."

For an instant his resolve wavered, uncertainty flickering in his eyes. Then pride—or fear—snuffed it out. He lunged, thrusting high, too fast and too wild.

Their weapons clashed, Crythium shrieking against stone as sparks burst into the dark. The jolt bit into Aria's arms, driving her back a step. He struck again, reckless, his lance whipping the air above her shoulder, the shaft slamming into the wall hard enough to chip the stone. He pressed forward, desperate, forcing her dangerously close to the others.

Aria's teeth clenched. If she faltered, panic would tear through the prisoners like a tremor through hollow stone.

With a sharp breath, she surged forward, ramming her weapon against his. The clash rang loud, a single piercing note. She twisted, leverage tearing his lance from his grip. It clattered down the steps, the glow vanishing into the dark beneath them.

He gasped, scrambling with bare hands, but she drove her knee hard into his stomach. The air left him in a ragged cry, his body folding as she slammed him back against the wall. He clawed weakly at her shoulder, but she leaned into him, her weight and fury pinning him.

Their eyes locked—his wide with terror, hers hard, carrying the weight of what would happen if she faltered. She saw shame ripple through him, a boy crushed beneath duty he didn't believe in.

"Don't," she hissed.

The word stopped him. His lips parted as if to speak, but nothing came.

Hollow-face edged closer, glancing between them, his hands twitching toward his weapon but waiting for her command.

"Bind him," she ordered.

Hollow-face moved quickly, rough but efficient, as he gagged the young man and fastened his wrists behind his back. The soldier sagged when it was done, chest heaving, eyes still fixed on Aria as though she had carved herself into his memory.

When she turned, the others were staring at her with a new expression—not only relief, but a dawning trust, as if the fragile thread of hope had at last found something strong enough to hold.

"Keep moving," she said, her voice carrying in the hush.

And this time, they followed not because they had no choice, but because they believed she could lead them through.

At the bottom of the stairwell, a faint violet gleam caught along the stone. The boy's fallen lance had skidded to rest against the wall. The wiry prisoner hesitated, glancing toward it as though afraid to claim what wasn't his.

Aria gave a short nod. "Take it."

He seized the weapon, its glow sharpening the lines of his gaunt face. His fingers tightened, the weapon anchoring him with a resolve he hadn't shown before.

They gathered before the heavy door at the base of the stairwell. Aria lifted the key, but before she could fit it into the lock, Ansel edged close, voice low. "There might be more out there."

Her eyes remained on the door, fingers resting on the key, unmoving.

"I think we're clear," Hollow-face murmured. "I don't hear anything."

She turned—just slightly—and their faces swam in the dim glow, drawn and anxious, waiting.

The wiry man clutched his new weapon tight. The old woman leaned pale against the wall. Hollow-face stood with his jaw set, ready for whatever came.

Even the quiet ones watched her, eyes reflecting the same uneasy blend of dread and hope.

Every gaze pressed the same truth into her chest. They were waiting on her. Trusting her.

Her hand tightened on the key.

She leaned in and slid it into the lock. The mechanism turned with a muted click. She pulled on the door, opening it just a crack. It creaked—a soft, slow complaint that echoed louder than it should have. Aria froze, breath caught, waiting.

A sudden hiss split the silence. Steam vented from a pipe overhead, the burst echoing down the corridor beyond. Someone behind gasped and sucked in a breath. Hollow-face tensed, muscles coiling as his grip tightened around his lance.

Amber light spilled in from the corridor beyond, a low glow cast by ceiling lights that bathed the space in sickly warmth. Just enough illumination to send faint shadows creeping at their heels. Aria crouched and peered through the gap. The corridor stretched empty—no guards, no voices—only the faint hum of pressure valves and the metallic tick of cooling pipes.

She exhaled, forcing calm. Could she keep them all safe—these people whose lives now leaned into her every decision? The dread pressed cold against her chest, but she shoved it down.

The others remained silent behind her, but the air stretched taut with tension. One misstep, one breath too loud—any small mistake could shatter their fragile calm.

Her thumb brushed the lance's mechanism. A hum stirred beneath her palms, the violet tip flaring faint but ready.

No turning back now.

"Let's go," she whispered.

One by one, they slipped through. Aria kept to the north wall and the others pressed in behind her, a silent chain of bodies hugging the stone. Hollow-face guided the old woman close at his side, the wiry man clutching his new lance just behind them. Every step was measured, each breath checked as they followed.

They moved in silence. Past a sealed room on the left, into a narrow passage that bent toward the Ascender junction. The corridor widened, then opened into the tower's main floor. Doors lined the walls—administrative rooms, supply storage, the faint glow of an office shuttered tight.

Still no guards.

The great door to the Inner District loomed ahead, its iron braces catching dull lamplight. Aria's pulse climbed. Every step toward it felt too loud, too long, as though the tower itself was waiting to betray them.

At last they reached it.

Aria gripped the large handle and turned. The bolt gave with a weighted click, and the door swung open onto the night.

The cool air swept in—sharp and merciless, but clean compared to the stale corridors behind them. The prisoners inhaled as though surfacing from deep water, shoulders loosening, eyes lifting to the cavernous expanse above the District. For the first time since the stairwell, their steps slowed, touched with something close to relief.

Aria felt it too, the weight in her chest easing, if only for a heartbeat.

She had brought them out. Through locks, through silence, through fear. They were free of the tower, but danger still pressed close. They had to move quickly, before—

"Drop the weapons," a voice cut through the night. "You're not leaving this place."

A scarred soldier stepped into view, lance leveled with quiet precision, the violet glow catching hard in his eyes. His voice was calm, steady, certain. He did not shout. He did not falter. He simply stood barring their way.

The prisoners froze. Aria lifted her lance, forcing her voice even. "Move aside."

The man's mouth curved faintly, not in humor but in certainty. He advanced, each step deliberate.

Aria braced. Her arms still ached from the stairwell clash, and the hollow drag of a sleepless night clung to her. She set her stance as the soldier closed, violet light pooling in the dark.

Crythium rang as their weapons collided, sparks bursting against the night. His strikes were measured, heavy, each one pressing into her guard with suffocating precision. Aria met them, her training carried her through the first exchanges, but his rhythm was relentless, driving her backward.

The wiry prisoner lunged in, his stolen weapon darting for the soldier's flank. For an instant hope flickered—then the soldier pivoted with brutal ease, the shaft of his lance smashing into the man's ribs. The prisoner folded with a ragged cry, collapsing against the wall, his lance clattering out of reach.

Fear rippled through the group like cracks through brittle rock.

Aria countered, teeth clenched, but her thoughts slipped where her guard could not: Sylas and Heidi, dragged away into the Stratum.

If she didn't survive this—who would save them?

The fear knifed through her focus, sharp and cold.

The soldier pressed harder, calm in his control. Aria's chest burned with more than strain. The weight of so many lives depending on her pressed close, and in that flicker of weakness, his lance slipped past her guard.

Her boots scraped stone as her weapon was wrenched aside. Pain shot through her shoulder as he forced her back, his gaze locking on hers—steady, merciless—as he drove in for the finishing thrust—

Then he was wrenched away.

Pike burst from the shadows, slamming into him with bone-jarring force. His elbow cracked against the man's jaw, and the soldier's eyes rolled back as he crumpled to the ground—unconscious.

Three hooded Dwellers swept in from the darkness, weapons drawn, forming a perimeter around the prisoners. One carried the heavy curve of a war hammer, its head dulled by use rather than polish. He shoved back his hood, a broad hand tightening on the hammer's haft. The weapon looked forged for the mines, not the streets—but in his grip, it promised only ruin.

Aria's breath caught. The face beneath was thick-browed, jaw tight with a strain she remembered well. Bram. The drunk from the Cantina.

She had last seen him bent over his brother's cot, fists clenched in helpless fury while she tended to the man. Then, he'd been all anger and grief. Now his eyes found hers through the gloom, something unspoken passing between them.

"You," Aria whispered.

Bram didn't answer, but there was no mistaking the shift in him. Whatever scorn he once held had burned away, leaving only the weight of his gratitude.

Pike stood over the fallen guard, poised for the finishing blow.

"Wait!" Aria's voice cut through the night.

Pike froze, breath ragged, the blade trembling inches above the soldier. His eyes moved to hers, sharp, questioning. "You're not going soft on me, are you, girl?"

"We need him alive," Aria said. Her voice was steady, though her chest still heaved from the fight. "I need to question him."

Pike's jaw flexed, irritation sharp across his face. "That may be so. But you left yourself wide open." He exhaled slowly, the breath heavy with frustration. "I've told you a thousand times, girl—your adversary doesn't care how tired you are. In fact, he's counting on it."

The words cut deeper than his tone, dragging up every memory of his drills, the bruises, the endless repetitions meant to beat that lesson into her bones. Aria held his gaze, refusing to let him see the sting, but in her chest the truth of it twisted hard.

Pike's gaze swept over the rescued prisoners, counting them with a soldier's eye. His brow furrowed. "Where are they?" he grumbled. "Heidi? Sylas?"

His head snapped toward the tower, jaw set.

"They're not in there. Not anymore," Aria said quickly, cutting across his silence. She looked down at the unconscious guard, her voice firm. "That's why I need him alive."

Realization flickered across Pike's face, the fight leaving his posture. He glanced up at the open street, scanning the shadows, then back at her. "We can't stay out here in the open."

One of the prisoners pointed to a narrow alley choked with shadow. "There."

They dragged the unconscious soldier across the street and into the alley, shadows closing tight around them. The prisoners huddled against the wall, breaths still ragged, while Pike dropped the guard hard to the ground. His men fanned out at the mouth of the passage, silent but watchful.

Aria turned to him, her pulse still thundering, disbelief and something achingly close to relief breaking across her face. "What are you doing here?"

Pike snorted. "Saving your hide," he grunted. "Heard you were taken."

The words struck her harder than she expected. Gratitude welled sharp and hot in her chest, nearly choking her.

She had pulled off a daring escape, leading the prisoners out of the tower, but she hadn't come out unscathed. The sting of the soldier's lance still lingered—its slip past her guard, that breath of inevitability. If Pike hadn't arrived when he did, she wouldn't be standing now, and the others would still be trapped. Or worse.

It stung, needing to be saved. Yet beneath the pride lay a quieter truth—one she couldn't ignore.

She was grateful.

"Thank you," she said, her voice low.

Pike wiped a streak of dirt from his knuckles. "Anna said we still owed you one. So, as always, she talked Sebastian into sending me to risk my neck."

A short laugh escaped Aria before she could stop it.

"Not that you needed much help," Pike added dryly.

"I'll have to remember to thank Anna," she said, though her voice caught halfway.

"You do that."

Silence stretched between them, heavy and unbroken.

Aria's gaze caught on the lance in his hand, the faint Crythium shimmer seeping through the cloth wrap. "How did you get that up here?"

Pike's mouth tugged into something like a smile. "Not every road ends at a checkpoint or the Lift, girl. Some of ours stay hidden." His eyes narrowed. "Now—want to tell me where those two are?"

Aria hesitated. The word stuck like a stone in her throat, heavy enough to shift the ground beneath them. Saying it would escalate everything.

Finally, she forced it out, voice low. "The Stratum."

Pike's gaze darkened, the weight in his eyes heavier than any words.

"I'm going to get them back," Aria said, her voice cutting firm through the hush. "Even if it kills me."

"It likely would," he stated flatly. "You can't just barge into the Stratum and ask the Warden to hand them over."

"We have to—" she faltered, then steadied herself. "No, I have to do something."

Pike's gaze swept over the ragged line of prisoners—bruised, hungry, clutching stolen lances like children holding onto scraps of hope. He exhaled. "I understand. But you're exhausted and they're worse. The best way to help them is to regroup and get some rest."

"I don't have a choice," Aria snapped. "They don't have much time."

"Don't be stubborn." Pike tipped his chin at the unconscious soldier. "The Stratum's huge. You've never been up there."

Aria stepped forward, eyes locked on the bound guard. "That's where he comes in."

Pike's voice went flat. "And you think he'll just talk?"

Without warning, Aria slammed the tip of her boot into the soldier's ribs. Hard enough to wrench a groan from him.

"Let's find out."

She crouched low, the lance's glow throwing the guard's bruised face into restless light. His fingers twitched at the ropes; his eyelids fluttered. A coarse breath rasped from him, and he forced his jaw, blinking as if surfacing from a dream. He tried to push up, shoulders shaking, but the bonds held him fast.

"You'd better talk," Aria said. "Clock's ticking, and I've got a friend here who'd be happy to put a hole in you if I let him. Where are the prisoners held in the Stratum?"

The guard laughed, wet and ragged, his breath rattling in his chest. "You think you scare me? A girl playing hero with a stolen toy?" He spat at her feet. "Doesn't matter where they are. You won't live long enough to reach them. The Warden knows where you rats are nesting. Once that brat of a prince leaves, he'll burn you all out."

The word jolted through her. Gideon was still in the Stratum, but not for long. Relief cut against dread, sharp as her lance's hum. She kept it locked down, her expression giving nothing away.

"Where?" she pressed, sharper now. "Which level? Which wing?"

The guard only grinned—wider, more defiant.

Pike's voice cut in, flat as iron. "The only way to make him talk is to make him bleed." His hand dropped to the knife at his belt, the steel half-drawn before the guard's bravado cracked. The man's eyes flicked to the blade and this time the fear was real.

Aria straightened. "No. The fight's over."

Pike's eyes narrowed, his voice rising. "Over? The fight is never over, girl. Not while Drazic and his men keep hunting us. They'll gag us, gut us, and burn us to the ground without a second thought. We let this one walk, and it's another family left broken—another child without parents. Is that what you want?"

"No." Aria's throat tightened, but her voice held. "I know what that's like. My parents died because of men like him." She met Pike's gaze, her expression steady now. "I won't carry that grief into another home, not if I can help it."

For a moment, the alley fell silent. Even the guard's grin faltered—the words hung between them, heavier than stone.

Pike's gaze drifted to the far wall. For an instant, he saw flames where there were none—and the echo of a name he never said aloud. He blinked hard, jaw tightening, as if forcing the image away.

"Then what was all that training for?"

"To protect life, not to take it."

His reply came low, deliberate. "One day you'll learn, girl—you cannot protect life without taking it."

Aria's gaze didn't waver. "If that day comes, I'll know I've already lost."

Pike exhaled hard through his nose. "That's a fine way to get yourself killed. Drazic and his men won't play by those rules."

Her jaw tightened. "Then I'll just have to be better than them."

Pike's mouth twitched, humorless. "And how's that working out for you?"

Aria pushed to her feet, shoulders tight, her gaze unwavering. "So far, so good."

For a breath, the silence held. Then Pike slid the knife back into its sheath with a snap. "Enough. We're wasting time."

He turned to his men, jerking his chin toward the rescued prisoners. "Get them away from here. Quietly. And keep the lances—can't have them caught with weapons."

One of Pike's men stepped forward, collecting the lances from Hollow-Face and the wiry man, then slid back into place without a word.

Hollow-Face's eyes lingered on Aria, searching. Then he gave a small nod. "You promised to get us out," he said quietly. "You did."

Aria met his gaze, a small nod the only answer she could give in return.

The old woman leaned into him for support, her steps unsteady but determined. Ansel and the other prisoners gathered close, ragged and thin, but moving as one. At the mouth of the alley, Pike's men fell in around them, shadows guiding shadows.

Before turning away, Hollow-Face glanced back once at Aria. No words, just a look—an acknowledgment that promises mattered, and that this one had been kept.

The group slipped into the night, leaving the alley emptier, quieter.

Aria pressed her sleeve, feeling the faint edge of the vial hidden there. Her grandmother's face rose sharp in her mind, pale and waiting. Time was running thin.

Pike's voice broke the silence. "We'll figure it out. Let's go."

Aria's throat tightened. Sylas. Heidi. Gideon. The Stratum loomed in her thoughts like a black wall. But the cure was here and her grandmother was slipping away.

She forced herself to nod.

The guard shifted against his bonds, a muffled laugh rasping behind the gag.

Aria looked down at him. "And him?"

Pike's mouth hardened. "He gets what's coming to him."

Her eyes lingered on the soldier's bruised face, then back to Pike. "We don't kill him."

Pike studied her, incredulity sharp in his eyes. For a long moment, he said nothing—the faint grind of his teeth the only sound in the hush. At last, he exhaled and slid his blade back into its sheath with a snap.

"Then gag him and leave him here. The rats he hates so much will decide his fate when they find him."

Traces of the Unspoken

From the Songs of the Forgotten

In the hush of dusk, she lies, her breath a fragile thread,
Eyes tracing shadows shaped by long-forgotten dread.
Songs of youth still shimmer soft beneath the never sky,
Love's quiet warmth; a name that never dies.
Her heart hums low, children's laughter woven faint,
Moments carved in light, untouched by time's restraint.
Darkness cloaks her now, yet still her spirit sways,
Drifting through the years where her memory softly plays.
No fear clouds her gaze; no end can dim her spark,
She fades into the shadow, like a whisper in the dark.

Author: Unknown

26

The Silent Hawk Soars

Location: Cavandel, The Outer District

The house felt smaller with every passing hour, as if the walls understood how fragile the night had become, and inched closer to keep it from breaking. Aria's grandmother lay beneath the thin quilt, the rise and fall of her chest so slight it might have been imagined. Heat pulsed through the skin at her throat, wrong and steady, and below the collar there was the faint shimmer that had crept up over the last days, a sickly light that seemed to answer each unsteady breath.

Jace sat beside her, elbows on his knees, a damp cloth forgotten in his hands. The lamp in the corner guttered, throwing long, restless shadows across the cracked stone floor. His eyes stayed on her chest—too slow, too shallow. She seemed smaller than she had that morning, as if the illness had stripped her down to little more than breath and memory.

The hours ran like water through a narrow channel. Sometimes she slept; sometimes she didn't. A few times, she turned her face toward the door without fully waking.

Jace did not leave. He could not.

The shimmer beneath her skin caught the light—lavender at first, then darkening, like ink sifting beneath the flesh.

Her fingers twitched when he cooled her brow, followed by a cough—soft and dry, more breath than sound.

His knees ached from the hours, but he didn't move far. The dim light cast her face in amber, softening the signs of illness but not hiding them. He wasn't ready to let go—not yet. He didn't know if she could still hear him, but silence felt too much like surrender.

"Remember the year she tore up your apron?" His voice was low, rough with exhaustion. "Said she needed fabric for her mask," he let out a tired little laugh, soft and frayed at the edges. "Didn't even ask. Just snipped it while you were sleeping."

The corners of his mouth curved briefly, a tired shape that wouldn't hold. "She hasn't changed. Still rushing ahead before the rest of us can catch up."

He let the thought hang, then continued, softer now. "I thought you'd scold her. But you didn't. You sat with her in the lamplight, guiding her hands while she stitched crooked seams. She wore that mask two years straight," he laughed, almost to himself. "Said it smelled like you."

The lamp sputtered, shadows climbing higher over the far wall. Lucinda's eyes fluttered, her lips shaping breath without sound. Jace leaned close, catching the fragments. "Aria... alright?"

He swallowed, the lie rough in his throat. "She's alright. She'll be back soon."

"Safe...?" The word was little more than air.

He caught her hand, cradling it between both of his. "Yes," he whispered, though the word burned. "She's safe."

He did not believe it, not entirely. Aria should have returned hours ago. He had told himself she was with the Dwellers, that Anna still needed her or the cure wasn't ready. He had told himself that before another thought pressed in from the edges, the thought he kept shoving away. Guards. Patrols. Workers taken in the street. He felt the ache of it and refused to give it a name.

***

Far across the District, Aria, Pike, and Bram moved through narrow back lanes where laundry lines hung like nets and the stone sweated with night. The other two Dwellers caught up as the streets widened toward the market, shadowing the rear—faces set, silent, watchful.

Aria's throat tightened as she turned to Pike. "What he said back there—about knowing our location—think it's true?"

Their pace remained swift, boots striking hard against the narrow lanes as his men fanned ahead and behind. Pike's gaze stayed on the street ahead, but the line of his mouth thinned. "True enough. The Warden's got eyes everywhere. Always has."

Bram's grunt was low, bitter. He shifted the hammer in his grip, resting its head against the cobblestones with a dull scrape. "Aye. I've seen neighbors sell each other for less than a meal. The Warden doesn't even have to pay most of 'em."

Aria kept her tone even. "So you've known."

"A while now." Pike's voice was flat, but not careless. "A miner knows a miner, girl. When a shadow doesn't belong, you feel it. Drazic's men thought themselves clever, but we've known."

The silence between them pressed heavy as they wove through another alley, broken only by the hiss of a glow-lamp overhead. Aria brushed her sleeve, the glass vial cold against her arm. "So the noose tightens."

Pike gave a short grunt that might have been agreement. "Any tighter and the city'll snap."

Her chest ached at the thought—streets filled not with guards and rebels, but neighbors, women, children. One soldier had nearly undone her; she couldn't imagine the whole city unraveling at once. "And when it does?" she asked quietly.

Pike's answer was low, the scrape of iron on stone. "Then Cavandel eats itself alive. Not clean. Not quick. A thousand shadows turning on each other."

Aria's stomach turned. She thought of how close he'd come to striking the guard. "It doesn't have to be that way."

Bram let out a rough laugh, short and sharp. "That's what my brother said. Hope'll hold us together. Then he near bled out in the mines." His gaze cut to Aria. "Still breathing because of you. So maybe he wasn't all wrong."

Pike's eyes stayed fixed ahead, unreadable.

"The cure," she said, softer now. "Word's spreading. They're starting to believe."

"Belief doesn't stop a blade," he muttered as they pressed on, his eyes cutting to every rooftop.

"It can keep one from being drawn." She held his stare, steady despite the weight behind it.

His silence stretched, then broke in a dry, humorless breath. "There's fire in you, girl. But fire burns both ways. Hope can rally a city, but when it fails, it leaves nothing but ash."

Aria drew a sharp breath, her grandmother's face pressing behind her eyes. "Then we make sure it doesn't fail."

Bram spat into the dust, his jaw tight, the long handle of his hammer jutting over his shoulder. "Ash or not, better than bending our necks."

Pike said nothing, only adjusted the strap across his shoulder and kept his stride quick, sweeping the rooftops again. But the silence he left carried more than words.

By the time the heavier spires of the Outer District came into view, the first stirrings of dawn's shift were felt in the streets. A battered railcar rattled past, crowded with miners returning from the night shift, faces hollow with fatigue.

They boarded with the last of the crowd and stood in the crush near the door. The frame creaked under the weight and the railcar jolted as if it resented the extra burden.

It groaned as it pulled onto the track, a rusted beast too weary to keep moving yet too stubborn to stop. Inside, the air was sour with sweat and dust, heavy enough to cling to the back of the throat. Miners packed shoulder to shoulder swayed with each jolt, their tools clattering together in a weary chorus.

Aria gripped the metal pole by the door, her free hand fixed tight against her sleeve where the vial lay hidden, the small shape like a heartbeat she could not steady. Each jolt of the railcar felt like stolen time, each sway made the glass seem sharper against her skin, as if reminding her what she carried.

A man near her sagged against the wall, eyes closed, his breath coming out in ragged snores. Another muttered to himself, fingers raw and blackened from stone, counting in time with the grinding wheels. A woman in the corner rocked a sleeping child, her hand covering the boy's ear whenever the brakes screeched. Someone coughed—a deep, rattling sound that set the car quiet for a moment before the noise of iron drowned it again.

Aria could feel every detail, as if the world were mocking her urgency. The railcar stalled on a slope, gears clanking and then catching, dragging them forward inch by inch. Heat from too many bodies pressed in and the sway of the car made her stomach knot.

She shut her eyes and told herself to breathe, to endure the crawl, to imagine Gran still holding on. But the faces around her—all worn down, all dulled by waiting—only deepened the dread that time was running ahead of her, leaving her behind.

The ride stretched long, far too long.

Behind her eyes she carried her grandmother's face and worse—the imagined stillness if she didn't move faster.

"Almost there," she murmured, voice too soft for anyone but herself. "Just hold on."

***

Inside the little house, the air seemed to contract—the space smaller, darker, as if the walls leaned inward. Jace brushed back a loose strand of silver hair, his fingers trembling despite himself. Her breathing faltered once, then steadied—then quieted. Her hand slackened in his, and the silence deepened around them.

***

The railcar screeched to a halt. Aria jumped off before it stopped fully, Pike following without a word. The uneven stones of the District's edge rushed beneath her boots, her chest tight as the crooked outline of the house appeared. Too dark. Too silent.

She ran.

***

The door slammed open. Jace looked up sharply. For a moment he only stared, as if the sight of Aria were some memory dragged into the room. Then he stood and stepped back to give her space, his fists clenched at his sides without purpose.

Aria stumbled in, breath ragged, eyes falling to the bed. She dropped to her knees, pulling the vial from her sleeve with trembling fingers.

"I'm here," she gasped, her voice breaking. "Gran, I'm here. Please—please wake up."

The room seemed to narrow to the rim of the glass and her grandmother's mouth. She pulled the cork with shaking hands, tilting the vial to her grandmother's lips, pressing drops against them, willing them to be taken i n.

Nothing.

Pike stood in the doorway with one shoulder to the frame, eyes lowered, still as stone. Somewhere outside, his men shifted and settled.

No one spoke.

Seconds stretched, cruel and endless. Jace watched, hollow-eyed, unable to move.

Aria bowed her head against the quilt, sob catching in her throat. "It's not working." The words were small, and broke as they landed. She held the vial still in her grip as though letting it go would make the loss true.

Jace swallowed and found his voice. It came out rough, careful, almost apologetic. "Maybe it needs more time."

Aria shook her head once, tight and quick, not lifting her face.

Was she too late?

Jace let out a slow breath and looked at Lucinda's face in the uncertain light. His eyes met Pike's and Pike gave a small nod, nothing more.

Somewhere outside, a railcar groaned beyond the houses, the sound fading into stone. Pike moved just enough to speak without stepping inside. His voice was low, almost distant. "We'll keep watch."

Aria's shoulders lifted once as if to say something, then settled. Jace stood behind her, but did not try to pull her away. The lantern burned unevenly and the room held its breath with them, as if the walls had decided to keep the last of the night for a little while longer. She pressed her forehead to the quilt, her voice so faint it barely stirred the air. "I should have been here," she whispered. "I should've been faster."

Location: Cavandel, The Stratum

Gideon Everhart was a fool. Of all the fools in all the world, he supposed he must be the foremost, because only a fool would linger here. He had told himself he would not wait again, not after the last time, not after the silence stretched so long it became an answer of its own. He had sworn her off in the dark hours, resolved to return to Valmere where duty at least was predictable.

And yet, here he was.

His trunk was packed. At his hip rested his sword, its Crythium edge concealed within a plain, timeworn scabbard—a companion since Valmere. To outsiders it seemed an heirloom of ceremony, a prince's ornament. Those who knew him understood better—it was a weapon kept keen.

His cloak lay folded by the door, ready for the Ascender. Every excuse to stay had been stripped away.

He told himself it was only caution, that a clean departure demanded certainty. He had even ordered his guards down to the District with instructions to comb the lanes once more, to be sure she had not surfaced quietly while he wasn't looking. But he knew better. It was not duty that bound him here—it was her.

He remembered her refusal, quiet but steady: "I can't go with you." He remembered his own answer, spoken with more conviction than he'd truly felt. "Then I'll come back for you."

He remembered her eyes, full of hope and doubt in equal measure, as if she wanted to believe but could not afford to.

And then the waiting. The hours stretched thin beneath the archway; the air grew cold, the shadows long. He had told himself many things, until the excuses soured and only silence remained.

That should have been the end of it. A prince does not wait on a miner's daughter, does not linger in a city that is not his own, does not imagine futures built on fragile words exchanged under festival light. He should have left.

But he hadn't.

Now, standing in his chambers with his departure set in order, he could not even name what kept him here. Not hope—hope had worn itself out. Not duty—his duty lay above. What bound him was something more humiliating still, that the prince of Valmere, heir to a kingdom, could be held fast by the memory of a miner's daughter whispering *what's it like?* as if he truly held the sun itself in his hands.

He told himself he was a fool. And still, he waited.

His gaze lingered on the trunk. Beneath the folded layers lay her mask, hidden but never far from his mind. He wanted to take it out, to see its carved edges catch the light, to trace the lines she once held to her face.

He almost imagined it would still carry her—the scent, the faint warmth of her hands, the echo of her breath inside it—as if her question still lingered there: *What's it like? The lantern in the sky?*

Foolish notions and yet they tempted him.

She had given it with words that unsettled him still, speaking of promises and beginnings, of trust not lightly offered. Looking at it would summon back that night—her voice asking him about the sun, her eyes uncertain yet unafraid, her mask pressed into his hands like a piece of herself. He should have left it behind, left *her* behind, but instead he had tucked it away like a keepsake. Now it sat among his belongings, silent and accusing, binding him to a promise he had no right to accept and no strength to refuse.

"You seem restless, Your Highness."

The voice broke through his thoughts like a knife drawn across stone. Gideon turned. The Warden stood near the hearth, drink in hand, posture as rigid as the steel beams that ribbed the Stratum. His pale eyes studied Gideon without blinking, as though he had been waiting for just such a moment.

"You have been a most honored guest," the Warden said smoothly. "I trust your accommodations were acceptable? Not quite the luxuries of Valmere, I admit, but I do hope they've proven satisfactory."

"They've been fine," Gideon replied, clipped.

The Warden inclined his head, as though satisfied. "Good. It is important to me that visiting dignitaries, especially one of your station, carry home a clear impression of Cavandel's hospitality. His Majesty would not wish to hear otherwise."

His gaze slipped briefly toward the trunk at Gideon's feet, then back to Gideon. "It was reported," he said lightly, "that your guards were seen traveling down to the District this morning. I do hope all is well. Nothing amiss, I trust?"

The silence stretched. Gideon offered nothing.

The Warden let it linger just long enough to feel deliberate before continuing, his tone courteous but edged. "If they have business below, my men would be more than happy to assist them in any way possible."

It was a probe, wrapped in politeness. Gideon forced a calm he did not feel. "There were inquiries left unfinished. A matter of prudence."

The Warden's mouth twitched into something too small to be called a smile. "Prudence. Of course."

Gideon reached for his cloak, unwilling to grant him further satisfaction. "Shall we?" he said, and opened the door into the corridor beyond.

As they moved through the corridors of the administrative hall, Gideon heard it before he saw it—a scuffle, boots scraping, a muffled cry rising from the direction of the building's rail station.

"Let go of me!" A young man's voice, cracking with anger and fear. "I didn't do anything—"

The heavy thud of a fist cut off the young man's protest. Gideon's gaze snapped toward the station down the corridor.

Two guards dragged the boy between them, while two other prisoners stumbled beside them, wrists bound, their faces hollow with fear. Along the narrow platform, the metal track glinted beneath the overhead lights. The boy kicked and twisted, his boots screeching against the floor, curses echoing into the open air.

Gideon's breath stilled. He knew that voice.

Sylas?

He stepped forward, voice carrying. "Halt!"

A ripple moved through the platform—workers slowing, drawn by the sound. Conversations faltered. A few edged closer, others hung back, eyes darting between the prince and the Warden. The air thickened with that peculiar stillness that falls before violence.

The Warden's face darkened. "What is the meaning of this?"

The soldiers froze where they stood, still gripping Sylas but suddenly rigid, their eyes darting between the prince and their master. Neither dared speak. The Warden's glare pinned them in place, sharp enough to skewer. The silence stretched, broken only by Sylas's ragged breaths and the scrape of his boots as he fought against their hold.

"Well?" the Warden pressed.

"Apologies, Warden," one of the guards stammered. "Space just opened in the lab. We were ordered to move the next transfer from the Infirmary."

The Warden's eyes narrowed, a faint curl of disdain at the corner of his mouth. "And you thought to parade them through *here?*"

Gideon stepped closer, authority ringing in his tone. "Release him."

"Your Highness—" one began, but Gideon's eyes cut like steel. "Now."

Reluctantly, they let Sylas drop to his knees. He coughed, clutching his ribs, then lifted his head slowly. His eyes widened when he saw Gideon, disbelief colliding with urgency.

"Gideon!" he shouted, voice raw. "They took her—Aria's locked in the tower. Heidi too. Back there." His breath caught, urgency cracking through. "We have to save them!"

The words struck Gideon like a blow. For an instant, the corridor warped, blurring at the edges.

Aria. Captured?

Was that why she hadn't come? Not hesitation. Not refusal. Captured.

Could this be true?

The Warden's pale eyes settled on Sylas, his composure strained to the limit. "Enough," he hissed, his voice clipped. Then his gaze shifted to the guards. "Remove him. This is no time for theatrics."

He turned back to Gideon with a thin smile, the edge of irritation hidden beneath a layer of courtesy. "Forgive the disturbance, Your Highness. He was likely caught stealing. He will receive his just punishment and be released."

Sylas twisted on the floor, voice cracking with fury. "Liar!" He gasped, straining against the guards' grip. "Don't believe him, Gideon!"

The Warden's face hardened, but his voice remained smooth. "Ignore him, Your Highness. Fear can twist words into madness, and that is all you hear now—the ravings of a lunatic boy."

"Not true!" Sylas shouted, desperation breaking through. "They're feeding us to the Screechers. I heard them!"

The words hung sharp in the air, heavy and still. Gideon's brow furrowed at the unfamiliar name—Screecher—but he kept silent. For a moment, no one moved. Even the guards holding Sylas faltered, their grips tightening as if to smother the truth that had slipped free.

Gideon's jaw clenched, his eyes shifting from Sylas to the Warden. He said nothing yet, but the silence pressed like a weight, demanding an answer.

The Warden's expression did not change, though the faint twitch of his jaw betrayed the effort it took to remain composed. When he spoke, his voice was quiet, measured, as if dismissing a child's tantrum. "Nonsense. You see how desperation drives him, Your Highness. A prisoner will say anything to avoid punishment."

Sylas struggled harder, dragging a boot across the grated floor. "It's the truth!" he spat, his voice breaking. "I heard them. That's what they'll do to us! And we're all innocent!"

The guards shifted uneasily. One muttered under his breath, cut off at once by the Warden's glance.

Gideon felt heat rising in his chest, a surge that demanded action, demanded he strike the lie from the Warden's mouth. His fingers curled against his palms until his knuckles ached. He wanted to speak—wanted to demand answers—but years of court discipline held him still. A prince does not lash out at shadows. A prince waits, watches, forces the truth into the light.

He kept his silence, though every heartbeat pressed harder, though Sylas's protests cut sharper with each breath. If he gave himself over to anger now, he risked playing the fool in the Warden's game. His restraint was frayed, it felt thinner with every passing moment, stretched taut as wire.

Gideon's gaze lingered on Sylas, but in his mind it was Aria's face he saw. *Is this true? Is she truly locked away in some dark tower, starved and beaten? Was he truly about to abandon her when she needed him most?*

His jaw tightened, resolve settling in. "Tell me, Warden. Is there truth in what he says?"

The Warden turned smoothly, hands spreading as if to calm a restless crowd. "Surely you don't believe—"

"I'm not lying!" Sylas cut in, his voice raw. "I can take you to her!"

The words landed like a stone hurled into still water, the ripples spreading fast. The guards stiffened, unease flashing in their eyes.

Murmurs rippled through the gathered crowd, growing bolder with each passing breath. Faces turned toward the confrontation, eyes wide, whispers darting between them like sparks leaping through dry straw. Someone muttered the prince's name. Another inquired about the disturbance. The tension thickened, pressing against the Warden's composure like a rising tide.

For a brief moment, his poise cracked. The mask of courtesy slipped, and something harsher flashed across his face. His gaze swept the restless throng—his city, his order—now shifting beyond his command. The control he had once wielded so effortlessly was fraying before his eyes.

When he spoke, the polish in his voice was gone, stripped down to a snarl. "Enough of this insolence!" The words rang sharp, carrying not only anger but the edge of fear—the kind a man feels when a lie threatens to unravel, when power starts to slip from his grasp.

The echo of his voice climbed the vaulted arches, then faded into a taut and uneasy silence. He straightened, smoothing the front of his coat as though the lapse had never occurred. When he spoke again, his tone was silken once more. "Your Highness, for your safety I must insist you return to your chambers. This rabble is beneath your notice. My men will see the matter corrected."

Gideon's jaw tightened. *For your safety.* The words curdled. His reply came steady but edged. "My safety is not what concerns me, Warden. Just the truth."

Sylas thrashed in his captors' grip, voice raw. "Don't let him fool you, Gideon, she's there—I swear it! You know I'm not lying!"

The silence pressed like stone. Gideon's composure frayed, the image of Aria locked in darkness gnawing at him with every breath. His voice was low but unyielding. "You will take me to this tower. At once."

The Warden blinked, his mask slipping for the briefest instant. "This... tower?" he repeated, tasting the word. Then the false smile returned, stretched thin. "Surely Your Highness has not been so long below that he forgets himself. The ladies of your court are better suited to your station than some wench, some—Dustborn from the mines."

Dustborn. The word struck Gideon like flint.

I'm just a Dustborn, she had said, *I have nothing to offer...*

The memory wasn't gentle. It came like an echo torn from the past, her voice rising unbidden, carried on the insult he had just heard. His eyes sharpened, the weight of his stare enough to silence the entire building. "Watch your tongue, Warden."

The Warden's smile lingered, though the humor in it had turned brittle. "Or perhaps this *Aria* is the reason you linger. Perhaps that's why your guards have strayed into the District. This *matter of prudence*—to see her safely to you before you depart?"

Gideon moved before the last syllable faded. He seized the Warden's collar and yanked him forward until their faces nearly touched. Gasps rippled through the crowd, a living shudder that swept from the front ranks outward. The guards flinched, their Crythium lances snapping upright with a low hum, violet light bleeding from the tips as they waited for command. Whispers rose, brittle and electric, the people straining to see—some in awe, others in fear.

"You will not speak her name again," Gideon said, low and cold, each word honed like tempered steel.

The Warden's throat worked soundlessly. For the first time, his voice failed him. He felt the crowd's gaze pressing in—the weight of so many eyes pressing against him, witnessing the unthinkable. His authority, so long absolute, teetered in that breath, and the silence that followed was no longer his to command.

He barked a short, harsh laugh that did nothing to hide the strain at his throat. "And what do you intend to do, boy?"

Gideon's eyes narrowed. "Tread carefully, Warden."

The Warden's smile broadened. "It is you who should tread carefully, Your Highness. This is Cavandel, not Valmere. Those men answer to me, not to you."

"Then speak it," Gideon hissed, fury burning under restraint. "And see how quickly your head rolls when my father learns of this."

The Warden's smile quivered, but he forced it steady. He tilted his head, as if considering the polite option. "Your father sits far above, and Cavandel runs by my rules. People vanish here—collapses, fires. Accidents are common enough." He let the words hang, then added, softer and colder, "And this Aria—if she even exists—could vanish just as easily. One less voice in the da rk."

Gideon held the Warden fast, weighing his next move. To draw steel here, in the heart of the Stratum, with lances leveled against him—it would be a fight measured in moments. He could see the calculation in the guards' eyes, the tremor of unease as they awaited a command. Every option seemed edged with ruin.

Then Sylas moved.

With a sudden wrench, he drove his boot down hard on the instep of the guard gripping him, snapping his head back into the man's jaw. The soldier cursed and staggered, his lance jolting sideways. The chain between Sylas's wrists bit into his skin as he twisted, snatching the ring of keys from the guard's belt.

One of the other prisoners seized the chance, wrenching free of his escort; the second followed, stumbling into the fray as shouts rang out.

The second guard lunged for Sylas, violet light humming as the lance swung down. Gideon had only a moment to act. He released the Warden and stepped in, sword flashing free. Steel rang against the powered shaft, sparks skittering across the grated floor. Sylas scrambled behind him, gasping, ribs heaving.

"Run!" Gideon barked, shoving the guard back.

The other two prisoners scattered down the adjoining corridors, chains clattering as they fled into the crowd of onlookers. Sylas stumbled beside Gideon, clutching the key ring tight as they broke through the gap, boots hammering against stone and steel. Their path opened onto the narrow platform where the Warden's tram waited, its rails humming with the steady thrum of power.

The Warden's composure shattered at last. "After them!" he roared, his voice cracking into the air. "Don't let them get to that tram!"

27

Echoes of Prophecy

Location: Cavandel, The Outer District

The room felt hollow, as though even the walls listened for a sound that would not come. Aria sat rigid beside her grandmother, clutching the frail hand in both of hers, willing warmth into it. The shimmer of Shatterblight had climbed high across the old woman's throat, glowing faint beneath the lamplight, beautiful and cruel all at once.

Jace stood at the foot of the bed, head bowed, his weathered face heavy with years of loss. In the doorway Pike lingered, arms folded tight, his gaze fixed on the floor. In the glow's thin light, their eyes met once, a quiet exchange that said what neither wanted to—it was over.

Aria shook her head slowly, refusing to accept it. "No," she whispered. "You can't." Her words fell into the silence like stones into water, sinking with no ripple. She pressed her cheek against her grandmother's hand, whispering pleas and half-formed bargains. The vial lay empty on the table, bitter drops gone and still nothing stirred. Seconds stretched into minutes, the silence deepening until the weight of it pressed against her ears. Even the lamp's faint humming seemed too loud.

She kept listening. Kept waiting. Tears soaked the quilt beneath her face. Jace shifted once, as though ready to draw her back, but he stopped when

Pike's hand gripped the doorframe, halting him. Both men watched her, sorrow pulling at them, but neither broke the quiet.

Then, so faint she almost missed it—a squeeze. The fingers in her palm tightened, barely a twitch, but it jolted through her like lightning.

"Gran!" Aria gasped, sitting upright, gripping harder. "She moved!"

Jace's eyes lifted at the sound, startled, but Pike only shook his head. "Aria..." he said quietly, his voice carrying both warning and pity.

"No!" she snapped, desperate. "I felt it. She squeezed my hand."

Jace came to her side, kneeling with effort, his rough palm covering Lucinda's other hand. They waited, breathless. Nothing. The old woman's face remained slack, her chest unmoving. Jace's lips pressed tight, a silent verdict.

Aria's tears blurred her vision. "She did. I swear it."

For a terrible instant it seemed a delusion, grief conjuring something hopeful where none existed. But then—the faintest pressure again, deliberate and lingering, just long enough to steal her breath. Jace froze beside her, disbelief unraveling into a fragile, aching hope. Even Pike, whose doubts had sat like iron, leaned closer, his stare sharp and unyielding, as though daring the shadows to prove him wrong.

"She's here," Aria whispered fiercely. "It's working."

For the first time, Jace allowed the weight to drop from his shoulders. He straightened, voice low but urgent. "Get me a wet rag."

Aria stumbled for the basin, dipping the cloth into cool water before pressing it into his hand. Jace wrung it out, dabbing sweat from Lucinda's brow, coaxing her back with steady strokes. Pike shifted closer, his earlier doubt giving way to a restless energy.

"What else?" Aria asked, her voice ragged, wild with hope.

"Keep her warm," Jace said quickly. "Her strength's near gone. The cure bought her some time, but it won't fight for her." He reached for another blanket, layering it gently across the quilt. "Now it's her battle. We help however we can."

Pike eased the door wider, letting more of the hearth's warmth to drift into the room. His glance toward Jace held a quiet warning. She might live, but only if they held the line against the dark pulling at her.

Aria clung tighter to her grandmother's hand, refusing to let go again. "You'll stay with me," she whispered. "Please stay."

Location: Cavandel, The Stratum

The tram started down the line, sparks leaping where iron wheels met the track. Gideon gripped the side rail, knuckles white, the wind knifing through the tunnel. Sylas crouched at the front, teeth bared in something between a grin and a grimace.

"Faster," Sylas shouted, leaning hard into the lever. The gears shrieked in protest but obeyed, and the tram lurched forward, gathering speed.

Behind them came a shout. Gideon twisted just in time to see a soldier sprinting down the platform. The man lunged as the cart pulled away, catching the rear rail by his fingertips. His boots dragged sparks along the grating before he hauled himself up with a guttural curse.

Steel flashed in the dim glow—a short sword, the edge jagged from use. The soldier surged forward, swinging wide. Gideon barely ducked, the blade shrieking against the iron wall. The tram swayed violently, its wheels screaming around a bend. Gideon braced, driving his shoulder into the man's chest. They staggered against the rails, locked in a desperate tangle, the tunnel wall flashing past in bursts of light.

Sylas risked a glance back, eyes wide. "You planning to toss him, or have him carve you up?"

The soldier snarled, driving a knee into Gideon's ribs. Pain exploded through him, but he caught the man's wrist before the blade could land. They strained, muscles trembling, the edge hovering inches above Gideon.

With a roar, Gideon twisted, driving the soldier's hand against the rail. The sword fell loose and clattered into the dark. The man lunged again, grappling for balance as the cart pitched over a rough joint. Gideon seized the opening, heaving him backward.

The soldier clawed wildly, catching Gideon's sleeve for a heartbeat before his grip tore free. The scream that followed seemed to hollow the tunnel, a raw sound that lingered long after the man was gone. For a breath Gideon feared the worst, then caught sight of him scrambling weakly toward the platform.

"Ha!" Sylas laughed, half-shaken, half-impressed. He shouted over the roar. "I guess that answers it!"

Gideon stood there a moment longer, his breath deep and ragged, then leaned into the railing. When he finally turned to Sylas, a shaky smile crept through, as if even he couldn't believe he was still standing.

He pushed off and crossed back to the front of the tram, dropping onto the bench beside Sylas, chest still tight from the fight. The air whipped sharp against his face, the tunnel lights strobing past in flashes, as they headed toward the West Wing.

Sylas shot him a sideways grin. "Mr. Mudslide himself—I'm impressed."

"You should be," Gideon said, smirking despite himself. "I just saved your life."

Sylas snorted, jerking the lever forward. "Uh-huh. And who's driving this thing?"

Gideon leaned back, but said nothing.

Sylas shrugged, glancing over. "It's fine. You can thank me later."

Gideon drew a slow breath, unease settling through him. "We're not out of the woods yet."

"The what?" Sylas blinked.

"The woods," he repeated. "You know, the forest?"

Sylas frowned, muttering, "You're making things up again."

Gideon looked at him, momentarily lost for words. "Never mind."

The ride settled into a strained silence, each lost in his own thoughts. Gideon tried to steady his breathing, but worry for Aria clawed its way up again, sharper with every passing moment.

"I need to find Aria," he said, the words slipping out before he could stop them. His tone tightened. "Where is the tower?"

Sylas turned to him. "District. Down below. But listen—we've got to get Heidi first. She's in that filthy cell back there, with a bunch of others. We can't leave them."

"No," Gideon said, the tension in his voice returning. "I need to get to Aria."

Sylas's hands tightened on the lever. "And Heidi's in the Stratum. We can free her first. That's smarter—and faster."

The tram screamed around a bend, throwing sparks. Gideon clenched the rail, the argument grinding in him. At last, he gave a short nod. "Then we need to hurry."

Sylas let out a breath, half-laugh, half-relief. "Finally. Something we can agree on," he said, as the glow of the West Wing swelled ahead.

The tram shuddered over a joint in the track, the wheels shrieking before catching smooth again. Gideon leaned forward, bracing against the wind, when a crackle split the air. Above them, tinny loudspeakers buzzed to life.

"Attention, all residents of the Stratum," the Warden's voice rang, rich and cold, echoing off steel and stone. "An imposter has been walking among us. He wears the face of Valmere's prince, Gideon, but he is a fraud. He is armed and dangerous. He was last seen westbound on the northern line. He's in the company of a fugitive Dweller from the Districts below. They have struck at our city and must answer for their crimes. Our safety depends on their swift capture and punishment."

The broadcast ended in static, the words grinding with mechanical certainty.

Sylas cursed under his breath, knuckles tightening on the lever. "Great. Now every guard in this place will be sniffing for us."

Gideon drew himself straighter, his steel-blue eyes narrowing. "So, the Warden shows his true colors."

A new sound rose behind them—metal grinding on metal as alarms began to blare. Gideon twisted, catching sight of another tram bursting from a side tunnel, sparks flaring as it merged onto their track. Soldiers clung to its frame, lances braced, the faint shimmer of Crythium tips flickering in the dark.

"They're on us," Gideon said.

Sylas forced the railcar faster, the wheels shrieking as they rattled through the bends. The chase stretched on, rails hammering beneath them, every joint in the track rattling through their bones. Gideon turned, each flash of light throwing their pursuers into view—faces set, weapons ready, never losing ground.

"They won't fall back," Gideon muttered.

"Then we don't slow down," Sylas snapped, leaning into the lever.

A bend snapped open ahead and Gideon's chest tightened. A platform loomed, crowded with soldiers. Lances leveled in a wall of steel, their glow cutting through the gloom.

"Forward's suicide," he barked.

The track split just before the platform. One line drove straight into the blockade, the other veering into a side passage marked with hazard paint and warning sigils.

Sylas wrenched the lever. Their railcar slammed onto the spur, sending sparks flying. Shouts carried after them, sharp against the stone, before the new tunnel swallowed them whole.

The relief was short.

Gideon looked back—the pursuing tram had jolted onto the spur as well, its soldiers still clinging tight, their lances burning violet as they closed the distance.

"They're still with us," Gideon called out, breath sharp.

Sylas only growled and threw a quick look over his shoulder.

The tunnel changed as they drove deeper. Stone gave way to smooth plating, lamps glaring against whitewashed walls. Hazard stencils streaked across the archways, black and yellow warnings flashing past. The air grew dry, metallic, filled with the low hum of machines.

Sylas's jaw tightened as his eyes locked on the line ahead. "We're running out of track."

"I can see that," Gideon said, tension edging his voice.

Sylas hauled back on the lever. The tram screamed in protest, speed bleeding away as sparks spat from the rails. The end of the line rushed toward them—a sealed bay, empty of guards. The railcar shuddered, grinding nearly to a halt.

"Off!" Gideon snapped, heading for the platform.

They vaulted clear, boots striking the plated floor hard. Behind them the pursuing tram thundered closer, its soldiers shouting as their own brakes screamed against the track

"Move!" Gideon urged, already running.

They tore into the first chamber, a mechanic's bay reeking of oil and scorched metal. Chains clinked overhead while a lamp swung on its hook, casting jagged shadows that slid over them as they passed. Sylas bent mid-stride and snatched up a heavy wrench from the tools scattered underfoot.

"Finally," he said, hefting it as he ran. "Something useful."

Through a doorway at the far end of the mechanic's bay, they burst into a brighter corridor.

"Look—there," Gideon said, pointing to a tall cabinet braced against the wall.

Together they heaved from one side. The frame groaned, then toppled, crashing across the door behind them.

"That'll hold them," Sylas muttered, adjusting his grip on the wrench.

"Not for long," Gideon called out. "Keep going!"

Rows of narrow rooms opened on either side, their doors half-swung, the glow of lamps spilling across the floor. Figures inside looked up from their desks in shock—men and women hunched over ledgers, papers and inkpots scattered before them.

Then the spell broke.

A woman shrieked as chairs scraped back in panic. Another slammed a drawer shut and bolted for a side door. Papers spiraled upward as Gideon and Sylas charged past.

The cries of the clerks faded behind them as they pressed deeper. At the end of the hallway, they came upon a reinforced door surrounded by wide-eyed scientists in white coats. The door loomed massive—thick steel, long beams, a keypad glowing red. Gideon seized the handle. Locked.

"Open it," he snapped at the nearest scientist.

The man flinched, his hands trembling as he tapped the keys. The code blinked red with a sharp buzz. He tried again, faster this time, muttering under his breath. The pounding of boots drew nearer, voices rising in sharp orders.

"Hurry!" Gideon barked.

The man mistyped again, curses spilling from his lips. The guards were nearly upon them now, weapons clattering as they closed in. At last the panel flashed green.

"Inside!" Gideon said as he shoved Sylas through, dragging the scientist after him. The reinforced door hissed shut, locks clamping into place. Gideon brought the hilt of his sword down hard on the keypad, sparks spitting wildly as the mechanism cracked.

Stillness fell—then pounding. Soldiers hammered from the other side, the reinforced steel ringing with every blow.

Only then did Gideon turn, chest heaving.

Three scientists huddled near the walls, pressed against their equipment. One clutched a notebook to his chest, knuckles white, eyes fixed on Gideon. Another slid sideways along the wall, gaze darting between Gideon and the locked doors.

The chamber stretched wide, white light glaring off glass and steel. Brass gauges ticked on their housings, the faint hiss of pressurized air slipping from unseen vents. Beneath it all ran a low vibration, as though the facility itself were bracing for an unseen threat.

Gideon couldn't stop staring at the rows of reinforced enclosures lining the walls, long shadows shifting within. His breath locked in his throat.

"What... what is this place?"

The enclosures answered.

A sudden motion cut through the haze. Something inside hurled itself forward, slamming against the glass with such force the floor trembled beneath Gideon's boots. The pane boomed like a struck drum, shuddering in its frame. Gideon staggered back, hand flying to his weapon, breath catching in his throat.

His eyes caught sight of the monstrosity inside.

The creature's body unfolded in a blur of limbs—jointed too many times, each ending in claws that scraped deep lines into the reinforced pane. Its head tilted in short, jerking motions, mandibles spreading wide to reveal a maw lined with sharp spines. Within its eye sockets burned a light that should not exist, purple as molten Crythium and far too knowing for a beast.

Gideon's pulse hammered against his ribs, each throb echoing the unnatural glow of the creature's eyes burning through the glass. In Valmere, his lessons had spoken of history, of order, of kingdoms brought to heel. None of it mattered now. Confronted by the horror pressing against the pane, only one truth remained.

This was no courtly intrigue, no enemy that could be reasoned with.

This was raw hunger caged in steel.

Beside him, Sylas stood rigid, his face leeched of color, voice rough and splintered. "Screechers," he whispered, as if the word alone might summon more. His eyes did not leave the pane, and in their stillness Gideon glimpsed something else—fear rooted not in surprise, but recognition. "This is where they were dragging me."

Another impact rattled through the floor, harder than before, sending tremors up the braces and into the air itself. Gideon could taste the fear rising at the back of his throat, sharp and metallic. He fought to swallow it down, but the truth was already seared into him. The Warden hadn't simply built a prison. He had carved a sanctuary for nightmares and here they waited, testing the strength of their prison, waiting for the day it might fail.

The enormity of it struck colder than the creature's stare. They had hidden this from him—the Warden and his men, all of them with their polished words and careful smiles—while the innocent were dragged here like cattle.

He forced a breath past clenched teeth, anger cutting through the dread. It wasn't only the Screecher testing the glass. It was the lie itself pressing in on him, daring him to accept that this was balance, that this was order. The chamber reeked of deception more than science, every ticking gauge and glowing lamp a reminder of what power chose to bury rather than confront.

A tall man in a white coat stormed toward them, face taut with outrage. "You can't be in here. This is a restricted—"

Gideon cut him off, shoving him back against a console. "Save it," he growled. "What is this place?"

The man faltered, lips trembling, eyes darting to the enclosures as though the answer might be written there. Behind him, the other scientists stayed pressed to the walls, silent and pale.

Sylas's voice drew Gideon's attention. "Gideon."

He turned and saw where Sylas was staring. Not at the glass enclosures, but farther along the wall. At iron bars, black and unyielding. Behind them, faces crowded the gaps. Human faces. Gaunt, dirt-streaked, eyes wide and hollow with fear. Hands shoved through the bars, reaching as if a touch alone might drag them back into the world. Hoarse voices broke from cracked throats, not words so much as pleas, rising and falling in desperate rhythm.

"Prisoners," Sylas said flatly, his jaw tight with barely contained rage.

The word hung in the sterile air. Gideon's gaze swept over the barred cells again, the desperation etched into every face searing itself into his memory. Whatever fear had gripped him a moment before twisted deeper now, hardening into anger.

Gideon dragged the tall scientist toward the barred row, shoving him close enough to feel the heat of the prisoners' breath. "What are they doing here? Answer me."

The man blinked, sweat streaking his temple. "They're—the Warden has ordered—"

"Ordered what?" Gideon snapped.

The scientist winced, his silence speaking louder than any excuse could.

Sylas stepped closer to the cells, jaw tight, wrench still in hand. One of the prisoners gripped the bars, his voice a rasp. "Let us out... please."

Gideon looked at the lock, then at Sylas. The scientist tried to protest, but Gideon silenced him with a glare.

"Open it," Gideon said.

When the man hesitated, Gideon shoved him towards the bars. "Now."

The tall scientist swallowed hard. Then, with a jerky motion of his hand, he beckoned sharply to a younger man lingering near the wall. The subordinate hesitated, eyes darting between Gideon's blade and the barred cells, but at another impatient gesture he stumbled forward, fumbling at the keyring clipped to his belt.

From outside came a hiss, then the high-pitched whine of Crythium cutters biting into steel. Thin orange lines crawled outward from the seams, glowing hotter with every pass. Sparks spat against the floor, each burst a reminder of how little time remained.

Gideon's jaw tightened. *They're cutting their way in.*

The younger scientist's keys rattled against the lock, his hands shaking so violently he nearly dropped them. A prisoner gripped the bars, eyes sunken and wild. "Hurry," he rasped.

The lead scientist's eyes darted to Gideon, his voice cracking as he tried to protest. "Don't—don't open it. They've gone mad in there."

"Shut your mouth," the prisoner hissed through the bars. His face was gaunt, lips trembling, but the hatred in his eyes burned clear. "After what you did to us? Mary's gone because of you. You'll pay."

The man flinched, shrinking under the words, but Gideon only tightened his grip on him.

The key scraped, caught, then turned with a grinding click. The iron door creaked open and a prisoner staggered out, half falling into Sylas's arms.

There was no time to breathe. The others surged forward all at once, clawing for freedom, their gaunt faces twisted with rage and desperation.

Gideon wrenched the scientist back, dragging him clear as the tide broke over the open cell. Sylas lifted his wrench defensively, warding off the press of bodies. Then a pair of hands ripped it from his grip, the tool vanishing into the crush as others snatched for anything they could use.

The chamber erupted into chaos. Shouts, curses, and sobs merged with the crash of fists against consoles and the shriek of metal torn loose. Equipment toppled, glass shattered, and the air filled with the acrid sting of chemicals as jars and vials broke across the floor. The scientists scattered, tripping over benches in their scramble to escape, only to be pulled down or shoved aside as the prisoners seized whatever they could find to smash and destroy.

Gideon shoved the scientist ahead of him, "Sylas—this way!" he shouted, pointing toward a heavy door that led to the adjoining lab. Together they forced a path through the frenzy, prisoners shoving past them in every direction.

Then came the fire.

Gideon didn't see which prisoner had sparked it, only the sharp, sudden flare behind him. By the time he turned, it was already too late.

The sealed door gave way with a tortured groan. Sparks cascaded as the seam split wide and the Warden's men poured in, weapons flaring violet through the smoke. Their shouts collided with the roar of flames and the cries of prisoners as the chamber descended into pandemonium.

A cry cut through the madness. The senior scientist jerked against Gideon's grip, pointing with a trembling hand. "Stop him!" he shouted hoarsely.

Through the shifting haze, a prisoner wrenched down a heavy lever. Brass gears clanged, rattling like iron teeth. A deep shudder rolled through the floor, followed by a grinding rumble. Across the chamber, the reinforced enclosures shivered—then began to sink, lowering slowly into recesses in the floor.

The scientist's voice broke. "No—they're not sedated!"

Through the glass, the Screechers stirred violently, claws scraping, mandibles gnashing. Their eyes burned violet, following the widening gap above as the platform descended. Guards rushed to encircle the chamber, weapons ready, the glow casting hard light through the smoke.

For a heartbeat Gideon froze, the horror of it rooting him to the spot. In that instant the scientist tore free, vanishing into the smoke, his white coat lost in the chaos.

"Gideon!" Sylas shouted, his voice raw as another enclosure shuddered and began to descend beside the first. The creatures within slammed against the glass, their cries rising to a pitch that made the floor vibrate.

Gideon forced himself into motion.

A knot of white-coated figures darted for the side passage, shoving past overturned benches. Sylas sprinted after them, barely reaching the door in time. He wedged himself into the narrowing gap, bracing both hands against the frame as the scientists strained to pull it shut. His boots scraped across the floor, muscles trembling as the heavy panel pressed him back, inch by inch.

"Quick!" he shouted.

Gideon arrived and drove his shoulder into the door, the impact jolting it wider. Together they forced it back, opening it just enough to squeeze through.

They stumbled into the adjoining lab, wild-eyed and coughing in the smoke. Together they heaved the panel shut, the lock snapping into place with a hollow clang.

Silence pressed in, thick and heavy, broken only by the muffled roar of chaos raging in the chamber behind them. Through the seams they heard it—the faint crack of glass beginning to splinter.

Sylas leaned against the wall, chest heaving, soot smeared across his face. He pushed off again and nodded toward Gideon, his voice hard with urgency. "Let's go," he rasped. "We have to find Heidi."

Location: Cavandel, The Inner District

The shimmer of the Shatterblight seemed less fierce than before, dulled and faded in places. The breaths that came were shallow, halting—but they came. Now and again her fingers twitched faintly against Aria's hand, as if some part of her still clung stubbornly to life.

Aria leaned close, watching every tremor, every flicker of movement. The cure was doing something, she told herself; it had to be. But was it enough? Each heartbeat felt like the last, and she hated herself for not knowing whether she should stay at this bedside or head for the Stratum.

Her thoughts spun, refusing to quiet.

Heidi. Sylas. Still imprisoned, facing who knew what at the Warden's hands. Were they being questioned? Beaten? Or worse? The not-knowing pressed heavier than any certainty.

And what of Gideon? Had he returned to the surface, to his world, leaving this place—and her—behind? Would she ever see him again, or had she already slipped into memory for him?

She bowed her head, torn in two directions at once. If she left this bedside, she might never see her grandmother again. If she stayed, her friends would pay the price for her hesitation. Both roads looked like betrayal, and she had no map to help her choose.

"You'll drive yourself mad sitting like that," Pike's voice cut through the silence. He stood in the doorway, arms folded, his expression unreadable. Two of his men lingered farther back, ever watchful, their weapons at their sides.

Aria looked up, startled, but he only went on. "Get some rest. You'll need it. Same for you, Jace."

Jace stirred in his chair, dark eyes hollow with weariness. "I'll be fine."

"You'll be no use to anyone half-dead on your feet," Pike said flatly. "My men will stand watch. She won't be left alone, not for a moment."

Aria's gaze fell back to the bed, to the faint flicker of life that lingered there. It might not last. It might. She tightened her grip, whispering through clenched teeth, *"Gran..."*

She wanted to stay, to keep her hand there until morning, but Pike's was right. If she collapsed before the choice was made—whether to climb toward the Stratum or remain here—she would fail them all.

Her throat tightened.

Slowly, she lowered her grandmother's hand and drew the blanket higher across her chest. "I'll be close," she whispered. "Don't let go."

Pike stepped aside, making room for her. His men shifted in the hall, eyes sharp. The quiet murmur of their presence carried a warm reassurance. Someone would be awake, someone would be on guard.

Aria moved to her room, the narrow bed waiting there. She lay down without undressing, staring up at the dark ceiling.

Her body trembled with exhaustion, but her mind refused to still. Heidi and Sylas, trapped in the Stratum. Gideon—gone, perhaps to the surface, perhaps lost, perhaps still searching. And her grandmother...

She stayed like that for a long moment, held between fear and duty, until her exhaustion finally dragged her under.

28

Shadows in Midnight

Location: Cavandel, The Outer District

The knock drew her from sleep, steady and low against the wooden door. Aria blinked into the dim glow, her room still cast in the pale wash of the lamp. At first she thought it was a dream—then the sound came. A long metallic buzz, low and unmistakable, carried through the stone. It faded, then came again, colder the second time.

"Aria," Pike's voice came through, quiet but firm.

She swung her legs from the bed, the cool floor steadying her as she rose and pulled the door open. Pike stood at the threshold, shoulders squared as though he'd carried the night with him.

"It's time," he said, his voice taut with urgency. He gave a short nod toward her grandmother's room. "She's holding steady. Jace is with her. The men kept watch—no trouble. But this..." His chin lifted toward the unseen source of the sound.

Aria wrapped her cloak around her shoulders, relief loosening her chest even as unease pressed in again. "I need to see her," she murmured.

Pike stepped aside, silent, letting her pass.

Aria eased the door open, her eyes falling at once to the bed. Her grandmother lay beneath the quilt, her breathing steady, the shimmer beneath her skin dulled to a faint glow. Jace was slumped in a chair at her side, chin dipped to his chest, one hand close as if he had kept vigil until sleep claimed him.

Aria moved softly to his side and touched his arm. His eyes snapped open, sharp even through the weariness, then softened when he saw her.

"She's better," Aria whispered.

Jace rubbed at his face, then gave a small nod. "Aye. Stronger than she lets on."

"Thank you," she said, her voice catching more than she meant it to.

He leaned toward her, his words low. "Go on. Do what you must. I'll keep her safe."

Aria squeezed his hand in answer, then rose, letting her gaze linger on her grandmother's face one last time.

From the doorway Pike's voice reached her again, steady but edged with urgency. "We should move before the city wakes."

Aria closed the door gently behind her, the quiet of the room settling like a seal and turned to follow him.

They slipped into the street, the door closing behind them with a muted thud. Pike's men lingered at his shoulder, waiting for his word. He studied them a moment, then pointed to the first. "Stay here. See to Jace and the old woman. Get them what they need—food, medicine, supplies."

The man's jaw tightened, but he didn't argue. He murmured an acknowledgment and slipped back inside the house.

Pike turned to the other, scanning the lane once before jerking his chin toward the tunnels. "Get back to the base. Tell Sebastian the girl's safe. I'm heading for the Stratum—he'll understand."

The second man hesitated only an instant, then turned and disappeared down the alley.

Pike cast a final look at Aria and Bram before setting off down the lane. Lanterns cast pale pools of light, leaving the alleys swallowed in shadow. A chill lingered in the air, brushed by a hint of coal smoke and the murmur of distant voices. Cavandel was waking, though uneasily.

Their boots struck the worn stone in a steady rhythm, half-lost beneath the drone of the alarm.

At the rail station, a handful of citizens waited in tight clusters, their faces drawn, eyes darting upward at every fresh burst of the alarm.

The railcar screeched to a halt, metal wheels sparking faintly on the track. Guards who might normally have stood watch here were absent; only a lone pair lingered, tense but already half-turned toward the Inner District, itching to be gone.

Pike led them aboard without pause, the three settling against the side wall. The railcar jolted, then lurched forward, carrying them through the cavern's throat toward the Inner District. The ride was short, but the air inside felt close, heavy with unease.

They stepped from the railcar into a restless crowd and moved in silence as they pressed deeper into the Inner District, where the narrow lanes widened into fuller thoroughfares.

The alarm rang again, colder with each note, shivering across stone and iron. People pressed toward their doorways in tense clusters, their murmured fears running together as they hurried to get off the streets.

Two merchants hurried past, their shoulders hunched. Aria caught pieces of their muted exchange—smoke rising… fire in the Stratum… Screechers. The words tightened something low in her stomach. Pike didn't look at her, but his hand shifted near the edge of his cloak, brushing the haft of the lance he kept hidden there.

The city's glow-lights flickered weakly above, casting more shadow than light. Ahead, a column of guards forced their way through the crowd, lances slung across their shoulders, faces drawn and grim. Their boots struck in tight rhythm, urgency driving them toward the Lift. None spared more than a fleeting glance at the people they pushed past.

Aria drew her cloak tighter, her gaze following the guards until they disappeared into the turn of the street.

Closer to the Lift, the crowds thinned. The great structure loomed ahead, its chains stretching into the unseen dark above, gears still groaning from the last ascent. A pair of guards lingered at the base, stances taut, lances held upright as though sheer posture might make up for their dwindled numbers. For the first time, the way to the Stratum did not feel sealed by iron. It felt unguarded—fragile.

The three lingered in the shadow of a narrow alley, the Lift's silhouette looming ahead like a promise and a threat. Pike studied the guards posted at its base, measuring them the way a mason reads the cracks in stone. Bram leaned against the wall, arms crossed, his jaw set like a man already reckoning the cost.

The city's hum pressed around them, the alarm threading through the air in a steady, cold line.

Pike crouched against the rough stone, fingers on the haft of his hidden lance as if feeling its balance. "Two at the base," he said quietly. "Not many, but enough to raise a cry. We'd need to silence them fast. No hesitation."

"We could try blending in," Aria offered. "Merchants, officials, engineers—someone with business in the Stratum."

Pike shook his head. "Not with our faces. Our best chance is speed—quiet, before they can raise their voices. The alarm's pulling men higher. That's the gap we use."

The silence stretched, then Pike turned to her. "We're on our own from here. Remember your training."

As he spoke, her thoughts drifted to Gideon. If he was still in Cavandel—if he still had men with him—maybe they could help Sylas and Heidi. But that hope was too thin to lean on. For all she knew, he was already gone, carried back to the surface and leaving only memory behind.

She drew a breath. "Get me on the Lift. You and Bram can turn back. No reason for you to risk your lives for this."

Pike's mouth curved in a dry smile. "Ah. Our little adventurer wants to be the hero." The smile faded. "Not today, girl. I've got a score to settle—and if this is my chance, I'm taking it."

Aria turned her eyes to Bram, a silent question in them—*and you?*

He met her gaze, steady and unflinching, then gave the smallest shake of his head as if to brush off the very thought of leaving. His voice was rough but certain. "Then we quit talking and move."

They slipped from the alley, the Lift looming closer with each step, its chains creaking faintly in the cavern's hush. The alarm droned again, thin and metallic, thrumming through stone and bone alike.

Then came the sound of boots—too steady to be civilians, too close to be ignored.

"Hold," Pike murmured, his hand settling on the haft of his lance. Bram paused beside him, pulling the hammer from his back as three figures moved to block their path.

The first stepped forward, quick and sure.

Pike lifted his lance, steady as stone.

"Wait—" the stranger said sharply, drawing back a pace. He pushed back his hood, revealing hard, disciplined features.

Not a guard.

His gaze shifted to Aria, and something like recognition flickered there. "You're Aria," he said, voice low and urgent. "Prince Gideon sent us."

The other two dropped their hoods as well. "We were heading back," one added quickly. "He's waiting. We'll take you to him."

Bram's grip tightened on the haft of his hammer, suspicion burning in his eyes. He angled forward, as though daring them to take another step.

Pike's lance hovered, his eyes narrowing. "Aria," he said quietly. "You know these men?"

Aria drew a breath, pulse pounding, mouth dry. She searched their faces, her mind flashing back to the festival. "I know them. They were his companions. Gideon. He's from the surface."

The word hung there, strange even to her. Pike's eyes narrowed further, the lance still poised between them. "Surface," he repeated, the sound flat and heavy. "And you trust him?"

Aria hesitated. *Did she?* Her heart told her yes.

"I trust what I've seen," she said finally. "He made me a promise—"

"He kept that promise," the first man cut in, his voice quick and urgent. "We came back, but you were gone. That's why he sent us again." His voice dropped. "To find you."

The words struck harder than Aria expected. Gideon had come back. He had stood in the place where she should have been and found nothing. The thought hollowed her chest, leaving her wondering what his face had shown when he realized she was gone—anger, disappointment, grief. The guilt settled in, sharp and unyielding, an ache she hadn't been ready for.

But there was no time to dwell on it. She forced her thoughts back to the present—to Pike's eyes on her, to Bram's hand still tight around his hammer.

Aria straightened, her voice steadier than she felt. "I trust them. We take their help."

Pike gave a slow grunt—more warning than approval—but he lowered his lance a fraction. A dry sound escaped him, a laugh stripped of anything like humor. "More hands in the fire, then." His mouth pulled into something close to a grin, though his eyes stayed sharp.

Aria turned back to the strangers. "Can you get us past the guards?"

The tallest of the three stepped closer, his hood falling back fully. "We bear papers and the royal marks from above. We'll get you aboard."

Another spoke up quickly. "The alarm works in our favor. Most were pulled to the Stratum. Those left are too busy to question every face that passes."

As he finished, the Lift groaned above them, chains rattling as the cage descended into view. The moment was narrowing to a point.

Pike's eyes cut to Aria.

Her stomach tightened, but she forced her breath steady and met his gaze.

"I'm ready."

The words settled like iron. Pike gave the barest nod and shifted his lance back beneath his cloak. The strangers moved with quiet efficiency, drawing their cloaks tighter as the Lift's cage screeched into place.

Light spilled across the platform, revealing only two guards standing watch. Their faces were pale in the illumination, their eyes darting upward more than outward.

"Stay close," the tallest man murmured. "Walk like you belong and they won't look twice."

The gates of the Lift yawned open. Chains rattled above, the iron floor groaning under its own weight. Aria tightened her grip on her satchel and stepped forward with the others, every breath sharp in her chest.

One of Gideon's men stepped forward, cloak parting just enough to reveal the parchment in his hand. The effect was instant.

The guards stiffened, eyes darting to the mark, then to the faces of the men who bore it. One muttered under his breath, too low for her to catch, but his grip on his lance loosened all the same. The other swallowed, then stepped aside without challenge.

The strangers walked on as though the matter were settled, and Pike followed with deliberate calm. Aria fell in beside them, her pulse drumming in her ears as she passed the guards. Bram brought up the rear, his hammer resting heavy on his shoulder, his stare daring either man to so much as twitch.

The gates clanged shut behind them. Chains jolted, gears roared and the Lift lurched upward.

Location: Cavandel, The Stratum

The darkness above felt like a throat waiting to swallow them whole. For years she had passed the Lift and wondered what lay beyond its reach—the Stratum. Now it waited, not as a curiosity, but as a gauntlet.

Aria braced against the railing, her stomach tilting with the first rise. The city fell away beneath them—lanterns shrinking, rooftops flattening, alleys turning into narrow cuts of shadow. The metallic drone of the alarm echoed up through the stone, thin and relentless.

Her thoughts skittered to her grandmother asleep under Jace's watch, to the Dwellers fighting for their piece of Cavandel, to Heidi and Sylas in the Warden's grip.

Gideon's promise echoed faintly in her mind—he had come back, and she hadn't been there. The guilt still pressed sharp beneath her ribs, but she forced it aside. This was no time to mourn what might have been.

She forced her gaze outward, to the rise of Cavandel's walls as they slipped past. This was not the time for regret. Every chain, every creak of the Lift, carried her closer to the Stratum—closer to her friends. Closer to danger.

The cage groaned as it climbed into the unseen, each shudder a reminder that there was no turning back.

Pike stood steady at her side, eyes fixed upward as though he could already see what waited above. Bram leaned on his hammer, shoulders braced against the sway.

The climb stretched on, the chains groaning as if burdened with more than weight. Then, with a final lurch, the ascent slowed. The groan of gears echoed above, and the Lift jolted to a halt.

The gates clanged open.

The cavern opened into a vast, vaulted chamber—a city of brass and shadow, where light pooled like molten glass beneath iron arches that stretched far above them. Aria braced for the crash of voices, the rush of guards pouring toward them. Instead, a hollow quiet met them.

No crowd surged forward to board the Lift, no guards stood in neat ranks. The silence was wrong—thick, waiting.

The air was sour, heavy with smoke and something stranger, more bitter. It didn't take long for Aria to spot the reason. Far down one of the great thoroughfares, a dark plume uncoiled against the high ceiling like a serpent stalking prey.

Was that the reason for the alarm?

Finally, she tore her gaze from the haze above and took in the city itself.

The Stratum stretched wide before them, its avenues glowing faintly beneath bright lamps as buildings of tiered iron and glass rose on all sides—graceful yet imposing. Their rounded façades and domed towers spiraled upward, each level laced with balconies and framed by arched supports.

The entire district unfolded in layered walkways and bridges that crossed a vast concourse lined with amber light. Every pane of glass caught the glow, scattering it across polished rails that curved through the streets like drawn filigree.

A few trams sat idle at their stations, their lamps burning pale gold through the drifting mist. A faint, wavering hum threaded through the quiet—an echo of the alarm moving through the Stratum like a held breath. The air carried it in subtle tremors, mingling with the sound of hurried footsteps. The whole district seemed to breathe with that strained, uneasy rhythm.

One of Gideon's men murmured under his breath, "Where is everyone?"

Another pointed to the distance, where faint shouts carried through the haze. The noise was scattered, urgent, but not near.

Pike shifted his lance beneath his cloak, eyes sharp on every shadow.

Aria stepped from the massive cage, her pulse pounding harder than before. The quiet was worse than open confrontation; at least then she would know where the danger stood. Here, it could come from anywhere.

Heidi. Sylas.

She held their names in her mind like anchors, steadying herself. This was why she had come.

One of Gideon's men adjusted his cloak, scanning the gray-streaked avenue. "He's waiting," he said, voice low. "Let's go."

The others gave short nods, already moving.

The avenue stretched wide and hollow before them, lined with high façades that vanished into smoke. Their footsteps rang too loud against the stone, every echo carrying farther than Aria liked.

Then the air shivered with sound. The Warden's voice, magnified and cold, rolled through the arches above.

"Attention, all residents of the Stratum. An imposter has been walking among us. He wears the face of Valmere's prince, Gideon, but he is a fraud...."

Aria's chest tightened at the Warden's words. She had never seen the Stratum, never walked its broad stone and metal avenues, but the words settled like weight in her ribs. The announcement echoed on, spilling down side streets and bouncing from the high walls until they seemed to come from every direction.

Gideon's men froze as if struck.

One stopped so abruptly that Bram nearly shouldered into him. Their faces turned up toward the arches, confusion sharp in their eyes.

"What—?" one breathed. "Imposter?"

The other shook his head, muttering as though to himself. "No. No, this is wrong." His hand twitched toward the fold of his cloak, as if bracing for a fight that hadn't yet found them.

They glanced at each other, then back down the avenue toward the Administrative Hall. Their focus slid from Aria entirely, urgency etched into every line of them. One stepped forward, his movement sharp, near to breaking into a run. "We need to get back. Now. If they've moved against him—"

The others didn't hesitate. They set a hard pace down the avenue, moving as one, strides even. Pike and Bram fell in without a word, matching their pace.

Aria hurried along, her breath tight in her chest. Her thoughts spun too fast to hold steady. Gideon's name still echoed above them, bound to that single word—*imposter.*

The Warden's voice had carried it through every arch, branding him a fraud, a danger, a lie. She had trusted him—hadn't she? For a heartbeat, doubt lanced through her. Had he deceived her from the start? The man who had sparred with her in the chaos of Founder's Day, who had promised to come back for her—was he only a mask?

She pulled closer to the nearest soldier, her voice cutting through the footfall. "Wait—what was that back there? What are they saying about him?"

The man didn't look at her. "We don't know," he grumbled. "Not yet."

"Then slow down and tell me," she snapped. "What's going on?"

Another soldier glanced back. "We have to get back to the prince."

Aria blinked. "The what?"

The third man turned, urgency flashing in his eyes. "Gideon. The prince of Valmere. He's in danger. The Warden's turned on him."

She'd heard the word before, back at the Lift, but it still carried no meaning. *Prince.* It echoed in her mind with a strange, foreign weight. What she understood however, was the Warden's cruelty—and that was enough.

They broke into a run, veering off the main thoroughfare and into a side lane flanked by tiered walkways and shuttered shops. The lamps above them were dimmer here, as if the light itself were bracing for what lay ahead. Somewhere far off, another announcement rose through the smoke-hazed air, the Warden's voice repeating the lie like a curse etched into stone.

***

Gideon and Sylas had escaped the Research facility amid chaos, forcing their way toward the southern rail line. The fire had spread faster than either expected, licking through the rafters as prisoners fled in every direction—some with weapons torn from fallen guards, others half-mad with terror.

The rail ahead had been overrun with guards, leaving them no choice but to continue on foot. Eventually, they reached the waste management sector, dense with tunnels and machinery. It offered just enough cover for two fugitives to vanish, and the stench kept most others away.

The tunnels were narrow, damp and foul with the reek of old runoff. Pipes rattled overhead, dripping at irregular intervals. The metal floor beneath their boots was slick with mud, sloshing faintly as they moved through shallow puddles. Every sound carried like a warning through the dark—the ring of boots, the distant scrape of metal—each one setting their nerves on edge, daring them to breathe louder. Gideon pressed close to the wall, the sweat on his neck chilled by the current of stale air. Sylas kept pace beside him, flinching at every noise that broke the stillness.

For a time, neither spoke. The tunnel pressed in around them, broken only by the hiss of vents and the faint buzz of maintenance lights. Their glow was weak and uneven, throwing strips of pale color across the damp walls. Shadows shifted with each flicker, bending over the surface like restless shapes.

Somewhere beyond, a clang of shifting metal echoed—heavy and close, the kind that made thoughts louder than breath.

Sylas coughed, batting at the sour air that clung to the tunnel like rot. "This place smells like something died, got buried, then came back for revenge."

"Keep your voice down," Gideon murmured, glancing ahead.

"My voice *is* down," Sylas whispered. "And besides, it's not like anyone else is stupid enough to be down here."

"Speak for yourself," Gideon said evenly.

"Oh, I am," Sylas shot back. "You're just too proud to admit how well you fit in."

Gideon grimaced, more in resignation than annoyance. "Mind your footing," he cautioned. "This isn't the time for amusement."

Sylas's grin lingered as they pressed deeper. "You know," he drawled, pausing as if searching for the right words, "has anyone ever told you you worry too much—"

He took another step—and vanished into a pit of sludge. A wet crash rang down the tunnel, followed by sputtering and a string of muffled curses. When he surfaced, slick to the chest in muck, his eyes were wide with disbelief.

Gideon was at his side in an instant, gripping his arm and hauling him free of the pit. The sludge clung thick, dragging at every movement until Sylas collapsed onto the grated floor, landing on all fours.

He stayed there a moment, head bowed, chest heaving.

"You hurt?" Gideon asked, scanning him quickly.

Sylas shook his head, spitting to the side. "Who put that hole there?"

Gideon exhaled, the tension in his shoulders easing. "Good. I'd hate to lose you to poor footing and a puddle of refuse."

Sylas glared up at him, dripping, hair plastered to his face. "Go on, get it out of your system."

Gideon's brow lifted. "...What?"

"You're dying to call me Mr. Mudslide—aren't you?"

Gideon huffed a quiet breath that might've been a laugh. "And I was just starting to like that name."

Sylas pushed himself upright, muttering under his breath as he wrung out a sleeve. Sludge streaked the metal floor, thick and dark, hissing faintly where it touched the vents. He sighed in frustration as he wiped a hand across his face, only spreading the filth further. "Brilliant."

Gideon's mouth twitched.

Sylas was halfway through another retort when a faint metallic clatter echoed up the corridor—a vent shifting, or boots on steel. Both men went still.

"What was that?" Sylas whispered.

The sound came again, sharper this time, followed by a low murmur.

Gideon's brief smile vanished. He tilted his head, listening. "Voices."

"Guards?" Sylas asked, voice low.

"Not sure," Gideon murmured.

The sounds drifted closer—faint chatter and the rhythmic clang of metal on metal. They pressed against the tunnel wall as two figures rounded a bend ahead, their lamps throwing pale light through the haze. One carried a coil of line over his shoulder, the other a tool crate that rattled with every step. Their uniforms were streaked with oil and ash, faces drawn and tired. *Maintenance workers.*

One of them knelt by the piping, running a hand along the line. "If we can just bypass the regulator valve, that should hold till we replace it."

"What would cause it to overheat like that?" the other muttered.

"Looks like the intake's clogged," his partner replied, crouching beside a junction. "We'll have to go in and check it."

"Figures," the first said with a sigh. "But what in the pits could have done that?"

The words faded as they moved on, their lamps shrinking into the distance.

Sylas let out a quiet breath. "Not guards, at least."

"Keep moving," Gideon said softly. "Before they double back."

They slipped past the echo of footsteps, following the tunnel until it widened into a large maintenance hub where several runoff lines converged. Steam hissed from vents overhead, veiling the air in thin threads of mist. Glow-lights cast a weak violet glow over the standing water pooled across the floor.

A ladder rose from the far wall, bolted beside a rusted inspection sign. Gideon tested the first rung—it shuddered but held.

"Up," Gideon murmured.

The metal groaned under their weight as they climbed. The hum of the tunnels dimmed beneath them, replaced by the slow, distant pulse of machinery—the deep mechanical cadence of the processing sector above.

The ladder carried them upward through a narrow shaft, the air growing warmer with each rung.

Gideon slowed near the top, one hand braced on a rung as he peered through the slatted grate above. The light filtering down was brighter, steadier, tinged with amber from the maintenance lamps. The floor beyond was still—no movement, no sign of workers.

"Anything?" Sylas whispered.

Gideon shook his head slightly. "Hard to tell. It's quieter than it should be."

He lifted the grate with care, the hinges creaking against the frame. The sound seemed far too loud in the silence. A moment later, he climbed through.

The Waste Management complex stretched around them—rows of tall filtration tanks and catwalks crisscrossed by steam lines. A haze hung in the air, lit by the amber glow of the overhead lamps. Somewhere deeper in the facility, a warning bell pulsed once, then again, hollow and distant.

Sylas climbed up beside him, wiping sweat and grime from his forehead. "Well," he muttered, "at least it's an improvement."

"Barely," Gideon said, scanning the shadows ahead.

They stood for a moment, letting their eyes adjust to the amber light. The space felt wrong—too still, too warm.

Sylas studied the catwalks stretching in every direction. "Where are we?"

Gideon took a slow breath. "Lost."

Sylas frowned. "That's reassuring."

He moved ahead a few paces, squinting through the haze. A rusted sign hung from a nearby column, its letters faded, and streaked with grime. *North Hall*, it read, the arrow pointing toward a dark corridor ahead.

"Look at this," Sylas called, pointing to the sign.

Gideon followed his gaze, tracing the direction in his mind. "If that's north, then east should be this way." He turned toward a narrow walkway that vanished between rows of filtration tanks.

"East?" Sylas echoed. "That where Heidi is?"

"Yes. The infirmary's east of here," Gideon said, then glanced down the corridor. "If we move quickly, we can reach it before the guards regroup. Let's just hope they're still busy with those—whatever those things are."

He started down the narrow walkway, the metal creaking softly beneath his boots. Sylas followed close behind, the steady hum of machinery filling the space between them.

Rows of filtration tanks flanked the path, their glass panels clouded from within. A few pulsed faintly with light, the flow inside sluggish and uneven. Others were dark, their gauges frozen in place.

They followed the walkway deeper into the maze. The rhythmic hum of the chamber faltered at times, replaced by faint shudders that trembled through the metal underfoot. Steam hissed from overhead vents, mixing with the low pulse of the alarm.

Gideon slowed as they turned another corner. A length of piping ahead had been split open, the edges peeled outward like torn fabric. The metal still glistened, damp with runoff that trickled across the floor in thin rivulets.

They moved on, slower now, their footsteps muffled against the grated floor. The air thickened—hot, metallic. A faint chitter echoed through the ducts above, high-pitched and fleeting. Sylas froze.

"Tell me that was a vent," he whispered.

Gideon didn't answer. The sound came again, closer this time, scraping along the steel. A second later, something heavy shifted in the shadows ahead.

The light caught it for only an instant—slick scales, limbs splayed low, eyes like shards of amethyst burning in the dark.

"Run," Gideon said.

The creature lunged from the steam, its shriek splitting the air. Gideon shoved Sylas aside as claws raked across the walkway where he'd stood. Metal screamed, sparks bursting as the Screecher's limbs struck the rail.

Sylas hit the floor hard, then scrambled to his feet, heart hammering.

"Move!" Gideon barked, drawing his sword. The Crythium edge flared to life, casting violet arches across the narrow passage.

The creature hissed, shrinking from the glow before lunging again. Gideon swung low, the blade connecting with a sharp crack. One of its forelimbs snapped backward, but the thing barely faltered.

It screeched, the sound reverberating through the entire level. Gideon knew others would hear it—human or otherwise. He stepped back, keeping the sword between them.

"Go!" he shouted.

Sylas hesitated only long enough to see Gideon drive the Screecher back before turning and sprinting down the corridor. The walkway shuddered under the creature's weight as it struck again, claws tearing into the rails.

Gideon pivoted with the blow, using the momentum to drive it back a step. Its hide gleamed where the blade had scored it—a shallow wound that smoked but did little else. The thing's strength was monstrous; each strike rattled the walkway beneath them.

He swung, but the Screecher twisted, hurling him against the wall. The shock drove the air from his lungs. He dropped low as a claw swept past, gouging a line through the steel behind him.

The lights wavered above as Gideon raised the blade defensively, forcing himself to focus. The creature moved unlike anything he'd faced—too fast, too deliberate, its body coiling low like a serpent before it struck again.

He feinted left, then cut right, glancing a blow across one of its eyes. The creature reared, shrieking, the sound clawing through his skull.

His vision swam.

Then came the rush of heat.

The Screecher's next strike slammed into a pipe along the wall. Pressure gave way with a metallic crack as a jet of steam exploded between them.

The blast hurled Gideon backward.

He hit the floor hard, shoulder skidding across wet metal. The Screecher took the brunt of it—its carapace hissing as scalding vapor engulfed it. The creature shrieked, thrashing against the rails, blinded by steam.

Gideon forced himself up, lungs burning. His sword lay several feet away, the violet light flickering across the haze. He crawled for it, fingers closing around the hilt just as the Screecher began to move again.

"Gideon!" a voice called.

He looked up to see Sylas at the far end of the corridor, the door half open. "Hurry!"

The creature turned toward the voice, its movements jerky, skin blistered where the steam had struck it. Gideon ran. Each step sent pain through his side, but he didn't slow. The Screecher roared behind him, dragging itself forward, claws raking sparks from the floor.

Sylas reached through the gap and grabbed his arm, hauling him in as Gideon stumbled through the doorway. They slammed the door shut and dropped the locking bar into place. A heartbeat later, the frame shuddered as the creature crashed into the other side.

Steam curled from Gideon's coat as he leaned back against the wall, catching his breath.

Sylas's voice broke the silence, low and tight. "It's still in there."

The door shook again—one final, frustrated strike—then went still.

They exchanged a look—the kind that didn't need words—and started down the adjoining corridor.

They hadn't gone twenty paces before the sound of boots echoed from ahead. Two workers appeared through the haze.

"Hold it—who are—" one began.

"Screecher," Gideon cut in sharply, keeping his head down while pointing behind them. "Through those doors."

Color drained from the men's faces. They spun with muttered curses and bolted back the way they'd come, shouting warnings as they fled.

Sylas exhaled, dragging a hand down his face. "That was too close."

"We're almost there," Gideon said, his voice steady.

Ahead, the faint echo of retreating workers faded in the distance—shouts growing dim, then gone. Behind them, through the thick metal door, came a soft scrape... then another, heavier, like claws testing the f rame.

Neither man looked back.

29

Light Eternal

Location: Cavandel, The Stratum

The talk of Screechers had spread faster than smoke; it moved through the Stratum in broken whispers, bending the flow of people toward the housing complex.

Guards stood at intersections, their armor bright beneath the lamps but their discipline frayed. They barked half-hearted orders, too distracted by the rumours to notice shadows slipping between columns and railcars. One kept glancing toward the vaulted ceiling as if expecting something to tear through it; another argued with a merchant about closing the transit lines.

From where Aria watched, the exchange reached her only in fragments.

"Not up to me," the guard grumbled, voice thinned by strain. "You hear the alarm. Curfew's in place until further notice. Warden's orders."

Through this confusion Aria's group moved unseen, weaving along the outer platforms. Steam vented from the rails in pale ribbons, cloaking them in warmth and shadow. The hum of the Lift faded behind them, replaced by the eerie silence and the quiet thrum of unspoken fears.

As they pressed northward, the grand concourse narrowed into administrative lanes where the architecture grew more deliberate—arched windows latticed in iron, and doorways embossed with Valmere's crest.

They turned down a quieter avenue. The air here felt different—still heavy with heat, but no longer carrying the oppressive weight that clung to the Lift. Buildings rose in stately rows, their windows trimmed with brass and glass, catching the lamplight like burnished coin.

Somewhere above, the Warden's announcement replayed through the loudspeakers—Gideon's name carried again through the halls, branded with that single word.

Imposter.

The sound had thinned to a distant echo, yet it lingered in every corner, stirring unease in the few residents who still moved between the buildings.

"This way," one of Gideon's men whispered, motioning them toward a structure set apart from the rest—a tall edifice of dark stone and glass, its upper levels shrouded in steam.

They advanced in silence, keeping close to the shadows. The outer walkway of the Administrative Hall lay deserted except for two guards stationed near the archway, their lances burning a dull violet that cast a faint glow across their tired eyes. Beyond them, the corridor opened into deeper shadow.

Aria and the others halted just short of the light, breaths held, bodies angled low against the columns. For a moment, nothing moved but the slow coil of steam curling from a nearby vent. They edged closer, moving as one until the darkness swallowed them whole.

Silence.

Without warning, the guards were yanked backward into the shadows. A brief struggle followed—the muted clash of armor, the scrape of metal against stone—and then nothing. The corridor stilled once more, the violet light flickering faintly where the lances had fallen.

When the quiet settled, Pike and Bram slipped from the gloom where the guards had stood. Pike adjusted his cloak, his gaze sweeping the entry before he gave a low murmur. "Clear."

The others emerged behind him, their movements swift and wordless as they slipped through the archway and into the corridor beyond.

The interior was colder than the avenues outside. The lamps along the walls glowed low, leaving more darkness than light. One of the men moved ahead, checking corners, before giving a small nod. "Clear."

They passed down a short hall and stopped before a set of broad iron doors inlaid with gold trim. The nameplate bore no title, only Valmere's sigil etched into the metal. Up close, the barrier felt even more imposing, its polished surface catching the faint light that seeped from the gap below.

One of Gideon's men reached for the handle, hesitated, then eased it open just enough for the scent of parchment and oil to drift through.

Inside, the air was still and faintly perfumed. The lamps glowed at half-light, casting a soft amber wash across a space both austere and refined. A writing desk stood near the window, orderly save for a few open folios and a quill resting mid-sentence in its inkwell. A trace of warmth lingered near the hearth, where a kettle sat untouched beside a teacup that had long since cooled. Aria's gaze moved across the room—the folded cloak on the back of the chair, the travel trunk near the wall, the precision of everything.

Gideon had left deliberately, not in flight but in purpose. Nothing here spoke of panic, only absence.

"Your Highness?" one of the soldiers called, barely above a whisper. The quiet held. He checked the adjoining door, swept behind the curtain, then gave a single shake of his head. "Empty."

Another soldier glanced toward the desk and the folded cloak. "But his things are here. He wouldn't have gone far."

Pike's eyes shifted to the travel trunk near the wall, then to the door. "You heard the broadcast. West, on the north line."

The men exchanged a look that settled into duty. "Then that's our heading."

Bram remained stationed near the door, scratching his beard. "But can we trust the Warden?"

Aria said nothing. Her reflection wavered in the glass panes of the cabinet beside him, the faint shimmer of the light making her seem half part of the room's stillness.

She felt the weight of Gideon's presence here—disciplined, restrained, yet restless beneath the polish. She stood a moment longer, the room's quiet order pressing against the ache in her chest. "I need to find Heidi and Sylas," she said at last. The words were not loud, only certain.

"Our charge is the prince," one of the soldiers replied, not unkind but resolute.

Aria's gaze lingered on the quill resting in its inkwell, a faint glimmer of light tracing its edge. She only nodded.

"Then thank you," she said softly. "For getting us this far."

Her words settled into the stillness of the chamber, unforced and genuine. For a moment, the soldiers seemed uncertain how to answer—unused to gratitude in a place where orders usually came sharp and cold. One gave a brief incline of his head, and another shifted his stance, as if reminded that there were still manners left in the world.

Pike broke the quiet. "Do you know where the stockade is?" His voice was measured, not demanding. "Where they keep the prisoners?"

The nearest soldier frowned. "Not exactly. The Warden keeps those locations tight." He hesitated before adding, "But we've heard it's somewhere to the west."

Another man nodded, relief flickering behind his eyes as though certainty—any certainty—was a comfort. "That's the same direction."

Pike studied them for a moment, weighing what little they knew. "Then west it is."

Bram adjusted his grip on the hammer, then slung it across his back, silent agreement in the motion. Aria glanced toward the door, and for a fleeting instant she thought of Heidi's quick laugh, of Sylas trying to mask his fear with bravado. Her throat tightened.

She turned back to the others, ready to speak, but a faint noise cut through the quiet. The soft click of a heel against marble—hesitant, out of rhythm—followed by the shuffle of papers.

Pike lifted a hand for silence. The sound came again, closer this time—someone moving just beyond the threshold.

A second shuffle followed, the faint tap of a pen against metal. Then, from the hallway beyond, a voice muttered to itself. "Of course. Of course they'd wander off. Can't possibly stay where they're posted for five whole minutes, can they?"

The room stilled. Weapons rose.

There was a pause, then a sigh of exasperation.

A light knock followed. "Gentlemen? If you're inside, you'd better have a *very* good reason!"

Silence.

The voice returned, sharper now. "Gentlemen, I will remind you this post is active until further notice. The Warden expects accountability, not tea breaks."

The silence that answered only seemed to sharpen his irritation. "No discipline," he muttered under his breath. "None at all. Can't leave a corridor for five minutes without someone losing their—" He stopped. "This is far too much stress for my condition."

The door eased open. "Right, I'm coming in, and if I find either of you napping, you'll be reporting to Mr. Grask by morning—"

A narrow figure stepped through the door and froze, clutching the clipboard to his chest like a shield. His coat hung several sizes too large, the sleeves nearly swallowing his hands. His eyes—pale and quick behind small lenses—swept the room once before landing on the weapons trained toward him.

"Oh," he breathed, irritation folding swiftly into alarm. "This is... not ideal."

"Looking for someone?" Pike's voice came low, his grin thin and dangerous.

The man blinked, words tangling. "You're not the guards."

Pike's voice stayed level, edged with something predatory. "So it would seem."

The man swallowed hard, adjusting his grip on the clipboard as though it might save him. "Right. Good. Or rather—not good, obviously, but at least that's clarified."

"Who are you?" Pike asked quietly.

The man hesitated, eyes darting to the others in the room—Bram's steady stance, the soldiers' unreadable faces—before returning to Pike. "Nibs," he managed. "Assistant to the Warden. Though really, associate assistant, technically speaking, if we're—ah—being precise."

Nibs stayed rigid in the doorway, the clipboard trembling faintly against his chest.

No one spoke.

Pike let the silence stretch until the man began to fidget.

"You work for the Warden," Pike said. It wasn't a question.

Nibs nodded quickly. "Yes. Well—yes. Administrative support, mostly. Documentation, reports, the occasional scheduling oversight. Not that the Warden would, of course—but if he did, hypothetically speaking, I'd be the one to make note of it."

Bram arched an eyebrow, closing the door behind the man with calm finality. "You're saying you know what's going on out there."

"I know... am aware of... some things." Nibs's gaze darted from the floor to the door behind him, his head turning just enough to gauge the distance, as if weighing how quickly he could reach it.

Pike took a measured step closer. "Then start with this—where's the prince?"

"The prince?" Nibs blinked rapidly. "Handsome, yes—very handsome—but, ah, difficult question. Unfortunately, we can't—well, I can't help you with that just yet." He cleared his throat, his voice shrinking to a thin nervous rasp. "The prince is... missing."

One of Gideon's men stepped forward, his hand tightening around his lance. "What do you mean, missing? The broadcast calls him an imposter."

The others murmured, unease threading through their ranks.

Nibs flinched at the accusation, eyes darting toward Pike as if seeking permission to speak. Pike gave a single, measured nod.

Nibs hesitated, then stammered, "There was… a disagreement. Between them. A falling out, you might say. The Warden didn't appreciate how involved the prince had become in matters that were—well, not his jurisdiction, strictly speaking. Things escalated. Rather quickly."

Bram's brow furrowed. "So the Warden turned on him?"

"I wouldn't say *turned*, exactly," Nibs said quickly. "More like… adjusted his stance. Reclassified the nature of the relationship. Temporarily. I'm sure it'll all be sorted once they—ah—speak again."

Nibs's voice trailed off, his nervous optimism hanging in the air like smoke.

No one spoke for a moment. The soldiers glanced between one another, their unease shifting into restless purpose. One adjusted his grip on his weapon; another took a step toward the door.

Pike's hand lifted slightly, a wordless signal to hold. His gaze remained fixed on Nibs. "And the alarms," he said evenly. "What's that about?"

Nibs blinked, caught off guard by the question. "Oh—the alarms! No, no, that's—well, that's an entirely different disaster." He tried to laugh, failed, and cleared his throat instead. "Separate matter altogether. The fires, you see, and the—ah—containment breach."

From behind Nibs, Bram frowned. "Containment breach?"

Nibs nodded quickly. "Yes—the Rocknids."

The word hung in the air.

Every sound in the room seemed to vanish beneath it. The soft hum of the lamps, the faint tick of metal cooling in the hearth—all drowned beneath that single name. Pike's expression hardened, the sharpness in his eyes cutting through the dim light. Beside the door, Bram went still, his hand tightening on the haft of his hammer.

Aria felt the blood drain from her face. For an instant, she was back in the tunnels—the hiss of steam, the gleam of chitin in the dark, the shriek that could splinter thought itself. Her stomach turned. "No," she murmured. "Not here."

One of Gideon's men looked between them, confusion furrowing his brow.

Pike's voice came quiet but sharp. "What do you mean, Rocknids? There are no Screechers up here."

Nibs adjusted his clipboard, fingers slick with sweat. "Well—normally, no. Of course not. But the research facility—ah—had a few specimens. Contained, naturally." His words tripped faster, thinning with fear. "There was a fire. The prisoners escaped. And the Rocknids... that's all we know so far."

At the word *prisoners*, something in Aria snapped into focus.

Heidi. Sylas.

"Where's this place—the research facility," she cut in, her voice breaking through Nibs's nervous stream. "Where are the prisoners?"

Nibs startled, blinking rapidly as though she'd spoken too loudly for the room. "Ah—well, that depends, doesn't it?" He shuffled his feet, eyes darting between them.

"On what?" Aria pressed, her patience thinning.

"Capacity," he stammered, then paused, as if the single word explained everything.

Pike's tone dropped, quiet but edged. "Keep talking."

"Well—the Stockade," Nibs blurted, adjusting his spectacles with a shaky hand. "With overflow in the infirmary and the research center. Well... no longer the research center, I suppose, considering the recent events."

Aria's pulse hammered in her ears. "We have to go. Now."

"Not if we don't know where we're going," Pike said. He turned to Nibs. "How do we get there?"

Nibs blinked. "I—I don't understand—"

"The Stockade, the infirmary, the research center," Pike said, his voice low but unyielding. "How do we get to them?"

Nibs swallowed hard. "The—ah—the infirmary's not far from here. The Stockade and the research facility are both in the West Wing."

Gideon's men exchanged brief looks. One spoke, his tone clipped with resolve. "That's where the prince is. Let's move."

The three turned for the door, purpose hardening their steps.

Aria collapsed her lance with a snap and stepped closer to Nibs, her gaze cutting through him. "The infirmary," she said. "You said it's close."

Nibs blinked, startled by her sudden focus. "Yes—just east of here."

"How do we find it?" Aria pressed.

"You'll—You'll see the medical insignia above the arch."

One of the soldiers paused at the threshold. "We'll find the prince," he said, glancing back at Pike and Aria.

Pike gave a single nod.

The man returned it and disappeared through the doorway. The other two followed without a word, their footsteps fading down the corridor—steady, controlled, carrying purpose like armor.

When the silence settled, Pike turned to Bram. "Take her to the Infirmary. Find her friends."

Bram frowned. "You're not coming?"

"I'll meet you soon enough," Pike said. His voice was calm, but there was something colder beneath it, a weight that made Bram hesitate.

Aria glanced at Nibs, then back at Pike, searching his face. "We should stick together. What are you planning?"

Pike's reply was measured. "What we did in the Abyss. We've been waiting a long time for this." Then, softer, "Go."

She hesitated, the words striking deeper than she wanted them to. *The Abyss.* She remembered the heat, the shriek of stone on metal, the blur of movement and claws closing in around them. The Alpha had risen from the dark—massive, unyielding—and Pike had struck it down without hesitation. When it fell, the others had scattered.

Her breath caught. He wasn't talking about the Rocknids. He was going after the Alpha again.

Drazic.

She opened her mouth, but Pike had already turned away, his resolve ending the conversation before it began. Something flickered behind his eyes—an old heat, the kind that lingered long after the flames were gone.

Nibs lingered near the desk, glancing nervously toward the door. "You're not—ah—you're not going to kill me, are you?"

Pike regarded him for a long moment. "That depends."

Nibs swallowed hard. "On what?"

"On how useful you're willing to be." Pike stepped closer, his presence quiet but suffocating. "You know where Drazic is?"

The name alone made Nibs flinch. "Drazic? Mr. Grask? Why—he's probably with the Warden or in his chambers?"

Pike's expression didn't shift, but the silence that followed was heavy enough to make Nibs shrink back a step.

"Find him," Pike said at last, his voice almost a whisper.

The words lingered in the air like a promise.

Aria hesitated at the doorway, hearing the edge in his tone. She didn't ask what he meant—she already knew.

Bram's hand brushed her shoulder. "Come on."

She turned away, the sound of her boots joining his as they stepped into the hall. The light dimmed behind them, the door closing on Pike and Nibs—one man trembling, the other perfectly still.

The corridor stretched ahead, its lamps dimmed to a low, unsteady glow. Aria quickened her pace, the echo of Pike's last words following her like a shadow.

They exited the building and headed east down the thoroughfare, keeping to the deeper pockets of darkness. The air grew warmer as they moved, the noise of distant alarms dulling to a faint pulse beneath their steps. Then the Warden's message rang out again, threading through the quiet.

Steam curled from vents along the walls, carrying the scent of metal and ash. After several turns, the streets narrowed into a quieter lane lined with slate-tiled façades. Ahead, a carved symbol caught the light—a mortar and pestle encircled by a sprig of crushed herbs.

"The infirmary," Bram murmured.

Aria's pulse quickened. "Let's move."

Bram nodded, unhooking his hammer with a low scrape of metal on leather. Aria thumbed the hidden catch near her weapon's handle. The lance extended with a soft hiss, Crythium filaments breathing to life along its edge until it glimmered faintly in the half-dark. She steadied the weight in her hands—familiar, balanced, quiet.

Together they stepped through the doorway, swallowed by the dim glow within. The air changed immediately—thick with the scent of antiseptic and something faintly burnt. Their shadows stretched long across the tile as they advanced, every sound measured, every movement controlled.

The corridor opened into a maze of narrow wards and treatment alcoves. Glow-lamps cast a pale, sterile hue across tiled floors and metal frames. A sharp undertone of sickness clung to the space, settling against the back of Aria's throat.

A handful of physicians still worked among the cots—thin figures in pale coats, sleeves rolled to the elbow, their faces drawn tight with exhaustion. Their aides moved quietly between patients, tending to those who groaned or murmured in fevered half-sleep.

Conversation faltered as Aria and Bram entered. The sight of armed strangers in worn, dust-streaked clothes drew wary glances. One of the aides froze mid-step, clutching a tray of instruments. A physician murmured something to her in warning, then looked to Aria with measured caution.

"We're not here to harm anyone," Aria said softly.

No one replied, but the workers edged aside, clearing a path through the ward. A patient coughed, breaking the stillness.

Aria slowed beside one of the cots, her gaze sweeping the ward. "Where are the prisoners kept?" she asked.

The question hung there. A few of the aides exchanged uneasy glances; one of the physicians stiffened, his hands tightening around a vial.

Aria took a small step forward.

That seemed to break something in the room. The physician looked toward the far end of the hall—toward the reinforced doors where the light dimmed to a pale blue haze. His silence was answer enough.

Aria gave a short nod of thanks and moved on. Bram followed, his hammer held low at his side. Behind them, the aides resumed their quiet work, though none of them dared look up again.

The corridor narrowed into a holding wing lined with cells on either side. Each was fronted by a wall of iron bars, the spaces between them filled with cold light and shadow. A strip of glow-lights ran the length of the ceiling, their pale hue cutting the air into narrow bands that flickered faintly against the floor.

Figures shifted behind the metal—prisoners, some standing, others hunched on narrow bunks, their faces half-lit and hollow. None spoke. The only sounds were the hum of the conduits and the faint scrape of metal as someone stirred in their cell.

A single figure sat slouched in a chair, blocking the way.

Ponytail.

He leaned back with one shoulder against the wall, knife tracing lazy circles along the armrest. His mismatched gloves—one black, one brown—moved with unhurried precision, his lance propped within easy reach.

Aria stopped just inside the threshold, her voice low but firm. "Where are they?"

For a heartbeat, Ponytail didn't move. Then the knife stilled, the metal catching the ceiling light as he turned toward them.

"Well, isn't this a treat," he said, his tone dripping with satisfaction.

"Didn't think I'd see you again—so soon."

Bram shifted beside her, the faint scrape of his boot echoing down the corridor.

"We're not here for you," Aria said evenly. "Open the cells."

He laughed, low and sharp.

Aria's grip tightened on the lance. "Step aside. Final warning."

Ponytail leaned back, the grin still on his face. Then, with unhurried confidence, he slid the knife into its sheath and reached for the lance beside the chair. The weapon came alive with a low hum, its violet glow spilling across the floor in fractured bands.

"Still haven't learned, have you?," he murmured, leveling the tip toward them. "Let's fix that."

Bram lifted his hammer, shoulders squaring. "Bad idea," he grunted.

Ponytail tilted his head. "We'll see."

Then the hum sharpened, the glow brightened—and he moved.

The violet light rippled against the bars as Ponytail advanced, the hum of his lance swelling into a low snarl. Sparks danced across the blade when it grazed the floor, faint trails of heat marking his path.

Bram shifted to intercept, planting his boots wide, hammer angled low. The guard swung first—fast, precise, his weapon carving a streak of light through the narrow hall. Bram caught the blow on the haft of his hammer; metal clanged, the sound ringing off the walls. He shoved back hard, forcing the man a half-step off balance.

The prisoners startled at the commotion, shadows stirring behind the bars.

Aria darted in from the side, her lance whistling through the air. She moved differently—tight, economical. Her strike caught the guard's weapon near the base, the Crythium edges flaring where they met. The energy discharge washed the corridor in a brief, blinding pulse of blue and violet.

Ponytail twisted away, agile despite his size and swept the lance across in a wide arc that forced them both back. "Come on, then," he taunted, laughing.

"Two against one? Don't embarrass yourselves."

Bram swung again, a heavy downward blow. Ponytail parried, the impact shuddering through the metal floor. Aria slipped past his guard, her weapon sliding in low; he caught it on the shaft, turned it aside and tried to jab at her ribs. She pivoted, the motion smooth as water, letting the tip scrape harmlessly past.

The fight moved down the corridor in bursts of light and echo—steel striking steel, boots grinding on tile. Prisoners pressed closer to the bars, their faces ghosted by the shifting glow, eyes wide and silent.

Bram grunted as the next exchange locked the two weapons together. Sparks spat from the Crythium blade, showering over his shoulder. Aria circled, her lance lowered. As the guard shoved Bram back, she stepped in and drove the butt of her weapon into his knee. The impact cracked through the air.

Ponytail staggered with a hiss of pain. He swung wildly in retaliation, his strike glancing off the wall and carving a blackened line through the paint. Aria ducked under, rose and swept her lance across his, knocking the weapon hard to the side. The clash rang down the corridor, leaving his guard wide open.

Bram stepped in and swung. Ponytail lifted his lance just in time to block, but the hammer's impact cracked through the air. The force hurled him backward; he slammed against the bars with a harsh gasp and dropped in a heap, the lance still clutched weakly in his hand.

For a moment, only the hum of the overhead lights remained.

Bram exhaled through his teeth. "Get the keys," he said, voice low. "He'll be out for a while."

Aria crouched beside the fallen guard, searching his belt until her fingers brushed the ring of keys.

Behind her, Bram adjusted his grip on the hammer, eyes still fixed on the unconscious man. He bent to pick up the fallen lance. "Won't be needing this anymore," he muttered.

Aria rose, the keys cold in her hand. "Let's hurry then."

She rushed to the first cell. "Heidi? Sylas? You in here?" Her voice carried low but urgent, echoing down the row of bars.

The prisoners stirred, then surged forward—hands reaching through the gaps, voices rising all at once. Pleas overlapped in frantic cries for release, for mercy, for anyone who would listen.

Aria stepped back, heart pounding, scanning the faces—none she knew.

Then, from somewhere near the last cell, came a disbelieving whisper. "Aria?"

She froze. The voice cut through the noise like a thread drawn taut.

"Heidi," she breathed, already moving.

The clamor of the others dimmed behind her as she hurried down the row, fingers trailing the bars until she reached the last cell. A shape shifted in the gloom—someone pushing upright, unsteady on her feet. When the light caught her face, Aria's chest constricted.

"Heidi," she said again, steadier this time.

Heidi blinked, as if her eyes couldn't quite trust what they were seeing. Then her breath hitched, and she stumbled forward, gripping the bars. "Aria? You're—how did you—"

"Not now," Aria said quickly, lifting the key ring with trembling fingers. "It's all right. Where's Sylas?"

Heidi's mouth opened, but no answer came—only a small, helpless shake of her head.

The lock clicked, and the sound seemed to fill the hall. Before Aria could pull the gate wide, the corridor erupted. The prisoners surged forward, spilling through the open cell, their footsteps pounding against the tile as they ran past—some weeping, some silent, all desperate for air and light.

Aria hardly noticed. She stepped through the doorway and caught Heidi as she stumbled into her arms. For a long moment neither of them moved, the chaos around them fading into a dull, distant roar.

When she finally pulled back, Aria's gaze swept over her—bruised, pale, trembling. "Are you hurt?"

Heidi shook her head, breath uneven. "They took him," she whispered. "Sylas. I don't know where."

Aria's throat tightened. She cupped Heidi's face, forcing her to meet her eyes. "We'll find him," she said, the words quiet but unshakable. "I promise."

A rustle from the back of the cell drew her attention. Hogan stood there, half in shadow, broad but seeming smaller than she remembered, his hands clenched at his sides. His eyes darted between them—nervous, pleading, ashamed.

For a moment, Aria said nothing.

Then she stepped aside, letting the corridor light fall across his features—broad and heavy, yet somehow shrunken beneath the weight of everything he'd done. "If you're coming," she said, "let's go."

Hogan hesitated, then nodded once and stepped forward.

Aria turned back to Heidi. "Stay close."

Behind her, Bram was already moving, working the other locks one by one. Gates slid open and more prisoners spilled out, some too stunned to move, others bolting for the corridor. When he reached the end, he dragged Ponytail's limp form from where he lay slumped and dumped him into the now-empty cell. The clang of the door rang out with quiet finality.

"That should hold him," Bram muttered, sliding the key into his belt.

Aria nodded, steadying Heidi against her shoulder. The faint wail of alarms carried from somewhere deeper in the infirmary—a reminder that their time was bleeding away.

"Let's move," she said.

They turned toward the exit, the released prisoners scattering ahead like shadows breaking apart, leaving only the four of them—Aria, Bram, Heidi and Hogan—moving fast into the narrow corridors beyond.

***

The constant drone of alarms pulsed in the distance—low, rhythmic, the heartbeat of a city bleeding in its own light.

The metal duct rattled faintly under their weight as they crawled forward, elbows scraping against the narrow walls. Every few feet, a seam hissed where the pipes met, venting faint warmth with the treated air.

Sylas paused at a slotted panel ahead, pressing his eye to the gap. Below them lay a wide chamber—the infirmary ward.

They had slipped out of the waste management sector hours ago—soaked, hunted, and half-blind from the smoke. Since then, they'd crawled through maintenance tunnels, crossed the underbelly of the administrative wing, and kept to the places where the city's light couldn't reach. Every turn had been a gamble—patrols moving in pairs, weary-eyed workers drifting between shifts, too many eyes that might still recognize the prince.

By the time they'd found the utility shaft behind the infirmary, exhaustion had dulled everything but instinct. The climb carried them upward through a web of pipes and vents until they finally reached the narrow duct above the ward.

Sylas shifted beside Gideon, his breath rough. His clothes—already worn thin from the mines—were now little more than rags, heavy with the stench of wastewater. His hair hung in tangled clumps, his skin streaked gray with soot and grit. Every movement left a faint smear along the metal.

Gideon wasn't much better. The fine fabric of his coat was torn at the sleeves and frayed at the hem, the once-deep blue now dulled to ash. The silver embroidery along the collar was blackened, the last traces of Valmere's grace buried beneath dust. Sweat had carved pale lines through the grime on his face, and his eyes—tired yet sharp—caught the glow from below like shards of glass.

They hadn't spoken in some time, but the silence between them felt different now—less distrust, more endurance shared.

Sylas exhaled sharply. "Dead end," he whispered.

Gideon leaned past him, checking the obstruction. "No way through."

His gaze dropped to the vent panel below, where faint blue light leaked through the seams. "Then we go down," he said, voice low.

Sylas followed his eyes, hesitating. "Into the ward?" he whispered.

Below, physicians moved among the cots, their voices low and steady, unaware of the two men crouched above them.

"Unless you see another way."

He didn't.

Sylas leaned close. "I know this place," he whispered. "They brought me through here. The holding cells are a few corridors down."

They both listened—the hum of the lights, the quiet murmur of physicians below, and no sign of guards.

Gideon tested the panel with one hand; the metal flexed but held. "Thin sheet," he murmured. "Two supports across the middle. We hit center, it'll give."

Sylas wiped a smear of grime from his brow. "You sure this is a good idea?"

"It's not," Gideon answered, "but it's the best we've got."

They repositioned themselves, bracing against the narrow walls. The duct groaned softly under their weight.

"On three," Gideon whispered.

Sylas nodded. "One."

"Two."

"Three."

***

The corridors ahead were washed in pale blue light, the hum steady and low. Aria moved at the front with Heidi close beside her. Bram guarded the rear, while Hogan lingered somewhere between them, his eyes darting at every sound.

The faint echo of alarms pulsed through the ducts above, distant but constant, a rhythm that seemed to chase them from behind.

Heidi stumbled once, and Aria caught her by the arm, steadying her before she could fall.

"I can walk," Heidi murmured.

Aria didn't let go. "I know."

They slowed as the hall opened into the infirmary ward—the same one they'd passed earlier, though now something in the air felt altered. The physicians moved between the beds with a kind of hushed resignation, their motions tighter, more restrained.

Rows of patients lay beneath the light, their skin pale in the steady hue. Some slept fitfully; others stared blankly at the ceiling, their breaths shallow. The scent of medicine mingled with something more human—fear, fatigue, the quiet decay of those waiting for relief that never came.

Aria's gaze swept across them, catching the faint shimmer of lesions along one man's neck—the familiar pattern of Shatterblight. Another patient's hands trembled as he tried to lift a cup of water, the motion weak and uneven.

It struck her then, sharper than she expected—the Stratum was not untouched. The sickness that ravaged the Districts below had climbed even here, into the place she once believed untouchable. The gleaming towers, the ordered streets—she'd always thought them certain, perfect. But disease cared nothing for boundaries or wealth.

It had found them too.

Her hand tightened unconsciously around Heidi's.

"The cure," she said softly. "We can help them—all of them."

For the first time since they'd entered the Stratum, she felt something cut through the fear and exhaustion. Pity.

Bram gestured ahead, drawing her attention back to the corridor. "We should keep moving," he said quietly.

Aria nodded, though her eyes lingered a heartbeat longer on the rows of beds before she turned away.

Then came the sound.

A metallic groan rolled through the ward.

Aria's head snapped up as the metal above them split apart.

Two figures crashed through the ceiling in a rain of fractured paneling and dust. The glow-lights flickered wildly, throwing the ward into stuttering bursts of brightness and shadow. Patients cried out, some scrambling from their beds as debris clattered across the floor.

Aria threw an arm over Heidi, shielding her from the falling fragments.

When the air began to settle, she looked across the room. A man was already on his feet, sword drawn, his face streaked with ash and grime. Behind him, another figure pushed up from the floor, dripping, filthy, his hair matted and his clothes torn beyond recognition.

Aria blinked, disbelief freezing her where she stood.

"Gideon...?"

He turned toward her voice, eyes widening, exhaustion breaking beneath recognition. "Aria?"

Sylas froze mid-motion, his head snapping toward the sound. "Heidi! Aria!"

The noise in the room fell away. For a moment, none of them moved—their eyes locked across the pale, ruined ward, the distance between them filled with everything they had survived to reach this place.

Then Sylas moved—crossing the space in long, uneven strides, shock giving way to something deeper. "You're here," he breathed, half a laugh, half a tremor.

Aria and Heidi caught him in a fierce embrace, the kind that left no room for words. He was soaked through, reeking faintly of metal and sewage, his shirt torn and stiff with grime—but they didn't care. He was alive.

When they finally pulled apart, Sylas still held Aria's shoulders as if afraid she'd vanish. "We thought—"

"I know." Her voice was rough. "So did I."

Heidi leaned closer, sniffing him. "What happened to you? You smell awful."

Sylas let out a tired laugh. "Don't want to talk about it."

Gideon approached more slowly, sword at his side. He looked older somehow, the grime and exhaustion deepening the edges of his face. The silver trim of his coat was scorched black, the color leeched from the fabric. Yet even in ruin, there was something unyielding in the way he carried himself.

"You're safe," he said, almost to himself.

Aria nodded, still catching her breath. "For now."

He followed her gaze to the others—Heidi, pale but standing; Bram behind her, hammer in hand; Hogan hovering uncertainly in the background.

Then Sylas saw him and froze.

His expression hardened, disbelief flashing into anger. "You," he spat. "You almost got us killed!"

He took a step forward, but Aria caught his arm. "Not now, Sylas."

He strained against her grip, eyes locked on Hogan. "He got us into this—"

"I know," she said sharply. "And we'll deal with it later. Right now, we've got bigger problems."

Heidi stepped between them, voice low but steady. "She's right."

Hogan said nothing. His hands twitched at his sides, guilt flickering across his face like a shadow he couldn't shake.

The silence that followed was taut, brittle.

Then Bram's voice cut through it. "We need to move. This place'll be swarming before long."

Aria nodded, the moment slipping from stillness back into urgency.

30
Beneath the Ashes

Location: Cavandel, The Stratum

They stepped out into the lane, where the air sagged under its own weight and the light struggled to push through it. The haze had deepened since they'd entered the infirmary, creeping in from the western sector like a slow-moving tide. The usual hum of trams and machinery had withered to a distant murmur, swallowed by the smoke. Each breath carried the sting of grit and a metallic trace of copper.

A sudden screech shattered the muffled quiet—raw, sharp, and far too close. The sound cut through the haze and ricocheted along the stone before breaking off, leaving the air quivering in its wake.

Hogan yelped and stumbled back, his heel catching on the uneven ground. He went down hard, the clatter rolling down the laneways. The group swung toward him—an instinctive mix of alarm and exasperation.

"What was that?" Hogan hissed, his voice unsteady. He peered toward the west, searching the haze as if expecting something to push through it.

Sylas drew a slow breath through his teeth. "Not so brave now, are you?"

Bram moved past him, reached down, and hauled Hogan upright, steadying him with a firm grip. "Easy," he murmured. "You're in over your head."

They shifted their attention toward the western lanes, where the haze trembled but held its secrets. The silence that followed was thick and expectant.

"That was one of them, wasn't it?" Sylas whispered, edging closer to Gideon.

No one answered.

Two figures hurried past them out of the haze—a man clutching the hand of a younger woman—their faces pale, eyes wide with the kind of fear that needed no explanation. Neither looked back as they bolted toward the housing complex.

Then silence again.

Only drifting smoke and the faint rattle of something distant, carried on the tremor of unseen movement.

More shapes emerged—half a dozen prisoners who'd fled the infirmary. They moved in a tight, disoriented cluster, scanning the lanes like trapped animals desperate for a way through.

Aria pointed south, where the haze thinned toward the transit lines. "Head for the central platform," she said. "Follow the rail until you see the gate lights. That'll take you back to the Lift. Keep to the alleys and move fast—don't stop for anything."

She turned to Hogan. He was pale and trembling, dirt and sweat streaking down his face like guilt made visible. "Go with them," she said quietly. "Stick together. Stay out of the open."

Hogan blinked, uncertain. "They won't let us on."

Aria's gaze moved over the small group—their torn clothes, their hollow eyes. Then she reached into her belt pouch. "This should cover all of you," she said, pressing it into his hand. The weight of Grottos clinked softly inside.

He stared down at it, throat working. "Aria..." His voice caught, rough and low. "I'm sorry."

She held his gaze for a moment, then nodded once. "Then don't waste it."

He hesitated only a breath before turning to the others. Together they slipped into the smoke, their footsteps fading toward the south until the haze swallowed them whole.

Gideon's gaze stayed on the dark arches ahead. "We got away once," he said quietly. "Don't want to face those things again. Keep moving."

The words hung for an instant before sinking into the muffled hum around them. Aria pressed the crook of her arm to her face, her steps slowing as they pushed through the haze. The Stratum felt smaller now, its vastness lost to the shifting gray. The lights above burned weakly, reduced to trembling halos that turned distance into guesswork.

Gideon slowed halfway down the incline, his gaze fixed on the shadowed arches ahead where faint voices drifted—guards, or perhaps only echoes. When he finally spoke, his voice was low and deliberate.

"We need to get to the surface," he said. "My father must know what's taking place down here."

Aria's steps faltered at the word. *Surface.* It cut through the haze like something she'd only ever dared to imagine. Hearing it now—spoken not as myth but destination—sent a strange current through her chest, a mix of hope and disbelief and something sharper than both. But as quickly as it rose, the feeling fractured.

Gideon scanned the lane ahead, listening to the muted hum buried in the air. He started forward without waiting for agreement. Bram followed, steady and wordless, while Heidi and Sylas exchanged a look balanced between doubt and exhaustion before trailing after. Aria lingered for a moment, her eyes drawn to the faint outline of the infirmary before she turned and followed the others into the gloom.

They moved through the lane in silence, following the gentle curve of the rail line until it widened into the Ascender concourse. The emptiness struck first. No guards at their posts, no operators at the terminals, no voices cutting through the stillness. The chamber stretched upward into shadow, the great platform suspended in quiet, the ceiling lost beyond the glow-lamps.

"Quickly," Gideon said, already moving. His voice carried a sharp edge, urgency wrapped in control. They followed—Bram, then Sylas, and Heidi with Aria close behind—their footsteps echoing across the steel floor.

"Get on," he ordered, breaking away toward the console. The others climbed aboard, the grating shifting faintly under their weight. Gideon's hands moved across the controls, tracing the arrangement of levers and switches as he tried to recall the sequence he had seen attendants use before. "It's this one... then the release," he murmured under his breath.

Aria gripped the railing, her heart tightening in her chest. Was this it? Was she finally going to see the surface, everything she had only imagined through her grandmother's stories? Or was it a trap, an illusion of escape before the Warden's men appeared to drag them back? She searched the shadows for movement, but nothing stirred.

A click broke the silence, then another. Gideon's motions grew quicker, his focus sharpening with frustration. Still, the platform didn't move.

Sylas frowned. "What's going on? It's not moving," he whispered.

"I'm doing everything right," Gideon said, his voice tight. "But it's not turning on."

Heidi stepped off the platform and hurried to the console. Her eyes moved quickly over the gauges and conduits. "Hold on," she murmured, brushing past him. A few seconds later she stepped back, her expression darkening. "He's right. No power. The Warden must have shut off the feed."

Then a low crackle filled the air, followed by the clipped hum of the loudspeakers. The Warden's voice unfurled through the haze—measured, almost gentle, the way it always was before he issued an order.

"Attention, residents of the Stratum," the voice intoned. "The fires in the West Wing have been contained. The western rail is closed until further notice. All residents are to remain indoors until inspection teams confirm safety in your sector. Anyone found outside will be detained. The fugitives responsible for tonight's disruption remain at large. City guards are to resume search operations immediately."

The message looped once, then cut out, leaving the chamber steeped in its own echo.

Bram turned toward the open lane, the distant haze shifting in the light. "Can't stay out here," he said, his voice clipped. "If the guards return, we won't have a way out."

Gideon stood at the console, one hand braced on the metal as if willing the machinery to respond. The dim light caught the edge of his profile—anger, frustration, a faint tremor of exhaustion beneath both.

Aria stepped down from the platform and crossed to him. "Gideon," she said quietly. He didn't look up at first, his focus fixed on the lifeless gauges. "We'll find another way," she went on. "But standing here isn't it."

His hand slipped from the console, fingers curling at his side. The silence pressed in, heavy with the realization that he was waiting again—for orders, for rescue, for his father's approval. He had come here to prove he was ready for responsibility and now he was standing in the ashes of a city his people had helped bury. What kind of prince waited for someone else to fix what was broken?

Gideon's jaw tightened, the weight of Aria's words pressing harder than she intended. *We'll find another way.* He wanted to believe her, but something in him rebelled at the thought. Another way to run. Another way to survive. Was that all he'd done since stepping into this place?

Her words lingered in the quiet and for a moment all he could hear was the faint hum of air somewhere deep in the walls. He could still see her from that night in the square—the lanterns, the laughter, the way she'd looked at him when he'd spoken of hope. *You work, you survive, you pretend it's enough.*

He had thought her cynical then, someone hardened by the darkness around her. Now he understood she had only been honest. The truth of Cavandel wasn't in its speeches or its machinery; it was in the people who refused to stop moving, even when there was nowhere left to go.

He straightened slowly, the exhaustion still there but reshaped into purpose. No more waiting. No more running. This was his kingdom too, and he was done watching it fall apart.

For a long moment, no one spoke. The smoke drifted lazily across the concourse, thin threads curling around the motionless platform. Gideon stood near the console, his hands at his sides, his expression distant but no longer uncertain. When he turned, the hesitation that had shadowed him since his arrival was gone.

Sylas noticed first. "You've got that look again," he said quietly. "The kind that usually means we're about to do something stupid."

Gideon's gaze shifted toward the archway leading to the Administrative Hall. The shadows there seemed to breathe. "If Thaddeus wants control of this city," he said, "he can answer for it face to face."

Heidi's eyes narrowed slightly, measuring him. "You think he'll just let us walk in there?"

"I think he's forgotten his place," Gideon replied.

Bram said nothing, but the way he adjusted his hammer was answer enough.

Sylas gave a nervous laugh. "So what's the plan? We barge in, kick down his door, arrest him, and tell Cavandel the Warden is finished?"

Gideon did not smile. He drew his sword from its scabbard, the Crythium edge bleeding a faint purple through the haze.

"Something like that," he said, his voice cold and low.

Aria hadn't moved. She watched him in the half-light, the change in him as tangible as the quiet around them. When he finally met her eyes, she said nothing. She didn't have to.

He turned toward the walkway, pausing once beside the dormant platform. "Come on," he said, almost to himself. "I'm done running."

They followed him into the haze, their footsteps fading through the arch. Behind them, the Ascender remained still—an empty promise left in the dark.

Somewhere in the distance, a low tremor rolled through the earth, faint but steady. The sound deepened, a shudder that seemed to move with the smoke itself. Aria glanced toward the western tunnels, where the haze was thickest. For a moment she thought she saw movement—something skittering across the far beams, too fast for the eye to catch.

No one else seemed to notice.

Bram moved first, the soft scrape of his boots breaking the stillness as he fell in behind. Heidi adjusted the strap of her pack and followed without a word. Sylas hesitated only a heartbeat before letting out a quiet breath and stepping after them.

Aria lingered where she was, her gaze fixed on Gideon. The change in him was subtle but undeniable—something steadier in his stride, a resolve that reached past the weariness in his shoulders. For the first time, she believed he might not only survive this place but change it.

Her hand found the switch on her lance, the faint hum rising as the Crythium tip came to life. Pale light cut through the dim air, meeting the faint violet of Gideon's blade. Two narrow flames against the dark.

Then she followed, her steps quickening until their rhythm became one.

Behind them, from the west, the sound came again—closer this time.

***

The corridor outside Drazic's quarters was quiet, the light from the glow-lamps pulsing in uneven intervals. Steam drifted from a ruptured pipe, clouding the air with the scent of oil and rust. He stopped at the door, one gloved hand hovering. For a moment he simply stood there. The night had stretched too long—reports, patrols, the fire, the Warden's tirade over the comms. His reflection in the metal panel looked older than it had that morning.

He nudged the door open and stepped inside.

The room greeted him with low light and silence. His armor rack gleamed faintly against the far wall, tools laid out in rigid rows. A lance leaned against the table, still flecked with soot from the earlier patrol. Drazic shut the door and unfastened his breastplate, setting it aside with the care of habit.

"Long night," a voice murmured from the darkness.

He froze. The sound came from the corner where the light didn't reach.

His hand dropped to the hilt of his sword, the motion slow and deliberate. He knew that voice immediately.

Pike.

"So," Drazic muttered, his tone sharpening. "You've finally come."

"I said I would," Pike answered from the dark.

"You always were predictable."

"Not as predictable as you," Pike replied. "Still hiding behind a title and a uniform."

Drazic's jaw tightened. "You talk like you've changed, Pike. But I know what you are." His voice carried the edge of old disdain, honed by years of resentment. "Just another thief, taking what was never meant for you."

"She didn't think so," Pike said calmly. "She made a choice."

Drazic gave a low, humorless laugh. "And she suffered for it." He searched the shadows, eyes narrowing as if the dark itself might move. "You think I don't remember why you ran? You couldn't live with what you did. Neither of us could."

The room seemed to contract around the silence that followed.

"What I did?" Pike's voice rose, sharp and sudden, breaking through the quiet like a blade through glass.

The room went still again, fragile, as if even the walls were listening.

"We're both to blame," Drazic said finally. His voice lowered, almost thoughtful. "Scarlet—"

"Don't you dare say her name again," Pike growled. His voice cut through the dark like steel drawn across stone. For a heartbeat, only the hiss of the lamps answered.

Drazic's expression shifted, caught somewhere between anger and disbelief. His grip tightened on the hilt of his weapon, knuckles whitening. "You think I wanted that fire, Pike?" he said, the words rough, almost defensive.

"I think you needed it," Pike said. "To do what you couldn't. Because she didn't choose you."

Drazic scoffed. "And you're here to punish me for it?"

The reply came low and menacing. "I already did."

The words landed like a closing door. A faint smile touched Drazic's mouth, bitter and knowing. Instinctively, his hand rose to the deep scar along his face—the one Pike had placed there.

For an instant, neither moved. Then Pike stepped forward, the light from the wall catching the edge of his blade. "Just finishing what I started," he said, his voice low and rough.

Drazic's hand dropped to the hilt at his side. The sword came free with a whisper of steel, its Crythium edge burning a cold blue against the walls.

"Then let's finish it," he said.

He struck first, quick and deliberate, the blade sweeping through the narrow space. Pike slipped aside, the motion smooth as shadow. The second blow came harder—he caught it with his dagger, the clang ringing through the room like a struck bell. Sparks scattered across the floor.

Drazic pressed forward, using his reach, each swing an assertion of strength. Pike gave ground, weaving between the strikes, letting them glance off the table's edge or cut through empty air. He waited for rhythm—a flaw, a pattern—and found it.

When Drazic raised the sword for a downward strike, Pike stepped inside it. The movement was small, efficient. His shoulder drove into Drazic's chest, turning his own momentum against him. Drazic stumbled, colliding with the side of the table.

He staggered back, teeth bared, anger overtaking control. He swung again, wild, catching the edge of Pike's coat. The blade hissed through fabric.

"You always did run your mouth before losing," Pike said, his tone flat.

Drazic growled and lunged, the sword cutting low. Pike leapt back, catching the blow with his dagger, but the impact jarred his wrist. The weapon slipped from his grip, clattering to the ground.

For a heartbeat, Drazic's grin returned.

Pike didn't hesitate. He reached behind, grabbing his lance. The Crythium tip flared to life, casting a violet glow that met that of Drazic's sword.

The room filled with color and sound, their weapons clashing in bursts of light that danced across the walls. Each strike drove them closer to the door until, with a final clash, Drazic shoved back and broke free into the corridor.

Pike steadied himself, breath measured, then followed. The echoes of pursuit carried down the hall as the two disappeared into the corridor beyond.

The lights overhead flickered, stretching Drazic's shadow in broken fragments as he ran. Behind him, there was only the sound of pursuit—steady, unhurried, the rhythm of a hunter who knew precisely how this would play ou t.

"Keep running, Drazic," Pike's voice echoed down the hall, calm and cold. "You've been doing it your whole life."

Drazic's jaw clenched, but he didn't slow. He cut down a side passage, past the narrow maintenance rooms, and shouldered through another hatch. Cold air hit him, sharp with the stench of oil and refuse. He'd reached the outer walkway—the waste overpass that slanted down toward the District below.

The space opened wide and uneven, half metal, half ruin. The grated path angled dangerously toward the void, slick with grime and scattered waste—scraps of twisted piping, torn fabric, and fragments of shattered crates that had caught on the railings instead of falling clean through. Beyond that barrier, the drop stretched far into the haze.

Below, the District glimmered faintly through the smoke, its glow diffused by drifting dust. The trash that didn't make the fall lay piled along the slope, a jagged river of debris that disappeared into the darkness. The hum of the Stratum's machinery vibrated through the metal underfoot, steady and low, as though the city itself were breathing.

A gust swept past, carrying the thin smell of rot and the faint clang of something tumbling down the incline. Drazic steadied himself, his boots slipping slightly on the slick surface.

Pike followed, his footsteps measured and deliberate. The glow of his weapon met the cold blue of Drazic's sword, two lights drifting closer across the fog.

Drazic stopped near the railing, his breathing rough. He turned, sword raised, the light painting half his scarred face in steel and shadow.

"This is where it ends, Drazic," Pike called out, his voice calm, the sound almost lost in the wind.

"Not yet," Drazic answered.

From the far end of the walkway came the sound of boots—two guards rushing into view, drawn by the noise. Drazic's mouth curved faintly. Then he laughed, deep and guttural.

Pike's grip tightened on the lance, but he didn't move.

Drazic's smile widened, thin and deliberate. "Show him what happens to those who cross me."

The guards charged, their Crythium lances flaring to life, blue light cutting through the fog. Pike shifted his stance, the violet glow of his own weapon spilling into theirs until the air between them shimmered with fractured color.

The first blow came fast and low. Pike pivoted, catching it with a downward sweep that sent sparks scattering across the grating. The second guard was already closing in; Pike twisted, parried, and struck back in the same motion. The clang of metal reverberated through the walkway, swallowed by the wind and distance.

They circled him—measured, disciplined. Pike's breathing slowed, his movements honed and deliberate, each step placed with the precision of someone who had survived too many fights in too little space. He let them press, deflecting strike after strike, letting their rhythm betray them.

The first guard lunged again. Pike dropped low, deflecting the strike, then rose sharply, using his shoulder to drive the man off balance. The other came from behind, Crythium edge flashing; Pike spun, parried, and forced him back with a short, efficient strike.

"This ends tonight, Drazic," he called out, his voice steady and sure. "One way or another."

For the first time, Drazic's smile faltered. His grip tightened around the hilt of his sword, knuckles whitening beneath the haze. "You should've stayed buried," he muttered.

The guards regrouped, panting, the blue light of their weapons flickering against the haze. Pike exhaled, his breath slow and measured, though fatigue had begun to pull at his arms. His stance held, but his shoulders burned from the repetition.

He needed to end it—quick.

Another clash of light and metal. Sparks scattered like fireflies, the sound filling the hollow air. Pike met a strike, twisted the lance from one guard's hands, and used the man's own forward momentum to drive his shoulder into him. The guard stumbled, hit the railing hard, and went over.

His cry echoed down into the chasm, ending in the muted crash of debris below. Pike glanced over the edge just long enough to see him caught in the slope of refuse and pipes along the wall.

"That the best you can offer, Drazic?" he called over, his voice steady despite the burn in his lungs. "You're running out of bodies to hide behind."

Drazic watched from a few paces back, sword lowered but ready, eyes narrowing as the faint light caught the edge of his scar.

Pike turned back, the second guard already advancing. Their lances met again in a blur of light and motion. The guard pressed hard, but his strikes were slowing—less precision, more panic. Pike ducked beneath a thrust and swept the man's legs out from under him. The guard hit the grating hard, rolled, and came up swinging, desperation replacing discipline.

Pike caught the blow with his lance and shoved him back, his teeth clenched. "Should've stayed down," he muttered.

The two locked for an instant, Crythium flaring where their weapons crossed. Pike drove forward, forcing the guard to stumble, his boots scraping against the slick metal.

Breathing heavy now, Pike stepped in. The next strike was clean, decisive. The guard barely caught it on his weapon, his arms trembling from the impact.

Pike didn't give him another chance.

He moved in.

A hiss split the air. Something coiled around his ankle.

Pike glanced down just as Scarlet tightened, locking his foot against the grating with a snap. The handle gleamed in Drazic's hand.

"Still fast," Drazic said, voice low, "but not fast enough."

Pike twisted, trying to pull free, but the whip held firm. The guard closed in again, his movements renewed with confidence. The first strike came high; Pike caught the blow on his lance, then blocked another, the effort dragging at his balance. Every shift of his weight sent the whip biting deeper against his boot.

Drazic watched, calm and composed, Scarlet coiled in his grip like a living thing. "She's missed you," he said. "Always did have a mind of her own."

Pike ducked under another swing, brought his lance up, and drove the guard back a step—but his footing slipped on the slick grating. The guard saw it and pressed hard, slamming Pike's weapon aside.

The impact jarred through Pike's arms. His back hit the railing, metal biting into his spine. Sparks danced in the fog as the guard's next strike came down. Pike caught it at the last instant, locking the lances together, the glowing tips quivering inches from his chest.

The guard leaned in, sweat streaking down his temple. "End of the line, rat."

Pike's gaze flicked toward Drazic, who stood watching with cold amusement. "You talk too much," he rasped.

He twisted his wrist, breaking the guard's lock just long enough to shove him away—but the whip yanked him back off balance.

Pike's muscles burned with the effort of staying upright. Every movement pulled against the whip, its coils biting deeper, each vibration running up through his leg. He knew he couldn't last much longer like this.

The guard pressed forward again, the Crythium edge flashing. Pike caught the strike and shoved it aside, but his balance was failing, his weight anchored by Scarlet's pull. His mind raced.

He could keep fighting and lose, or free himself and gamble everything on one opening.

Another blow came down. Pike ducked under it, let the motion carry him into a crouch, and with a quick, brutal twist he reached for the whip. The leather burned his palm as he tore at it, yanking hard until the coil slipped from his boot. Pain shot through his leg, but the tension snapped.

Scarlet came loose.

Drazic's expression changed, a flicker of surprise breaking his composure. Pike seized the moment. He yanked the whip's loose end hard, ripping the handle out of Drazic's grip, and flung it across the grating. It clattered against the walkway, the coils twisting lifeless in the mist.

For a heartbeat, Pike was free.

Then the guard lunged.

The first blow forced him down to one knee. The next he barely caught, the Crythium lances locking together in a shower of sparks. Drazic stepped in now, his sword gleaming in the haze.

Pike's arms trembled under the weight of the guard's weapon pressing down on him. Metal shrieked, the noise cutting through the fog. His footing slipped again, his knees striking the grating as he tried to hold him off.

The guard snarled, driving his weapon lower. Drazic stepped closer, slow and deliberate.

"Look at you," he murmured, his voice calm, even. "On your knees again. Right where you belong."

He leaned close, his tone measured, deliberate, cruel.

"I'm glad she burned," he said softly, the words trembling with quiet fury. "Better that than watch her waste herself on you."

For a moment, the world went still. The clang of the fight, the hum of machinery below—everything receded. Pike's grip slackened on the lance, not from weakness but from the weight of the words. He stared at the grating, his jaw tightening until the muscle in his cheek twitched.

When he finally spoke, his voice was low and dangerous. "We're finally on the same page," he growled.

Pike moved.

The shift was sudden. He twisted, catching the guard's weapon and driving it aside. The blade scraped across the railing in a burst of sparks. Before the man could recover, Pike slammed the butt of his lance into his chest, sending him sprawling backward.

Then Pike rose.

The look in his eyes had changed—no fury, no shouting, just a quiet, deadly focus.

The guard lay where he'd fallen, breath ragged, eyes wide. He looked at Pike, then at Drazic. Whatever loyalty had bound him broke in that instant. Without a word, he scrambled to his feet, seized his weapon, and ran—boots clanging across the walkway until the sound was swallowed by the fog.

Pike didn't watch him go. The quiet that followed was heavier than before, the kind that pressed against the skin. Only the low hum of the machinery below remained, faint and endless.

Drazic stared after the guard, disbelief flickering in his eyes before settling into contempt. "Coward," he muttered. His gaze snapped back to Pike. "You're a disease. You know that? Everyone you touch ends up running, bleeding, or burning."

Pike said nothing. His lance hung loosely at his side, its glow dimming in the fog.

Drazic began to pace, his sword still drawn, voice tightening. "You think this means anything? I've rebuilt everything you've ever tried to break."

Pike's eyes didn't leave him. "You've built nothing. You've just buried it deeper."

That stopped Drazic. He turned, the faint light catching his scar, the anger behind it finally visible. "You think you're better, don't you? That's why you left me with nothing. You and her both."

"She made her choice," Pike said quietly.

"And you took her from me!" Drazic's voice cracked, raw and human now. He stepped closer, the sword trembling in his grip. "You think she loved you? She pitied you. You were her cause—something to fix before she outgrew it."

Pike didn't flinch. "At least she never feared me."

That landed. Drazic froze. His lips parted as if to speak, but nothing came. Then his expression twisted—anger, grief, something between the two. He raised the sword again, but his hand shook.

"You don't get to talk about us like that," he whispered. "You don't get to say her name."

"I haven't," Pike said. "You're the one who can't stop."

Drazic laughed—a hoarse, broken sound that barely held together. "She's still here—I can hear her."

Pike's expression didn't change, but his fingers tightened on the lance. "That's not her you're hearing," he said flatly. "That's your guilt talking."

Drazic's eyes darted toward the whip lying where Pike had thrown it. His breath quickened. "She's still mine," he murmured. "She'll always be."

The sound of footsteps echoed faintly from the corridor behind them. Aria and the others appeared at the far end, weapons raised, their silhouettes blurred by haze and light. They didn't speak.

Drazic didn't seem to notice them. His focus was fixed on the whip, lying coiled in the mist like something alive. He took a step toward it, then another. Pike followed his gaze, then looked back at him.

"She's gone, Drazic," he said, his voice steady. "It's time we let go."

Pike bent, reached for the whip, and held it for a moment. The leather was cold, heavier than he remembered. Then, without another word, he turned and flung it over the railing.

The sound of it falling was swallowed almost instantly.

Drazic stared, his face blank at first, then twisting into disbelief. "No," he whispered. "Don't—"

He lunged forward.

"Scarlet!"

His voice cracked the air, the sound echoing down the chasm as he dove after the whip. For an instant, his figure hung against the glow rising from below—then it vanished into the dark.

Silence reclaimed the walkway.

Sylas was the first to move. He hurried to the railing and looked over, the glow of the city reflecting faintly in his eyes. "Is he...?"

Pike stood beside him, his voice flat, empty of triumph. "I hope not," he said coldly. "He deserves to live with what he's done."

He turned away, the mist swallowing him as the hum of the Stratum returned—steady, indifferent, endless.

31

The Hidden Flame

Location: Cavandel, The Stratum

The scent of smoke lingered faintly in the vents, sharp beneath the sterile chill of the Stratum. Somewhere beyond these walls, the West Wing still smoldered, though the fires had been beaten down to embers. Thaddeus Blackthorne sat in the stillness of his office, a glass of dark liquor in hand.

Across from him, the great relief of Cavandel loomed against the wall. The veins of Crythium threaded through the carved stone, once steady in their glow, now flickering in uneven pulses. Their light wavered over ledgers, scattered papers, and a cracked seal that no one had dared to replace.

For the first time in a long while, he met his own reflection and drank. The Dwellers were a problem he understood, predictable in their defiance. But since the prince's arrival, the balance had fractured. The West Wing lay in ruin. The Stratum in chaos. And now the Screechers pressed at the gates.

He set the glass down and stood, watching the amber beads along its rim. Reports and memoranda cluttered the desk—records of containment that no longer meant anything. Order had always been an equation, one he alone could solve. Now the numbers refused to add up.

He turned toward the relief of Cavandel—his city—and saw not a monument but a map of fractures. The flickering light reached only so far, leaving the edges in shadow.

For a long while he stood there, listening to the hum in the walls. It sounded weaker tonight—distant, uneven—like a machine struggling to recall its rhythm. The silence that followed pressed inward, close and heavy.

Balance is not peace, he thought. *It is control. It is the hand that keeps the scales from tipping.*

His hand drifted toward the decanter, then faltered. The drink had stopped burning. Everything had.

Then a voice—his voice—crackled through the speaker above the door, distorted but clear enough to cut through the quiet. "Attention, residents of the Stratum," it began, though the Warden wasn't sure he heard the rest. He turned toward the sound, the words settling into the room like dust.

He turned away from the speaker, the noise fading into static, and crossed toward the relief on the wall.

Determination gathered behind his exhaustion, slow and deliberate. Control could be lost—but it could also be rebuilt. He had done it before. When the mines collapsed in the early years, when riots swept the District, when starvation had nearly torn the city apart, it had been his hand that restored order. The people had learned then that balance required cost, and he had been willing to pay it. He still was.

He returned to the desk, gathering the scattered papers into neat piles, smoothing their edges until they aligned. The tremor in his hand steadied with the motion. The act was small, almost meaningless, yet it reasserted something within him. Chaos began here, in the mind. Control began with its correction.

He glanced again at the relief of Cavandel, the flickering Crythium throwing fractured light across the stone. In those brief flashes, he imagined the city returning to form—streets cleared, sectors restored, silence reclaimed. The Dwellers would be rooted out, the Screechers destroyed, and that prince—he would be rid of him once and for all.

Order was not gone; it merely slept. And he would wake it.

He adjusted his coat, straightened his cuffs, and reached for the control console. One command at a time, one correction after another, until the city remembered who it served. Balance could still be restored. It had to be.

He had just begun to steady his breathing when the sound reached him—faint at first, like the city shifting in its sleep. Then came the clearer rhythm of boots against metal, the scrape of something heavy dragged across the floor outside. Voices, low and urgent.

He froze.

For a moment he told himself it was his own men returning, some last fragment of discipline clawing its way back to him. But the pattern was wrong. Too many steps. Too little hesitation.

He turned toward it, his pulse quickening despite himself. Beyond the door came muffled voices—his guards, calling for identification. A reply answered too low to catch. Then movement. A sharp scuffle. The crack of impact. A grunt of pain cut short. Another thud, heavier, final. Silence followed, clean and absolute.

He stared at the door, and the room seemed to recede, the world narrowing to that single slab of iron and whatever stood beyond it.

The first blow bent the hinge inward. Dust sifted from the frame and fell across the floor.

The next came harder. Metal rang through the chamber, the vibration running up the legs of the desk and through the floor beneath him. Another impact followed, then a fourth, each one steady, measured—as if the city itself were knocking for permission to enter.

Thaddeus didn't move at first. He watched the door flex under each strike, the hinges shuddering, the seal beginning to warp. Dust trembled loose from the rafters and drifted through the light, yet his expression remained unchanged.

He drew out the chair and sat, slow and deliberate, aligning himself behind the desk as though preparing for a meeting. His hands folded neatly before him. The reports, now stacked with precision, waited at his elbow.

Across the room, the carved map of Cavandel still glowed in uneven rhythm, its reflections twitching across the floor like faint heartbeats.

Another blow. Louder. The lock began to twist.

He leaned back slightly, studying the door with quiet detachment, the faintest curve of disdain tightening his mouth. *They will come in shouting,* he thought. *They always do. And then they will realize what victory costs.*

The hammer fell again—one deep, final strike. The lock gave way with a sharp metallic snap, the door crashing inward against the wall.

Smoke from the corridor drifted in first, carrying the sting of oil and iron. Bram emerged through the haze, his hammer still raised, shoulders squared against the dim light. Gideon followed, then Aria, Heidi, and Sylas—faces drawn, eyes set with exhaustion and resolve.

Thaddeus remained seated.

For a fleeting instant, the room seemed to hold its breath.

Pike appeared in the doorway. "I'll keep watch."

Gideon gave a single nod.

Bram swept his gaze across the room, measuring the Warden in silence. A low grunt escaped him—half acknowledgment, half warning—before he turned to join Pike in the corridor, leaving the door ajar.

As Aria stepped inside, her boots crunched over shards of the shattered lock. The air was cleaner than anywhere she had ever breathed in Cavandel—dry, sterile, stripped of the dust and sweat that clung to life below. Yet beneath that purity lay something colder.

This was where it began. Every command that bled down into the District, every quota that broke a miner's back, every order that sent guards into the tunnels to drag someone away—it all started here, in this quiet room. The thought turned her stomach.

Nothing was out of place. The walls were lined with precision. Shelves of ledgers. Instruments polished to a gleam. Even the light felt controlled, confined within the edges of its fixtures, as if afraid to spill where it shouldn't.

No one spoke. Even the machinery in the walls seemed to quiet in his presence. Aria felt the weight of the place closing around her—the office where lives were reduced to numbers, where balance was measured in suffering.

She thought of her grandmother. Of miners who never came back from the depths. Of the cages and the cells and the way the city had learned to bow beneath the sound of this man's voice. And now here he was, sitting before them with the stillness of stone carved too long ago to remember what it was meant to guard.

The Warden's gaze shifted from face to face, his expression unreadable, as though taking measure of the ones who had come to end him.

"Welcome," he said at last, his voice calm, almost courteous. "I was wondering when you'd arrive."

Gideon stepped forward, stopping just beyond the desk. The others stayed close behind, their silence filling the space where words might have gone.

"I thought I understood you, Warden." His voice was calm, almost gentle. "I don't think I ever will."

Thaddeus didn't answer. He reached instead for the decanter, the movement slow and precise. The glass tilted; amber light caught in the pour. He filled it higher than before and drank, the swallow hard enough to echo faintly in the stillness.

Gideon watched him, something tightening in his jaw. "It didn't have to come to this."

Still no reply—only the faint clink of glass against the desk as Thaddeus set it down.

Gideon's tone sharpened, no louder but colder now. "You must answer for your crimes, Warden—against your people and the Crown."

The words hung between them, heavy and final, the kind that couldn't be taken back. The Warden's gaze lifted at last, the faint glimmer of light reflecting in his eyes. Whatever he might have said next, it was not apology.

Thaddeus rose slowly, the chair's legs scraping against the floor. For a moment, no one moved. He reached across the desk and lifted a shard of Crythium from its stand, the fractured crystal glowing faintly in his palm. Its light bled through his fingers, pale and steady, washing the lines of his face in violet.

He studied it in silence before turning and walking toward the shelf at the far wall. Each step was deliberate, unhurried. He set the shard carefully in its place among the ledgers and instruments, as though returning a sacred thing to where it belonged.

When he spoke, his voice was quiet but carried easily through the room.

"Do you know what happens when a Crythium vein collapses?"

The question came soft, almost conversational. Thaddeus didn't turn from the shelf, his fingers still resting on the shard's stand.

"The miners—the ones who survive—they speak of silence. Not the absence of sound, but its opposite. A pressure so absolute it feels like the mountain is screaming. Everything that held the stone apart simply... lets go. And then the weight remembers itself."

He turned slowly, hands clasped behind his back. His tone stayed even, but there was an edge beneath it.

"You've never heard that sound, have you, Your Highness? You don't know what it means to live with that kind of pressure. Every man down here does. It's what this city is built on. We keep the mountain from remembering. We hold back the weight."

He made his way back to the desk, each step steady, as though the ground itself demanded proof he still belonged there.

"Have you ever gone a day without a meal, Your Highness? Ever watched someone fade into the dark and know they'll never come back? It happens every day down here. Sometimes it's Shatterblight. Sometimes it's a mineshaft. But you learn to keep moving, because stopping won't bring them back."

Across the room, Aria felt the words settle in her chest. It wasn't pity she felt, but a strange, hollow understanding. These were the things that had shaped him—the wounds that had turned him into what he was. It didn't justify what he'd done, but it made sense of it.

She stepped closer to Gideon, her voice low, unsteady. "We all live with it, Warden," she said. "You just made sure no one ever forgot it."

Thaddeus's gaze cut toward her, sharp and measured. It lingered only a second, but the meaning was clear. Then he turned back to Gideon, the movement calm and deliberate, dismissing her as though she hadn't spoken at all.

"You think you know what it takes to hold this city together," he said, his voice steady again. "Think you know what it means to make sacrifices."

He let the words settle, his gaze fixed on Gideon.

Gideon's reply came quiet but certain. "I don't need to stand in a collapsing mine to know it kills people," he said. "And I don't need to live down here to know what you're doing is wrong."

Thaddeus regarded him for a long moment, then exhaled softly. "And what, exactly, is so wrong about it?"

Sylas's voice broke the stillness from near the doorway. "How about locking us up for no reason? Preventing us from sharing the cure? Cutting the Crythium quotas in half while your guards hoard the rations?"

Thaddeus didn't so much as glance toward him. "Discipline," he said flatly. "Without it, the city starves. Chaos does not feed the hungry."

Gideon took a step closer. "I've seen the creatures."

That drew Thaddeus's attention. "Then you understand why they cannot be allowed to live. They undermine the mines, spread infection, and keep the people in fear. Eradication isn't vengeance—it's prevention. Progress. Cavandel's survival depends on it."

Aria's voice cut through the air, soft but unyielding. "You call it survival. It sounds a lot like slaughter."

Thaddeus's eyes shifted toward her, brief and dismissive. "You've never had to choose between a dying city and a dying conscience, girl."

Gideon's tone cooled. "And when that choice came, you decided it was easier to feed innocents to the things you feared. Tell me, Warden—was that for their safety too?"

The Warden's jaw tightened. "Foolish boy." His voice was low, but the calm had begun to fray. "Every decision I've made was for the greater good. One life traded for a hundred others. That's what it means to be a leader."

Gideon didn't move. "No, Warden," he said. "That's what it means to be a coward."

The Warden flinched. For a heartbeat, no one spoke. Then Sylas's voice cut through the tension, raw and unfiltered. "And don't forget he tried to kill you," he said. "Us too, while he was at it."

Thaddeus's gaze landed on Sylas, expression unreadable. A faint curve touched his mouth—not amusement, not regret, something colder. "You're still breathing," he said. "So I must have failed."

Sylas shifted, jaw tight, but Gideon raised a hand, stopping him.

"That's not something to be proud of," Gideon said.

Thaddeus's eyes returned to him, the dim light glinting across their surface. "It isn't pride," he said. "It's proof that mercy only delays the inevitable."

Gideon regarded him for a long moment, the silence between them steady as stone. When he finally spoke, his voice was quiet but carried through the room with unmistakable authority.

"Thaddeus Blackthorne," he said. "By the authority of the Crown of Valmere and in the name of the people of Cavandel, you are to be taken into custody. You will stand trial for your crimes—against your people and against the throne."

He took a slow step forward, his words deliberate, unflinching. "If you resist, you will answer here instead."

From the corridor, Bram's voice cut in—dry, impatient. "I say we just bash him and be done with it."

The room didn't flinch.

Thaddeus's gaze shifted, briefly, toward the open door. A trace of disdain touched his face, as if the comment proved something he'd always believed.

Gideon didn't turn. His voice remained level. "He stands trial."

Bram muttered something under his breath—half protest, half surrender—but he didn't push further.

The silence that followed was tighter than before, drawn like wire between restraint and fury.

For a heartbeat, the Warden said nothing. Then a faint smile touched his lips, brittle and humorless.

"Without me," he said softly, "there is no Cavandel."

Before anyone could move, he gripped the edge of his desk and heaved. The heavy wood crashed forward, scattering glass, papers, and a half-spilled decanter across the floor. The sound filled the room, swallowing their collective breath.

When the dust cleared, the Warden was gone. The wall behind his desk stood ajar, a narrow door sealing shut with a hiss of pressurized air.

"He's gone," Sylas breathed.

Gideon was already moving. "Bram."

Bram stepped forward, hammer in hand. The first swing dented the reinforced panel; the second buckled it. On the third, the door gave with a shriek of tearing metal. Heat rolled out from the gap, the air dense and dry.

They pushed through with Pike in the lead, weapons drawn, following the echo of retreating footsteps.

The corridor beyond was narrow and low, the pipes trembling faintly against the walls. Red emergency lights pulsed in uneven rhythm, throwing their shadows forward in stuttering bursts. The air smelled of iron and hot machinery, edged with the faint ozone bite of burning Crythium.

No one spoke. Their footsteps rang hollow, swallowed by the low hum that lived in the walls. Aria glanced toward Gideon but said nothing.

They pressed on, the passage tightening, the heat rising with every turn. Then, faintly through the haze, came the flicker of pale light ahead. Beneath it, distant and echoing, came another sound—the rasping cry of something alive. It rose and fell through the metal corridors, carried on the pulse of machinery.

Pike lifted a hand, halting them. The motion was small but sharp. "Hold," he murmured. His head tilted toward the noise, his expression unreadable in the red light.

Another cry followed, closer this time—a wet, grating shriek that crawled along the walls and set the pipes vibrating.

Sylas swallowed hard. "Is that what I think it was?"

"Quiet," Pike said, his voice low.

The air shifted with the hum of pressure vents opening somewhere ahead. Aria felt the heat pulse once, steadying herself as Pike took a cautious step forward.

They moved as one, boots whispering over metal, the pale light ahead growing stronger with every step. The sound came again—several voices now, layered and uneven—and the realization settled over them like a weight. Whatever was waiting in that chamber wasn't just machinery.

The passage widened abruptly into a circular chamber that dwarfed the hall behind them, the Power Station stretching out in tiers of walkways and turning turbines, the air alive with the thrum of machines. Steam hissed from ruptured vents, curling through the crimson glow.

The Core dominated the center, a massive sphere of metal plates and pulsing Crythium, suspended above the grated floor by four thick pillars. Its light washed across the walls in deep, uneven violet waves, making every surface gleam as though alive.

The space was vast, built in concentric rings that stole their breath. Outer control rooms lined the curved walls, some with doors thrown open and light spilling from shattered panels, while closer to the Core another ring of glass-walled chambers surrounded the generator, linked by grated catwalks that shimmered with heat. At the far side, facing the Core directly, stood the main control room, its broad window catching the violet glow and throwing it back across the chamber like a fractured mirror.

The heat was staggering. Engineers sprinted along the walkways, scattering tools and papers as they ran. Among them, guards in tarnished armor fought to hold the platforms, their Crythium lances flaring with unstable light as they swept the haze in defensive arcs.

"Hold the line!" someone shouted, but the command dissolved in the noise.

A guard stumbled near the base of the stairs, armor scorched, another dragging him upright just as a cry tore through the air—a sound jagged and inhuman that rolled through the chamber and made the pipes shudder.

Every head turned upward.

Through the haze, something moved along the upper catwalk—a blur of pale limbs and glinting eyes. The Core's glow caught on its slick hide as it slithered down the railing and landed hard on the grating below. No one spoke. The creature crouched low, its movements slow and deliberate, revealing another form sliding through the haze behind it.

Aria's grip tightened on her weapon. Pike stepped forward a pace, deliberate and steady, the reflected glow tracing faint lines across his face.

Sylas whispered, "There's more than one."

Pike didn't take his eyes off the movement ahead. "You and Heidi fall back," he said. His tone was quiet but final. "Stay in the corridor. If these things get through, you run."

Sylas hesitated, glancing toward Gideon, but one look at Pike's face ended the discussion. Heidi caught his arm and pulled him back, both retreating toward the doorway as the light from the Core flickered across their faces.

A nearby guard's lance flared brighter as he raised it. The motion broke whatever spell had held the room. The creatures reacted at once—slick bodies unfurling, claws scraping metal as they turned toward the light. Orders collided, metal rang, and the chamber erupted into motion—guards closing ranks, engineers scrambling for the exits, steam bursting from vents in frantic plumes.

Through the chaos, Aria's gaze lifted to the far side of the chamber.

Across the expanse of heat and noise, she saw him—Thaddeus Blackthorne. The Warden moved along the upper tier with calm precision, untouched by the panic around him. He walked beneath the red light and drifting smoke as if none of it existed, heading straight toward the main control room.

She gripped the railing, the heat pressing fierce against her skin. "Up there," she called out, her voice nearly lost in the roar.

Gideon's eyes tracked the Warden's steady ascent along the catwalk. "I see him."

Pike swung his weapon, driving one of the Screechers back, then glanced toward them. "Go," he shouted. "We'll hold them off."

Gideon met Aria's gaze. "Stay close."

She nodded once, and together they moved toward the narrow stairway that wound upward along the Core's edge.

The stairway curved along the inner wall, narrow and steep, its rails hot beneath their palms. Below, the battle raged—a flicker of light and movement amid the smoke. Pike and Bram fought beside the guards, their silhouettes flashing in and out of sight as Crythium lances cut through the haze.

The noise rolled upward, distant but steady, while the Core remained calm. Its great sphere pulsed at a measured rhythm, light flowing in even waves across the plates and cables that bound it to the pillars.

"Keep moving," Gideon urged as they climbed, tracing the curve of the chamber. The air thickened, light sliding across their faces in bands of violet and shadow. Sweat burned at Aria's eyes, but she pressed on.

She glanced over the railing and saw the fight below—the Screechers weaving between the pillars, flashes of violet sliding over their slick hides.

Then one of them broke away.

It vaulted up the side of the structure, claws biting into steel. The sound of tearing metal echoed through the chamber as it climbed, fast and direct, closing the distance in seconds. The walkway shuddered under its weight.

Aria's lance snapped open with a hiss of light. Gideon drew his sword beside her, the violet glow glinting along its edge. "Stay back," he warned, eyes fixed on the creature's shifting silhouette.

It struck first—fast, a blur of pale limbs. Gideon met the blow, the impact ringing through the metal beneath them. Sparks scattered into the air. The catwalk was too narrow, leaving no room to flank or retreat; one misstep meant the drop.

He parried again, steel glancing off carapace. The creature's reach was longer, its strikes relentless. Each clash drove Gideon closer to the railing until the grating slipped beneath his heel.

The Screecher reared up, claws sweeping down.

Aria lunged forward, catching its arm with her lance. Crythium light burst where metal met shell. The creature hissed and staggered, giving Gideon space to breathe. She vaulted past him, landing between him and the beast.

The air trembled with the hum of the Core. Aria thrust and withdrew in quick rhythm, the creature matching every move. It was too strong, too fast, its limbs folding and unfolding with sick precision.

"We can't beat it like this," she said, breath sharp.

Gideon braced behind her, sword raised. "We don't have a choice—"

But she was already moving.

Aria collapsed the lance and sprinted toward the Screecher. Its right claw slashed across the space where she'd been, scraping the rail. She vaulted, caught the edge and let her momentum carry her over the arc of its strike.

Landing in a roll, she twisted beneath its body and reactivated the weapon mid-motion. The lance extended in a flash of violet light, driving deep into its flank.

The creature shrieked, tail lashing wild. Its second strike came around and clipped her side as she cleared the space. Pain tore through her ribs, but she didn't stop.

The Screecher turned on her, rage breaking through its rhythm. It struck again and again, claws hammering against the lance as she fought to hold it back.

Gideon moved as it pressed forward. He caught its blind side and swung once. The Crythium light flared white—then vanished as the strike hit true. The creature convulsed, limbs folding in on themselves before it toppled backward into the mist below.

For a moment, the air was still—only the steady hum of the Core and their breathing.

Aria leaned against the railing, one hand pressed to her side, her face drawn with pain but steady.

Gideon looked up. "Are you hurt?" he asked, closing the distance between them.

She shook her head, as if denial could make it true. "I'm fine," she said quietly. But when she shifted her weight, her knees weakened. Gideon caught her before she could fall.

The warmth from the Core surrounded them, the metal beneath their feet vibrating with life. For a moment, neither spoke. Her breath came shallow, controlled. He saw the strain in her face, the way she fought to stay upright.

"You saved me," he said quietly.

Aria managed a faint, weary smile.

He studied her for a moment, torn between urgency and something heavier. "Don't scare me like that again," he whispered, his voice hoarse.

"Getting hit wasn't part of the plan," she managed, a flicker of humor crossing her face.

Gideon adjusted his hold on her arm, steadying her. "Can you walk?"

She nodded once. "I don't have much choice."

He looked up the winding stair. The control room loomed above, its broad window flashing in rhythmic bursts of violet light.

"Then let's move," Gideon said softly.

They started upward together, her steps slower now but sure.

Through the drifting steam, Aria caught sight of motion on the upper catwalk. The Warden was there, his coat trailing behind him as he crossed the final bridge—untouched by the chaos below.

An engineer inside turned toward him. Thaddeus didn't slow. He caught the man by the collar and hurled him through the doorway, sealing it behind him.

Aria's voice cut through the noise. "What's he doing?"

Gideon's eyes stayed fixed on the upper tier. "Doesn't look good," he said. "We have to stop him."

Behind them, a voice called out through the din—small but unmistakable. "Aria!"

Heidi burst from the corridor entrance, breathless, grease streaked down her arm, eyes wide with determination. Sylas stood at the threshold below, gesturing frantically for her to return, but she ignored him and ran forward, reaching the base of the stair.

A shrill tone pierced the air—thin at first, then multiplying as warning lights along the walls began to flash. The steady rhythm of the Core wavered, its glow quickening into erratic pulses that painted the chamber in fractured color.

Gideon froze halfway up the stair. "What is that?"

The engineer who'd been thrown from the control room scrambled to his feet near the sealed door, eyes wide. "He's overloading it!" he shouted, his voice breaking through the noise.

He struck at the glass with his palm. "Warden, stop! You'll rupture the Core!"

Inside, the Warden didn't look up. His silhouette moved with deliberate calm, hands working across the panel, adjusting dials and levers with mechanical precision.

The engineer turned toward Gideon and Aria as they reached the top of the stair. "He's forcing a power surge through the containment grid," he said, breathless but coherent. "If he keeps at it, the Core will breach. There won't be a city left."

Below, the machinery began to change pitch—a deep, rising hum that crawled up the walls and through the metal under their feet. The light from the Core brightened in pulses, every beat sharper, more violent.

Aria's voice was low, strained. "He's going to destroy it all."

Gideon's jaw tightened. "We need to stop him."

He moved toward the door, eyes fixed on the Warden's silhouette within the flickering light.

Gideon reached the door first and tried the handle, but it refused to give. A mechanical lock clicked from within, sealing it. Behind the glass, Thaddeus continued his work, moving with methodical precision, his reflection flickering in the pulse of violet light.

"Warden!" Gideon shouted, striking the glass with the flat of his sword. "Stop this!"

Thaddeus didn't turn. He flipped a final switch, then rested both hands on the console, watching, waiting.

The engineer pressed close beside Gideon. "He's rerouting the regulator feed—he's going to push the Core past containment."

The hum from the generator deepened, vibrating through the walls and into their bones. Aria stepped closer, shielding her eyes against the glare. "He's not listening."

Gideon raised his sword again and swung. The blade struck the glass with a sharp crack. A web of fractures spread across its surface, the sound slicing through the noise. He swung again, harder, and the panel shattered inward.

Heat burst out, the air rolling past them in a wave that smelled of metal and ozone.

Thaddeus turned at last. His expression was calm, almost curious, as if they'd simply interrupted a meeting.

"Prince Everhart," he said. "You're just in time."

Gideon climbed through the broken frame, glass crunching under his boots. "Turn it off," he said.

"I can't," the Warden replied. "No one can now."

Gideon seized him by the collar. "What have you done?"

Thaddeus regarded him for a long moment before nodding toward the console. "I've stopped holding the weight of the mountain."

Aria stepped inside behind Gideon, the heat washing over her as she spoke. "You'll kill everyone."

Thaddeus didn't look at her. "Everyone, or no one. The mountain decides."

He lifted his hand slowly, revealing a broken lever.

The engineer cried out, "He broke the release handle! We can't vent it now!"

Thaddeus straightened, the faintest smile on his lips. "Without me, there is no Cavandel."

32

Chains Unbound

Location: Cavandel, The Stratum

Gideon didn't hesitate. He hurled Thaddeus away from the console. The Warden hit the floor hard, the sound lost beneath the rising whine of machinery.

"Tell me how to stop it!" Gideon shouted to the engineer.

The man pushed past him to the console, hands flying over the dials. "You can't shut it off from here—the regulator's jammed! When he broke that lever, he disabled the discharge circuit."

Aria steadied herself against the doorway, the vibration in the floor deepening beneath her boots. "How do we fix it?"

The engineer looked up, sweat running down his temple. "We can't," he said, pointing toward the broken lever. "We need to get out of here."

He started for the door, but Gideon caught his arm, stopping him. "We're not running," he said, voice firm. "Tell me how to stop it."

The man hesitated, torn between fear and duty. "You can't," he said again, quieter this time.

Thaddeus pushed himself to his knees, a low, humorless laugh slipping out.

Gideon turned on him with a growl. "Stay down."

The lights flickered, shadows sliding across the glass. Alarms shrieked as the readings climbed higher. Steam hissed from ruptured pipes, curling across the floor in pale, glowing trails.

A crash sounded behind them. The door burst open and Heidi stumbled in, hair damp with sweat, streaks of grease across her face. She froze at the sight—the shattered glass, the failing lights, the Core blazing through the window like a storm held in glass.

"What in the pits did he do?" she shouted over the roar.

The engineer didn't look back. "He overloaded the Core. Snapped the release handle too—it's locked in surge mode. We can't vent the charge unless it's bridged again."

They stared at him, confusion cutting through the panic.

"I tried de-energizing it," he said, voice raw, "but it's too late—the oscillator's in a feedback loop."

Heidi met his gaze. "So what are you saying?"

"I'm saying—if we can't discharge it ourselves—Cavandel's finished."

Aria pressed a hand to her side and winced as she stepped forward. "There has to be a way."

The engineer held up the broken lever. "Not without this."

Heidi's eyes narrowed. "Can't we just bypass it?"

"Maybe." The man hesitated. "But we'd have to access the circuit directly."

He pointed to the access panel, and Gideon quickly tore it free.

"Tell me what to do," Heidi said, already crouching.

He rifled through a drawer, grabbed a wrenchlike tool, and tossed it to her. "Use this. Find the relay cluster—three lines, one blue, one black, one copper. Unfasten the grounding bolt from the blue feed and secure it to the copper conduit beside it. That'll bridge the gap. I'll de-energize the line," he said, already turning back to the console.

Heidi caught the tool and dropped to the floor, sliding under the console. "Got it."

The Core's hum deepened, vibrating through the floor as she reached into the nest of wires. "Blue feed, copper conduit—easy enough," she muttered, more to herself than anyone else.

"Good. But don't touch both ends at once," he warned.

"Noted," she called out, reaching deeper. A sharp spark cracked from beneath the panel, and she jerked back with a curse. "That was not supposed to happen."

"Careful," the engineer snapped, eyes darting between her dangling feet and the console's readouts.

Another spark rang out, and Heidi hissed through her teeth but she didn't stop.

"Keep at it," he urged. "Once you've got the bolt in place, tighten it hard—it'll reroute the draw into the conduit loop."

The Core's glow surged, washing the room in violet. Heat pressed against their faces.

"Almost there!" Heidi called, twisting the wrench in short, precise motions. A final metallic click cut through the hum.

"Done!" she shouted.

The engineer leaned over the console, checking the gauges. "Good. We've got a connection. The discharge circuit's live again."

Heidi slid out from beneath the panel, hair frizzed and eyes bright.

Gideon helped her to her feet. "Good work," he said.

Aria stepped closer. "So how do we discharge the—whatever it was?"

He didn't look up right away. "The oscillator," he said, voice thin. His gaze drifted toward the window, to the Core blazing behind the glass. For a long moment he simply stared, violet light trembling across his face. Then, slowly, he nodded in its direction. "In there."

Silence held the room. The light pulsed against the glass, each beat sharper, louder, as if the Core itself were listening.

Heidi frowned. "Are you insane?"

The engineer finally looked at them, weariness clouding his expression.

"That's where the oscillator's housed. It's the only way to discharge it."

Heidi stared at him, disbelief tightening her voice. "You're trying to kill us."

The engineer shook his head slowly. "I'm sorry," he muttered. "It's the only way."

Heidi shook her head, incredulous. "You really want one of us to walk into *that* thing?"

The engineer cleared his throat. "In theory, nothing should happen, really. It's standard procedure in case of an overload."

"In theory?" she shot back.

He swallowed, glancing again toward the Core as if choosing his words carefully. "The oscillator runs on high voltage, but the draw is low—barely enough to arc if the charge has a proper ground. Whoever goes in just needs to stay connected to the plate while it drains. It creates a skin effect and should bypass them entirely."

"*Should?*" Heidi repeated, her tone caught somewhere between outrage and disbelief.

He didn't answer that—only adjusted a gauge with a trembling hand, the whine of the machinery swelling around them.

Aria took a step forward, her limp pronounced now, pain threading through her voice as she said, "I'll do it."

Both Heidi and Gideon turned to her. The words seemed to hang in the charged air, caught between the hum of the Core and the shriek of the alarms.

Heidi shook her head sharply. "Not a chance."

Gideon looked at Aria—the stubborn set of her jaw, the exhaustion shadowing her face—and something in him settled, firm and unyielding. If the Core went, the mountain would fall with it. Cavandel, Valmere, everything he was meant to protect would be gone. What kind of prince turned away while his people burned? What kind of man called himself a leader and let others bear the cost?

Before Aria could argue, Gideon stepped forward.

"Then I will."

The light from the Core struck his face in shifting bands, outlining the steadiness in his expression. "You said it's safe if the person's grounded," he said, eyes fixed on the Core. "Show me how."

The engineer gestured toward the catwalk that stretched from the control room to the Core. "Behind the hatch," he said. "You'll see the oscillator chamber. We just need to short it."

Gideon's gaze followed the path of the catwalk, where heat shimmered through the air like rising glass. "How?"

"Anything long enough," the engineer said. "Metal. It just needs contact."

Aria took a step closer. "No, Gideon."

He turned to her, confusion flickering across his face. She reached up and placed her palm gently against his cheek, her touch light against the grime and heat. "Thank you," she said quietly. "But you can't—"

His voice softened. "Aria..."

"This isn't about courage," she murmured. "You still have a life waiting above—something beyond all this." Her hand slipped from his face to her side, pressing lightly where the fabric was torn and darkened.

He reached for her, his hand closing around her arm, steady but careful. Their eyes met, the Core's light flickering between them. "I can't let you," he said, his voice low—almost breaking against the sound of the rising hum.

"You're not letting me," she said, her tone almost gentle. "It's my choice."

The engineer hesitated, glancing between them. "It has to be done soon," he warned. "Once the charge peaks, there won't be time to—"

The Core's pulse deepened, swallowing his words, the sound vibrating through every beam and bolt until it became the only thing left.

For a moment, the world seemed to fall away. The alarms, the heat, the shuddering metal—all of it blurred into silence. Aria's hand rested against his arm, her touch trembling, though her eyes held steady on his. In them he saw everything she couldn't say—fear, defiance, a kind of quiet grace that left him breathless. He wanted to stop her, to find some other way, but the truth pressed between them like the heat from the Core. Slowly, wordlessly, he nodded. It wasn't surrender—it was understanding.

Behind them, Thaddeus stirred. No one noticed as he dragged himself toward the wall, his movements small and deliberate. His coat brushed the floor as he crept along the base of the consoles, keeping to the shadows, eyes glinting with spite. When he reached the door, he paused only long enough to cast one last look toward the others—then slipped through the opening like a rat fleeing the light.

"Hurry," the engineer called, voice strained above the rising hum. "We're running out of time."

He pointed toward the catwalk. "That hatch needs to come off," he said, voice strained. "Help her."

Gideon stepped onto the catwalk, the metal trembling beneath his boots. The heat struck him at once, rising in visible waves. He lifted an arm to shield his face as light flared around him, arcs of violet electricity snapping across the rails like lashes of liquid fire. Each pulse from the Core came harder than the last, vibrating through the steel until it thrummed beneath his feet.

Behind him, Heidi moved to Aria's side. Without a word, she caught her in a fierce embrace. Aria froze for a heartbeat, then managed a small, crooked smile. "Okay," she whispered, half to Heidi, half to herself. "This is happening..."

Heidi gave a breath of laughter, soft and broken, then drew back, her eyes wet but shining. No words passed between them; none were needed.

Aria straightened, setting her face. The retractable lance hissed open in her hand, the Crythium tip blooming with a faint violet glow that mirrored the Core's heart.

The engineer's voice carried over the roar. "Stay grounded. Keep one hand on the railing—don't let go, no matter what!"

Aria nodded once, the motion sharp, then stepped onto the catwalk. The metal rang beneath her weight, echoing into the chamber.

Gideon reached the panel and wedged his sword into the seam. The metal shrieked in protest as he forced it open, bolts rattling loose until the hatch gave way with a harsh, echoing clang. A rush of light burst out, searing and alive, flooding the catwalk in violent pulses.

Inside, the oscillator came into view—a chamber of mirrored metal split cleanly down the center, twin coils pulsing in rhythm with each other. Sparks leapt between them, stray arcs tearing through the air like lashes of molten glass.

Gideon stared at the two halves, realization settling cold and heavy in his chest. If only his sword were long enough—

For a fleeting instant the thought flickered through him, but the distance was too great. He forced it aside, jaw tightening as the heat pressed in around him.

Aria reached him, each step a struggle. The catwalk trembled under her boots, the metal burning hot enough to sting through the soles. She kept one hand clamped to the railing, using it to steady herself as she moved closer. Every jolt of the structure sent a pulse of pain through her side, sharp and breath-stealing, but she pressed on. By the time she reached Gideon, her face was pale with strain, her breath uneven.

She tightened her grip on the railing, knuckles white, the violet light flaring in her eyes. For a moment, neither spoke. The roar of the Core filled the space between them, a rhythm too vast for words.

He looked at her, searching for something—maybe the strength to stop her, maybe the courage to let her go. Whatever he found, it left him silent.

She steadied her breath and nodded once. With her free hand, she extended the lance toward the coils. The tip glowed fiercely, its light merging with the storm inside the chamber. She stretched farther, the heat searing her skin, but the distance refused to close. Her arm trembled, but the lance slipped just short of the mark.

Gideon saw it—the inches that separated them from survival—and acted. He caught the railing with one hand, anchoring himself against the shaking metal, and reached for her with the other. "Grab on to me!" he shouted over the roar.

She hesitated, shaking her head. "No—"

The Core shuddered violently, a wave of light bursting outward, rattling the catwalk beneath them. Sparks cascaded across the rail, scorching the metal.

"Now, Aria!"

She hesitated for the briefest moment, then reached for him. Their hands met, fingers locking tight. The vibration built to a deafening roar, swallowing sound, breath, and thought alike. The light flared once, searing against their faces—and then everything fell away into darkness.

***

The Warden ran.

He had escaped Gideon and the others, only to find himself hunted again. His footsteps skittered across the metal floor, the sound sharp and uneven, panic breaking through the practiced control that had once ruled every gesture. He risked a glance over his shoulder and caught sight of them in the flashing light—Pike, lean and relentless, with Bram close behind, his silhouette broad and unyielding.

Thaddeus turned a corner and spotted a door ahead. Salvation. He lunged for it, the echo of pursuit closing in behind him.

And then, all at once, the lights failed.

The world fell into darkness.

He stumbled through the doorway by memory, slammed it shut, and threw the lock. His breath came ragged, his pulse pounding in his ears. He pressed his back to the cold metal, eyes searching the black for any sign of motion. Nothing. Just the echo of his own breath and the faint hum of systems struggling to restart.

He had escaped. He was safe.

When the lights returned, it was only a flicker at first—a stuttering pulse along the walls. Through the narrow viewport, he saw shadows move past the corridor outside—Pike and Bram, scanning, searching—but what he didn't see was the thing standing behind him.

The light steadied just long enough for him to notice the reflection on the glass—tall, curved, and wrong.

Then the Screecher moved.

***

Darkness.

It pressed against everything—thick and absolute. For a time, there was no sound but the slow crackle of cooling metal and the soft hiss of steam escaping broken vents.

Then, faintly, came a sound.

"Aria?"

A voice reached her through the dark, thin and frayed at the edges. She tried to move, but the world shifted away from her.

"Aria, can you hear me?"

Was it Heidi? Sylas? The words bent and folded in her mind, distorted by the ringing in her ears. She opened her mouth, but no sound came.

A hand brushed her shoulder. Another voice now—deeper, steadier, urgent. "Quick, she's hurt. We need to get her to the surface—"

Gideon?

The sound faded.

For a while there was nothing. No light. No heat. Just the soft echo of boots against metal, the weightless drift between waking and falling away.

Then motion—steady, rhythmic, rising.

When she opened her eyes again, she was cradled in Gideon's arms. The world swayed around her, the walls of the Ascender gliding upward in slow, graceful motion. Through the haze, she saw his face—pale, streaked with soot, eyes fixed on her with quiet determination.

"You're safe," he said softly. "It's over now."

She tried to nod but couldn't quite manage it. Her body felt distant, every breath a tremor. The wound at her side burned beneath the torn fabric and her left hand throbbed with dull heat. She lifted it slightly, wincing at the sight—a blackened scar winding across her palm.

"You'll be all right," Gideon said again, though his voice trembled faintly. "Just hold on."

The Ascender broke through the last layer of rock and light flooded in.

It was blinding—sharp and colorless at first, then spilling into gold. Aria turned her face away, tears springing forth as her eyes tried to adjust. The air felt impossibly cool and alive in her lungs, carrying scents she had never known—earth and water, and something else.

Heidi and Sylas stood beside her, shielding their faces, laughing weakly in disbelief. Bram was near the edge of the platform, his broad frame outlined in the glare, a dark silhouette against the sky. Pike lingered a few steps behind him, silent, watching, waiting.

Aria stirred and looked up at Gideon. "Put me down," she said softly.

He hesitated, tightening his hold as if afraid she might vanish if he let go. "You can't stand yet."

"I can," she whispered. "Please."

For a moment, he searched her face, then nodded and slowly set her on her feet. The motion sent a wave of weakness through her, and her legs gave out. Gideon caught her before she could fall, one arm steadying her around the waist.

She drew a careful breath, leaning into him for balance, then lifted her gaze to Pike.

She didn't speak. She didn't need to. The question was there in her eyes, unguarded and full of hope.

Pike met her gaze and smirked faintly, a glint of his old irreverence returning. "I'm not ready for this adventure yet," he said. "There's still work below."

Her expression faltered—disappointment flickering across her face before she could hide it. Pike's smirk softened into something quieter, more sincere. "Don't worry," he said gently. "You'll see me before long."

Bram shifted beside him, resting the hammer across his shoulder. "We'll keep things steady down there," he said. "Make sure you've got a city to come back to."

Gideon stepped closer to Aria, urgency tightening his voice. "We need to get you to the Palace—"

"I know," she said softly. "But first..." She turned back to Pike and Bram, her voice steadier now. "Tell Jace and Gran I'll return soon."

Heidi squeezed her arm. Sylas gave a small, quiet nod.

Aria managed a faint smile. Heidi and Sylas moved in close, each slipping a shoulder under her arms as Gideon adjusted his grip. Together they turned toward the slope leading away from the Ascender, the air bright and unreal around them.

Pike raised a hand in parting, and she returned the gesture weakly, her fingers trembling.

The wind swept across the platform, carrying the scent of pine and rain. Aria lifted her face toward the open sky, the light still too bright, too vast to feel real. After a lifetime beneath stone, the horizon seemed endless—alive and waiting.

They began to move, the others steadying her as they climbed the slope. Behind them, the Ascender stood like a relic of another world, half-shrouded in mountain shadow. Ahead lay Valmere, its towers gleaming in the distance, bathed in gold.

But as they walked, the questions pressed close. Would Gran be all right? What of the Dwellers—would Cavandel hold together without the Warden's hand, or fracture even further? Could the city ever heal from what it had endured? And the surface—this new world of sky and light—would it welcome her, or would part of her always remain below, bound to the dark that shaped her?

She looked up at Gideon, at the quiet strength in his expression, then at Heidi and Sylas beside her—their faces drawn but bright with wonder. Whatever waited beyond the slope, they would face it together. That much she knew.

The tunnel widened until, at last, they stepped through the mouth of the mountain. Heidi gasped, one hand lifting to shield her eyes. Sylas stopped beside her, awe softening his usual grin.

Aria followed their gaze.

The valley stretched out before them—vast and golden, light spilling across the peaks like the dawn of something entirely new. The world felt impossibly large, its colors too open, too bright, as if the mountain had exhaled and revealed something it had hidden for centuries.

"I can feel it," she whispered, lifting a hand to her brow. "The sun?"

"The sun," Gideon echoed, his voice quiet, reverent.

A small smile touched her lips—fragile, unshakable. "Wait till Gran sees this," she murmured.

The wind caught her words and carried them upward, letting them vanish into the light.

Epilogue

Three Days Later
Location: Valmere, The Skyport

Sunlight flashed off the airships moored along the Skyport, their brass hulls shimmering with reflected sky. Wind coursed between the towers, snapping pennants against their poles and carrying the clang of hammers through the docks. Crewmen shouted over the thrum of engines as ropes strained and propellers turned in slow, gleaming arcs.

Sylas leaned out from a gangplank, a pair of sunshades far too large for his face slipping down his nose. "Heidi! Come on! You can't spend your life clinging to the ground!"

"I most certainly can," she shouted back, lowering her own tinted lenses to squint up at him. "That thing looks like it's held together by wishful thinking."

"You'll love it! It's like you're walking on air!"

"That's supposed to make me feel better?"

Gideon's laugh cut cleanly through the din. "It's the only way you'll ever see what's in the engine room!"

Heidi froze halfway up the ramp, torn between terror and curiosity. "That's not fair," she called back, but the edge of a smile betrayed her.

Sylas grinned from the rail, the oversized lenses catching the sun in a bright, ridiculous flare. "You can see the whole world from up here!"

She glanced toward the palace—the high balcony where Aria was still recovering. For a moment she lingered there, eyes tracing the glass spires, the wind lifting her hair. Then she drew a slow breath and took one tentative step onto the ramp.

Sylas whooped loud enough for half the dock to hear as Gideon extended a steadying hand toward her.

Five Days Later, Morning
Location: Valmere, The Palace Infirmary

The infirmary was filled with filtered light, soft and gold through the high windows. The steady hiss of vapor valves kept time with the quiet pulse of the machines along the wall—gentler cousins of Cavandel's engines, their cadence closer to breathing than to labor.

Her grandmother lay beneath linen sheets pale as mist, her chest rising and falling in calm, even measure. Jace sat nearby, shoulders rounded in exhaustion that looked almost like peace.

"She's stronger each day," he said without looking up. "The healers say she'll walk again before the month's out."

Aria touched the edge of the sheet, feeling the warmth that lingered there. A faint smile pressed at her lips. "They'll have a hard time keeping her in bed once she can."

He chuckled under his breath. "That's what I told them."

He leaned back, hands loose on his knees. "Cavandel's holding—for now. Kegan's trying to play commander, but the miners won't follow. Most still look to Pike and Sebastian. And if anyone can steady things, it's them."

Aria's gaze lingered on her grandmother's face. "Then they'll find their footing again."

Jace nodded. "They always do."

She brushed a stray hair from her grandmother's brow, the warmth of her skin grounding her more than the room's golden light ever could. "So will we," she murmured.

Five Days Later, Evening
Location: Valmere, The Palace, Aria's Rooms

Evening settled softly over the palace, painting the walls in muted gold. The hum of the city drifted through the open window: distant laughter from the courtyards, the faint chime of glass carriages gliding along the avenues below.

On the table between them lay two masks—one dark, one silver—catching the glow of a single lamp. Their edges had dulled with travel and smoke, yet each still held the faint shimmer of the world they'd left behind.

Aria traced the curve of hers with a fingertip. "I should return this," she said quietly. "I didn't know you were—who you were," she corrected.

Gideon leaned back in the chair across from her, the lamplight falling across his face in slanted bands. "Isn't that the point?"

She shook her head. "You're a prince, Gideon. Your life isn't your own. I don't want to hold you to promises made in the dark."

He studied her for a long moment, the kind of silence that felt more like thought than hesitation. "I meant them," he said at last. "All of them."

Her gaze drifted to the window, where the last traces of daylight burned along the rooftops. She rose and crossed to the glass. Valmere unfurled below—vast and golden, alive in ways she still couldn't name. Its light pooled against the pane, spilling over her hands like something she couldn't quite hold.

"This place, Gideon—your world. It shines, but it doesn't feel like mine."

She turned back to him, uncertainty flickering in her eyes. "I'm not sure I belong here," she admitted.

He rose, closing the distance between them. When he spoke, his voice was low. "Then it doesn't matter where 'here' is," he murmured. "As long as we find it together."

Aria looked up at him, the words catching somewhere deep inside. "And if I can't?"

"Then I'll remind you," he said simply.

The last light slipped beyond the rooftops, leaving the city aglow with its own quiet pulse. Gideon stood beside her, their reflections overlapping in the glass—two shapes suspended between shadow and gold. For a long moment, neither spoke. The silence felt less like uncertainty and more like understanding.

He didn't reach for her at first. He stood with the kind of careful stillness she'd come to recognize—not hesitation, but respect, as though her comfort mattered more than anything he might want to say.

"Aria," he said softly.

She turned toward him, her hand lifting to rest lightly over his heart. He covered it with his own, their fingers settling together as though the gesture had always belonged between them.

When he eased back, the room felt steadier for it, anchored by something quiet and sure.

He squeezed her hand once before letting go. "I'll give you some rest," he said, voice low but gentle. He stepped toward the door, pausing with his hand on the frame.

She nodded, the faintest smile softening her features.

Gideon held her gaze a moment longer—steady, certain—then slipped from the room, closing the door softly behind him.

THREE WEEKS LATER
Location: Valmere, The Palace, Aria's Rooms

The sky above Valmere shimmered with airships drifting through the sunlight, their brass hulls gleaming as they passed between the towers. From the balcony, Aria watched them glide in lazy arcs over the city, shadows sliding across the palace gardens below.

Jace had brought news earlier that morning—her grandmother was walking again, slow but steady, and Cavandel was holding.

She lifted a hand against the brightness, then slipped on the tinted lenses Gideon had called sunshades. The world beyond the mountains was vast and dazzling—too beautiful, too open to seem real.

Far below, in the royal gardens, Gideon walked beside his mother. The Queen's gown caught the light like a spill of glass, her laughter faint beneath the hum of the airships. They moved with an easy rhythm, their conversation calm, though from this distance Aria couldn't hear the words. When Gideon glanced up, their eyes met for only a heartbeat before he turned back to his mother, their quiet exchange continuing.

Aria's gaze dropped to the bandage wrapped around her left hand. Beneath it lay the scar—dark at first, now fading to silver—the mark of what she had survived and what it had cost. Her lance was gone, lost to the surge that had nearly taken them all. A piece of her past, buried in the mountain.

She brushed her fingers across the gown she wore—soft, flowing, pale as morning. It reminded her of the dress from Founder's Day, the day she had felt like an impostor in her own skin. Even now, standing in a palace of light, she wasn't sure it belonged to her. Yet she felt no urge to shed it. Perhaps belonging wasn't a place or a people—it was something carried forward.

She turned back into the room. Gold filigree lined the walls, curtains spilling like water from the ceiling, a bed large enough for a family to live in—so different from the cot she'd slept on in Cavandel, where the hum of machinery had been her lullaby.

Sylas sat at the edge of a long banquet table, devouring a meal fit for a small army. Heidi tinkered beside him with a strange half-assembled thing—a device of gears and crystal tubing. A clock, maybe. Or one of the Vox-communicators Gideon had tried to describe. Aria couldn't tell.

Her hand rose gently to her chest. And Gideon—this feeling that lived quietly between them. Somewhere in her night chamber, on the bedside table, lay his mask—dark, worn, familiar. Could she truly imagine a future with him? A Dustborn girl from the mines and a prince who walked in sunlight?

She looked back toward the garden, but Gideon and the Queen had vanished from sight. Only the rustle of leaves and the drifting hum of an airship filled the air.

For a moment she lingered on the balcony, letting the warm wind sweep through her hair—gentle and alive. Then she stepped inside, her hand brushing the doorframe.

She took one last look at the sky beyond the balcony—the golden light, the airships gliding between the spires—before closing the door behind her.

And for the first time, she didn't fear the darkness.

She simply turned toward the light.

This has been:
Escaping The Darkness, by Adam Inkwell.

Copyright 2025 by:
Adam Inkwell

If you enjoyed this book, please consider leaving an online review.

Doing so helps other readers discover, and enjoy this book as well.